WINDFALL

KIRBY JONAS

WINDFALL

KIRBY JONAS

Cover design by Clay Jonas

Howling Wolf Publishing
Pocatello, Idaho

Howling Wolf Publishing
1611 City Creek Road
Pocatello ID 83204

For more information about Kirby's books, check out:

www.kirbyjonas.com
Facebook, at KirbyJonasauthor

Or email Kirby at: **kirby@kirbyjonas.com**

Manufactured in the United States of America—*One nation, under God*

Publication date: February 2022
Jonas, Kirby, 1965—
Windfall / by Kirby Jonas.

ISBN: 978-1-891423-41-3
Library of Congress Control Number: 2021916505

To learn more about this book or any other Kirby Jonas book, email Kirby at kirby@kirbyjonas.com

To Kristi Roberts, for her graciousness,
friendliness to an absolute stranger, and for her beautiful smile.
I couldn't ask for a more perfect "Eva Galanti"

To Doug Larson, who again was kind enough to let himself appear on a book cover whose content he knew little about

And to Lance, who portrays himself really well

CHAPTER ONE

♦ *1973* ♦

Rock Springs, Wyoming, August 13

EVA GALANTI WOULD HAVE liked to think her sixty-nine Plymouth Valiant truly was what its name implied: valiant. After all, the station wagon had cost her two hundred and fifty dollars in cash, money won hard and ugly by pretending to be nice to the miners, oil roughnecks, drunks, and perverts down at Benny's Bar and Grill, where the waitresses were pretty, and the customers weren't—or at least that was the story from non-customers.

But as the so-called alpine white (but in reality more "fetid cream") wagon squatted at the roadside, pouring smoke out from under the hood and front wheel wells, with its dull round headlights staring out at her like the glassy eyes of a dead snake, *valiant* wasn't one of the words of choice she smeared it with. In fact, she had named it a lot of other words in the last three minutes, and none of them started with the letter V. If she could have found an appropriate V word, she certainly would have, since she had used up most of the alphabet already in search of all the most-fitting words for her car and still needed more.

Already smelling smoky, and possibly a little sweaty, even before getting to Benny's Bar and Grill, the smoke-filled den of iniquity on the outskirts of Blairtown which she called her workplace, Eva pushed loose strands of dark hair back from her high, round forehead and fought back tears. The scene before her—and the one that awaited her at work—were only now striking home, and both were harsh. Even cruel.

Benny Fitz, the owner of Blairtown's infamous and seedy bar and grill—whose real name was Fitzgerald except that he was too lazy to use the entire thing—was going to pop a cork over this. Not that it was Eva's fault she was going to be so late, but that would make no difference to Benny. It would merely be one more thing he could yell at her for, and that seemed lately to be his calling in life.

Eva couldn't deny that she had been late for work five or six times in the last month, because every other day something seemed to go haywire in her life. It was like a recurring nightmare—which was ironic, since she actually *had* recurring nightmares about that very thing: being late for work. To say nothing of her even more terrifying nightmares about Benny Fitz *away* from work.

Having to face Benny Fitz, whose appetite for greasy burgers, fries, and Schlitz beer was enormous and well-known, and whose appetite for his hired girls was huge and notorious—like Benny himself—would be a nightmare in anyone's book. But it was magnified in Eva's case, because for reasons all in his own head, Benny considered himself Eva's jilted lover.

It hadn't been so long ago when Benny used to tell Eva that she was far and away his most beautiful girl—meaning barmaid—and Eva believed he had meant it, mostly because she had heard words like that most of her grown-up life from a lot of others of the male gender— "grown up" meaning from about fourteen on to her current thirty-eight years of rough and rocky, always broke, always hungry, nearly always sore-footed life. But Benny Fitz was not something Eva would have given her leftover, questionable, happily no-longer-married virtue to, not even if he offered her thirty dollars an hour in cash to work for him—which was almost twenty-eight dollars over Wyoming's minimum wage. Some things in life simply weren't worth any amount of money.

Benny Fitz housed his three hundred fifty pounds of hog lard and soft muscle under a black-haired, mole-sprinkled hide that seemed constantly to stream with sweat, smelled like he had issues in the men's room that no amount of soap could eradicate, and always seemed to be accidentally smearing up against one of his waitresses, and occasionally a female customer, especially those who were too inebriated to think of anything but love, even if that love might be with a creature that was part orangutan, part gorilla, and part enormous, peeled cantaloupe.

The bad part was Benny had fired his full magazine of come-ons at Eva since she first started working for him and missed with every one. He now had an empty gun and a chip on his shoulder the size of Russia, and today would be the latest Eva had *ever* been to work. She knew that because she was almost late already, it would still have been two more minutes to get there by car, and now she had to walk . . . in flats that provided little cushion between her feet and the road . . . in the sweltering hell of mid-August. But the hell out here could not compare to the hell waiting inside Benny's.

Turning in desperation, Eva started her journey. She made it only ten or fifteen steps from the car before whirling back and jetting her wad of keys as hard as she could at the Valiant, which sat there gawking and smoking like a fat man in front of a cheap cigar store, and was now drooling some kind of fluid out onto the road that she didn't recognize and wasn't sure she wanted to.

Another twenty steps and she remembered that most of the keys in that fat wad were the keys to her house, her shed, and her hope chest.

She laughed, actually laughed, as she turned around, broken in spirit, and started back after the keys, thinking about the hope chest. It was ironic in the extreme for Eva Galanti to own something of that name, for at her age Eva had years since used up all the hope she had put in it and couldn't seem to find much to replace it with.

On a weekend, or an evening, Eva guessed somebody more than willing to pick her up would have stopped before she made it to Benny's. Rock Springs and the area surrounding it were in the middle of a boom and had already more than doubled in size in the last year or two—although not in a good way. But this time of day most of the new residents were out working on the construction of the billion-dollar Jim Bridger power plant, the coal strip mines or trona mines, or exploring for coal, oil, or gas. Anyway, most people didn't come driving out to Blairtown unless like Eva they absolutely had to.

In reality, although Eva didn't like the idea of being late again, she wasn't so sure she would want very many of the area's new residents to come to her rescue anyway. There were far too many stories in the news these days of some hapless woman being beaten up, raped, or murdered in this town or in Green River, to the west. Rock Springs, especially in the nighttime hours, had become a dark, dangerous place to call home.

With the sweltering sun slamming down on her all the way, Eva walked along the side of Blair Avenue toward her unfortunate place of employment with the railroad tracks on her right and a brushy expanse of desert on her left that ended abruptly against broken, ragged gray clusters of rock not quite tall enough to be called cliffs or escarpments yet large enough to block any of the city in that direction from her view. Ahead, she could already see the dusty, sprawling heap of stockyards, box-es, crates, and wind-beaten trailer houses that bore the non-descriptive name of the armpit known as Blairtown. It was on the closest edge of that collection of civilization's dregs where Benny Fitz had chosen to live out his life as an entrepreneur.

At ten minutes after one, the doorbells jingled as Eva eased the front door of the lounge open, peering around the metal door frame to see what kind of crowd already populated the dim-lit main room. Ironically, the first thing she heard was Helen Red-dy singing, "Leave Me Alone", three words she would have loved to use on just about anyone who was likely to accost her in this place.

Henri Kropeshek was a tart, tasteless blonde in a too-tight pink dress whose lower half was hidden by a white apron, her hair permed big enough that she should have had to pay her hairdresser three times. A pen and order pad in her hands, Henri looked Eva's way as the sunlight splashed blue into the smoke-filled room. She gave Eva a vicious frown.

Henri was never the friendliest girl in the place, but her ex-pression this afternoon seemed particularly vile, which could mean a number of things and possibly all of them: one, Benny was already taking Eva's being late out on her; two, Henri had been trying to juggle a crowd much too big for one girl, espe-cially a girl of Henri's limited talents and mental capacity; and three, Henri was angry that even hot and sweaty, with smeared makeup from the tears she had fought without success to hold back, Eva still looked five times as attractive as she did.

Eva allowed herself a rueful smile. She shouldn't think things like that; she wasn't a boastful or proud woman. But sometimes she had moments of spite when it came to Henri, be-cause all too often Henri, in her jealousy, seemed to go out of her way to make Eva's life miserable, and it was Henri's attitude which contributed to her ugly appearance more than it was any God-given homeliness.

Moving through the too-loud, shadowy room as she tried to avoid eye contact with any of the eight or nine men and one female customer scattered about the place, Eva passed beyond the bar, trying to hide a limp from having walked so far in bad shoes. With a deep breath, she put her hand on the greasy aluminum door, which was covered in brown waxy paper printed in faux wood grain. She exhaled, then pushed on inside.

Benny Fitz, in all his sweaty, oily, hair-matted glory, whirled toward her from in front of the huge cast iron griddle, a spatula in his hand. His wet-looking, savagely curly black hair, hanging limp almost to his shoulders and held only slightly in place by the idiotic-looking white paper chef's skull cap he wore, whirled with him. Eva could think of no better word to describe Benny's fun look at the moment than incensed, even as she was imagining all the disgusting hairs that might be falling onto the griddle to mix with the burgers.

"Okay. Where the hell have *you* been?"

The mousy-looking barely seventeen-year-old dishwasher standing beyond Benny looked as if he wanted to disappear like a tadpole down the drain.

"I'm sorry, B—" She almost said his name. Maybe she should have, to try and earn some points, to try and save herself some of his coming tirade. But the feel of Benny's name sliming across her lips always left Eva feeling sullied. "My car broke down."

"Again? My hell! Get a new car—*Eva.*" He spat her name like a used-up wad of tobacco or a bitter peanut.

I would if my boss paid me a decent-enough wage to afford one, she wanted to say. A dollar thirty-five an hour plus tips wasn't exactly living the high life. Instead, Eva gave him a nervous, hopefully placating smile. "I will soon. It won't happen again." She once more stopped short of saying his name, cringing inside because even to think it made her queasy.

"Right." Benny turned fully to her, looking as huge across the middle from in front as he did from the side. He was only missing the cute little muffin top on his chef's hat for her to want to compare him to the Pillsbury Doughboy, or at least a demonic version thereof. The dishwasher behind him had completely vanished from sight at this point, like a spindly aspen sapling hidden by Mount Benny. "You know what, Eva?"

Whatever he had intended to say was cut short when the lounge door banged open again, allowing the entrance of Henri, all stubby five foot one and fourteen feet of button-straining chest girth of her. Her voice was petulant, and her glare toward Eva as hot as smoking tar. "I don't s'pose it's too much to ask for some help out here."

You need more help than I can give you, Eva thought, but the hot water she was standing in was deep enough already. "Sorry, Henri. I'm hurrying."

So she hurried. Right past Benny, who stood there with one hand on a hip, the other clutching the spatula. Eva cringed as she passed him. She didn't need to wonder what walking behind a greasy, erect crocodile might feel like. In keeping with the African references, the dishwasher who once more appeared beyond him had the appearance of a petrified meerkat.

Jerking her apron off a hook on the wall, a hopelessly stained, gaudily frilled apron that tried to pretend it was still white when in fact it was a mix of beige, yellow, and splotches of light brown, she slipped the strings behind her back and was tying a bowknot in them as she pushed through the door and into the racket of the lounge she loved to hate, where Charlie Rich was now crooning out "Behind Closed Doors". She should have smiled at the appropriateness of the song, but she had an eight-hour shift ahead of her, and she was already dreading the close of the shift, when Benny would be free to unleash all his wrath—and probably finish whatever he had started to say when interrupted by Henri.

Benny wasn't a man to stew forever and not say anything to someone he felt had wronged him. He was not what one might call non-confrontational. The grossly fat man, about eight years Eva's senior, and over three times her weight, seemed to thrive, in fact, on opportunities to cut down, berate, and otherwise demoralize his employees every chance he got—especially if they were employees who had shown the audacity to ward off his charming advances. This made Eva, his one-time favorite girl, now his favorite target.

Benny had told her last week that she had used up her last chance; Eva had not heard the last about her late arrival today.

Eva agonized over the slowness of her tour of duty, but at least the bar's constantly renewed supply of drunks and future drunks, cads and soon-to-be jilted lovers delayed her unpleasant rendezvous with Benny Fitz. Every time he would try to corner her and finish chewing her out—or groping her, whichever he deemed appropriate—Henri would come in screaming about getting behind, or some customer would accost Eva, probably in hopes of avoiding being served—and smiled at—by Henri, who if she were standing at the base of a tree would charm a raccoon into leaving the ground and climbing to the very highest branch.

There was no chance that Eva wouldn't have to face the music before she went home, but putting it off as long as possible she hoped would make Benny forget how angry he had been. It had pretty much worked, on average, about zero of the few dozen times she had tried it before.

Most of the men in Benny's, like most of the men now in any other drinking place in town, were residue either from the railroad, the mines, oil fields, or from the mass of construction going apace in and around Rock Springs, in the face of potentially the town's biggest boom since its beginning in the 1880's. Many of the faces in here she had never seen, and many she would never see again. There were plenty of other bars and lounges around the area that had more to draw customers than Benny's did—live music in most of them, for starters.

During Eva's last break, of three she took out in the lounge rather than in back—with her intention to avoid close contact with Benny being obvious—she made a phone call using a number she had committed to memory forever, a number many people claimed she should never have dialed one time, much less memorized. The number belonged to Brandon Lucky, one of Benny's four part-time dishwashers, and the only person who worked at Benny's besides the night cook, Jud Shouter, that Eva would have given more than a broken fingernail for. Brandon Lucky was the guy Eva referred to as her "Lucky miracle", which always made him laugh. Besides the dishwashing job, where it seemed like he worked fewer and fewer hours with each week, Brandon was a fulltime mechanic at Dino's Mechanical, thus the fulltime winner of Eva's heart, because he knew how to fix troubled automobiles, and none was more troubled than her Valiant.

Brandon was also married, but in spite of that fatal flaw, he was possibly the best real friend she had in this town.

Brandon's voice came over the other end of the line. *Hello?*

"Brandon!"

Hey, Evie! It hardly took him a moment for her identity to register. She guessed that probably meant her car broke down far too often. *You okay?* His voice had gone quieter. That most likely signified that his wife was home, and to Karen Lucky, Eva Galanti was nothing better than a worm in an apple—Brandon being equivalent to the apple. Karen had no grasp of the concept of a man and a woman being mere friends. Perhaps most people didn't.

"Kind of. Yeah. Well, no," said Eva, fighting back a sudden rush of tears that angered her and made her bite her lip.

The station wagon again, huh? said Brandon.

"Yeah. Brandon, it's on the side of the road on Blair, maybe a half mile or so from here."

So maybe across from the cemetery? asked Brandon, for clarity.

"Maybe that area. I couldn't see anything over the rocks. Brandon, I don't know what to do. If I get fired . . ." Her voice trailed off. She didn't even want to think about what she would do if she lost this job, much less talk about it. She had applied at many other places over the last three months, most of them much closer to home, but with no luck finding an opening or, when there was one, having to face the fact that without gener- ous tips from men almost too drunk to walk, much less think, she would never be able to pay her bills on the income from one job—at least not any job she was qualified for.

It'll be okay, Evie. Brandon never called her by her real name. *I've got you, right? I ain't your Lucky miracle for noth- ing, right?* He said those words, then swore quietly. Eva knew what that meant: Karen had overheard even his quiet voice.

"Hey, don't get yourself in trouble. Stay my Lucky miracle."

Yeah, right. Brandon was trying to sound casual now. *What time you off work?*

"Nine, but I was half an hour late. Benny might try to keep me over."

Got ya. I'll be down there at nine. He'll be fried about it, but I don't think he'll give you quite as big a hassle if I'm with you. Hey, I just got home from the shop, so I'll get something to eat and clean up, then I'll see you in a couple hours. Good?

"Good." Eva swiped at the tears that welled up in her eyes. "Good. Thank you, Brandon. I have no idea what I would do without you."

After she hung up, she found herself feeling far too glad that she didn't have to hear the certain-as-death explosion happening right now at the Lucky apartment. In all the areas of life where Brandon might have been lucky, his choice of a spouse wasn't one of them.

Around 8:45, two things happened. The first of them took Eva's breath away—not in a good way—and the second took her to the floor.

CHAPTER TWO

EVA GALANTI WAS WAITING on a table, and evading unwanted advances from five guys who had too much beer and too little chivalry, when the phone started to ring. Every waitress in the place—which now meant three of them, Eva, Henri, and a brunette who slathered herself daily in makeup and perfume and called herself Teton Belle—was busy, but finally, in disgust, Belle went and yanked the black phone off the wall. "Y'ello! Benny's." Her voice had a decidedly southeastern twang to it— today. Some days it had a Scottish lilt or might sound like she was from the Australian Outback, depending upon who she wanted to impress. Most days she just sounded like she was from the Wyoming desert. "Yeah, hold on." She turned with a smile that would make reservation dogs dry heave. "Yo, Eva. Yore boyfriend."

Glad to leave the table full of oglers, Eva turned and hurried across the room. Her step felt light now that it was almost quitting time and she knew Brandon Lucky would be here soon.

Belle stood with one hip cocked, twirling the phone around in her hand like a lasso and staring Eva down as her jaws tried to negotiate three truckloads of gum.

Eva choked out a thank you, and with an ugly smile for Belle she took the phone. Belle didn't bother to tell her who it was, not beyond being "her boyfriend", and she didn't like speaking with her enough to ask. "Hello?"

Hey, Evie, it's me!

It was Brandon Lucky, and Eva felt instantly sick. She tried to hide it. "Hi, Brandon. Is everything okay?" She knew it wasn't. He wouldn't have called if it was.

"Well . . . I kind of got delayed a bit. You going to be okay if I don't get there till fifteen after?"

Eva cringed and crammed her eyes shut, fighting to hold back a gust of air that tried to escape her lungs. She composed herself and took another calming breath. "Sure, Brandon, you bet. I'll be fine. Is everything all right?" She waited with every muscle taut.

Yeah. Yeah, his voice was more than normally quiet. *Yeah. I'll be there soon. I promise. I just . . . Hey—be there soon.*

She could tell he didn't want to hang up, but he did. For a long moment she stood holding the phone to her mouth, pretending someone was still on the other end. At last, she took a deep breath and smiled. "Okay," she spoke soothingly to the beer-scented phone receiver that didn't care about her any more than it would a dead goldfish. "I'll see you soon then. Thanks for calling."

Teton Belle was standing ten feet away, by a table, pretending to care what its patrons were saying to her—that is if they were speaking simple enough English for her even to understand. Henri looked over from her own table and gave Eva an expression somewhere between a snarl, a sneer, and her earlier frown—a really sweet face, no matter how Eva thought about it.

Eva took a deep breath to try and prepare herself for a come-to-the-blackboard meeting with Benny Fitz. It was then that the front door opened, and *he* loomed inside.

Eva's mouth dropped open as she saw the monster of a man who eased the door back on its hinges until it shut with a *click*. The big, bearded newcomer, who stood over six and a half feet tall and looked like a Dallas Cowboys lineman, scanned the room, with a gaze that was slow and cautious and intent. He wore a short-sleeved blue plaid shirt, splayed wide at the top to make room for a massive neck that would never agree to his trying to button a collar around it. His Levi's were snug, with very little flare to the bottom, marking him a man who didn't care for modern styles, and he wore well-used brown harness boots.

In spite of a young, boyish look to his face, Eva couldn't remember ever seeing a bigger, stronger-looking man, and she found herself praying he wouldn't be another of those who came in here wanting to meet her, as so many had professed to her was their initial reason for setting foot inside Benny's. For once, she wanted to meet a big, strong, kind-hearted stranger with no ulterior motives, a man who wandered into the place by chance.

Eva glanced at Henri, then at Belle. Both of them looked from their tables full of patrons to her and smiled with great satisfaction that she had to take a turn waiting on someone. Henri even added the special charming touch of waving her on with a flick of her pen.

Taking another deep breath, Eva started toward the newcomer. "Hello. I'm Eva," she said over the yelp of someone laughing back at one of the pool tables and Lobo singing, "Me and You and a Dog Named Boo". In order to meet what turned out to be sharp, clear, gray-blue eyes, she looked up—way up, sort of like she was standing at the bottom of the Empire State building and trying to see how far up it went.

The big man nodded. "Hello, ma'am. Lance." Eva was surprised to recognize the shyness in his smile. He was eying her alertly, but not the way a wolf would, as she had seen from so many others. The faintly boyish look about Lance's face was offset by the closely trimmed brown beard, a few deeply etched wrinkles on his forehead, and the cautious blue eyes of one who had seen enough trouble to torture any naivete into submission.

"Nice to meet you, Lance. If you want to pick yourself a table, I'll be right with you."

Big Lance looked toward the bar, his eyes seeming to rest over-long on the mirror behind it.

"Okay if I sit at the bar?"

"Oh, sure. Sorry, I wasn't even thinking."

The loud clack of someone breaking balls at one of the two pool tables far back in the cigarette smog at the right side of the long room caused Lance's head to jerk that way. Eva noticed that his right hand came partway up to his belt line. He tried to look nonchalant lowering it back down as he shot her an embarrassed smile and lumbered to the bar.

Eva walked around behind the bar, and Lance settled onto a stool. She heard it creak, coming to grips with his weight, and she had to hold back a smile of amazement. She looked over at the clock. Still ten minutes left. Could she possibly stay occupied with the newcomer until Brandon Lucky arrived to save her from Benny's concentrated wrath?

She didn't like to make casual conversation with many of the male customers who came into Benny's. She had found the hard way that it gave inebriated men the wrong idea—and in this town where many of the men who lived here had no permanent address, some of them living out of tents or out of their vehicles down along the Blacks Fork River, it could be a deadly idea. But there was something different about Lance, besides the fact that he hadn't had time to become inebriated yet, and right now it didn't seem like she had a lot of choice. She already knew what she faced with Benny Fitz, and she had yet to find one truly sympathetic, sober customer in the bar who hadn't been leering at her like a piece of bacon. At least this big young man with the shy smile was an unknown—and he had kind eyes.

"What can I get for you, Lance?" she asked, feeling a smile naturally light on her lips.

"Do you have Jack Daniels?"

"Of course." She started to turn away, then turned back, thinking about buying time. Her eyebrow went up a little, a tic she had developed when she felt a little uncomfortable—not in danger, just on the edge. "Are you adventurous with your drinks, or is it only ever J.D. for you?"

After studying her for a moment, one corner of the big man's mouth came up in a little smile of amusement. "Adventurous? I don't know. Sometimes, I guess. Why?"

"Oh, I discovered one a week ago that I really like. Maybe you haven't tried it. Windsor Canadian?"

He pursed his lips thoughtfully. "What's it like?"

"I guess kind of spicy-sweet, maybe like a light rye. I can let you taste just a little—see if you like it."

He shrugged one shoulder. "Ah heck. No, go ahead and pour me a glass. I wouldn't want you to think I wasn't adventurous or didn't trust you."

Lance's demeanor was so soft and casual that Eva couldn't help continuing to smile at him. He smiled back, then sloped his eyes away.

Eva dragged out the act of getting the bottle from under the bar, and she poured even more slowly, glancing at the clock.

"You must get off at nine, huh?"

Her eyes jerked over to him. "What?"

"You get off at nine? You seem pretty interested in that clock, and I know how it is about quittin' time."

She let a light laugh escape her. "Sorry—I didn't know I was so obvious. Bad manners."

He grinned. "It doesn't bother me. I'd be looking too." Three fingers of Lance's left hand made the shot glass seem to vanish. "Well, here's to quittin' time. But I'm sorry I got here so late." He raised the glass to his lips and took a long sip, set it down on the bar again, looked thoughtful for a moment, then smacked his lips. "Hmm. I don't think I would ever have chose that if you didn't tell me to."

"Oh, sorry! You don't like it."

"No! No, it's really good. Kind of more like dessert than real whisky, but good." He looked at her and broke into a grin, then looked back down.

"Do you want me to get out the Jack Daniels?"

He looked back up at her, studied her eyes for a moment. "You know what? No. I think I might let you show me some more new ones. Maybe I've been in a rut too long."

She laughed. "Only you can know that. So . . . what do you want to try?"

"Well . . . Okay, first let me see how much I have in my wallet. I don't want to get bounced out of here."

Eva laughed again. "Well, we don't have *one* bouncer here, and it would take three or four to throw *you* out. So I wouldn't worry about it." She suddenly realized how her words might have sounded and felt herself blush.

"Sorry! I didn't mean that in a bad way. I just mean—"

Lance was laughing. "It's okay. I knew what you meant. I'm used to people thinking I look like a Volkswagen and Godzilla had a baby."

Eva was glad she didn't have a mouthful of anything. Even as it was, she was sure she probably sprayed spit on big Lance when she busted out laughing. She was soon laughing so hard she could barely see, and covering her mouth with her hand as she tried to keep from choking.

Lance laughed too, but not nearly as hard as she was. Her embarrassment at knowing she must be making a fool of herself only made it worse. It was as if all the tension of the day was finally releasing itself at once.

The big man sat there watching her with his intense but smiling blue eyes as CCR started singing, "Looking Out My Back Door". Finally, he said, his voice quiet, "You think you'll be okay?"

She managed to stop laughing as she studied him. When she saw the twinkle in his eye, she let out another laugh, then wiped her eyes. "Sorry. You'd better watch what you say—and don't do that when somebody is drinking."

"You kiddin'? That's the main goal at huntin' camp—makin' somebody spray whisky out their nose."

Eva forced back a laugh as she shook a finger at him. "Okay, Lance, that's enough. You have to learn to fight fair—and pick on someone your own size."

Lance grinned, a fun-loving endearing grin. Eva had no idea what this Goliath might be like drunk, but sober he seemed nothing like the other men she had been dealing with since the start of her shift. It suddenly felt very safe in Benny's Bar and Grill.

Lance seemed then to remember he was holding his wallet on the bar top. He flipped it open to check for bills, and as he did Eva saw metal flash. What made it registered a moment after his big fist closed over the object, hiding it from prying eyes. He counted ten one-dollar bills and a ten in the billfold. "Looks like I could get drunk, if I wanted to."

She eyed him for a moment. "But I hope you won't. So what do you want to try next?"

"I don't know. Surprise me."

With a twinkle in her eye, she took his glass and turned her back on him. Taking out a bottle of Old Crow bourbon, she poured two fingers in the glass and then put the bottle under the bar so he couldn't see it. She handed it to him, and after studying her for a moment, he looked down at the glass. "You didn't put anything in this, did you?"

She laughed. "Of course. Alcohol."

He matched her laugh. "Touché. All right then." He put the glass to his lips and sipped it once, then again. He set it down. "Dang. Jim Beam, right?"

"No."

"No?"

She shook her head.

"How about—"

The sharp sound of Benny Fitz's voice cut Lance off in mid-sentence. "Eva, do you know you're off the clock? I need to see you as soon as you finish there."

Eva's eyes flew to the clock. He was right; she cringed at sight of the ugly minute hand sticking straight up. She looked over at Benny. "Sure. Just finishing up with this gentleman."

Benny eyeballed Lance. In weight, Lance was a good fifty pounds lighter than Benny. In height . . . Benny almost had to look up to meet Lance's eyes, and Lance was seated on a stool. Clearing his throat, Benny gave Lance a nod and squeezed back through the doorway into the kitchen.

Lance looked at Eva. "He doesn't look happy."

She gave a little shake of her head. "No."

"He looked like someone took a big crap on top of his birthday cake."

Eva tried to laugh. The sound was pathetic, and she knew her expression was too.

Lance's face grew serious. "Hey. You all right?"

Eva nodded quickly. "Sure. Of course."

A moment passed, and then Lance raised the glass to his lips again and sipped. He set it down. "Okay, I give up."

"Old Crow bourbon," Eva said. She realized the tone of her voice had dropped since Benny's intrusion.

"Ahh . . . the cheap stuff," exclaimed Lance. "Well, it's pretty good if it can pretend it's Jim Beam."

She forced a smile, then cleared her throat. "Hey . . . I have a question for you. You don't have to answer. Just curious."

"Shoot."

"That's a bad thing to say if your answer is yes."

He gave her a laugh. "Well, shoot anyway."

"Was that a badge in your wallet?"

He looked down at the wallet, which was still curled up in his hand, then looked back at her. "You weren't supposed to see that."

"Security?"

"No. Cop."

"Oh. Where?"

"Here. Rock Springs P.D."

The feeling of lightness grew inside her. She didn't know that Benny was going to do anything she would need a policeman for. But just in case, knowing Lance was a cop made her feel safe, even with angry Benny around.

After she hadn't replied for a few moments, a shadow came over his expression. "Not a fan of cops?"

She popped out of her state of reverie and gasped, "No! I mean, yes! No!" She laughed and, after a moment to digest her reaction, he did as well, although his wasn't the huge, rollicking kind, the kind that matched his size. His was more reserved. That made her wonder if being the quiet type came naturally, or if things he might have seen in his career had made him seem a little distant. "I'm sorry, Lance. I was just thinking."

He smiled. "Thinkin's good. So . . . you're headin' out, huh? And I just got here."

"I'm waiting for a ride," she volunteered. "My car broke down on the way in."

"Oh yeah? Cream-colored station wagon? A ways up on the side of Blair Avenue?"

She stared at him, then laughed. "Oh, great! That obvious, huh? I guess at least it's still there then."

"Yep. Still there."

"I have a friend who's a mechanic. He was supposed to be here at nine and had something come up."

"So he's not comin'?"

"No, he said maybe fifteen after." She paused, then took a leap of faith. "Hey, can I ask you for a favor?"

"Sure."

"Is there any way I could sit with you at a table for a while? Or maybe we could leave together?"

"Your boss, huh?"

She gave him a nod. He had read in her demeanor what she didn't say with words.

"Yeah, I figured. I've heard ugly things about that guy. I instantly didn't like him."

"Good intuition," she said quietly.

"I'll stay. If he wants to talk, how do you think he'd act if I came with you?"

The thought gave her a moment of paralysis by fear. What *would* Benny do? Maybe it would help. Or maybe he would be all right tonight, then unload both barrels on her next shift.

She hesitated too long, so he nodded. "I get it. Too much rockin' the boat maybe."

After a few more moments, she nodded. "Yeah. Maybe."

He cast a look past her, and it was obvious he had caught a movement. She stiffened but didn't look. "Is he here?"

"Not this second, but I think he peeked out. Maybe you better go. Just make sure he knows I'm still waitin'."

"Yeah. Okay. Thanks . . . Lance. I'm glad you came in."

"I'm not goin' anywhere. Tell you what—I'll hang out there by the door. If it gets loud I'll come in."

She had to blink hard at the tears that tried to fight their way into her eyes. On a whim, she reached across the bar and gave his forearm a squeeze. It was hard to fathom the sinewy massiveness of it. She mouthed the words, *Thank you,* then turned, walked to the kitchen door, and passed through with a deep breath. She sensed Lance only a step behind her.

Benny was standing by the griddle, feet splayed, arms folded across his soft, massive chest, draped over his immense belly. He was already glaring her down, and once more the dish washer was shrinking away behind him, trying to look even smaller than he really was.

"What are we gonna do about today, Eva?"

She froze. There were times when she had felt so brave standing up to this man, but this wasn't one of those times. She could feel herself truly on the brink of losing her job. She had also taken to mowing lawns around town, pushing a rickety old red Briggs and Stratton from door to door when she saw grass that looked too long. But she didn't have the guts to charge enough for those jobs, and there was no way doing yard work could pay her rent, not when those customers were mostly sober.

Eva had too many people depending on her. She couldn't afford to lose this job, no matter how she dreamed every day of throwing her apron in Benny's face, kicking him in the impossibles, and walking away.

She walked as close as she dared, like a subservient wolf submitting to the Alpha. If she had had a tail she would dutifully have put it between her legs. Instead, she put her hands together in a motion of pleading. "Benny, I'll get the car fixed. I promise. Brandon's coming to get me right now."

Benny glared at her. She sensed there was much more on his mind than only the car, and only her being late. And Benny never could keep anything inside.

"Who's the big fat oaf out there, Eva? I can smell trouble a mile away."

She instantly bridled up. She had only known Lance a few minutes, and already she could tell he was ten times the person Benny was, and that he actually cared about people. The difference in the gaze of his eyes and Benny's was like a rotted piece of meat compared to a peppermint: It didn't take a moment to see which was sweeter. And *fat?* The fire of her Italian blood roared to life. She had to drop her gaze to the floor to hide it.

"Just some guy, Benny." She felt dirty. She had actually said his name, twice now, and on her tongue it felt like acid. "I've never seen him before today." She instantly regretted admitting that.

"You'd better stay clear of him if you know what's good for you."

She nodded, unable to meet his eyes. More than any other time, it seemed, her hatred for Benny Fitz surged up inside her. "Okay. What about today?"

"That's what I asked you, Eva. What are we going to do about it?" She had succeeded in shifting his gears, for now.

"Brandon will fix the car."

"How many times has that scrawny piss ant fixed it already? If you ask me, he should be a full-time dishwasher and forget being a mechanic. I'm surprised the garage keeps him."

"Ben— He'll fix it." She managed again to stop herself before saying Benny's name and wondered if he ever noticed when she did that. "He will, I promise."

"This is it, Eva." Benny's voice had grown harsher, maybe because she wouldn't look up at him.

She nodded.

"You hear me?" Harsher still. "Look at me, Eva! I want to hear you say it. This is your last chance, I swear."

Benny had told her that at least three times before, but this time his demeanor seemed worse than ever. He had embarrassed himself too many times trying to get her to bed, or even merely on a date with him, as if to him there was even a difference between the two. She had a feeling he really was getting close to the end with her. He hadn't tried to touch her and had said nothing flirtatious in at least five shifts, and that couldn't be a good sign. She knew she should be happy, yet she needed this job so bad. Her family would starve without it.

She dragged her eyes up to meet his. "I understand. It won't happen again."

She managed to meet his gaze long enough that Benny somehow found encouragement in it, and his eyes softened. Before she knew it, he was stepping closer. "I know you didn't mean to be late," he said, and his big arms closed around her in what he must have thought was a comforting embrace.

But inside, Eva found herself instantly quivering with the need to run, to hide. Benny smelled like some foul animal, maybe a pig, had mated with a goat and their offspring had rolled in hamburger grease. She felt bile rise up in her throat, and she couldn't bring herself to put her arms up and encourage his embrace. Even if it meant her job, there were some lengths to which she couldn't go.

And Benny hated that. When he stepped away, his arms fell like two worn-out hammers, and he glared through her. "You'd better be here on time tomorrow, Eva. Maybe even early."

She nodded and turned to go. To put away her apron, she had to walk past him, and she couldn't bring herself to do it. She had gotten clear to the door when his voice stopped her. "What—takin' the apron home? Scared to walk past me now or somethin'? Come on, girl. I won't bite."

Yet he would. And much more. Eva froze, staring at him.

It was at that moment when the door pushed open, and the head of a bear poked through, seeming close to touching the top of the doorframe. "Hey, Eva, you about ready?"

Eva stared at Lance, wanting to cry out with joy. "Oh yeah. Just a sec, Lance. I just have to put up my apron."

She felt Lance watching as she walked toward Benny, untying the apron with shaking fingers. The betrayed look in Benny's eyes would have cut her in half if his eyes had been drill bits. Tomorrow she was going to pay for Lance stepping in like this right after Eva had acted like he meant nothing to her. But perhaps tomorrow would be worth it.

Tonight she was safe.

CHAPTER THREE

BRANDON LUCKY MIGHT NOT have been everyone's first idea of a great catch, at least not in the looks department. He had narrow, mistrusting slate-blue eyes and straight, thin, nearly black hair, prematurely graying along the front, where it was generally pressed down for so many hours a day by a ball cap that it tended to look greasy, even when it was clean and dry. She had once overheard a customer describe Brandon's face, with its long, hooked nose, as looking like it had been slammed sideways in a door. The other person in that conversation had gone on to say it made Brandon's eyes look like they almost wanted to touch each other in the middle. Eva had angrily stalked away from the conversation before they could say any more. It had been all she could do not to chew them out, for she knew what a great person Brandon really was, and she knew the way his loving smile lit up his face like no other.

Brandon was a huge fan of the musical trio, Peter, Paul, and Mary, especially Paul Stookey, who was the inspiration for a reddish mustache and goatee in which Brandon took great pride.

Brandon Lucky, with Stookey goatee, wide-legged black polyester pants, tattered black tee shirt and all, had been Eva Galanti's savior so many times she couldn't count them, and from the beginning he had been the perfect gentleman. The two of them had worked together at Benny's for almost a year, and never once had he attempted to touch her inappropriately, something she couldn't even say for all the barmaids. Brandon had never been flirty, but always sweet and kind, and always there for her in times of need, even if he had to skip out on his other job—or his not-so-understanding wife—to make sure of it. And one thing nobody could take away from Brandon was that marvelous, warm smile he always had for the people he liked, which lit up his entire countenance, like the sun breaking through on a a cloudy day. When Brandon exploded into that smile, he looked to Eva, if not handsome, at least sort of roguishly attractive, and so kind that it made his looks a non-issue. Anyway, who wanted a man who looked like a model? Her ex-husband had looked like a model, and she would have traded ten of him and a box of donuts for one Brandon Lucky.

In spite of his last name, an *un*lucky childhood and lack of sound parental guidance had left Brandon roaming the streets of Missoula, Montana, at a young age. Curiosity had led to his test-driving of many cars, which would not have been an issue except generally the cars' owners had no foreknowledge of the test drives.

His little hobby had given him many hours of entertainment that unfortunately never caught up with him in his youth, and the first time he was arrested, stoned on heroin and "test-driving" a car without the knowledge of its owner, he was five days past his eighteenth birthday.

He landed in a courtroom with a judge that had no sense of humor nor of mercy, and he spent the next seven years of his life in the Montana State Penitentiary, in Deer Lodge, learning in the hardest way at least one valuable lesson that many of his fellow convicts never did: He had no wish to spend the rest of his life behind bars with a bunch of lost, sleazy souls he wouldn't give a dime for the lot of—at least any of them but the one old man, serving life for murder, who had taught him to be a mechanic.

Brandon came out of the pen as straight as the road to hell, not outwardly worse for the wear other than being decorated with cheap prison tattoos on both shoulders and thin as a flamingo ten days into a full-on fast. But he was hard put to find a human soul on the outside that he dared trust.

Like most ex-cons, he had trouble finding jobs, but one man, Dino Priest, the aging owner of a mechanic shop here in Rock Springs, had decided to give him a chance. He had taken Brandon under his wing, fixed up a back room in the shop where he could stay until he got on his feet, and basically given the young man new life. That man was the brother of the pen-bound mechanic who had so kindly taught Brandon all his skills, then died of a heart attack only two months before Brandon's release from behind bars.

The trust from Dino Priest and his brother was something Brandon would never forget.

Even now that Brandon was married to Karen, and although he had to have a second job to keep ahead of the bills (Karen was a medical disaster around every corner and an illicit drug user waiting for every moment when Brandon made the mistake of looking away), he and his wife lived in a modest apartment on the east end of downtown, and he continued working for the old man. He most likely would until the old man, like his brother, was gone, and Dino's Automotive was closed down.

Eva had gotten weak in the knees when Brandon pulled up to the front of Benny's in his primer gray 1958 Chevrolet Delray, a car in whose trunk Brandon liked to joke that he could hide a whole family of dead bodies. Brandon had fixed the car up, sanded it down, smoothed it out, and sprayed it with primer, then clear-coated over the primer because he never could afford to have it painted the cherry red color he dreamed about, "but someday he would".

Brandon and Eva said goodbye to the man Eva knew only as "Lance" and headed out toward the loneliest stretch of Blair Avenue, where a now even lonelier Plymouth Valiant waited for them, broken down on the shoulder. For several minutes, they didn't speak.

"Hey, Evie," Brandon said at last, both hands firm on the steering wheel even though before her he had never been in a car like this with two huge bench seats and a girl this beautiful.

She looked at him and wasn't going to speak, simply because she was enjoying the feeling of escape from Benny Fitz. When she spoke she merely said, "What?"

"You okay? Benny give you the biz for bein' late?"

"He tried."

"I'm real sorry. I really meant to be there."

Eva couldn't have failed to notice the red, swollen place on the left side of her friend's face. "No, Bran, please don't worry about it." She reached over and squeezed his leg, then left her hand resting there. "Lance was there with me. Did I tell you he's a policeman?"

Brandon looked over at Eva and grinned, softening and warming his sliver of whiskered face as always. "Yeah. You did."

He eased the Delray up to a stop sign and she gave his leg another squeeze. His heart lurched. He knew Eva meant nothing by it other than a sign of her friendship, but a woman that looked like Eva shouldn't do things like that. He was only a man.

"I guess I did. Sorry," Eva said sheepishly. "I guess that doesn't matter. Cop, firefighter—garbage man. Whatever he does for a living, I think he put a scare into Benny. And Benny can't fire him like he can you."

"True. You're prob'ly better off. But I can't help thinkin' what could have happened if that guy wasn't there to step in when you needed me and I promised you I'd be there."

"Bran! Stop! It turned out fine. I'm okay. Really." Eva smiled her reassurance.

Brandon chuckled and gave her a lopsided grin, stretching his reddish mustache to its thinnest limits. "Okay." He pulled onto Blair Avenue and drove in silence for half a minute before clearing his throat. "Hey." He didn't go on, but Eva wouldn't hear of that.

"What? Brandon, what?"

"Oh, nothin'. I was just thinkin'." He was thinking about the red spot on his cheek, which might easily turn into a bruise, as hard as Karen had hit him. He wanted to lie to Eva about it, to tell her he was crouched down checking someone's tire when they inadvertently opened their car door and hit him. Maybe it was better if he said nothing.

Eva finally squeezed his leg again, then dragged her hand away and left his blood to go back to normal. His heart, however—that was another thing. If he lived to be a hundred, he would never lay a hand on sweet Eva Galanti, but he well knew his heart would never recover from knowing her.

The Valiant crouched like a blond tiger in the shadows, waiting to pounce on the first unsuspecting car to drive by on this barren stretch of deserted road. Too bad it was a broken tiger. Across from them to the left loomed the dark, rectangular forms of sleeping boxcars, but other than those and the sprinkle of lights back toward Blairtown, here in the darkness there was little sign of civilization.

Brandon wheeled his Delray around and pulled over into the weeds in front of the Valiant, leaving his headlights shining on the other car, the motor running.

He didn't shut his door when he got out, because he knew Eva well enough to know she wasn't going to sit and wait for him to look at her car. She had told him she used to watch her father work on cars, and although she had never learned enough to fix them herself she always wanted to. At the rate she was going with this well-abused Plymouth, whose main entertainment seemed to be breaking parts of itself, she might get enough experience in another year to open her own mechanic shop.

Brandon popped the hood, and Eva stood and watched as he rubbed his hands together ceremoniously, then started looking around. "Start 'er up, Evie. Try, anyway."

Eva got in and turned the key. The engine revved after three short bursts of firing. It purred, and she hated it. When did a car ever continue running badly when a mechanic looked under the hood? Now they weren't going to figure out a thing.

"Got it!" Brandon called.

Surprised, Eva jumped out. "Really? You want me to leave it running?"

"Sure. Come here and look."

Leaving the door open, she hurried to the front. Brandon pointed and looked over at her. "Fan's frozen."

Eva's first thought was happiness. In less than two seconds, they knew the problem. Her second thought was more pessimistic. "Is that huge? Expensive?"

"Not necessarily."

Her heart seemed to fall. *Not necessarily,* in Eva Galanti's world, always seemed like it should be followed with the words, *but in your case it certainly will be.*

"How long will it take to fix?"

"I can come back in the morning and drag it over to the shop so we don't take a chance of damaging anything driving it over there. I bet it's done by mid-afternoon."

"I have to work at one again."

"I figured. It's okay. I'll come get you."

She looked at him, almost frozen. Her eyes jumped to the red place on the side of his face. "Brandon . . ."

"Hey. Stop, Evie. This is my choice, all right?" So he knew she had guessed where the red mark came from.

"Bran, have you ever . . ." Her voice, with her thoughts, trailed off. She was eating off someone else's ice cream cone. Brandon was a big boy. Only he could know when enough was enough.

"Ever what? Thought about leavin' Karen?"

Eva felt her face flush, and she looked away, then forced her eyes back to him. "Do you love her?"

"I think I used to."

"Okay. I guess that answers my question. Why are you staying, Brandon? I don't think it's going to get any better."

He shook his head. "Who else would ever have a guy like me, Evie? I mean, come on."

Her instant thought was to say, *I would,* but she couldn't say that. It wasn't true. She didn't want to be a shallow person, but she had promised herself that if ever she married again it would be the last time. And it would have to be everything she had ever dreamed of. She truly did love Brandon Lucky, but only as a friend, or as a sister might. She could never give him all her devotion, and pretending she could would only hurt them both.

"Someone would, Bran. You're a pretty great guy."

Even in the darkness, she saw her friend's eyes sadden, and she wished she could love him the way he deserved to be loved. He had had a rough start in life, but he had done a complete turnaround. Brandon deserved so much better than what he had. He deserved someone who might not believe he could walk on water, but who would support him if he tried.

"Come on, let's get you home. I'll bet your family's gettin' worried about you."

Eva smiled and touched his arm. "Thank you, Brandon. I don't know what I would ever do without you."

Brandon pulled the Delray up in front of Eva's house on Ridge five minutes later and leaned over to look toward it, where its living room lights glittered yellow through a screen of cottonwood branches and leaves. He straightened up and looked at her. "Want me to walk you in?"

"If you want."

They got out and stood together looking toward the house. Eva could see her grandmother moving across the living room, her movements as slow as a praying mantis stalking its prey. Her eyes misted over.

Isabella Rossi, the withered, wonderful old lady Eva called Nonni, which in Italian was short for Nonnina and was a term of endearment meaning "little grandmother", was in her twilight years of life. Eva knew it, and her mother knew it, and although neither ever spoke of it, it was a thought that filled their hearts with anguish.

"Your Nonni's gettin' around pretty good, huh?"

Eva smiled. Brandon was trying to make her feel better. "Yeah, she's doing okay. She's eighty-five now, you know."

"I didn't! Wow, then she's *really* doing good."

She took a deep breath and sighed it out. Yes, maybe that was the right way to look at it. Brandon was always trying to make her feel good. Anyway, when it came Nonni's time to go, it would be okay. She was a strong believer in the after-life, and she had been missing her husband, Pierro, for a long time, and speaking of him more lately than she had in years. She had to know her time was close. Perhaps she was excited about it, although it would be hard for her to leave her loved ones behind.

They walked to the concrete steps, which were old and crumbling, a hazard to anyone fool enough to walk down them without great care. On the porch, Eva paused long enough to watch Nonni through the window as she sat down on a ragged brown couch that was at least half Eva's age and had seen the abuse of dogs, cats, children, and even an occasional passing rabbit from the hutches Eva and her son Tyke used to keep in a shed behind the house. Dirty diapers had been changed on that couch, Kool-Aid had spilled there, and on that couch their old Irish setter, Giuseppi, had breathed his last faithful breath. Eva still mourned him two years later.

Turning, Eva looked at her friend, who appeared wistful, somehow lonesome, and a bit sad. Haltingly, she reached up and touched her fingertips to the red place on his cheek, and Brandon put his hand up and laid it over hers, pressing her hand close to his face. It was the closest thing to physical touching besides a hug that Brandon had ever taken the liberty of. He smiled at her, spreading his fine reddish mustache out until a slender nail could have been stuck into the midst of it almost anywhere without touching one hair.

"I guess I'll see you in the morning, Evie. I'll come at eight."

"I guess I'll be up." She stood on her tiptoes, and it didn't take much for her five foot five to reach his five foot ten. She kissed him softly on the cheek, in the middle of where the redness was. When she stepped away, he was staring at her, his smoky blue eyes suddenly moist. "No one should ever hit you, Brandon. You're too nice of a guy."

CHAPTER FOUR

EVA HAD HELPED HER father pull a car with a chain several times, and it never got any less nerve-wracking. She would almost rather have paid a tow truck to take her wagon to Dino's than to sit behind that wheel trying to keep the right tautness in the tow chain without dragging Brandon's car down. And she lost track of all the times slack got in the chain, in spite of her best efforts, and then when Brandon sped up it jerked Eva as if it were trying to yank off her front bumper.

Brandon dropped her back off at the house around nine o'clock, in time for her to sit at the little round table in the kitchen, just big enough for the five family members, and have breakfast, which as always was a very traditional old country affair. It consisted of *caffé latte*, that being nothing more than hot milk with coffee, along with *fette biscottate,* a cookie-like hard bread. Tyke, Eva's jet black-haired fifteen-year-old, had graduated from the typical children's drink of *caffé d'orzo,*

Nonni's traditional Italian name for hot chocolate, to a sweetened mixture of hot milk, cocoa, and strong coffee.

Nonni toddled in from down the hall, all smiles for Eva. Her
eyes disappeared almost completely from sight behind a network of wrinkles given her by two countries, three states, and
half a dozen cities of residence. She spoke to Eva in Italian because she only knew perhaps ten words of English, none of
which she used with any frequency because most of them were
curse words, and Nonni was a devout Catholic who didn't believe in swearing—unless absolutely necessary. Eva spoke back
to her in the same polished Italian she had learned along with
her English, as Nonni stopped behind her and put her gnarled,
beautiful old hands alongside Eva's neck, caressing her silky
hair.

Eva's mother, Bianca Galanti, turned from the stove, wearing a floor-length, flowered red dress and an apron that covered
the front of it down to just above the knees. She shook a spoon
good-naturedly at Eva. "Too much Italian around here, you two.
Tyke and Leo will never learn which is which."

When Nonni looked a question at her daughter, Bianca repeated the admonition in the old language. Nonni giggled and
squeezed Eva's neck, holding to the table's edge for support as
she moved to her own chair.

Bianca Galanti was tall, even taller than Eva, and had once
been elegant, some fifty pounds of rotundness ago. She kept her
black hair, now streaked loosely with silver, pulled harshly back
from her face and rolled in a bun at the exact back of her head.
The lack of loose hair accentuated the sixty-year-old's triangular
face, especially her broad, well-shaped cheekbones and fine but
proud Italian chin. Bianca couldn't arch her eyebrows too much
to change her expressions because they already had almost the
perfect high arch to them, and her deep chocolate eyes, the same
eyes with which she had gifted her daughter, were the jewels

that Bianca used to show her moods. Sometimes they were joy-ful, sometimes sad, and other times full of wrath at the thought of some injustice, even if it was an injustice that only she or one of her generation might consider as such.

"Before you start to eat, cara," —this was Bianca's term of endearment usually saved especially for her daughter, meaning simply "dear"— "you should go and see if Leo is awake yet. He was stirring ten minutes ago."

With a glance at the clock, Eva rose and set her napkin down, then made the short trip along the hall on the rough, hag-gard gray carpet that was so old and battered by shoes that it felt like she was walking across a fallow farm field. The last bed-room on the left belonged to Tyke and her three-year-old, Leo.

When Eva looked into the bedroom, Leo was sitting up on the bed, his fine, thin, milk chocolate-colored hair radi-cally unsure which direction it wanted to go in, thus choos-ing a hundred different directions at once. Besides the messy hair, the other perpetual thing about Leo was the smile plastered on his face, although no one had even been in the room. It seemed like most days Leo woke up with the same smile on his face that was there when he closed his eyes to sleep.

Leo Marcos Galanti was his mother's little angel, born in 1970 as what the pediatrician referred to as a Mongoloid, which was typical terminology until a year or so later, when they start-ed referring to his condition normally as Down Syndrome. Eva's mother had told her that doctors in her day had had a much more horrible-sounding term for the condition. They once referred to Down Syndrome babies as Mongolian idiots. Just the sound of the term applied to her beautiful boy made Eva cringe.

When Leo was born, her own obstetrician, upon helping de-liver him, had told Eva her baby suffered from a condition known as Mongolism, where a baby was born with an extra set of chromosomes that started him or her out in many ways a few lengths behind fellow racers in life. That moment, looking into the obstetrician's sad face, was the first hint she had had that anything about her baby was abnormal.

"Hi, buddy," said Eva, crouching down to get her face in his line of sight.

Leo looked up, blinking his almond-shaped eyes, which were slanted a little upward at the outside corners. When his vision came into focus, his smile grew to monstrous proportions, and she went to him and picked him up off the bed. She wondered whose embrace was tighter, hers or her baby boy's. Leo's favorite thing in life was hugging, and it was an art at which he excelled above all others Eva had ever known.

Standing up, Eva returned to the kitchen with her little treasure and tried to put him in his highchair. She should of course have known better. Leo started to squawk. One of the few things that would get this reaction from him was an attempt to keep him from hugging any and every loved one who came within his sight.

Dutifully, Eva took Leo around and let him give his hugs. Tyke held his brother longer than all the others. He had a soft spot for anyone who was challenged in any fashion, a trait he had displayed since long before Leo's birth, and Tyke was his baby brother's greatest champion, as well as his lifetime hero.

They finally settled down to eating, and Bianca took a bite of her *fette biscottate*, followed it with a little sip of nearly boiling coffee, and chewed for a few moments. She looked at Eva, who was lost in sipping her coffee and gazing at her baby boy in his worn-out highchair, which had come all the way from New York City some two decades past.

"How is the car, cara? Will Brandon be able to fix it?"

Eva didn't want to think about, much less talk about, the station wagon. "Yes. He thinks so."

Bianca waited. "When? Soon?"

"I don't know, Mama. I don't know for sure."

Bianca took another little bite of her sweet, hard bread and looked down at the steam curling out of her cup. She must have sensed Leo watching her, and she slanted her eyes over to him. The moment she did, a huge grin exploded over his face, and she matched it. "It's okay, piccolo" —a pet name she often used for Leo, meaning "little one"— "Don't you worry. Your Grandma Bianca isn't sad. Just thinking."

Leo's grin grew larger, although often that feat did not seem possible. He would have gotten out of his highchair for another hug if he could have.

Isabella looked at her daughter for a while, her black eyes shining out of a field of wrinkles. Finally, she asked her something in Italian. Bianca replied, and then for a while the only sounds at the table were the clinking of cups against saucers or the chewing of sweet hard bread.

The phone rang, and Tyke was the first one up. He must have been expecting a call, as he would never have been out of his chair so fast otherwise. It seemed he was trying to make the most of the last two weeks of his summer vacation and was probably expecting friends to call. He was a popular boy in the local high school.

"Hello? Umm . . . Yes. Please hang on." Disappointment had fallen over the boy's face, and he put a hand over the mouthpiece and looked at his mother. "Your boss, I think."

Eva was glad her son knew better than to speak Satan's name in her home.

Gravely, she got out of her chair, setting her napkin down near her plate, and went to pick up the phone. "Yes? This is Eva."

Eva. Benny. Somebody called in sick. Can you come in early?

The last thing Eva wanted was to see Benny so soon, and the thought of an extra few hours with him was akin to the thought of having the vomit of drunks spewed over her—an experience she wasn't proud to say she had been through more than once. But how could she turn down overtime when she and her family struggled every day to know how they would put decent food on the table, pay the rent, and buy clothing to keep them warm in the winter?

"I'll have to find a ride." She took comfort knowing that Benny would be taking orders and preparing food. Otherwise, he doubtlessly would have offered to come and pick her up. As of yet, she had avoided his ever coming to her home to soil it with the sweaty filth of his presence.

Fine, said Benny. *It could make a big difference in the conversation we still have to have about yesterday. Call me back as soon as you know when you can get here.*

"All right. Thank you." She managed not even to think of saying his name, and hung up as she heard him start to add some last comment.

She had the strange urge to wash her hand that had been holding the phone. Maybe she needed to put bleach on her ear as well. She went back and sank into her chair, smiling in response to her mother's concerned look and avoiding everyone else's eyes.

Why did her life have to be this way? Where was the end of the rainbow? When did the mythical ship that was supposed to be out there waiting for her come into dock?

"You have to go in early?" Bianca finally spoke what the others were thinking.

Eva nodded. She felt too depressed to reply out loud.

"It might be for the best, cara," said Bianca. "I was waiting to tell you Mr. Jensen called."

Eva felt her face pale. She stared at her mother, searching hopefully for some good sign in her eyes about her conversation with their landlord and finding none. "What is it now?"

"He's pretty angry about the last fourth of the rent money. He wants it right away."

Again, Eva only nodded, looking down at her steaming cup and wishing herself into oblivion. Mr. Jensen had promised her another week. Apparently he had forgotten.

After a long moment of silence, Bianca added, "He said he's thinking about putting an advertisement in the paper for new renters."

Eva could tell it took all her mother's strength to add that last part, and of course she didn't blame her. She would not have wanted to share that news with loved ones either. Keeping the news from Eva this long didn't help matters, but on the other hand it really didn't help Eva knowing it either. Coming up with enough money to pay the rest of the rent right now meant they were going to have to figure out for a couple of weeks how to get by on beans and ketchup—and hope there was enough of that to fill them all.

In complete silence, Eva finished her breakfast, sipping the last of the coffee that was almost cool now, and like the hard bread had lost all flavor. She partook of it because for a moment it helped her not to think of cold-hearted old Mr. Jensen, of Benny Fitz, and of the smoke-filled bar and grill.

A thought came to her, a desperate thought. She got up and went down the hall to her room. On her dresser top lay a calling card, face up. She was a little ashamed to admit that when the card came to her she was preoccupied with other thoughts, and she really hadn't looked at it. Now she did.

Lance Cartwright, it said in bold black letters, *First Class Patrolman, Rock Springs Police Department.* Following those bold letters, in smaller type, was a phone number, apparently to the police department.

But there was another number at the bottom, this one written with a pen. In front of it, it said simply: *In case you need me.*

Eva's heart was already pounding, and now it sped up. Need him? She needed him. Bad. She had been planning on calling the station to see if she could reach him. Could she be so lucky as to find him home?

She went back to the main room, unplugged the phone from the wall without a word to anyone, and took it back to her room. Here, she plugged it into a seldom-used jack, then sat down on the bed, holding the phone in silence for several minutes while she tried to breathe deeply and get her nerves and heart under control.

Finally, she dialed the pen-scrawled number. It rang. And rang. Then it rang. And rang. Ten times. No answer.

She noticed she was shivering as she reached to push down the button and disconnect, and yet the temperature in the room wasn't cold. In fact, it was warm, as most summer days in the Galanti household were, since insulation in this ancient, decrepit house had apparently seemed like some mystical concept to the builders, back in 1925.

She sat still for a while until finally gaining the courage to dial the police station number. This time it picked up after two rings. *Rock Springs Police Department. This is Rhonda. May I help you?*

"Yes, thank you. I'm hoping to reach Officer . . . Cartwright?" She almost smiled when the significance of the name struck her. Cartwright! That was the family name of one of her father's favorite television programs, *Bonanza,* which she had spent many enjoyable hours watching with him, in what now seemed like another life. And oh, how the name fit Officer

Lance, who seemed as massive to her as middle brother "Hoss" did in the television series.

Well, we don't . . . The woman stopped whatever she had been about to say and paused for a moment. *Would you like to leave a message for him, and I'll see if he can call you back? Also, may I ask what this is in reference to?*

Eva wasn't sure how to reply, so she opted for something cryptic, but potentially interesting enough for this receptionist to feel like it was important to get the message to Lance. "He asked me for some information on a person he is investigating, and I think I've got what he needs." It sounded like a great lie, big enough to garner immediate attention.

Seeming interested, the woman took Eva's name and number. She was saying goodbye when she suddenly stopped. *Oh, miss? You're in luck. Officer Cartwright just walked in . . . Oh . . . Okay, miss? He says he'll give you a call right back. Please stay near your phone.*

The woman didn't have to beg. A minute later, even though she was expecting a call, Eva jumped when the phone rang. When she picked it up she hadn't been able to stop her heart from pounding. Why did it feel like this was an illicit call?

"Hello?"

Eva! Benny.

Her heart crashed to the floor. "Hi."

You find anybody? I really need you in here—now.

"I'm trying. I'm waiting for a call back right now."

Well they better hurry. You've got a lot to make up for, I'm warning you.

"Okay. I hope I can be there soon." She hung up the phone gingerly, knowing if she used the emotions she felt for Benny Fitz right now she would have driven the handset right through the base and then would have to go buy a new phone.

Almost immediately the phone rang again, and this time Eva swore and blushed. She normally saved her colorful words for her car on its every-other-daily breakdowns. This time the phone seemed as much her enemy as the Plymouth.

She almost didn't want to pick it up, but she did. This time, her voice in her own ears sounded almost plaintive when she answered.

Hi. Is this Eva?

"Yes. Oh, hi, Lance!"

Hey, I tried to call a little bit ago, but it was busy. You okay?

"Yeah. Sorry, it was my boss on the phone. I thought it was you calling."

Are you all right?

"I am, but . . . Well, I was hoping you might be off work."

No, I work an eight-hour shift of overtime today. I'll be on until four.

She didn't seem able to pick her heart up from the floor where it had fallen. "Oh, sorry! Well, I guess I should let you go then."

Wait! Why did you call, Eva? Are you sure you're okay?

"Yes. Well, no, not really. My boss wants me to come in right now and work because somebody called in sick. But Brandon has my car at the shop."

Oh, well shoot! Where do you live? I'll come pick you up.

She seemed to seize up, staring at herself in the mirror.

You still there?

"Sorry! Yes, but . . . Lance, I don't want you to get in trouble. It's okay. I can try to find somebody else to get me there."

Hey. Eva? You're going to make me feel really bad if you don't let me come and get you. Don't make me look your address up.

She laughed. This was really embarrassing, and it was a blow to her pride. But she had few people around here she trusted except for Brandon, and she couldn't bear to drag him away from work.

"Okay. I can't tell you how much I appreciate it. How will I repay you?"

Lance's big laugh came over the phone. *By not acting like a dope. By letting me come and take you to work. I'm supposed to be a public servant, and you're as public as anybody, right?*

When she hung up, Eva had to fight back tears. There was no doubt in her mind: God had sent Lance Cartwright to her yesterday. And in all likelihood she would always feel indebted to him for his generous kindness to a woman he hardly knew.

Taking a deep breath, she stood up, dabbed her tears away, and went to take the phone back to the other room.

She found Leo smiling at her, his little arms coming up for a hug, and for a brief moment the world was a happy, perfect place.

CHAPTER FIVE

OFFICER LANCE CARTWRIGHT SET the phone down on the hook, a little smile on his face. He couldn't help it. It was seldom in life that a man met a woman as beautiful as Eva Galanti, and now after only one time meeting her she was calling on him, of all people, for important favors. It sure made him wonder what God had in store for his life next.

Lance had a report to fill out, and he had been hoping to get it done at the station, and also to get a bite to eat. But he doubted that Eva Galanti had chosen lightly to call on him for a ride, and if it was that important to her to turn to a near stranger, he wasn't going to question it, nor stall in going to pick her up.

"Officer Cartwright."

The voice was that of Police Chief Howard Buyer, and it startled Lance from his thoughts. He turned to see Buyer standing in his office doorway, a good-looking man somewhere in his late fifties, with short-cropped hair that was an even blend of brown and silver, stretched over a broad skull. Buyer's build was a mix between that of a natural strong man and a wrestler, lithe and lean but muscular and taut. Lance was seven inches taller than his chief, and probably twenty years younger, and yet he still would not have cared to take him on face to face, for the damage he guessed his chief might inflict before going down.

Howard Buyer smiled at Lance, showing long creases down both sides of his mouth that had started out as dimples. "I'd like to talk to you for a minute."

Lance cursed, in his head. He didn't feel like he had been on the department quite long enough to put his chief off, but he knew Eva Galanti was desperately awaiting his arrival.

"I was just heading out to meet someone, Chief. I don't suppose we could wait until I come back." He was taking a chance, but life was all about taking chances. If he angered the chief, then so be it. At least he had tried to do the right thing.

"It'll only take a minute," replied the chief, motioning Lance into the office with a wave of his muscular arm. The chief's office door was open, but the door on arguments was fully shut.

Lance walked into the office and remained standing when Chief Buyer sat behind his wide desk of deep red wood. "You can sit, Lance," said the chief, which in Chief Buyer vernacular meant, *Sit your butt in that chair.*

"Yes, sir. Thank you." Lance drew away from the front of the desk the padded vinyl chair meant for Chief Buyer's *sub-*

jects. He had to get it back far enough so his knees wouldn't hit the front of the desk.

As Lance sank into the wooden chair, although stout enough, it creaked and groaned, in the language of chairs probably pleading with him or calling him and his nearly three hundred pounds a bunch of names that would have hurt Lance's feelings if he had understood furniture-ese.

"Lance, you're a good officer." Lance couldn't remember many times when the chief had called him by his first name. Two of the very few had now been spoken two sentences in a row.

"Thank you, Chief."

"I've been watching you pretty close, especially lately. You have a good head on your shoulders. A level head. You don't get in fights, except if you have to. I like that."

"Thank you." Lance's mind was drifting back to Eva, even while he was soaking up the chief's praise and wondering when the *however* part was coming.

"There's only one thing I'd like to see you improve on."

Lance laughed inwardly and cringed at the same time. Here it came: the *however.*

"What's that, sir?"

"Okay, two things you can improve on," said Buyer, his dimple-creases deepening with his smile. "First, you can stop saying 'sir' all the time."

This time Lance laughed out loud, but it was hard to feel much sense of humor sitting in Chief Howard Buyer's office. Lance had a lot of respect for the man, but he never failed to make him nervous, as if Buyer were always watching to see if he would make a mistake.

"Okay. No more of that."

"Good. So Lance, I'd like to see you writing a few more citations."

"Sir?"

Buyer frowned, but it was a good-natured expression.

"Oh, yeah! Sorry. So . . . more citations? I've tried to write any that I thought were deserved. When Rick trained me, he said we didn't have any quotas."

The "Rick" Lance was talking about was Richard Cohen, the five-year Rock Springs officer they had put in charge of Lance's rookie training three years before.

Chief Buyer frowned. This time it wasn't good-naturedly. "I don't particularly like to hear that word used. Now please understand that Officer Cohen is correct. No quotas here. But . . . You simply need to write more of them."

The laugh inside Lance Cartwright now wasn't any more good-humored than the chief's frown. This was more of the double-speak he hated from government agencies. Even down here at the bottom of the totem pole where police were, apparently it couldn't be escaped. More citations. In plain language, it meant more revenue. Anyone with any sense knew that. And it meant quotas—no matter what name some official might try to ease his conscience calling them.

"I'll do my best, Chief," Lance replied. "So you're saying you want me to write people even if they don't seem like they deserve it?"

"If they're breaking a law, and you stop them for it, that pretty much makes it cut and dried, doesn't it? What did you choose to wear a badge for, Officer, if it wasn't to uphold the law?"

"I know what you mean, but—"

"No 'buts'. Lawbreakers get tickets. Plain and simple. This office has to have integrity, Lance. This badge has to stand for something—for upholding the law for all people equally, with no preferential treatment. We are in this job to make sure people are safe, and people are kept safe because we enforce traffic laws. It's that simple. There are plenty of people around Rock Springs breaking traffic laws every day, and causing wrecks. We have to do our part to curb that.

"Here," said Buyer, reaching into a desk drawer to pull out a stack of citations and throw them in front of Lance. "Take two other officers for example: Glattner and Hinshaw. Every one of those tickets is from this past two days alone, and from those two officers. I want you to follow their example."

"Yes, sir," said Lance. He knew he said "sir", and he made no attempt to correct himself. His chief might claim not to like the overuse of the title, but right now he was acting differently. "Is there anything else?" He wanted to lunge up off the chair but didn't dare do so yet.

"Actually, yes. There's a warehouse up on the left side of Elk Street that I'd like you to start doing a closer patrol of, if you would. It's the first building after Springs Drive—Primo's, it's called. I think it's thirteen-O-three. They make custom auto parts, and lately we're starting to get calls from them about prowlers in the area. They're worried about break-ins. So do me a favor, especially on weekends, and keep an extra eye out there, would you? Anyone around there who doesn't seem to belong, I'd like you to call me. Immediately."

Lance stared at him, trying to register the command. Most prowling wasn't done until after dark, which left an obvious question.

"Call *you,* sir? You mean even if you're off duty?"

"Yes. Even then." Chief Buyer didn't seem to mind being called "sir" any longer. He reached over to a wooden business card holder at the front edge of his desk, drew out one card, and handed it to Lance. "That's my home number on the bottom. Don't hesitate to call it."

Lance continued staring until the chief shrugged. "The owner is a friend of mine. I owe him a personal favor."

That explained everything in two sentences. "Okay. Understood." Lance stowed the card in his pocket, hoping he never had to call the chief at home and test out his command.

"Oh, and one other thing," the chief said. "The owner is kind of particular about what goes on in the building—being a custom car parts guy and all. Maybe secretive is a better word than particular. Anyway, do me a favor and don't try to go inside. Just patrol around the outside and make sure there's nobody suspicious lurking around. If there is, make contact with them and get their information."

"Good as done, Boss. I should head out," Lance said, then waited.

"By all means," said the chief. "Go keep your appointment. And keep up the good work. Oh—and one last thing: Keep going like you are, doing the right thing, and we have a little incentive program here in the department we usually don't let the guys in on for a while. We'll talk about it more some other time, but just understand that I know it can be pretty hard to make it on a cop's wage. And good, loyal work has better benefits than you might think. It's one of those 'don't call us, we'll call you' things. I'll bring it up again when the time looks right."

This thought brought a grin to Lance's face. Even though he had no idea what the chief's revelation entailed, making money was always a welcome thing. "Okay. Thanks, Chief."

The chief stood and thrust out a hand, which Lance took. Although the chief's hand was much smaller than his, it was every bit as hard and muscular, impressive especially for a man of his age.

"Oh," the chief said suddenly. "There is one more tiny thing: I'd still like you to think about shaving off that beard. I've had a few older folks ask about it, and I could tell they didn't think it was very becoming on a police officer."

Lance only grinned. "I'm thinkin' about it, Chief. I just don't know how much you'd like me lookin' like I'm fifteen years old."

Lance shut the chief's door behind him. Out in the main hall, which technically was the hallway of the Rock Springs municipal building, Lance almost ran right into one of the chief's superheroes, "Glatt" Glattner, whose real name was Jacob, although it was seldom used.

"Jeez, big guy," scolded Glattner pleasantly. He was a drastically handsome man with chocolate brown hair, wide shoulders, and lean hips, at six foot two formerly the tallest officer on the department, before Lance came along. "You're like a plow horse."

Lance grinned. "Sorry, Glatt. I shouldn't be allowed indoors."

Glattner laughed. "You said it, not me! Say—you want to grab a bite to eat later on? Four hours or so?"

"Sure, buddy," said Lance. "Sounds great." The invitation made him happy. Like everyone else in the Rock Springs P.D., he had high respect for Jacob Glattner, the most senior officer in the department now except for their two detectives, Plancher and Deroe. The only downside Lance could think of about Glattner was how he always felt like he was under a little bit of scrutiny when he was with him, as if Glattner was his supervisor and always trying to gauge his effectiveness as a cop. It was close to the same feeling he got with Chief Buyer.

Out in his patrol car at the curb, Lance tried to maneuver his two hundred ninety-five pounds of six-foot-seven frame around to a position of semi-comfort, then shook his head and grinned at himself. Comfort! Some things simply weren't meant to be.

Eva Galanti gave Leo another hug, then waved at the rest of the family and ran out the front door the moment she saw the patrol car pull up, a black and white Ford LTD. She would have liked to introduce Lance Cartwright to her family, but she had already taken too long getting to work, and Benny was going to be jumping up and down and frothing at the mouth. Besides, there would be plenty of time yet ahead if she and the policeman became friends as she hoped they would.

Lance unfolded himself out of the driver's side, making the Ford visibly level out. Had it been human, she guessed it would have given a sigh of relief.

"Hi, Lance. Thank you so much for coming."

"Sure thing. I hope I wasn't too long. The chief stopped me on my way out to give me a scolding."

She gave him a surprised look but held any other reply until she was seated. As he sat down, the whole car rocked his way, and she couldn't help let out a little laugh.

Lance flushed. "Sorry about that."

"It's okay. I hope you aren't in trouble with your chief," she said.

"Nah. He just wanted to tell me I don't write enough citations."

She looked her amazement at him. "I thought I had heard the quota thing was a myth."

"Funny, that's what I told him." He pulled back into the street. "He said there really isn't a quota, per se, but he wanted me to write more tickets."

That made her frown, puzzled.

"I know. Sounds like double-speak to me too. I guess they just don't like the word 'quota'. They must have some other word that means the same thing, like 'goal'."

The ride to Benny's, down A Street, then down Blair Avenue, was fairly fast, perhaps too fast. Eva had no desire to get there even as soon as they did, but she knew Lance was only doing his best to make up for his earlier delay. He pulled up and got out, probably meaning to come around and open her door, but she got out first and met him at the hood.

"You gonna be okay? You want me to make an appearance in there real quick?"

She started to tell him no, but almost instantly changed her mind. Maybe it would be good at that if she kept the big officer on her boss's mind. Who knew when Benny might need a jolting reminder?

"Is that okay? Can you pop in in your uniform?"

"Of course. I just can't buy a drink. It's the least I can do for taking so long to get you."

They stepped to the door, and he opened it for her. The first person she saw when her eyes got used to the shadowy, smoky interior, which today for some reason also smelled like rancid grease and Brut aftershave, was Benny Fitz. He had seen her as well, and he was glaring her way. She guessed that was because by now Lance was also inside with her, his silver badge probably shining bright through the darkness.

She turned to thank Lance, but before she could get any words out, he asked, "What time do you get off?"

"I'm not sure. It was supposed to be nine again."

"Do you have a ride home?"

She started to nod. Brandon had said he hoped to have the Plymouth done. But there were no guarantees. "I'm supposed to, but I don't know. It's okay, though. I'll call someone."

"I'll be here at eight thirty," he said, seeming not to have heard her. "Sharp. I'll be in a white and black Bronco—in my street clothes. If you hear from your ride in the meantime, just try to give me a call."

Eva couldn't help but smile. So often lately she had felt like everything was against her. Lance Cartwright was the best thing that had happened to her besides Brandon in weeks, if not months.

By the time the door shut behind Lance, blocking out the bright sunlight from beyond, and Eva turned around, Benny had vanished. She scanned the bar, then the lounge. No Benny. That meant he would be waiting in the back, like a spider lurking in the shadows beyond its web.

Wait for the kill . . .

CHAPTER SIX

THE LINGERING SCENT OF rancid hamburger grease and French fry oil in the lounge became an assaultive wall upon pushing through the swinging door to the kitchen, although the smell of Brut vanished completely. Back here, the light smog hanging four feet down from the ceiling was a mixture of oils burning and Benny's Camel cigarettes, and it swirled and spun in blue wreaths that made it resemble even more the sticky webs of Benny's that Eva feared right then so much.

In the midst of the web, his ever-present spatula in hand, stood Benny Fitz, his apron smeared with blood and black grease. Sullen anger smoked in his eyes the same way the cigarette jutting from a corner of his mouth smoked up the room. Eva saw the dishwasher who had been standing behind Benny make a quiet exit out the back door and would have bet Benny told him to.

"We're gonna talk later, Eva." Benny stared her down, his eyes looking as greasy as his lips and cheeks. "The place is too busy right now, so get your fat butt out there." It was funny how someone with a hind end as large as Benny's could use such an insult on a woman as fit-looking as Eva, but oh how often that seemed to be the way with such insults.

Stepping back, Benny glanced sideways, found the hook beneath a piece of masking tape with her name on it, and yanked her apron loose, throwing it at her. "We're gonna talk about bringin' uniforms around here too."

By which of course he meant uniformed officers.

Feeling numb, Eva backed up, turned with the apron in her hands, and walked back into the lounge. With her hands shaking, she could barely get the knot tied in the apron strings behind her back. Her mind was whirling. The whole room was a fog of smoke and fumes and shadowy, blurred faces, a din of noises from Kenny Rogers on the hi-fi croaking out to *Ruby* not to take her love to town, to clinking glass, to raucous laughter, to the click of billiard balls on the far end. It all seemed to spin around Eva with the blend of smoke like a miniature carnival and a house fire mixed in a gigantic blender.

"Hey. Eva!" She felt a hard slap on her backside, and someone squeezed her buttock. She turned, trying to bring the man into focus as his hand fell away from her. "I need a JD in the worst way."

She blinked, and the face of a man she knew only as "Pop" came into focus. Pop was an oil man, she understood—a roughneck. A lean and sinewy little man not much taller than her five foot five, with powerful hands and veins that seemed to rage to the surface of his leathery skin like little ropes, any place a vein could be. He had a full head of wavy hair that should have been gray but which he kept dyed a light reddish brown, because somehow he seemed to think it made him handsome for the ladies.

"It'll be a minute," Eva said, trying to stay calm, still feeling the brazen touch of his hand on her. It was nothing new. In the rage of the current boom, men had come to Rock Springs from literally all over the globe, to build and to mine, and most of them knew they had immunity in this town because it wasn't likely the law would ever catch up to them for any crime they might commit. But being slapped, grabbed, and groped by greasy, whiskey-breathed men never got easier, never got tolerable, no matter how used to it Eva might be.

She was tying her apron as she made her way through the swinging gate, back behind the bar. She snatched up a shot glass and a square bottle of Jack Daniels Old Number 7, its amber fluid glowing provocatively in the smoke-stained yellow lights lined up along the top of the mirror on the wall behind the bar.

In sharp contrast to moments earlier, all of a sudden every sight, every sound, and every smell in the room now seemed crystal clear, set apart from everything else around it. Even with the noises in the background, and the sound of Pop's raunchy comments she was trying to block out, the tinkling sound of the whisky flowing into his glass was accentuated like a cold mountain stream in a high-country dawn.

She handed Pop the glass, he handed her two dollars back, telling her to keep the change, and then made a comment that she had to grit her teeth over and roll her eyes. He tried for a few more sentences to engage her, but she excused herself as politely as possible and moved on down the bar.

Bill, Jerry, Wayne, Stratton . . . She knew many of the regulars strung out along the mahogany by name, and some only by face. One blond-haired man well over six feet tall looked like he had had a board tied to his face for the first five years of his life. His profile was something like a rough concrete wall, and his gaze was a million needles through Eva's skin.

She stopped at Wayne, the most polite of the men she recognized, and tried to make conversation and pretend the blond-haired man wasn't even there, but that wasn't in the cards.

"Hey, doll. Don't forget me." The blond man's voice was low and sullen and sounded like he had wads of toilet paper stuck up both nostrils.

Eva poured the blond-haired man's order under his leering stare and knew this shift was going to be as slow as sitting nude in a snowdrift waiting for the sun to come up.

"Hey, Eve," she heard a feminine voice beside her, and a too-familiar hand brushed her backside. She would almost have preferred Pop.

She gritted her teeth and turned to look at a short, compact-looking yet pretty barmaid by the name of Joyce, whose hair was cut short in the pageboy style, with the word "boy", in Joyce's case, being particularly meaningful.

There were too many customers close for Eva to warn the twenty-five-year-old Joyce about inappropriate touching, so Eva replied only with, "Hi, Joyce," then steeled herself and went back to serving the crowd along the bar, who all seemed to be enjoying their weekend away from the construction sites and the railroad, the coal mines and the oil fields, perhaps a little too much, as usual.

A man sauntered in whose build was athletic, and his golden-blond hair short-cropped yet still running strongly to a wave. He had a fine reddish-blond mustache and large, expressive eyes that shone an exquisite crystal blue even in the shadows of the bar. The stranger was a man Eva had never seen, much to her surprise because he seemed like a man completely at ease, comfortable in his environment, confident in himself perhaps in the extreme. Plainly put, he didn't look like someone walking into a crowded bar for the first time.

When the man saw Eva, a little smile came to his lips, as well as his crystalline eyes, and he sauntered her way, careful never to seem like he was giving way to anyone in his path. He went to a place down the bar, separated from the nearest patron by three feet of inexplicable no man's land.

Eva was drawn to the newcomer, who was watching her intently, with that almost imperceptible smile on his lips. She walked down to him. "Hi. I'm Eva. You new here?"

"Not to town. But to Benny's, yeah."

"Then welcome. What can I get for you?"

"Colt .45, if you have it. No glass."

"Coming up." Eva smiled at the stranger's very specific taste, choosing the malted liquor over anything else in the bar; they carried most brands of any notoriety.

She popped the top on a twenty-two ounce bottle of Colt. 45 and handed it to him, and he took a long swig and smacked his lips. "I guess I'm rude," he said with a grin. "Eva, I'm Chris. Chris Hinshaw."

"Hi, Chris." She felt compelled to extend her hand. He held it for a few moments, and she found she didn't mind.

"So, Chris, you say you're not a stranger to town?"

"No, but sometimes I wish!" he said with a chuckle. "I'm a veteran of this place, actually. Used to do construction here."

"But no longer?"

"Nope. Physical labor stinks."

The comment surprised Eva a little. With Chris Hinshaw's build and powerful forearms she figured he must have a fairly physical job, or else he spent a lot of time at the gym, which wasn't all that common a pastime. Her curiosity, and Chris Hinshaw's gentle, friendly way with conversation, made her want to press him further on his line of work, but she guessed he would have volunteered it if he wanted it known.

"So what brings you into Benny's?" *It can't be the reputation of the owner!* she thought.

"Good reviews." The little smile he gave her was cryptic.

"Really? Wow. Well, that's good to know."

"Should be. They were about you."

She stared at him until she could wrangle her tongue loose again. "About *me?*" She hated knowing it, but she was blushing and was glad for the dim light in the place.

He laughed. "Sorry, that prob'ly sounds creepy. But no, a friend of mine said—and I'm quoting him, so don't slap me—there was a beautiful, sweet girl working here who was even humble on top of everything else. That's not something I see much of around the Rock, so I had to come see for myself."

After recovering from another moment of amazement, Eva let out a giggle. "Well, the part where you said 'girl' tells me he was talking about someone else."

He grinned. "No, his description was pretty specific, and he named you by name. As soon as I saw you I knew who he was talking about."

A gut feeling hit Eva, making her feel strange, but not in a bad way. "I don't suppose your friend might be a great big guy named Lance."

Chris Hinshaw grinned bigger. "I guess he would. He talks pretty highly of you."

A flood of feelings and thoughts rushed through Eva. She had been around long enough to hear a lot of flattering things passed around about her, and some things passed around that embarrassed her and made her feel sick, depending upon who was doing the talking. Something told her that anything Lance had said she wouldn't have minded a bit. But being called a girl still made her laugh.

"So then if you're friends with Lance, I'm guessing you're a police officer," she said, leaning closer and lowering her voice.

"Yep, a cop. You're a good guesser. And I'm telling you what—you found a pretty good guy as a champion. That big brute has a heart of gold." He raised his Colt .45 and sipped deeply, giving her a wink, and Eva basked in the warmth inside her. Now she wished she had someone she could brag about Lance Cartwright to. Not that the two of them would ever make a pair, because she must be at least ten years his elder. But he certainly was a sweet young man.

Eva was forced to move on eventually, and Chris Hinshaw sat and drank alone. After half an hour or so, when she had found only three more short moments of peace to chat with him, he got off his stool and swept the room with his eyes, the shrewd eyes of a cop, with the same judgmental gaze as Lance Cartwright.

Eva made her way back over to Hinshaw. "I hope you'll find more chances to come in. And your friends are welcome too. This place doesn't always seem like the safest place in the universe. It's nice to have good guys around now and then. And I especially like you guys coming in because my boss doesn't. He refers to you as 'uniforms'."

"Sheepdogs," said Chris Hinshaw, grinning.

"Sheep— Oh! Yes, sheepdogs. That's a good way to put it. And thank you for what you do. I don't imagine you ever get enough thanks."

He shrugged his broad shoulders. "Don't worry. Thanks from just one lady like you makes up for all the rest. See you around, Eva. I'll keep the word going around about Benny's. We'll be sure and put this joint on the map; it sure is in a weird place for a bar."

Later that afternoon, a uniformed officer with a bulky, clean-shaven jaw and a flattop haircut came in and stood in the doorway for a while, scanning the room. He was a big enough man, and seemed like he could handle himself, but there was a nervousness about his glance that she couldn't dismiss. After a while, the officer saw her and walked to the table she was serving. Eva smiled. "Can I help you?"

"Maybe. I'm Officer Stone. You must be Miss Galanti, right?"

She smiled again. This feeling of being watched over by the entire Rock Springs P.D. could get addictive. "I am."

"Good to meet you." Officer Stone nodded at the patrons who stared at him from their round table and said, "When you're done here, I'd like to have a minute of your time." He went back and stood by the front wall to wait for her.

When she had finished taking the orders at the table, passed them on to Benny, in the kitchen, and brought them their drinks, she went to Officer Stone, where he waited patiently at the front. She wiped her hands on her apron. "So what can I help you with?"

"Well, I want to show you a few pictures, if you have a minute. I should have tried to talk to you somewhere else. This isn't the best place to do this, but I don't have your personal information, or I would have called you at home to set something up."

"We can wait if it's better," she suggested, highly curious as to what photos he was going to show her that he wasn't bothering to show anyone else in the room.

"No. No, I'm here now. I don't suppose you've seen this guy around before," he said, glancing around to see if anyone else was paying attention, then holding up a xeroxed photo of a sour-looking, balding man who wore a tie he seemed to be using to bind the middle of his collar together on a neck that was too large to let him button his shirt. In the upper right corner was written the name Lucas "Lookie Luke" Borders, a date of birth and brief description.

"I haven't," replied Eva, shaking her head. "Sorry."

"No problem. How about him?" The second photo was of very poor quality, as if someone had made a copy of a copy of a copy. From what she could see, this one had a slightly friendlier look, and wasn't a homely sort, other than having strange eyes. The name on his picture was Gavino Berretti, alias Galletto.

"No, not him either."

He nodded. "Okay. Last one."

Again, the third photo was of pathetic quality, like a shot taken of someone in a dark room with nothing but a candle glowing to illuminate him. It was another man she didn't recognize, at least from this photo, a dashing, handsome gentleman, from what she could tell in the picture, who wore his suitcoat and tie well and had a kind hint to his gaze. In the corner of that xeroxed page it said, Ambrosio Procopio.

"I'm afraid not. But I'm sure curious about something."

"What's that?"

"Why me? Why did you think I might know them?"

He looked at her for a few seconds, then scanned the room again. His earlier nervousness seemed to return. "Can you come outside for a minute?"

"I guess. Sure."

She followed Officer Stone outside, and they stopped half under the shade of the green- and white-striped awning, half in the hot sun. "I'm sorry about all the secretiveness, Miss Galanti. By the way, my name is Buck."

"And you can call me Eva." She held out her hand, and he took it and held it for a few seconds. Her willingness to shake his hand seemed to affect him emotionally, for a film of tears came into his eyes before he cleared his throat and blinked them away. His unexpected show of emotion shook her. She had to guess there was much more to it than she could know—likely more than he was going to tell her.

"Thank you, Eva. I appreciate that. I have to say I wish I had seen you somewhere else, but here I am."

"I don't understand. Why does it matter where you saw me?"

He looked around again, cautiously. "Because we probably shouldn't be letting anyone see you talk to me."

"Oh." His words scared her, but maybe more so the way he was acting. His words, his close-to-the-surface emotions, his furtive glances around. It all added up to something she wasn't sure she even wanted to understand.

"So why me? What made you think I'd know any of those men?"

"I can't exactly say, other than you work at this place, and . . . Well, I guess it sort of has a reputation I'm trying to unravel, even though I don't know enough to talk about it yet. A friend of mine told me about you. A fellow officer. He said you worked here, you seemed trustworthy, and . . . Okay, I'd better stop there. I don't want to say too much yet. Just be careful, Eva. There are things going on in this town that I can't talk about, but they're pretty scary. Be careful who you talk to in this place, and what you say. All right?"

In spite of the heat of the day, a chill ran through her. "Sure. I will. Thank you."

He dug into his shirt pocket and fished out a business card and a pen, flipping the card over to scratch a number on the back. "This is my personal number: two, six-five-two-seven. Please don't share it with anyone. And please don't mention I talked to you, okay? Not to anybody."

"Except other policemen," she put in.

He stared at her for a long moment, then scanned all around them once more before meeting her eyes again. "Listen. Like I said, I don't want to scare you. But when I say anyone, I mean *anyone*. Don't tell a soul we talked. No family, no cops— *nobody*. Hopefully all those drunks in there will forget I was here. But if you see any of those guys I showed you, please call me right away. Unless you see them, this isn't going to matter.

But if you do, it might. At least then maybe I can find out more. I wish I could tell you more, but I really can't."

"So do I even get to know who those men are?"

Buck Stone smiled. "I wish I even knew for sure who they are. All I can say is I got an anonymous note from someone, along with these three photos. The note said I'd be getting more information later. That was two weeks ago, and just yesterday I got a phone call—anonymous again. This disguised voice told me some stuff about Benny's, and some other scary stuff I won't mention, especially because I don't know if it's true. But I was specifically told to ask around down here and show these photos, just to see if anyone knew them and would be willing to talk about them. Until I found out about you, there wasn't any-body I actually dared talk to."

She smiled. "So all because of Lance."

"Yeah. All because he told me about you, and he seems like he trusts you."

"But . . . You're not sure you trust him."

Officer Stone gave her a rueful look. "It's a lot more complicated than that. It's not that I don't trust him. He's been a really good friend, and I'm pretty sure he's a good guy. I just don't know anything for real anymore. Heck, I don't even know why I'm telling you all this, to be honest."

"Because I'm a good listener?" She smiled.

"Yeah. I guess that's it. And I guess because I'm trusting you."

"Why?"

He stared at her, his mouth clamped shut. Finally, he shook his head. "I don't know. Something in your eyes?" He shrugged.

"Okay. Then thank you. I guess that will have to be good enough for me."

He took another deep breath. "Eva, there's one other thing I should say, and this is going to sound weird: I honestly don't know one single thing about the guys in these photos. Not a thing. I wasn't just saying that. For all I know they could be federal agents or something, okay? I'm not trying to scare you if they ever show up here."

Eva nodded. His words gave her a strange modicum of comfort. "Okay. Thank you for that."

For the first time, she began to realize that the look on Officer Stone's face was not simply caution, or even worry for her. The look might not even be as much nervousness as it was actual fear. Officer Stone was flat scared, of something. He was trying to protect her from the same fear he had inside him.

She folded her arms quickly across her chest. "Okay. Buck, right?"

"Yeah. Buck. And thanks for talking to me, Eva. I hope if we see each other again it's at a party or at the store or something."

"Me too, Buck. Hey, I'd better get back in."

"Yeah. Thanks again." He turned and walked to his waiting patrol car as she went back into the lounge, feeling a strange apprehension she hadn't felt before meeting Officer Buck Stone.

She walked straight to the girl's room, went inside the stall and sat on the edge of the toilet seat, staring at the door. Her heart would not stop pounding. What in the world could be going on in this town? Whatever it was, she prayed she would never know. Trouble plagued her life enough already.

For some reason, maybe because she managed to stay up at the bar most of the time instead of having to fetch sandwiches from the kitchen, where Benny Fitz lurked, the rest of the shift seemed to go by fast, and she was able to push the cryptic visit from Officer Stone far to the back of her mind.

Then came the last hour of her shift. During that hour, she couldn't help looking at the clock every few minutes, seeing it tick closer and closer to eight-thirty, when Lance Cartwright had

said he would come for her in his Bronco. The minute hand
seemed to take forever to move.

When she remembered Lance coming, she couldn't help also
remembering what Buck Stone had said about not telling anyone
he had been to see her, or what they had talked about. She felt a
little queasy. Why not tell Lance? He couldn't possibly cause a
fellow officer any trouble. She had always been a good judge of
people, and she had no doubt that Lance was a good person.
Wasn't he?

She cursed herself, and she almost cursed Officer Stone. He
had planted the seeds of doubt in her mind. She had been so
happy to meet a guy like Lance. Now, even if it was far back in
the recesses of her mind, a little question would nag her about
him. She wished Officer Stone had never come here at all.

She felt the odd apprehension grow stronger inside her
chest, and fighting it back didn't help. It felt like she was
living in an episode of *Mannix* or something. Why couldn't
she tell Lance anything Buck Stone talked about? The fact was
she didn't know. She just couldn't. If she couldn't keep a confidence with Officer Stone, she could keep it with nobody else.

Her head whirled. What did she know about Officer Stone,
anyway? She closed her eyes and gritted her teeth. She had to
get these thoughts out of her mind. All they could do was drive
her insane.

At eight-twenty, Benny's night cook, Jud Shouter, came in,
and Eva happened to be in the back collecting a tray of sandwiches for a table full of boisterous patrons she would just as
soon have poured boiling coffee on as be involved in conversation with.

Benny had gone to the restroom and left Eva temporarily in
charge of flipping burgers. She was at that stage of night where
she would almost have sold her soul for a shower and some
shampoo. She smelled like a piece of smoked ham.

"Hi, Jud," she greeted the stocky, thin-haired man who came in through the front door wearing a once-white tank top and 501 jeans, with grease-splattered tan work boots on his feet.

"Hi, Eva. How you doing?"

"Good. Really good. I'm almost off."

He grinned. "Lucky!"

Jud Shouter, a married man with two kids, was one of the few people at Benny's that Eva could trust, could carry on a conversation with her that didn't turn to flirting, and who actually seemed to care how she felt. In fact, he and Brandon were probably the only two here she trusted completely, or as completely as she trusted any man; her ex-husband, who made her despise his name so bad she took her old one back, had left a bitter taste in her mouth toward most men, although few would have guessed it because she knew how to treat men to make them like her. It was the only way to survive—and thrive in—the life of a barmaid.

The toilet flushed in the restroom, and Benny came out too fast to have washed his hands, unless he had done it in the toilet. He kept a bottle of rubbing alcohol on a shelf above the stove, and he screwed the lid off, splashed some on his hands, and rubbed them together, eyeing Jud.

"You good for the night, Jud? It's eight-twenty-five. I think I'm gonna take off."

Eva's heart soared. She couldn't have been much happier than to think she was going to finish her shift with no Benny around, and, with that being the case, she guessed no harsh talk with him either. That wasn't like Benny, who usually kept his word when he promised his employees they were going to have one of his "talks". But Eva was not one to question a gift horse.

"Got it covered, Boss," replied Jud, clapping his hands and rubbing them together as he turned to the smoking triple row of burgers.

"All right. Good job." Benny turned his sweaty, hairy face to Eva. "You're off too. Hang up your apron; I'm giving you a ride home."

CHAPTER SEVEN

EVA GALANTI KNEW HER job hung in the balance. A job she hated like none she had ever had, under a boss she despised like almost no one she had ever known. And yet at home Tyke needed new shoes, along with new clothes for school, she needed to pay the overdue rent, and she needed to keep her car running, to say nothing of buying food. She could not lose this job, not without something else being already promised.

She knew the moment Benny spoke that she should run. Her mind whirled to the thought of standing in line for food stamps, of begging churches for secondhand clothing, or even standing on street corners with her hand out for change.

No. She wouldn't run. But she would be strong. She had stood strong before, and Benny hadn't fired her. She could do it again. She *had* to.

Then, amid the fog in her brain, she remembered Lance Cartwright! Lance had said he would be back at eight-thirty, and it was now twenty-five after. Lance didn't strike her as the kind who would be fashionably late. If anything, the big patrolman was already outside. Eva drew a deep breath and forced back a relieved smile. She wasn't going to think about the implications of anything Buck Stone had said to her right now. Lance Cartwright was a good person. She knew that as much as she knew anything.

Putting on a stoic face, she said to Benny, "Oh. Thank you," then walked past the fat man and Jud, untying her apron as she went. She could feel vibes from both of the men—vibes that were one hundred eighty degrees apart. Benny's vibes were obvious. They went back and forth from furious anger to lust. Jud's were sorrowful, sympathetic. He knew what Eva was headed into and there wasn't a thing he could do for her—or at least he wouldn't. Eva couldn't blame him. He couldn't afford to be without a job either, and he was replaceable.

But Jud didn't know about Lance Cartwright. Eva was going to be fine—at least for tonight.

When Eva hung her apron and turned, Benny was standing there with hands on his hips at the door going out, watching her. She walked toward him, mind in a whirl, trying to imagine what this night could have turned into if Lance weren't here to pick her up. She would have been frantically planning ahead, trying to decide how far she would go to stop this man. It had only ever taken words from her before, but she had always known one day that would change.

Eva stared at the door as Benny turned and smiled a greasy smile at Jud. "See you tomorrow, Jud. Take good care of the place."

Benny Fitz thought he had a date. She could hear it in his voice. Again, she held back a smile as they walked out into the lounge.

Eva didn't know why Benny often parked out front, when most of the others with the exception of Jud parked in the back lot, and went out that way. It was probably Benny's way of giving his lounge employees one last evil eye, making sure they knew even if he wasn't actually watching them he would certainly be thinking of them.

She scanned the room for Lance. It took five seconds to see he wasn't in here, so he must be sitting in his Bronco out front. She guessed now that she probably should have told Benny Lance was coming back for her, but in a way she was glad she hadn't. She was going to relish the look on Benny's face when he saw the big policeman there waiting for her.

The odors of the kitchen and the lounge lingered on Benny and Eva as they stepped out the front door and let it shut behind them. Benny stopped and drew in a lung-filling breath, seeming not to notice the rotten smell of methane from the stockyards. "Man, what a night!"

But not the night you think it's going to be, Eva thought. She scanned the curb in front. As she looked over the one on the opposite side of the street, her heartbeat started to rise fast. *Black and white Bronco . . . Black and white Bronco . . . Black and white Bronco . . .* There was no Bronco in sight, black and white or any other color. *Lance! Where are you? Stall,* Eva said to herself. *Stall!*

"Oh, Benny?" She stopped and pivoted on her heel. "I should have used the restroom before I left." She tried to get past him.

Benny just laughed as he grabbed her upper arm and spun her back around. "Oh, come on, Eva! What are you, a four-year-old? We're five minutes from your house. Let's just go."

She tried to pull away from him, but Benny had been a hod carrier for a mason for years before he started up the bar, and there was no pulling away from his grip.

"You're hurting me! Let go, please."

"Come on." He dragged her toward his car. "You can use the bathroom in a few minutes. I'm not gonna wait around."

"Then I'll call for a ride."

"From your friend the cop?"

She froze. "I guess."

A little smile came to Benny's lips, the kind of smile someone gets when they know something you don't.

At that moment, a car pulled up across the street, and a sleazy-looking, rail-thin man with filthy, longish blond hair and a Levi jacket got out, looked either way along the street, then started at a saunter toward Benny and Eva. After an initial leer that took in all of Eva, from head to foot, his gaze settled on Benny.

"Got that thing done, Benny."

"Oh, good! Good, Willie. Here." He reached into his back pants pocket and pulled out a business card, flipping it over to show dirty Willie some scrawled writing on the back. "Show that to one of the barmaids. It'll be good for a burger and a few beers. Oh! And—" Reaching into his pocket again, he drew out a folded bill and slipped it into Willie's hand. "Thanks again. See you around, Willie my man.

"Come on, Eva," Benny said. "I don't think you're gonna be able to find a ride home, so let's go."

Eva felt sick as Willie went away from them and she was alone with Benny once more. Had Benny and Willie's dealing had anything to do with Lance? Certainly not. No one could have known Lance was coming back to get her.

She started walking with Benny's hand on her arm. After a few yards, his hand fell away, but she kept walking. She was trained now.

Eva drew in a deep breath. Okay. She had maybe another minute. Maybe Lance was running late. He couldn't be that late. He would be here. Of course he would.

Yet what if he wasn't? What if Eva was truly getting into Benny's car, and they were heading across town together?

Was this the night of sink or swim for Eva Galanti? If it was, fine. Fine. Maybe it was time this all came to a head. If she ended up without a job, then so be it. But why assume the worst before it happened?

She guessed she was probably a fool as she made up her mind to give Benny a chance to take her home, like he said he was going to. She couldn't simply end everything right here and now, quit her job and put herself and her family in poverty because she thought she could tell the future. She would give Benny a chance to hang himself. If she ended up unemployed, that was something she would just have to deal with. She had felt it coming for some time anyway.

Benny stopped five spaces down the row of cars at a silver-green sixty-eight Pontiac Le Mans sedan. He didn't come around and open Eva's door, which was the first thing he did right; she wanted no favors from this man. She wanted a paycheck for slaving away for him—nothing more. She cringed when she slid onto the vinyl seat and wished she had a newspaper to sit on.

The Pontiac was as filthy and scarred up as Benny was, and the seats as greasy and hairy as his skin. It stunk of stale food and spilled alcohol, bad breath, dirty carpet, and cigarette smoke—in short, everything Benny Fitz. Even the smell of the stockyards was preferable to this.

Benny threw the shifter in drive and pulled away from the curb, after a few turns getting onto Blair Avenue. They drove up to the downtown area, where Benny chose a route that could get them to Eva's house but was a way she would never normally take home because it would force them on a convoluted path packed with traffic, slogging along between downtown businesses and blocks of tight-packed residences. It would take them easily twice the time to negotiate as her normal route. Still, they could get to her house this way, but he would have to turn in two or three more blocks.

Rows of closed businesses flashed by on either side of them, with windows glowering and dark, staring Eva down with an almost human malevolence. With bated breath, she waited for Benny to ask her for directions, but he never did. The disturbing question came to her: Did Benny already know where she lived only because she had had to put her address down on her application? She wasn't sure she wanted to know that answer.

They were creeping along behind a beat-up Ford pickup that looked as if it intended to park in the middle of the street—M Street, to be exact. The crawled through a cramped, dirty neighborhood Eva had never seen, and a neighborhood she would just as soon not ever have seen.

At the end of the block, Benny darted left. Eva gave him a sharp glance. "Why are you turning?"

"Because."

"Benny, where are you taking me?"

They drove all the way down Euclid buried in his silence until he turned left onto L Street, in what appeared to be the absolute seediest part of town, and pulled over to stop at the curb.

"Why are you stopping?"

"We're here."

Eva turned to look at the grungy white house in front of which they were stopped, a seedy-looking property with a lawn of dirt and a vaguely familiar beat-up Olds sedan parked along the side.

"Who lives here?" She felt the alarm rising sharp inside her.

Where was Lance? she screamed inside her head. He had promised her to be at Benny's before she got off. He should have come for her. And what about Brandon Lucky? Her car should have been done. She had heard nothing from him either.

"Benny. Where are we?"

"Settle the freak down." Benny sounded like it was all he could do to hold back a growl. "We've been needin' to talk. Why do you think I let you off early? To be nice?"

"Why don't you come in for a bit, Eva?"

She froze, staring at him. "You . . . live here?"

"Sure! Why? Not nice enough for you? Not as nice as your little place, of course." He gave a chuckle, but there was no humor in it.

"No, I'm sure it's nice. But you told me you were taking me home. Come on, Benny. Please."

"Eva, just shut your damn trap. You even capable of that?"

She didn't reply. She only stared at him, her heart racing but her breath not seeming willing to come.

"All right. Thank you. Listen, Eva, I've been doing a lot of thinking about you. That car of yours. Wow. What a heap of trash, huh? You'd probably like something newer and more reliable, wouldn't you?"

She shrugged, feeling courage seep back into her a little at a time. "Sure I would. I don't see how, though." Her racing mind sought some way out of here.

Benny stared at her with cocksure eyes. He chuckled and scratched above his ear. "Well, I do. At least that's what I've been thinking about. You know, Eva, that bar is running me ragged. Hell, there's times I'm so busy I can't see straight. I've been thinking for quite a while that I could use some bigger help than what I've got."

"What do you mean 'bigger help'?" she asked. Maybe she would play along with him for a while, and in the meantime keep hoping she could think of a way to get away.

"Like a manager. Not just me, ownin' and managin' and everything all by myself. How'd you like to be my manager? I'd give you a raise, maybe even a couple hundred a month, if you do a good job. Wouldn't even be a whole lot more work most of the time. You know, just now and then when I need a day off or want to go home early, or if I have to take off and go to the bank or somethin'."

Eva couldn't stop staring at him. "Well . . ." This was a trap. It *had* to be a trap. First off, if he only wanted to ask her to manage the bar and grill, he could have asked her at work, or on the way to her house. He had no good reason to have brought her to his place.

"Come on. Let's go in, have a nice little drink. We'll talk it over. What do you say?"

Headlights of a car coming off Front Street onto Noble, in front of them, got closer and closer for a few seconds, then made the turn onto L Street, splashing bright into Benny's and Eva's eyes. Benny swore. "Turn the brights off, idiot!" he said with a growl, as if the other driver could hear him.

They waited for the glaring headlights to pass, both of them looking down at the dash. But the vehicle didn't pass. It pulled over in front of Benny's car and stopped.

They looked up at the same time as a door slammed shut. Eva's heart leaped.

Brandon Lucky was walking toward them out of the headlights' beam.

CHAPTER EIGHT

"WHAT IN THE HELL?" Benny Fitz's exclamation was followed on the instant by his flinging open his door, and lunging out onto the street. "What are you doin' following me around, Lucky?"

Eva had jumped out her side of the car and stood with a hand on the roof, staring at Brandon in shock mixed with huge relief.

Brandon jerked his thumb behind him. "I took Eva's car down to the bar so she'd have it for tomorrow. They, uh . . ." He paused, suddenly frozen and seeming unsure.

"They what?" growled Benny.

"Well, they told me you left together."

And Brandon was smart enough, knew Benny Fitz well enough, to know he would take Eva here rather than home. God bless Eva's Lucky miracle! Bless him for knowing where Benny lived. She wanted to leap on Brandon and hug him.

Benny glared at his dishwasher, almost grinding his teeth in his fury. "So why'd you come *here?*"

Brandon stared back, his mouth unhinged. How did he answer that question? They all knew why Brandon had come here rather than go to Eva's. Only a fool who wanted a spotlight on his foolishness would have asked such a thing. But then only another fool who didn't care about losing his job would answer it, so Brandon chose instead to stand there looking like a petrified mackerel.

"Ah, to hell with you!" Benny barked. "Go sit in the car, Brandon. Eva and I have to have a talk. And turn off those damn lights!" Benny turned back to Eva and jabbed a finger downward at the car. He didn't have to follow that signal with words.

Eva slid back into the car she had hoped she was escaping forever. Benny got in and slammed his door as if he wanted to pull it all the way to his right side. Eva shut hers so softly it didn't even latch. The lights of Eva's Valiant slowly faded out.

For a long twenty seconds that seemed more like minutes, Benny sat with both hands on the steering wheel, staring down, trying to collect himself so he could speak past his ire. At last, he drew a big breath, and Eva heard his teeth make a cracking sound as he ground them together.

"Did you know he was comin', Eva?"

She shook her head. "Well, earlier I thought he might. But he never called, so I gave up."

"But you were hopin', huh?"

"Benny, I didn't even think anything about it after we left." She wasn't lying. She had only been thinking of how to get out of Benny's clutches. It didn't escape her that she had spoken the much-despised name of her boss, that she had done so far too many times in just one day.

"Well, I hope that car works good, Eva. I don't know what else to do but send you down the road if you're late one more time. Got it?" He lanced her with his eyes. They seemed to go right through her face and out the back of her head.

"Got it. I won't be late. I'm sure he fixed the car up good." She had heard it running, because Brandon didn't shut it down when he got out. She had heard rougher-sounding kittens.

"Well. I sure hope you're right. I have half a dozen girls with applications in, and all of them live close enough to the place that even if they broke down they could walk to work pretty fast. One more time, Eva. One more and you're done."

To judge by the look in Benny's eyes, this time he meant it.

He scoffed. "Get out of my car and go home. Be to work at one tomorrow. Better yet, ten to one."

"Okay, Benny, I hate you." That was what she said in the fantasy in her head. Her real words were much more mundane and overly submissive: "I'll be there. Thank you."

She pushed her door open, while Benny stayed in the car. She clicked the door shut and walked toward the passenger side of her own car, fearing at any moment that Benny might change his mind and come raging after her.

By the time she reached the station wagon, she was once more shaking all over, and breath was hard to draw. She pulled her door open and fell inside, barely shutting it and not even looking over at Brandon before she said, "Go! Please go!"

Brandon barked the tires pulling back into the street. Eva hadn't even known the Valiant could do that.

They drove to Noble, then back to Front Street, where Brandon turned right without a word. After another block, he said, "You okay, Evie?"

She gritted her teeth, fighting back tears. Looking out the windshield, she sank her head against the seat. She could do nothing but nod in reply. She couldn't even meet his gaze. She could only think of one thing: her close call with Benny Fitz.

It took ten minutes, because of the crowds downtown, for them to reach Eva's. When Brandon pulled the station wagon up in front of her house and turned off the key, pulling it out and holding it in his lap out of habit, he looked over at Eva, sitting beside him with her eyes shut. She drew a deep, chattering breath and looked at him, impulsively reaching over to grab and squeeze his hand.

"I'm glad you came looking for me, Bran. Tonight was the first time I was really scared. You're my guardian angel, you know."

He laughed quietly. "No, your Lucky miracle, remember? Ah, jeez. It was nothin', Evie. I just wanted to get your car back to you for tomorrow. It's runnin' good."

"I heard. It sounds really nice—as far as station wagons go. And as far as future broken cars go." She laughed, and he laughed with her.

"You're going to take me home now, right? Or at least back to the shop."

A moment of disappointment hit Eva when she realized she had forgotten that Brandon would be without a car to get himself home. She had been looking forward to going inside to see her kids and her mother and grandmother. "Of course! Yeah! So why'd you bring me here then?"

He smiled and handed the keys to her. "I don't know. Guess I was trying to give you some time to get hold of yourself."

She laughed. "Yeah. That was probably a good idea."

"And I didn't want to let you go yet." She smiled at that, and he rushed to add, "Plus I thought maybe you'd like to get one of the kids or somethin'. You know, so . . ."

She sucked in a breath. "Oh! Right. Because of Karen, huh? That's smart. I'll be right back then. Or do you want to come in?"

Brandon stared at her. They both knew he shouldn't, but Eva knew Brandon didn't get many chances to experience real joy in his life. He knew it too.

"Do you think it'd be okay?"

"Of course it would, silly. Come on."

They got out and went to the house, seeing Bianca through the lace curtains holding Leo as she walked across the living room, and Tyke sitting watching TV. Eva and Brandon stood watching the scene for a while, Eva's heart in her throat.

"Pretty sweet, huh?" said Brandon.

She smiled, looking at Leo through the tears in her eyes. "It sure is."

Eva threw the door open as her mother was setting Leo down on his feet by the sofa. Even as a three-year-old, her little boy couldn't walk unaided quite yet, but he liked to sidle along the couch, especially if someone like his big brother was there to smile at him as he passed.

Hearing the door open, Leo turned and gave Eva his huge grin and started working his way as fast as he could along the sofa, making sure not to let go of its support.

Eva met him halfway and swept him up in her arms, holding him tight. Tyke rose and stood by them until Eva reached an arm out and hugged him close as well. Tyke loved his hugs as much as his little brother did, even if he was too macho to admit it.

Bianca stood with a smile on her face, watching them. "Everything good, cara?"

"Yes, Mama. Good. Brandon fixed the Valiant."

"Oh! That's wonderful news!"

"Yes. But I have to take him back to get his car."

"Oh." Bianca looked confused. "Then why did you come here?"

"Brandon wanted to go for a drive and make sure everything was working well." She hated lying to her mother, but she wouldn't have dreamed of worrying her with the truth about the evening, and Benny Fitz.

Bianca turned to Brandon, and reaching out, she took his hands. "You are an angel, Brandon. Thank you for helping."

Brandon grinned, then laughed. "An angel? That's what Eva told me! If you're telling me the same thing I guess it must be true."

"Excuse me?" cut in Eva. "So are you telling me my opinion isn't worth anything?"

Brandon blushed, then laughed again. "Oh, come on! I can't win for losin'."

"Hey, Brandon, how would you like to eat with us?" asked Bianca.

After a moment of confused-looking contemplation, he shrugged. "I— Are you sure there's enough?" Unfortunately, Brandon knew too much about the financial situation in the Galanti household.

"Well, of course there is. And now that you said that, I insist," said Bianca, waggling a finger at him.

"Okay then. Yes. I'll be glad to."

When Bianca turned back to the kitchen, Eva drilled Brandon with her worried friend look. "You sure it'll be okay, Bran? What about Karen?" Her voice was quiet.

He shrugged. "It'll be fine. Promise."

But Eva had heard that kind of promise before, and her eyes swept across the red spot on his face. "All right. I'll have to believe you know what you're doing. Hey. Do you mind if I make a phone call?"

"Of course not. I can visit with Tyke and Leo or just watch TV. Go ahead." He motioned her on.

Eva took the living room phone to her room, plugged it in, and pulled Lance Cartwright's card out of her pocket, peering at his home number and repeating it over a few times in her head as her heart began to pound. This was a big moment. This was the first time she would have heard Lance's voice since her visit by Officer Stone. She dialed the number and waited only a ring and a half.

Hello? This is Lance. He sounded all right. He sounded good! Nothing could make Eva believe this could be the voice of a person who had anything to hide.

"Lance! This is Eva. Are you all right?"

An oath came over the line, and then he apologized. *I'm really glad you called, Eva. I'm so sorry I wasn't there to pick you up tonight. Did you make it home okay?*

"I did. That's where I'm calling from, and you don't have to apologize. I was just worried about you."

Well, for good reason, it turns out. When I came out to the Bronco to drive down to Benny's and get you, I had two flat tires. Slashed *tires. I tried to call you.*

It felt like someone dumped a gallon of acid on Eva's stomach. "You did? Who did you talk to?"

Some guy. I had a feeling it was your boss.

Eva called Benny a terrible name, making herself blush even though he couldn't see her. "I'm sorry. Lance, I have to tell you something. Can I come by in about an hour? Will you be home?"

I will. But you don't want to keep me waiting that long, do you?

"Kinda. I think I should tell you this in person."

After she got Lance's home address on Liberty Street, and they hung up, she returned to the kitchen and helped Bianca get supper on the table. She hadn't seen her grandmother since getting home, and after a while, starting to feel apprehensive, she asked about her.

Bianca gave a little shrug as she picked up a pot of freshly made red sauce and carried it to the table, Eva following her with fresh white bread, baked on a cookie sheet in the way of the old country.

They set the pot and the bread on the table as Eva kept watching her mother. When Bianca turned back to the kitchen, Eva took her arm, pressing on. "Mama? What about Nonni? Is she all right?"

She recognized the old cryptic expression on her mother's face. It was an expression she got when she was trying to hide something she didn't want anyone to know.

"Mama?"

Bianca met her daughter's eyes with a sad frown, glancing past her at Brandon Lucky and the boys. "She's . . . You know, cara, she's tired. She's just tired."

But behind Bianca's eyes there was more. "Mama, stop. If there's something wrong with Nonni, you have to tell me. I'm not a baby."

A rush of tears came into Bianca's eyes, chilling Eva instantly. Her mother was not often quick to get emotional. "You're *my* baby. Listen, cara. Maybe we should talk later, okay? After the boys go to bed tonight. Don't you think?"

"Mama, just tell me—something. I won't even be able to eat now unless you tell me. What's wrong?"

Bianca drew a deep breath and wiped her hands nervously on her apron, then patted the sides of her tightly drawn hair, as if to straighten it. She looked past Eva at the others, who all seemed to be glued to the television. "All right," she said in a lower voice. "Just really brief—Grandma is having her pains again. Okay? I think it might be her heart."

Eva stood in shocked silence. Perhaps "sad" was a better word than shocked. She had been expecting something like this for a while. Her grandmother was never one to complain about things, but now and then over the past several months she had caught her with an expression on her face that could only be one of pain. Every time she asked about it, her grandmother played it off, but deep down Eva knew something was going on. She didn't ever press it, because it scared her too bad.

"Then we need to go to the doctor."

"Oh, cara. I know. I knew you would say that. But you know we don't have the money. Tyke has had that bad tooth for more than two days, and sometimes the pain is so bad he can hardly sleep. We can't even take him to the dentist, so how can we afford a doctor for your grandmother?"

The sick feeling in Eva's stomach grew. She knew her mother was right, but they couldn't let Nonni suffer in pain. Wouldn't the doctors take payments? For that matter, wouldn't a dentist? They had to do something. She hadn't realized Tyke's tooth was even bothering him that much—another secret they were keeping from her.

"Mama, why haven't you told me his tooth was getting so bad?"

"Cara . . . I didn't want to bother you, all right? You have so much to worry you already. I was going to try and find some way to take care of it."

Eva smiled ruefully. "And how would you do that?"

Bianca smiled in return and reached out to squeeze Eva's arm. "I don't know. But we'll find a way. We will."

Eva drew another deep breath and whirled around, fighting her emotions. Her mother didn't need her daughter's tears to add to her woes.

Find a way? Eva had been trying to "find a way" for a long time now, but the pieces never seemed to come together. How were they going to find a way when it seemed like every new day another piece to their life's puzzle came crashing to the ground?

CHAPTER NINE

AFTER SUPPER WAS OVER, Eva went back to where her mother and grandmother shared a bedroom. They even slept together in the room, in a queen-size bed that took up the majority of the open space in the musty-smelling room, which often smelled of garlic as well, a staple in any Italian household.

Isabella Rossi lay on top of a cranberry-red silk counterpane, her head on a pillow with a case of the same fabric, her hands folded on her chest. Her grandmother's skin looked more gray than normal, mixed with a pale purple hue in the dim light. Eva stopped and stared. She waited to see her grandmother's chest rise.

When the subtle movement finally came, a gust of breath escaped Eva, and she fought back tears of relief. "Nonni?" Her voice was soft. "Nonni? *Stai dormendo?*" In the only language her grandmother knew, she was asking her if she was asleep.

Isabella's eyelids fluttered open, like a butterfly landing on a leaf. She produced a wan smile, reaching a trembling hand toward Eva. "I am awake, *mia colomba,*" she said in Italian. Mia colomba meant "my dove", and it was the term of endearment she used most often for her granddaughter.

Eva took her hand and held it, and she didn't try to fight the tears that swam in her eyes. Her grandmother was so dear to her. She couldn't imagine having her gone, especially when medicine might potentially help her stay around for years longer, if only they could afford it.

"Your heart is hurting, Nonni?"

Isabella nodded. "Maybe a little. But it is nothing. It will stop soon. Mostly, I am only tired."

Eva swallowed hard. Her grandmother's words could be taken with a double meaning: *It will stop soon* could have referred to her heart, not her pain.

"Yes, you do need to sleep. I'm sorry I woke you."

"Oh, my dove. No, no. You didn't wake me. I was simply resting my eyes and thinking of tomorrow and all the things I want to do." She smiled again, this time bigger. She was gathering her strength into that smile, trying to fool Eva into thinking she was okay.

Eva leaned closer and put a hand along the old lady's cheek, then bent and kissed her on the forehead. "You sleep, Nonni. I will tell Mama to bring you some broth. It will relax you."

Isabella nodded and closed her eyes. "Okay, my dove. That will be okay." She took a deeper breath, and she was snoring by the time it came back out.

Slowly, watching her grandmother all the while, Eva backed out of the room and nudged the door shut with a soft click.

She went to her mother and took her hand. "She's sleeping. But still smiling. Maybe when she wakes up you could give her some broth."

Bianca had a smile of her own at those words. "All right. Hey, we will be fine, cara. You'll see. Something will come up."

"Yes. It will. Mama, would you like some alone time with Leo? I think I'll see if Tyke wants to come with me to drop Brandon off at the shop."

"I think that would be a good idea," Bianca replied. "I don't think Brandon's wife is a very nice person. It won't do to have you be alone very much with him."

Bianca took her daughter's shoulders and leaned slightly down to kiss her on the cheek. Straight and elegant in spite of her extra weight, Bianca at five foot nine stood four inches taller than her daughter. "You're a good girl, cara."

Eva giggled. "Girl? Mama, you are getting senile. I haven't been a girl in over twenty years."

Bianca took a deep breath. "I told you: You will always be your mother's little girl. Always."

Eva drove the station wagon along the dark, dangerous streets of Rock Springs like a shark patrolling a twilight reef. She had decided to take Brandon back to Dino's Automotive on Elk Street first so he could get his car without telling him she had to go over to Lance Cartwright's afterward. She knew he would insist on going with her, and she was afraid she had already put him in enough danger of another run-in with Karen by keeping him as long as she already had.

After thanking Brandon again for all he had done, especially for saving her from Benny, she and Tyke drove to Lance's house on Liberty. As he had said, the two driver's side tires of a black and white 1970 Bronco parked at the curb were flat. No sooner had she pulled to the curb beyond it than the front door of a small white house came open, and the wall that was Lance Cartwright closed off most of the yellow light that otherwise would have come from the house.

Tyke jerked upright. "Wow! Is that Lance?"

"Yes."

"Mom, he's huge!"

She smiled. "Yes, he is, isn't he? Like a Cowboys lineman."

Tyke gave her a grin. He knew his mother wasn't into football, but she used the reference because he liked it and she knew it would mean something to him.

They got out at the same time, and by then Lance was standing at the passenger side of the Valiant. "You saw the tires?"

She nodded. "Can we come in for a minute?" When he said yes, she introduced him and Tyke to each other, and they walked back to his house, where a dog the size of a stunted horse met them inside the door, ominously quiet, keenly observant.

"That's Moose," Lance said. "He's a quarter each of Great Dane and Saint Bernard, but you can't really see the Saint Bernard. We think his dad was a Mastiff. He'll take a minute to get to know you, but once he decides you're part of the pack you'll be his best friend."

"I sure hope so," said Eva. "Has he eaten supper yet?"

Lance laughed. "Come on in. You want me to lock him in his room?"

"No! I love dogs. I just never had a rideable one."

Remembering the personalized license plate she had noticed on Lance's Bronco, Eva said, "I saw your plate says 'Bar Jay'. What does that mean?"

"Oh, Bar J is my grandpa's brand on his ranch."

"Wow, your grandpa has a ranch?" asked Tyke, his mouth agape.

"He does."

"That's cool!"

Lance grinned. "It is, huh? It was a great place to play, growing up."

"Hey," Tyke said, "Can I ask you a question?"

"Sure."

"How tall are you?"

Lance laughed. "Six foot seven. Sometimes taller."

Tyke looked confused. "How can you get taller?"

"Well, I keep smacking my head on things, and the lump on top of my head is startin' to turn permanent. At least that's what the doctor told me."

All three of them laughed, but Eva saw Lance unconsciously rubbing the top of his head a moment later.

Eva went and sat on a couch upholstered in heavy brown corduroy, while Tyke took over a slick blue La-Z-Boy and started getting acquainted with Moose.

Lance seated himself against the arm of the couch so he could face Eva. "So . . . what's the big secret you've been making me sweat about?"

"Well, it's something weird. I don't know if it will help."

"One way to find out."

"Right. So when I was at Benny's, he was basically trying to kidnap me. I'm not sure what else you could call it."

Lance bristled up. It was the first time Eva could remember seeing fire in his normally friendly blue eyes. "He *what?* What happened?"

"It's okay. Nothing bad, but . . . Well, I told him I was going to go back in and call for a ride, since I didn't see you outside. He asked me if I was talking about 'my cop friend', and it was just really weird how he said it. He had a look like he knew something I didn't. Then some guy pulled up across the street and came over to Benny. He said something to him about 'getting that thing done', or something along those lines. Then Benny handed him some money and sent him inside to get a free dinner."

Lance had settled back hard against the arm of the couch now. He was pondering what she had told him, his jaw muscles bunched up hard. "Okay. What'd this guy look like?"

"He had longish blond hair—really kind of stringy and greasy. And he was super skinny. About five foot seven or so. He wasn't a lot taller than me."

"What was he drivin'?"

"Oh, boy. You would ask that. I don't know. Something kind of dark, and long. A two-door? Sorry. I wasn't paying much attention. It could have been something like an older Lincoln or even a Cadillac. But nothing nice. Oh—and Benny called him Willie."

Lance swore. "Oh. Huh. I know who it was. Willie Baker. A real class act. Willie Baker, or Willie Fry 'er."

Eva stared at him for a few seconds, then started laughing. "What did you say? Will he bake her or will he fry her?"

Grinning, Lance repeated the words. "That's what I first heard my friend Rick Cohen call him. Sorry—that just stuck in my head since. So yeah, Willie Baker is a real sleaze ball character. We know he's a druggy, and I'm sure he's a lot worse, but it's hard to catch him at anything because he seems to slide through the cracks. We like to call him Slick Willie."

"Do you think he could have flattened your tires?"

"I'm sure he could have. Did you tell Benny I was coming to get you?"

"No! I never said a word about it. But he sure jumped to a fast conclusion when I told him I was going to call somebody. It was like he was already thinking about you."

"Yeah, it does seem weird, huh? Especially if Benny was acting suspicious and then gave him money. Wow. That guy really wanted to take you home himself, huh?"

Eva froze. She was positive that Tyke, although he didn't seem to be paying attention, was hanging on every word. Suddenly, she wished he wasn't there. "Uh . . . Yeah. Yeah, he really wanted to take me home."

Lance caught the change in her voice and studied her face for a moment, until she flung her glance toward her son. Lance nodded knowingly. "Well, hey, Eva—do you want a drink of water or anything?"

"Umm . . ." She thought he was actually offering her a drink until he motioned for her to get up with him. "Yeah, sure. Hey,

Tyke, do you want a drink? I'm going to go in the kitchen with Lance for a minute."

Tyke looked up from scrubbing the top of Moose's head with his fingertips. "Uh . . . No, Mom, I'm okay. Thanks."

"Okay. Be right back."

She and Lance went to the kitchen, which was in another room, behind a closed door. "All right, what happened?" said Lance. "You didn't tell me everything."

"I'm scared, Lance."

"Of what?"

"Benny. He wasn't taking me home—at least not to *my* home. He said he was, but then he drove me over to his house—on L Street—and tried to get me to go in with him."

"How'd you get out of that?" asked Lance, and she could see a rising temper in his eyes.

"That's when Brandon found me. He had gone to the bar to bring me my car, and when they told him I left with Benny he was smart enough to go right to his place instead of mine."

"Yeah. Smart. I don't think your Benny's going to forget how smart Brandon is."

"What do you mean?" Eva looked into Lance's eyes and felt fear rise up inside.

Lance shrugged. "Sorry, I shouldn't have said anything. I just have a feeling that guy's pretty vindictive. And if he can hire somebody to slash a cop's tires, right in front of his house in broad daylight . . ."

Eva nodded soberly. "Yeah. I see what you mean. I guess I should warn Brandon."

"I have a feeling your Brandon knows the score. I've seen his kind. He's been around enough to know the streets, and that Benny guy is the roughest kind of street thug, from what I'm seeing. Except now he has enough money he can pay his dirty work done."

As Lance talked about how he viewed Brandon, Eva found herself wanting to tell Brandon about her visit from Officer Stone. He had been in the society of rough men. What if he knew something about the guys Stone had shown her? Yet she knew she had no right to ask. Stone had asked her not to talk to anyone.

"Are you going to be okay?" Eva asked Lance. "How will you get in to get both tires fixed?"

He shrugged. "I have a friend, a tire guy that owes me some favors. I'll have him bring a truck over. It'll be fine. Promise. I'm more worried about you."

"Yeah. Me too. I don't suppose you could come by tomorrow, could you? Maybe just swing in and check on me? I'll be there at one."

"Sure. I'll be working some O.T. again, but that's okay."

"What about next week?"

"We'll figure something out. What I wish is that you'd go find some other place to work."

"I've tried," she said. "I've put a lot of applications out. Nobody wants me, I guess."

He stared at her and for a moment said nothing, but she could see the wheels spinning in his eyes. Finally, he just said, "Huh." He was too much of a gentleman to say what he had been thinking, so she was left feeling foolish for the comment she hadn't thought all the way through.

"I mean . . . They don't want me to *work* for them."

Now he grinned. "I knew what you meant. I guess there's no accounting for taste, right?"

They returned to the front room, where Tyke was having so much fun getting acquainted with Moose that Eva decided to stay a little longer. She and Lance filled the empty space with small talk for a while before the subject came around to her car and Lance asked her how it was running. Even though she said it was purring, he thought she should buy something else, which brought them around to a topic they both loved.

Eva told Lance about watching her father fix up and paint cars and about all the different ones they had owned, at least those she could remember, the last one being a brand-new sixty-six Chevy Chevelle, which they had been forced to sell shortly after his death.

Lance whistled. "Man, that's a car I'd like to have. What color?"

"My dad's was red. Fire engine red, pretty much. But if I could choose I would get black."

"Nice, nice. You should get one."

She laughed. "Right. Me in a Chevelle. Like I could afford one anyway. And I don't exactly see the nice sixties models for sale in every lot."

"Have you looked?"

"Okay, no. When you're making one-thirty-five an hour you don't do a lot of car shopping. It just makes you more depressed."

He smiled his understanding. "You got me there. Sorry, Eva. I bet somethin' turns around for you soon, though."

From the look in his eyes, he really didn't believe it. And neither did she. But he was kind for saying it.

In the morning, Eva came out of the bathroom to see her mother giving Tyke some aspirin. Bianca shoved the bottle back in the cupboard when Eva saw her, and turned away. Eva gritted her teeth and walked to her son, smelling fresh, strong coffee. The smell did almost as good a job of waking her up as the caffeine would.

"Hey, Tyke. Your tooth still hurting?"

"Yeah, a little."

Eva knew with Tyke what "a little" meant. It was something tough, polite kids said when they knew their mother had no extra money to pay a dentist bill. Maybe on Monday, one of her two days off, she would go out and try to see if she could drum up some business mowing lawns. It was hotter weather now, and the grass wasn't growing very fast, but there had to be *someone* out there who would take pity on a pretty woman shoving a rickety lawnmower around the streets begging for work.

"See if you can hang on just a little longer, sweetie. We'll figure something out."

What Eva needed was to meet someone who had all the answers a destitute woman could ever need for a way to come up with extra money—and good money, at that.

Lance Cartwright, doing his shift of overtime, picked that quiet Sunday morning to drive around to the business on Elk Street that Chief Buyer had asked him to keep an eye on especially on weekends.

The area of Elk where the business sat, which the chief had called a warehouse, was much quieter and more open than the area of town he spent most of his time in. It was out beyond the old part of town, away from all the sleazy businesses and run-down homes, with few other places of business nearby until the road led to the Kasbah lounge and the places that surrounded it. It had almost no landscaping to speak of, only a curbed parking area some hundred feet from it with a row of flowering crab trees, and some overgrown and pointless-looking, flowerless rose bushes along the front wall.

The building indeed appeared to have been built as some kind of warehouse, probably the kind the federal government used to house BLM fire crews, their equipment, and the like. It was wood-sided, painted pale gray with white windowsills, windows that likely hadn't been opened in years from the look of them, and over the front door was an arch-shaped sign that said PRIMO CUSTOM AUTO PARTS.

In keeping with the look of a retired federal or highway department property, a lot of empty space surrounded the building and a few outbuildings, a dusty, gravel-covered yard keeping them separated from the street by a gentle stone's toss. There was no sign of life in front of the building, but when Lance drove around back he was surprised to see two vehicles, a pale yellow mid-sixties Dodge short-bed pickup, and a Plymouth Roadrunner, possibly a sixty-nine, bearing Nevada license plates. It was painted the ugliest greenish-gray color imaginable for such an otherwise nice-looking car, with a black hood and redline tires.

Chief Buyer had told Lance specifically not to go inside the business, only to check around outside and make sure everything looked in order. But that didn't mean he couldn't get a closer look at the Roadrunner.

Parking his LTD and leaving it running, he got out and went to walk around the car, whose paint job, although not the prettiest color, looked almost pristine. He peeked in the window to find a nice new stereo inside, a perfectly cared-for bench seat with cloth inserts, a manual gearshift, and a speedometer that went only to 120, which made him smile. This era Roadrunner had a 383 under the hood, and he was sure it could do better than that.

Lance felt someone watching him, and he jerked his eyes up to look at one of the two large, solid glass windows on either side of a metal door. Even as he looked, a flat black drape dropped back into place over the right window, concealing whoever had been looking out.

With an uneasy smile at having been caught, Lance went and got back in his car and backed away from the building. As he started around to the only side he had yet to see, he glanced back and saw the drapes opened on the other window now, and a face watching him. The face appeared to be dark, but a longer look showed the window itself to be tinted a fairly dark shade. That was something he wasn't sure he had ever seen before on a structure.

He idled the LTD around the far side of the building, which had two more windows, these the double-hung kind with multiple panes. They too were stained a darker color than normal glass, and also screened with black drapes. This friend of the chief's really *was* secretive about his custom-made auto parts. Lance was going to have to find out more about this place. Who knew what kind of treasures they might be able to make for his Bronco, if he ever got any money ahead?

He drove a few hundred more yards up Elk Street, going slow on purpose, until he got to a spot where he could pull over and sit. He got out a pair of binoculars he kept in a leather case under the front seat and cranked around to train them once again on the building. Like any good cop, strange, overly cautious people made him curious.

As he had suspected, there was someone standing outside the front door of the business now, also watching him through binoculars. With a grin, he waved at them, laid the binoculars down, and drove on up the street to have a look around the Kasbah. Even on a Sunday, they were bound to have some good country music playing, and maybe even a live band. Heck, it wouldn't even hurt to look around inside for a while.

CHAPTER TEN

EVA'S SUNDAY CAME AND went without much incident. She took the family to early church services, got everyone home in time for her to change into her work blouse and skirt, and it was back to the bar and grill again. The Plymouth was running like a proud Arabian stallion.

As Lance Cartwright had promised, he showed up at the bar shortly after one, coming inside in his uniform. After he left, there was a certain aura in the air among the other customers, for all had seen Lance acting in a very friendly manner toward her, and most of them were still fairly sober—therefore smart enough not to do anything that might draw the unfriendly attention of big Officer Cartwright.

By the time they started to become a little more "under the weather" and started to discuss things amongst themselves and resent the fact that some giant cop was coming into the bar to hang out with their favorite barmaid, a stranger showed up, a bright-eyed young man who couldn't have been much over twenty-seven or twenty-eight, wore a short, dark haircut, thick sideburns, cute dimples in his cheeks, and a pencil-thick mustache in the center of his upper lip, trying unsuccessfully to make him look more handsome than he was cute.

The young man, who stood five foot ten or a little taller, walked to the bar in a smooth easy gait after studying the room for long enough to spot Eva.

Liking this man from her quick study, she walked down the bar, polishing water spots off a glass. "Hi. I'm Eva."

"I know." The young man grinned. "I guess by now every man I work with knows."

Eva looked at him quizzically, scanned his face and what she could see of him above the bar, and laughed. "Okay. Another police officer—right?"

He grinned back at her. "So obvious, huh?"

"Pretty obvious, especially when you started talking about 'every man you work with'. You're a friend of Lance's, I guess."

Still grinning, the man put out his hand. "Rick Cohen. I trained that big galoot."

She shook his hand, then recalled something Lance had said. "Rick? You wouldn't be the same Rick with the funny saying about Willie Baker, would you?"

Rick Cohen laughed, making his deep chocolate eyes twinkle. "Willie Baker, or Willie Fry'er? Yep, that would be me. Is that dang Hoss stealing all my good one-liners again?"

For a moment, Eva was confused. "Hoss? Oh! Hoss! I have wanted to call Lance that, but I didn't know how he would take it."

"Don't worry, I'm sure he's heard it his whole adult life. I started callin' him that the day we met. I mean come on! Six foot seven, almost three hundred pounds, and a last name of Cartwright? How do you not call the guy Hoss?"

"Right. How do you not? So what will you drink? You're off duty, right?"

"I am. Just give me something hard and on the rocks. No beer. I can't stand the smell."

She had to laugh. "Well, you might find this funny, considering where I work, but that makes two of us!"

"I bet. If you're like me, after some stupid drunk pukes on you once, the stench of beer gets pretty offensive. Oh! Sorry; that was gross."

Giggling, she said, "It was gross. So are stupid drunks." She popped a hand over her mouth and looked quickly around. "I guess I should keep my voice down, right?"

He winked at her and leaned closer so his now quieter voice could be heard over the crooning of Stevie Wonder. "I wouldn't worry about it. All the stupid ones will think you're talking about other guys."

While Rick Cohen sat at the bar, then eventually went and played a couple games of pool with one of the few sober patrons, Eva continued waiting on other customers, but made her way back to Rick as often as she could manage to without drawing Benny's attention. Luckily, he didn't come out of the back very often, and by three o'clock, when Jud came in to take over cooking, Benny got ready to go home. The entire day, he hadn't given Eva so much as a sneeze. She wished every day could be so good. And she hoped it wasn't a sign of some coming storm.

Rick Cohen watched Benny Fitz go out the front door, turning to scan the room just before it closed. Benny's cold, leering eyes settled on Eva, but when he realized Rick Cohen was watching him he scowled, turned and let the door swing shut behind him.

Rick raised his eyebrows. "Wow. I keep hearing creepy stories about that guy, all over town. Now I can see why. Nice guy, huh?"

"Yeah. Nice. Hey, Rick—thanks for coming in. I never asked, but Lance sent you, right?"

"Well . . . No. I mean . . . Yeah, okay, he might have suggested it, but I mean . . . Well, come on, Eva, I would have had to come in eventually anyway, the way he goes on and on about you."

Surprised, she studied his eyes. "He does? Really?"

He frowned and looked her up and down. "Uhh . . . Yeah. He does." He looked at her for a bit longer, an incredulous look in his eyes, then laughed. "Wow. Are you for real?"

She couldn't help sharing his laugh. "For real why?"

"Just are you for real? Look at you, you— Well, never mind."

Eva had a feeling that whatever Rick had on his mind would only embarrass her, so she didn't push it. She thought about Lance Cartwright, though. And this good-looking, baby-faced Rick Cohen. Both of them were at least ten years her younger. But no matter. It felt good to think maybe she could still make a member of the opposite sex notice her once in a while, even if it never turned into anything more—especially when they found out about Tyke, and more especially when they found out she had a Down Syndrome child, a child she wouldn't have traded for every eligible bachelor in Wyoming.

"I guess I'll take off," Rick said, after she hadn't responded for a while. "Lance and I have the night shift tonight, so I'd better go get ready. You'll be okay now, right? With the boss gone?"

"Sure. I'll be okay. Thank you for coming by."

"The pleasure was all mine. I promise."

"And tell Lance hi for me. He's doing two shifts back to back again, huh? That's going to be a *long* day."

After Rick Cohen left, the place kept rolling, life as usual. Smoke wreaths swirled among the smoke screen; the stench of rancid fry oil vied for superiority with a dozen brands of cigarettes; burgers tried to smell tempting among the resulting smog; billiard balls clacked, ever-more-inebriated men told loud stories and laughed boisterously through the tones of Led Zeppelin screeching out "Whole Lotta Love", and alcoholic beverages tinkled without end into eager glasses.

Eva had no friends in the lounge today, at least no one she completely trusted except for Jud, who seldom came out of the back. Regardless, when she took her last break, she chose rather than going to the staff breakroom to sit at one of the tables at the rear of the room, seated to one end of the bar against the wall facing the front door. She wasn't even sure herself why she made that choice. It simply felt like she needed to be around people, even people she didn't care one way or another about.

The crowd kept doing what drunk crowds do, although for some bizarre reason no one came to her table to bother her. And then she saw him coming through the front door.

There are some men who could stroll into a crowd of dashing male models, and even at average height stand out like a Goliath. Some men whose charisma reaches across rooms, across ages, across galaxies, like actors Clark Gable or Rock Hudson, Robert Redford or Robert Conrad. This was one of those men.

Eva didn't know if she could adequately have described this man if a policeman had had reason within the hour to ask it of her. Sure, she could have told the policeman he had rich, thick, wavy brown hair, thrown loose and full to the right from a part on the left, not too curly, but with a potential to get unruly in the wind; that he wore a perfectly groomed brown mustache that just covered his entire upper lip and that even from a distance she suspected would not have a single hair out of place, or even a millimeter longer than any other; she could have told them his wide, strong shoulders and lean hips were covered by a nearly form-fitting, thinly striped black suit of the highest quality brushed wool, with a tie whose solid black was broken only by a tasteful paisley pattern. He stood perhaps six-foot one, and if Eva were any judge must weigh somewhere in the neighborhood of a very well-toned, muscular two hundred pounds.

On second thought, she guessed the police should be very satisfied with the detail she would have given them.

Yet she could not have described the other qualities of this man, the qualities that made him pop out of the bar crowd like a ring-necked pheasant strutting through a barnyard full of scruffy leghorn chickens. Of course she was already looking at the man, and much of what she felt came from his appearance, but part of her wondered if she were facing the opposite direction, would she have felt him come into the room? The aura surrounding him was that strong.

The man had removed gold-framed sunglasses, and after a long, slow search his narrow, deep-set eyes landed on Eva, perching there as if they had been seeking a long-lost home and at last had found it. His chest expanded with a deep breath, which she knew only because she was studying him so closely. With a faint smile lifting his lip corners beneath his mustache, he tugged on the right lapel of his perfectly tailored coat, then glided toward her. It almost looked like he was approaching her on a conveyor belt.

The man stopped at Eva's table, and two things struck her now that he stood so near: first, the strange thought that some-where, sometime, she had seen this man before, and second, something made her feel like she should stand up to meet him. She made to do just that.

He raised a casual hand, palm out to her. "No, no, miss. Please. Stay seated. May I?" He waved at the chair across from her, his deep eyes shining out at her. She was trying to decide if they were really blue, when at a distance she had thought they would be the color of mahogany.

"Sure." She found herself wondering if she would have had the strength to tell him no if she had wanted to.

He turned and scanned the room once more, from one far wall to the other, then pulled out the chair and lit on it like an Everglades kite coming to rest on a branch. Was everything this stranger did going to appear so flawlessly smooth?

"You are Eva, I believe. My name is Ambro. Ambro Procopio—Ambrosio, actually, but I usually try not to overwhelm people when I first meet them." With a sly smile, he slid a hand through the air between them, and she couldn't have resisted it if it were covered in tar. His grip was gentle, yet the hand itself was large and firm and strong.

She hadn't let go of his hand before it struck her, like a hammer inside her head: *Ambrosio Procopio!* This man hardly looked the same in real life, but the name was one of the three on the Xeroxes Officer Buck Stone had shown her. She wanted to be alarmed, and yet she wasn't. After all, hadn't Stone told her himself that he didn't even know who this man was, that he might be some kind of officer? From the man's kind, clean-cut looks, demeanor, his build, and the general sensation she got from him, he certainly fit the part of a cop.

Eva felt breathless, but not scared, and not even worried, only intrigued.

"I don't suppose you're a police officer too." It was the first thing that came to her mind, spilled across her lips without her preparing to hear it, and she was instantly shocked at herself. Shocked most because she didn't know where she found the strength to speak to this over-powering man whose name she had not been prepared to hear from his own lips.

Ambrosio Procopio looked at her a moment. He must have been surprised at her words, but his face revealed no expression beyond the mild amusement that seemed to live ever in his eyes. Finally, he smiled, and the deep creases on either side of his face came out of nowhere. He must not have been one who smiled frequently, because he had the feel of a man in his forties, perhaps even early fifties, and yet the creases created by his smile vanished completely when he went sober again. Other than the brownish shade of a thick beard beneath his skin, and a small scar outside his right eye, Ambro Procopio seemed to have nothing that tarnished his perfect olive-toned skin.

"A police officer? Hardly."

"I'm sorry! I'm not sure why I said that."

"There is nothing to be sorry for. Nothing. In fact, as a boy I used to dream of being a policeman."

"Thank you." She felt the need to explain herself: "It's just that for a few days it seems like every man who comes to introduce himself to me is an officer." Of course she wasn't fool enough, even while so mesmerized, to tell him of Stone's visit, or to tell him she had already heard his name.

"Then I will submit to you that this must be your lucky day, Miss Eva. May I call you Eva?"

"Of course." Foolishly, she wondered how she would reply even if he asked if he could call her Mud.

"Is it your break time, Eva?" Ambro asked. "Is this a bad time for you?"

"No, of course not. I have a few minutes left." Yet she wondered why she volunteered this information. What was Ambro Procopio here for? Whatever it was, it did not seem like it was casual. He did not seem like the type who did very much for casual reasons. Should she excuse herself and try to make a call to Officer Stone while this man was still here? She stared at Ambro Procopio for a while longer, and then a part of her started wondering if she should feel some kind of guilt, or even feel foolish, because she found herself not wanting to tell Stone this man had been here at all.

"Do they let you partake of alcohol while you're working? I know some these days don't," said Ambro.

"No, I can. A little."

Ambro swiveled at the waist, and the first barmaid in his line of sight happened to be Teton Belle. For a moment, both of them froze, and Eva saw a little flicker of recognition in the woman's eyes. Or had she imagined it? Whatever it was, it was gone on the instant.

Ambro casually beckoned Belle, who came over, bashing Eva with a perturbed glance but showing Ambro her gleaming teeth, after a moment of silence. "Hello, sugar. Can I get you something?"

"Of course. For me, some light wine. Do you have any Sauternes?"

Belle stared Ambro down, her jaw for the moment unhinged. "Are you serious?"

He gave her a patient smile. "I do not often to joke around, at least not about my choice of alcohol. Yes, very serious."

"For both of you?" asked Belle when she found her voice.

Ambro looked at Eva. "You really should try it. It is a taste you will never forget—and possibly may never have a chance to try again. Frankly," he said, looking back up at Belle, "I am surprised you have any here and that you know what it is."

Eva wondered if Belle was bright enough to know she was casually being put down, or at least to Eva it sounded that way. "Oh, I do, hon. I do. I had a chance to look through the wine locker just last week, and our boss pointed it out to me and told me if I broke it I would be paying him money out of my salary for the next two months. And we have only one bottle, by the way."

Ambro chuckled. "Yes, of course. Eva?" He looked at her again, and his will seemed irresistible.

"Sure. I'll try it."

So Teton Belle strutted off, and when she returned a few minutes later she had a sealed bottle containing a rich-looking amber-yellow wine, sealed off with a golden foil cap. She set two wine glasses on the table, struggled like a novice to open the bottle, then carefully filled Ambro's glass three-fourths full. She filled Eva's up to half.

"All the way, thank you," directed Ambro, motioning with his head toward Eva's glass.

The fake smile plastered to Belle's face grew slightly. "Oh, of course. I'm sorry." She filled Eva's glass to the same level as Ambro's. "That will be thirty dollars," she said. She waited until Ambro produced a fancy-looking leather wallet and slid out three crisp ten-dollar bills, then a five, handing them to Belle as if they were no more than blank pieces of scratch paper from off the floor that he wanted her to discard. Belle didn't seem to notice the tip, which was over three times what she made in an hour.

She stood as if entranced after re-corking the wine bottle. Ambro had to nod politely and say, "That will be all, Belle," before the woman turned and wandered away, for some reason looking numb. It took a moment for it to hit Eva that Ambro had called Teton Belle by name. None of the barmaids wore name tags.

Ambro turned back to Eva and squared himself in the chair. Eva was staring at him, still trying to digest the man's familiarity with Belle, as well as the price of the glass of wine in front of her. How could anything taste good enough to cost fifteen dollars a glass?

"I am still rather shocked that a place like this would carry something like Sauternes, but I have learned that it always pays to ask."

"Sure," replied Eva, as if what he said made perfect sense, and it made perfect sense for a bottle of wine to cost forty dollars or more.

"So let me see. Here is to new acquaintances," said Ambro, raising his glass across the table to Eva. "May ours be fruitful to all."

She raised her glass, letting it chime against his, then pulled it back and put it to her lips, mimicking Ambro. She felt oddly nervous about doing anything that would make her seem less in his eyes.

"What do you think?"

"Excuse me?"

"Of the Sauternes. What do you think of the Sauternes, Eva? Do you approve?"

"I—" She didn't even know if she approved. She had so many jumbled thoughts wrangling around in her head at once that its flavor hadn't even registered on her. "It's delicious. The best I have ever tasted," she said.

By his smile, she knew she had given him the right review. What she didn't tell him was that she had never tasted any wine that cost more than ten dollars a bottle, and very little of that.

"Eva, may I ask you a question? Oh—first, are you still good with your time? I promise you if you have to go, it will be fine. I mostly only wanted to make your acquaintance today. Be honest: It's no issue."

"I . . ." Again, she froze. Until now, she hadn't noticed, but her time was up. Her curiosity was on high alert, and it made her almost sick to think of sending Ambrosio Procopio away without hearing why he had come. The way he was acting, it almost seemed like he had come here to offer her a job or something.

"Actually, I guess my break time is up. But . . ."

She didn't finish her thought, so he did: "But when will you see me again?"

Blushing, she nodded. "Yes. You have me so curious."

"Yes, I suppose I would. Tomorrow. I will come tomorrow."

Her heart fell. "I'm off for the next two days."

He frowned sadly. "Oh. I'm sorry to hear that. Then you will work Wednesday?"

"Yes." Would she have to wait until Wednesday to learn what this was about? She didn't dare ask that, but her disappointment must have showed in her face, to judge by his next words.

"But you must eat food on your days off as well, don't you?"

After a foolish moment of staring at him, she laughed. "Yes, of course."

"Then tomorrow. Tomorrow on your day off I will find you at your house at six in the evening and treat you to the finest Italian supper in town."

Eva couldn't think of one Italian restaurant in this town, but it wouldn't have mattered; no one made better Italian than her mother, so wherever he took her, his promise would fall flat.

"Okay. Sure. That would be nice. I'll see you tomorrow." Eva Galanti had never agreed to a date in her life with a man she hadn't known more than ten minutes. If when Officer Stone told her about a man named Ambrosio Procopio he had also told her she would be accepting an invitation to dinner with him the first time they met, she would have laughed.

Feeling weak and foolish, yet somehow giddy, she lunged up clumsily and started away, hearing Ambro get up behind her.

"Oh, Eva?"

She turned back. "Yes?"

"I am very good at finding what I want in life, but I think if I had your address it might make things easier for me to pick you up tomorrow."

CHAPTER ELEVEN

"AMBROSIO PROCOPIO?" LITTLE ISABELLA Rossi repeated the name Eva had told her. "Procopio? That is a name of the old country, my dove. You knew this, no?"

"Yes, I thought so, Nonni," replied Eva in Italian. "I thought that perhaps you would like that."

"Well, I do . . . and I don't."

"Why is that?" Eva looked mischievously over at her mother, who was listening in.

"Because, baby girl, you never know when you can trust an Italian man. They are hot-blooded, you know."

Eva couldn't help laughing. "I also knew you would say that, Nonni. It is okay. You and Mama have raised a strong girl who doesn't let hot-blooded men have their way with her. Besides, the man I married was named Pedersen, no? Scandinavians are not known to be so hot-blooded, and look at all the trouble I had with him."

Isabella smiled, making her eyes crinkle up until they vanished behind folds of wrinkled flesh. She patted Eva's hand. "You are so right. And yes, I know we raised a good girl, dove. You will need every ounce of your strength, too. Do not forget that. You have never gone on an outing with a true Italian, have you, child?"

"No, Nonni, I don't think that I have."

"Then you just remember. If you start to get in trouble, you think of me, okay?"

"I will. I promise."

Isabella smiled again and held her arms wide, calling Eva in for a warm embrace. She kissed her cheek. "Okay. You go. Have fun. And think of me and your mother."

As her grandmother imparted her advice, Eva pushed a nervous, almost guilty feeling way in the back of her mind knowing that she had yet to make a decision whether or not to call Officer Stone about Ambrosio Procopio's visit. And now he was going to take her to dinner. Was she playing with fire?

Bianca's glance darted outside the front window, and she gasped, making Eva and Isabella turn also. "Cara, do you know what this Ambrosio drives?"

Eva had no idea, but she wasn't expecting the car that sat outside where asphalt met the lawn. The car was a sleek coupe, a convertible with a dark cream-colored top, whose body was the most exquisite, deep orange-tinted gold she had ever seen. Thanks to her father and his love of nice cars, Eva was confident in saying that this was a new model Pontiac Le Mans Sport, and beyond question one of the most beautiful automobiles she had ever seen.

The driver's door opened, and Ambro Procopio eased up out of it, smooth as a wisp of smoke, sleek as a sack of otters.

"My," breathed Bianca. "My. Eva—you had better be careful. This one, he is no ordinary man."

Eva could only nod. She didn't know a lot of things, but she knew that. *Call Officer Stone. Call Officer Stone. Call Officer Stone.* The admonition rang in her head, even as suddenly she knew she would not.

"Let him come to the house, cara," said Bianca, with a firmness she normally saved for when she was about to chastise Tyke, or already in the middle of chastisement.

"I don't think he would want me to go out to him anyway, Mama. He's not that type," Eva managed to reply, as they watched Ambro Procopio stroll up the broken walkway toward the front door, his jaw, neck, and shoulders seeming too wide to be on a normal man—but then Ambrosio Procopio was no normal man.

"I don't trust him," said Isabella. Eva looked at her grandmother, whose chin was firm, her jaw set. Her lower lip was threatening to ride up over the top one, thanks to her lack of top front teeth.

"But Nonni, you don't know him." She found herself stumbling on her Italian, which she hadn't done in years. Then again, she would likely be stumbling on English right then as well. She hated to admit it, but she was feeling flustered only because of the nearness of Ambro Procopio.

"I do not need to know him, Eva," replied Isabella. "I see him."

To herself, Eva smiled. Her grandmother was an old woman, a proper lady, from the old school. What could she remember of how a young woman felt for an intriguing, suave gentleman?

The three women stepped back away from the window as Ambro Procopio's measured knock came on the front door, three sharp taps. Tyke was starting to walk in from the hallway when Bianca motioned him back and shushed him.

"I will answer the door, Eva," said her mother. "You go down the hall with your son, and I will call you."

Without waiting for her daughter to protest, Bianca went to the door, and Eva disappeared into the hall.

"Hello," Eva heard Bianca say as she swung the door open. "You must be Mr. Procopio."

"I am," said the man's muffled voice. "I am at your service, madam. And you are Miss Galanti's mother." Eva smiled, because Ambro Procopio had won instant points. Her mother hated it when men tried to flatter her for her youthful looks by pretending they thought she and Eva were sisters.

"Yes, I am," Bianca replied. "Mrs. Galanti. Bianca Galanti." The words surprised Eva. Her mother wasn't prone to giving out her first name offhandedly.

"Oh—this is my mother, Mr. Pro— I don't suppose you speak Italian, do you?"

"Very poorly, I'm afraid. If it has to do with food, the answer is yes—or perhaps cars. Little more."

"That is all right. I think we only ever speak it because of Mother. This is Isabella Rossi." Eva heard her grandmother mumble something, and the last words surprised her, as they sounded like *thank you,* two of the very few English words Isabella understood and could say.

"Would you like to sit down, Mr. Procopio?" The surprises kept on coming. "I will call Eva."

"Yes, I would. Thank you."

Bianca soon appeared in the hallway and walked along it to where Eva stood waiting with Tyke at the far end. "He is a very smooth gentleman," she whispered with the shrug of one shoulder. "Go to him. Let us see if we can find out more of what sort of man he is."

Taking a deep breath and straightening her dress against the fronts of her thighs, Eva went down the hall, feeling breathless. She turned the corner, and Ambro Procopio spied her and stood up from the sofa, giving her a slight bow. In the lighting of the living room, his deep-set gray-blue eyes now seemed even more blue than she had imagined while sitting with him in the dim-lit lounge. "It is so good to see you again, Miss Galanti."

"You can call me Eva," she told him, for which she received a sharp jab in the ribs from the thumb of her mother, who stood a little behind her.

"Thank you—Eva. Your mother has invited me to sit for a while, so if you would like . . ." He motioned with a wide sweep of his hand toward the furniture. Since he would not know which piece she would choose, he took the high road and offered her all of them.

Eva walked to the La-Z-Boy and sat down, demurely turning her knees to point away from Ambro as he sank back down on the sofa.

After bringing strong coffee for the four of them, Bianca sat on the opposite end of the couch from Ambro. She sipped her coffee as she fired a warning glance toward her mother, who sat on a love seat that was at right angles to the sofa.

"So how was your day, Mr. Procopio?" Bianca asked before Eva could think of anything to say.

"Marvelous. Thank you for asking. And yours?"

"Very good, thank you," replied Bianca. "Eva? How about you?"

Eva had been more than prepared to let her mother carry the conversation. She didn't normally have an issue with talking to people, but she felt self-conscious with Ambro.

"It was . . . fine."

She didn't dare tell him she had spent the day dressed like an urchin, pushing her rusted red Briggs and Stratton around the streets on the north end of Rock Springs, knocking on strangers' doors and begging them to let her mow their lawns. At least she had come away with twenty-seven dollars, which was the most she had made in one day since early June.

Needless to say, she also didn't dare tell him she had spent a good part of the day going back and forth trying to decide if she owed Officer Stone the consideration of giving him his requested phone call to say Ambrosio Procopio had indeed come into her life, so out of the blue.

"What kind of car is that?" she thought to ask. "I'm guessing a Le Mans Sport?"

Ambro stared at her, blinking a couple times before he smiled in amused surprise. It was the first time Eva could recall seeing him taken aback by anything. "You impress me more and more, Miss Galanti—Eva, I mean. My. Yes, it is a 1972 Pontiac Le Mans Sport, to be exact. The paint is called quetzal gold. Exquisite, is it not?"

Eva smiled back at him, trying to hide how pleased she was to have obviously impressed this man who was so sure of himself. "It *is* exquisite. My father was a lover of great automobiles," she said. "He passed that love on to me."

"A smart man," said Ambro. "There are not very many women who can find their way around a car even enough to change the oil—no offense intended."

She smiled. "None taken. I think you're right."

Ambro's lips parted to say something, but he stopped and looked over at Bianca, seeming only then to have remembered there were others in the room besides Eva. "So your husband was a car man. What did he own?"

"We have owned many," Bianca said. "We once had a fifty-seven Hudson Hornet. A fifty-seven Bel Air. A Buick Road Master."

"Nice. Another fifty-seven?"

Bianca laughed lightly. "No, that one was a fifty. We've had many cars that weren't fifty-sevens. He used to fix them and sell them. I don't think we ever made much, but he got a lot of enjoyment from it."

"That is certainly what life is all about, right?"

Bianca measured Ambro with a long look, then nodded. "Yes. Yes, it is, Mr. Procopio." When he responded with a warm smile, she said, "I hope you will forgive me, Mr. Procopio, but I am very interested in your given name. Eva tells me it is Ambrosio?"

"So it is," he said, smiling over at Eva. "And what is it that interests you so?"

Bianca shrugged. "Well, it is simply so magical, don't you find? Remind me of its meaning, would you?"

Ambro grinned. "It was my mother's way of trying to keep me alive forever, she told me when I was a boy. It means 'he who is immortal'."

"Oh, yes! Yes. I do remember now. He who is immortal—or eternal. Ambrosio. Enchanting."

"Thank you, Mrs. Galanti. If you would, please call me Ambro. I try not to weigh anyone down with my long name if at all possible."

"Ambro. Okay, I can only try. But Ambrosio is so beautiful, it may take some effort. So. Will you have my daughter for long tonight?"

An amused look came into Ambro's eyes. "What is your wish? I will bring your daughter home at whatever time you say." His glance cut over to Eva, to whom he gave a half wink.

Again, Bianca laughed. "She is a grown woman. I'm merely curious."

"Eleven. Or sooner," said Ambro. "Promised."

Bianca gave him another smile, which Ambro returned— one of those smooth, charismatic smiles Eva had been stunned by at her first meeting with him. He looked over at her, and that was Eva's signal to rise if she was ready, which she was.

She stood and moved closer to him. Tyke came in from where he had been lurking in the hallway and stood shyly before his mother and Ambro, and the man looked at him. "Hello, son. I am Ambro Procopio." He held out his hand, which Tyke shook as he tried to hold the man's gaze.

He smiled. "I'm Tyke."

Ambro raised an eyebrow. "I like that. It's different."

Tyke's eyes flicked over to Eva, a little color coming to his face. He had hated his name for years. "Thanks," he said.

"Hey, Tyke. Did you check on Leo?" asked Eva. Ambro looked a quick question at her but held his tongue. "Oh! I'm sorry. Leo is my other son."

"I checked on him, Mom. He's asleep."

"Okay. Make sure you tuck him in good, will you?"

"I will."

Tyke spied Ambro's car outside and almost gasped. "Wow! Cool car!"

Smiling, Ambro said, "You can come out and drive it around the block—if you want."

"Oh no," Eva cut in. "Maybe next time. You'll be here all evening if you open up that can of worms."

Ambro grinned, and Tyke let go a shy laugh. "Yeah. I'd sure like to look at it closer sometime, though."

Looking at Eva with an appraising glance, Ambro nodded. "Well, I think your mother has just invited me to come back a *next time*. So you will get to look at it again—and closer."

Out at the Pontiac, like the suave gentleman, Ambro opened Eva's door for her and shut it when she was safely seated. She glanced down at his dash, surprised to see a phone mounted there. What would it be like to be among the world's wealthy?

Ambro came around, slid into his own bucket seat, and said in a casual voice, "You should probably buckle your belt." Eva, like most people, wasn't used to putting on a seatbelt, but she knew there must be a good reason for the request. She found it odd that even after his suggestion he didn't buckle his own belt.

They went two blocks down the street at a casual pace before Ambro turned left out onto Railroad Avenue, slowed, and came to a stop in the middle of the road, looking back toward Eva's neighborhood. It had vanished from sight. Here where they had stopped, the line of houses marched onward continuously on the left, but on the right, at least for a ways, was nothing but tan dirt, sparse straw-like grass, and shrubs.

Ambro glanced at Eva and smiled. "Okay, watch this."

Saying that, he screamed the tires and put up a cloud of smoke as they tore down the street, hitting sixty miles an hour past the row of houses almost before Eva knew what was happening.

As they once more came into an area with houses on both sides, Ambro let off the gas, a big grin on his face, his eyes smiling even behind the brownish tinge of his sunglass lenses. He eased his foot down on the brake, slowing back down to the twenty-five mile an hour speed limit. "Nice, huh? It has a 455 under the hood. There isn't a—"

Whatever he was going to say was cut short by the chirp of a siren. Eva whirled to look behind them as she heard Ambro say, "Oh, isn't that wonderful? What are cops doing hanging around up here this time of evening?" He whipped over to the right road edge and let out a long sigh. "Okay. Hey, Eva, could you drop that glove box open? I have my registration and insurance card in there. Thank you."

She did as he asked, and then, with the papers in his left hand, Ambro parked both hands in plain sight on the steering wheel, waiting. Eva couldn't hold back her curiosity. She cranked around to see Lance Cartwright's friend Officer Rick Cohen strolled up to them, his right thumb hooked in his gunbelt, an inch in front of the holster that held his revolver. She noticed that the thong had already been removed from the revolver's hammer.

Officer Cohen stopped at the back of Ambro's window, and before he could speak Ambro said, "I don't think I've met you."

"Do you meet a lot of policemen?" asked Cohen after a moment's pause.

Ambro laughed. "No, not many."

"Good. Well, this is a beautiful car, sir. Very nice. Any idea why I stopped you?"

Ambro nodded. "Yes. A pretty good idea."

"Okay. Do you know how fast you were going?"

"I have a pretty good idea," Ambro repeated, sounding as casual as if he were ordering breakfast.

"And what would your 'pretty good idea' be?" asked Cohen, trying to sound patient.

"Maybe . . . fifty-five?"

"Okay," Cohen repeated, this time drawing the word out. He sounded impressed. "Most guys won't admit their speed, but you're only five off. It was sixty, actually. You in a particular hurry?"

"No. I apologize, officer. I was showing off a little."

"A car like this is worth showing off—a little. I just wish you would have done it in somebody else's town. I'll need to see your driver's license as well," he said as he took Ambro's paperwork with his left hand.

"Certainly. I'll have to reach."

"Go ahead. Are you armed?"

Ambro hesitated a little longer than Eva expected. "No, officer. Not armed." He reached into the inside of his suitcoat and withdrew a long black billfold made of some fancy leather, a different billfold from the one he had had at Benny's. Flipping it open, he drew his license out and handed it to Cohen.

"Thank you. I'll be right back."

Cohen returned to his car, and a smile came to Ambro's face and stayed. But there was a set to his jaw and brow that made Eva think he wasn't smiling so much inside. After twenty or thirty seconds, he looked over at Eva and clucked his tongue. "Sorry about this. It certainly isn't how I hoped to start out our evening."

She smiled back at him. "I'm okay. Really. This thing sure is fast, though."

That made him grin again. "Yes. Yes, it sure is fast. Maybe not the best thing to show you on our first evening together. Especially since now it has me eating crow."

"At least *your* car will go fast enough for you to get a speeding ticket," Eva said with a little laugh. She was only partly joking.

Cohen returned five minutes later with a citation in hand. He gave it to Ambro to sign, again with his left hand. He hadn't leaned down to look inside the car, so he didn't know Eva was in here. She wondered if he would have remembered her if he had, and if it would have made any difference with the ticket.

"All right, Mr. Procopio," said Cohen, tearing off Ambro's copy of the citation and handing it to him. "I don't mind you speeding out on the highway somewhere. Please just don't do it in town."

"Yes, sir, officer. My lesson is learned."

At the last moment, Cohen leaned over and peered toward Eva. "Evening, m—" For a moment, he froze. "Oh! Hello, Eva Galanti. I had no idea that was you in there."

She smiled. "Sorry."

"No reason to be sorry," Cohen said with a shrug. "It's good to see you."

"You too. I hope you have a safe night."

Smiling and showing his dimples, Cohen nodded and walked back toward his car, and Ambro pulled sedately away from the curb.

"I had no idea you knew cops." She didn't think to remind him that she had mentioned at Benny's how police officers kept coning in to introduce themselves. "Why didn't you say hi to him sooner?"

"I . . . I'm sorry. I didn't think it was my place."

After a moment, Ambro shrugged, smiling at her. "Think nothing of it. I'm certain it will all work out."

After that, he drove on south in silence.

Eva sat trying to decide if anything Ambro had done yet should worry her. She wished Officer Stone had had more intelligence on him. If he had, perhaps she would not be here now.

CHAPTER TWELVE

AMBRO PROCOPIO DROVE HIS Le Mans Sport like an old lady after leaving the traffic stop. They drove all the way through downtown—which as usual was packed with pedestrians and traffic this time of evening—then up steep streets, through residential neighborhoods which like downtown were sometimes clogged with traffic the likes of which had never existed in this town prior to the boom. A minute or so into the drive, Ambro grew conversational once more, all of it small talk. The slow pace due to all the traffic made long conversations possible. Eva guessed in some cases, perhaps like now, that might be considered the one plus to Rock Springs' shocking growth in the last couple of years.

Ambro asked about Eva's father and mother, her grandmother, and about places she had lived before. He asked about her favorite car, color, and food. He kept her so involved in conversation that although she had noticed when they left the business district and headed into the neighborhoods, where of course there would not be a restaurant to be found, she never had a chance to ask him about it.

At last, they started climbing streets into the area of Rock Springs with the highest elevation around, a well-off neighborhood she had driven through only once before, out of curiosity. Many of the homes here were large and well-built, both they and their landscaping immaculate. On Palisades Way, at the extreme edge of town, Ambro at last pulled into a cul-de-sac and stopped in front of a massive two-story house of smooth red brick, with a deep emerald lawn and two heavy, decorative brick columns guarding the entry to the sidewalk. One of them housed a large mailbox. There were three cars already parked in a driveway spacious enough to have easily held another four or five, and all three were luxury automobiles, the nicest of them a blood red Chrysler New Yorker. The spaces between either side of the house and the nearest neighbors were expansive. At the back of the house the terrain seemed to drop over into a nothingness of barren desert.

They stopped behind the red Chrysler, and Eva looked over at Ambro as he threw the Le Mans in park. She wasn't quite sure how to take Ambro sometimes, or how to talk to him, for he seemed so polished, so refined. But then in their conversation he also seemed approachable and sometimes even warm. She decided to talk to him the way she would any other adult male who was far outside her social circle but treated her in a kind manner.

"So . . . We came to your *house?* This is where you live?"

Ambro smiled. "Oh no. No, no, Eva. I actually live in a duplex. A very nice duplex, mind you, but still a duplex. No, I promised you the finest Italian food in Rock Springs, but I am no accomplished chef. I don't even like to cook. You will soon see a true chef of the old country. As you probably already know, there really isn't a good Italian restaurant in this area, so we make do on our own—and quite well, as you will see."

Without waiting for any more questions, Ambro got out, and Eva, already guessing he would want her to, stayed in her seat. He came and opened her door, then took her elbow with a gentle hand as she climbed out, looking around the beautiful, tree-lined cul-de-sac and down the street, then in awe up at the huge brick home, where three dormers beat their chests in the upper story.

"This is the home of my . . . *employer,* Mr. Primo Santori, and his wife Serenella. And it is Primo, not Serenella, who is the lover of preparing fine Italian cuisine. But don't let on that I already told you so. He always likes to spring it on his guests as a big surprise."

He smiled, and still holding onto her elbow he walked her to the front door. Eva found herself a bit frantic trying to go back through her mind to sift information and remember if Primo Santori was one of the names Officer Stone had shown her. But he wasn't. She didn't remember the other Italian name, but she was certain that either the first or the last name started with a G, and it seemed like one of the two names had something to do with the name brand of a firearm.

As they reached the front door, Eva felt acutely aware of her attire, looking at Ambro's immaculate striped suit. "I wish you would have told me how to dress. I feel like a pauper next to you, and in this kind of place."

Ambro looked surprised, and he scanned down the length of her, then back up, not looking the least bit uncomfortable in the act of studying her, yet somehow not making her feel uneasy. She had chosen to wear her favorite dress, a paisley sea green affair with engraved buttons that resembled pewter, pocket flaps on the chest, a belt and pleated skirt that dropped to just below her knees.

"What?" Ambro looked astounded. "You have absolutely nothing to feel bad about, Eva. Look at you! I should have told you when I saw you earlier, I think you look nothing short of ravishing. And I'm glad you didn't wear any of those gaudy, ugly things women are starting to wear now. This stylish, more conservative look suits you perfectly."

A blush came to her cheeks. "Thank you, Ambro."

"You are most welcome."

He dipped his head in the manner of a bow, then turned and pushed a white doorbell button. Inside the house, they could hear a set of elegant-sounding chimes, and then the click of shoe heels on a tile floor. The door swung open, and a blonde lady of about Eva's height stood before them, her face hard-looking and a collection of seams and sags under her jaw and on her neck taking away some of her flawlessness and making Eva suspect that her real hair might not be blond either. She wore a form-fitting white blouse with a modern, over-wide collar and a floor-length black skirt.

"Good evening, Serenella," greeted Ambro, again with a slight bow. "May I introduce you to my friend Eva Galanti?"

"How do you do?" Serenella Santori ducked her chin, almost smiling. "Won't you come in?"

Ambro and Eva went inside, and the woman of the house eased the door shut behind them. Taking Ambro's coat as soon as he had it off, which revealed a solid-torso and bulging chest exploding against a slick-looking cream-colored silk shirt, she hung it up on a nearby hook on the wall, then led the two of them through an entryway that seemed to go forever, into the depths of a monstrously large house that Eva guessed must smell something like heaven. As near as she could tell, besides the aromas of meat, spices, and tomato sauce, the full potpourri also included a hint of peppermint and lemon.

As they turned a corner behind Serenella Santori into a cavernous dining hall with rich red Saltillo tiles on the floor and a deep brown, ornately carved table that would have seated twenty people, a man stepped from another doorway, letting a dark walnut door swing shut behind him. Eva was immediately certain that this was neither of the other faces Officer Stone had shown her.

"Ah, Ambro! Ambro. It is good to see you, *amico*. But of course—you are late." The man, who stood a few inches less than Ambro Procopio's height, had looks almost as startling as Ambro's, but in a different way. Whereas Ambro seemed supremely confident and at ease, in his world or in any other, there was a naturally warm look about his face, a look Eva felt like he might not want everyone to see, but couldn't help. The man now before her suffered no such failing. He had all of Ambro's supreme confidence, yet absolutely none of his natural appearance of warmth.

The man's hair although graying around the edges, was close to the same rich deep brown as Ambro's, although this man's enjoyed none of the waviness, and although it appeared to be thick enough on top, it was smoothed down and lay far enough back from a high, round forehead as to give the initial impression that it was receding. He sported a cautiously trimmed gray-brown mustache and silvering goatee and a silk suit, striped like Ambro's, and red paisley tie.

Eva saw all this with one sweep of her gaze, but the most startling thing about the man was his unsettling silver-blue eyes, with which he now skewered Ambro.

"I am sorry, *Capo*," Ambro used the Italian word for "Boss". "But I had a brief encounter with one of Rock Springs' finest. And besides, that traffic downtown is terrible."

The other man laughed, almost more of a silly giggle, completely incongruous with his austere visage and sharp blue, mockingly reproachful eyes. "Aww, Ambro, Ambro. You never will change. Ever. Showing off your fast car, no doubt. Now tell me—why did I have that telephone installed in your car if you weren't going to use it to let me know when you have done something ill-advised and as a consequence would be late? Should I have given the telephone to Galletto instead?"

"No! Please! Anyone but that cluck," said Ambro with a grin.

Primo chuckled, making laugh wrinkles appear outside his eyes and mouth, and clapped his friend on the shoulder. "You know I'm only having fun, Ambro. So this must be the young lady who seems to be the talk of the town. Miss Galanti? Allow me to introduce myself: Primo Santori—at your service."

With that introduction, and under the piercing study of the wintry eyes, Eva had to gather herself to reply. *Talk of the town?* She found herself taken aback by the comment, and she tried to digest what it could mean. "Thank you," she managed to blurt out. "I'm Eva Galanti. But . . ." She glanced over at Ambro, blushing, then back to Primo Santori. " . . . it sounds like you already knew that."

"Ah, yes. Yes, I did. Do not concern yourself, though." He must have read the look on her face. "It is just that Ambro can get a little talkative when he is taken with someone as he has been with you. Truly, he has talked of little else but you today."

Eva found herself blushing even harder. When she looked at Ambro, he gave her a little shrug. None of his composure had gone south, the way hers had. "This is true, Eva. I confess."

"But of course you cannot blame him," Santori interjected. "From what I understand, half of the city of Rock Springs has taken to visiting you at Benny's. And why should they not?"

Eva allowed herself an embarrassed laugh. She didn't have any interest at the moment in learning where all these claims were coming from, because it only promised to make her feel even more self-conscious than she already did. But she made a mental note to ask Ambro about it later, if the moment seemed right. Her biggest question was how Santori would know about the other visits unless he had some connection with the police department himself, since one hundred percent of the other visits were from officers.

Primo Santori, once the food had been brought in from the kitchen, seated Eva next to Ambro, with his wife to the right of his own chair at the head of the table. The aroma of the food had intensified with its proximity, making Eva as ravenous as she could remember feeling in weeks.

"Okay, first—the wine," announced Primo Santori, still standing at the head of the table, behind his chair. He opened a white-labeled black bottle and with a well-practiced hand filled each waiting glass to a line that it seemed only he could see. "So . . ." He gave Eva a deep, studying look from under oppressively low-hanging, almost unkempt eyebrows—the only thing she could see about him that wasn't perfectly groomed. "Would you like the wine-maker's presentation, or would you rather be surprised by the taste?"

For a moment, she could only gape at him. She looked over at Ambro to get his reassuring look, then back up at Santori. "I would very much like to hear your wine-maker's presentation." She didn't dare tell him it would be a first for her—and that it wouldn't mean anything to her in particular.

"Okay," said Santori with a large smile that still failed to soften his eyes, reaching down to take the stem of his glass with delicate-looking fingers. He was obviously proud of what he was about to do, and happy that she had asked him to. "Eva Galanti, if I were a true wine maker trying to sell this bottle of wine to you, I would use words something like these: This beautiful, burgundy-colored wine was made in 1935, in Fontanafredda—in the old country. It was first aged for three years in a cask of oak, before being bottled as it is now. It will give you hints of black cherry, tobacco, dried mushrooms, pepper, balsam leaves and mint, with velvety tannins and a bright acidity. It would be ideal with true Italian food that is heavy on red meat.

"And that, Eva, is what I would tell you—*if* I were the maker of the wine. I will not tell you that I haven't tasted delicious wines from other countries—even from here in the United States—but a true Italian should support his people. Do you not believe this is true?"

"Of course," replied Eva. Again, his will was strong enough that she wouldn't have dared answer any other way, although in the back of her mind she couldn't help feeling there was a deeper meaning to his question.

Santori swept them all with a broad smile, then raised his glass. "Now a toast: to good friends and companions, old and new."

Eva put her glass to her lips, careful to observe how much the others drank. It wasn't as if she had never taken part in a toast, or in the drinking of wine, but she had never done so in this kind of society. She didn't know why, but that made her feel somehow ashamed.

The wine was . . . interesting. Not her thing, really, but not hard on the palate either. She knew she would have felt ill to know its cost, but she knew beyond any doubt that was something no one in this house would openly discuss, and she had enough couth never to ask. Her guess was that the bottle must have cost as half a month's rent, maybe more.

The conversation at the table was surprisingly light. Even Serenella grew more conversational, especially after her second glass of wine settled. The food was indeed the most exquisite Eva could remember, although she would never have told her mother that. She had to guess this meal had taken Primo Santori hours to perfect. The only thing about the meal he apologized to her for was the cheese, which he regretted not having had imported from Italy.

Once dinner was over, Ambro and Santori lit up long, slender brown cigarettes and smoked appreciatively while all of them retired to twin sofas in a sitting room almost as large, and even more elegant, than the dining room. The walls, accented by white wood around the windows and pointless decorative trios of carved wooden frames surrounding absolutely nothing in the middle of three walls, were a deep red, almost as blood-red as the wine had been.

They continued their conversation, with both Ambro and Santori quizzing Eva about her job, about her aspirations in life, and her hopes for her family. Unsure if she wanted to see the reaction of the others to a revelation of Leo's Down Syndrome, Eva kept that to herself, but she proudly spoke of both him and Tyke, of her mother and grandmother, and of the father who had given her and the family so much joy and security, but had been called away far too soon.

When the conversation finally began to lag, Santori drew a deep breath. "Well, Eva, if it means anything to you, I think you deserve far more than what you have. As do those sons of yours. And your mother and grandmother should have the finer things in life. They will not be around forever, you know."

Eva nodded. "I hope things will change. Someday." She didn't know what else she could say. If Ambro had been building up to offer her some kind of job, as her gut instincts had told her, it had not been forthcoming. Perhaps he had changed his mind about her in the interim.

Then she caught a look that passed between Santori and Ambro, and she was almost certain Santori gave his friend a little wink, as Santori was standing up. The homeowner's move was everyone else's signal, and Ambro helped Eva up as Serenella struggled on her own to rise off the sofa.

"I hope you will come back and see us again," Santori said. "It has been a very pleasant evening, and you know, there is much more of that good food where tonight's meal came from. I am always looking for someone to practice on—someone who hasn't grown weary of my cooking."

Eva smiled and glanced over at Serenella. "I doubt anyone would ever grow tired of your cooking."

"Well, thank you. Your words are gracious. Let me show you to the door."

When Primo Santori was ready to say goodbye, he didn't beat around the bush. But it was all right. Eva was ready to get back to her simple, settled way of life, where she didn't have to be self-conscious of anything she said or did. She was ready to hug her family, and maybe sit and watch a little television before retiring for the night. The kind of things average people did.

She learned too soon that Ambro had no similar plans for her.

CHAPTER THIRTEEN

AMBRO PROCOPIO DROVE THROUGH the city and back toward the north end of town, the area where common—and less than common—people and most of the businesses could be found, as if he had only one citation left before the courts would take his driver's license away. When he passed the turn-off leading east toward Eva's house, she sat for a moment, first waiting to see if he would catch his mistake, then wondering at what point it would no longer sound rude to bring it to his attention.

A quarter mile past the turn, now well up past where A Street turned into Elk, she took a calming breath. "I should have pointed it out sooner, but did you know you passed the turn to go to my house?"

Ambro gave a little grin, throwing her a glance. "I did indeed."

That silenced her for a moment. Eva prided herself on sensing danger when she was in or near it, and she didn't feel it now. That left her only with curiosity, for by this point she hardly even let herself think about Officer Stone's visit anymore.

"Where are we going?" She was more than curious because other than some scattered small manufacturing and service-related businesses, and of course the wild country music lounge they called the Kasbah, there wasn't much more to see on the road ahead.

"It's a surprise," Ambro replied.

His demeanor was so innocent that Eva still wasn't concerned. He seemed perhaps a touch excited, but not devious. She waited. At last, after passing the rowdy crowd at the Kasbah and the onramps to the freeway, and now heading out into the middle of nowhere on Highway 187, Eva looked over at him.

"This doesn't go anywhere but through the Red Desert toward Farson," Eva pointed out.

Ambro took a long, calming breath and stopped the Pontiac in the middle of the road, then finally looked over at her, wiggling his eyebrows. "It doesn't go anywhere, but it sure goes there fast."

Throwing the car into first, he gunned the motor and popped the clutch at the same time, throwing Eva back against her seat. The tires barked on the pavement, but after that first second there was no room for barking or squealing. Instead, the tread of the tires, and the hundreds of horses under the hood, were shooting the Pontiac forward at such a speed on the dark, deserted highway that for five or six seconds Eva was merely thrilled. It had been years since she rode in a car this fast, or at least since a driver had volunteered to demonstrate the car's speed.

They were going seventy miles an hour when she looked over at the speedometer, and they weren't into the ride much more than seven seconds.

Eva's thrill grew to worry around ten seconds, when they hit ninety, and by the time Ambro threw it into the last gear, she was going back and forth in horror from watching the darkness ahead fly into their faces to the speedometer climbing to its final mark, at one hundred forty miles an hour. It wasn't that Eva had never driven a car this fast, but never had she done so in the dark.

"That's almost five hundred horses!" Ambro yelled over the roar of the engine. His eyes seemed to gleam, and there was an insane-looking smile frozen to his face.

"This is too fast!"

Eva's cork had popped. She couldn't hold her fear in any longer and regretted not speaking up sooner. It was one thing going over one hundred in broad daylight, but they were passing through country now that was home to at least three good-sized ranches, and they had no way to know what large animals, be it horses and cattle from the ranches, or some of the feral horse herd, might be out on this highway. At one hundred forty miles an hour, if anything appeared in front of them, it, and they, were dead.

Laughing, Ambro glanced over at her. The furious and frightened anger must have been painted all over her face, because the moment his eyes landed on her he let off the gas, then began to ease down on the brake pedal.

It seemed forever, and a lot of rattling and complaining by all five hundred horses, before Ambro had the car back down to seventy miles an hour. The little smile pulling at the corner of his mouth remained as the car kept creeping slower, but he didn't look over at her until they were down to sixty.

At the moment when he finally looked at her, a red light erupted behind them, and Ambro looked in the rearview mirror and slammed his hand hard on top of the steering wheel. *"What?* You must be kidding me!"

A siren sang to prove that no one was kidding Ambro.

Still furious, with her heart racing and her brain swollen with so much anger she felt like jumping out and walking back to town, Eva didn't feel the slightest bit sorry for Ambro for getting pulled over twice in one day. Without even asking her permission, he had taken both their lives in his hands. Only seven or eight times in her life had she gone over one hundred thirty miles an hour, and those times were with the man she trusted most, her father, and on a wide, empty, well-lit highway. No one but a maniac would drive one hundred forty miles an hour into an abyss full of untold stock and wildlife.

There was a long pause as they sat there idling, with the red light rotating behind them, before Ambro and Eva saw anyone. When they did, he appeared on Eva's side of the car, a tall, heavy-set man dressed in the uniform of a Sweetwater County deputy, and wearing a light-colored cowboy hat.

He motioned for Eva to roll down her window, which she did. After a moment of silence, as he looked at her face and seemed to be seeing someone he didn't expect to see, the deputy leaned down to look farther into the car.

"You mind tellin' me what in the hell that was—" The deputy stopped. His eyes seemed to focus on Ambro in the soft glow of his dash lights, mostly with the help of the officer's flashlight beaming into his face.

"Oh." He swore and dropped the flashlight beam out of Ambro's eyes. "Hello, Mr. Procopio."

"Hello, Deputy Miles. How is your evening?"

"Well . . . safe, I reckon. So far."

"You're expecting a change?"

"No, sir. At least I hope not."

"I hope not as well."   ,

A pregnant pause ensued. Both men seemed to be waiting—Ambro for the deputy to tell him he could leave, and the deputy for Ambro to ask if he could.

Eva spoke: "Deputy, can I speak with you for a moment?"

The deputy stared at her, and even in the darkness she saw a flicker of his eyes, and an expression of hesitation. Before he could speak, Ambro cut in. "Eva? What is the matter?"

"You know what the matter is, Ambro. You scared me half to death. No offense, but I think I want to have the deputy give me a lift home."

He smiled patiently, but she caught nothing except the beginnings of it, for she jerked her eyes away. "Please, Eva. I was only having some fun. I thought you enjoyed fast cars."

"I do," she snapped. "When they're driven by sane people."

The deputy had backed away from her door. He hadn't spoken for twenty seconds or more. "Are you two all right? I'm not going to have any trouble we need to clean up out here in the morning, am I?"

"No, Deputy Miles. No trouble." Ambro's voice was firm, and confident, as always. "You can go ahead and go about your shift."

The deputy hesitated, his eyes flitting toward Eva. She saw his jaw set. "Why don't you give me your information, Mr. Procopio—you know, so it looks like I'm doing my job. All the usual: license, insurance, registration. Ma'am, I would like to look at your license as well."

"Why?" asked Ambro.

"What's that?"

"Why hers?" Ambro repeated. "She wasn't driving. You don't have any right to look at her license."

The deputy stared Ambro down. All three of them knew Ambro was right.

"It doesn't matter," said Eva through tight teeth. "It's fine. He can look at it."

"I'm just trying to be safe," said the deputy, half mumbling.

He took their information back to his car and wasn't gone long enough to write much down before he returned. "All right. You can go, Mr. Procopio. But I sure wish you wouldn't drive like that on this highway. You know, I've seen dead deer along here, and elk—even a mountain lion once. I almost hit a whole herd of wild horses myself one time, not far from here. I don't want to be the one picking up the pieces, if you don't mind."

"It's no worry," said Ambro, his words measured. "I can handle myself. I didn't start driving yesterday."

"Yes, sir. But . . . Do you want me to give the lady a lift back to wherever she's goin'?" It seemed like it took all the courage the deputy could muster to ask.

"No, she's fine. Thank you for asking."

The lawman glanced back down at Eva, then once more at Ambro. Eva suddenly found herself lacking the strength to speak her own mind. The iron will of Ambro Procopio, like his employer Primo Santori, was too strong.

"Have a good night, Miles." This time Ambro seemed to forget the "Deputy" part. He turned the steering wheel hard and spun the car around on the highway without an overt glance behind them to see if anyone was coming.

They drove for a full mile before Eva managed to override her anger enough to take a deep breath. "You're taking me home, Ambro."

Ambro took a moment to reply. "Yes, Eva. I am. And I am truly sorry. I should have asked if you'd like to go fast. I had no intention of scaring you. I just knew you liked fast cars, and . . ." His voice trailed off. He seemed almost disconcerted.

She stared at him. She couldn't hide the look of incredulity that must be branded on every part of her expression. "How could you possibly think that wasn't going to scare me? It would have scared anyone—except a fool."

A flash of something Eva had yet to see went through Ambro's eyes—perhaps pride, perhaps anger, perhaps surprise. Maybe, and most likely, a mixture of all three.

He let the car slow down, rather than speed up once more as she had thought he might. After a ten-second silence, he said, "No one likes to be called a fool, Eva, and in that way I am no different from most. You should be more careful with your choice of words."

This time she didn't look at him. Instead, she stared at some flickering orange lights out her window in the faraway dark. She wasn't about to apologize, and she would not be intimidated.

They were back among the scattered businesses on the north end of town now, well past the Kasbah lounge and coming close to her turn. Ambro slowed the Pontiac a little more. "Eva?"

She cringed at her name being spoken by the man in the other seat. He repeated it.

"What?" She couldn't make her voice sound calm. She couldn't keep it from simmering with residual anger.

"I am sorry, you know." He slowed and made the turn. The car crept on for another five seconds before it paused at the last turn. "Eva?"

"What?"

"Aren't you going to talk to me anymore? I'm really sorry about the speed. I should have realized."

"Realized what?" she snapped.

"That it would scare you."

She scoffed. He made the turn. She was pretty sure he hadn't gone one mile over the speed limit since turning around after the traffic stop by the time he pulled over facing the wrong way a block from her house. She jerked her eyes over at him. Was he letting her off here?

"Eva? I still want to be friends. Please do not be angry with me."

"Please take me home."

"Okay. But remember, I'm truly sorry. I wish I could go back and make a different choice."

He drove the rest of the way to her house, and she jumped out her door before he could get out and come around. He still managed to clamber out and yell after her. "Eva! Please wait."

She whirled on him. "For what?"

"Can't you at least let me walk you to your door?"

"I can walk by myself. Thank you."

And turning, she did just that. Only when she was opening the front door did she hear the Pontiac pull away.

CHAPTER FOURTEEN

EVA HAD INTENTIONS OF sitting with the family watching a movie, then going quietly to bed, but she couldn't be so lucky. The moment she opened the door, Tyke came running from the hall, yelling, "Mom!" He was carrying Leo tightly in his arms.

Obvious signs of terror filled the eyes and voice of Eva's oldest son, and on the instant, her blood seemed to run cold. The skin of her face reacted by tightening up as she took three fast strides toward him, reaching out.

"Tyke! What's the matter?"

"Nonni! They came and took her to the hospital!"

Eyes instantly moist with the tears of fear, Eva scanned the room. "Where's Grandma Bianca?"

"Gone too. She rode in the ambulance."

Eva grabbed Tyke and Leo as one package, jerking them against her torso. She would have claimed it was to comfort them, but she needed the comfort as much as they did. Leo found one of his big surges of strength and struggled to turn until he could also get an arm around his mother's neck.

Tyke's grunt almost sounded like one of disgust when he finally pushed his mother away from him so his little brother could get himself turned all the way around and wrap both arms around Eva. But if it was disgust, it vanished quickly in a relieved laugh, as Tyke came back in to complete the three-way hug, managing to hide his teary eyes from his mother.

"It's going to be okay, boys," Eva soothed them, and herself. "It will be all right. When did the ambulance come?"

"At ten-fifteen," said Tyke, dropping a number that had obviously waited on the tip of his tongue for the last twenty minutes.

"Okay. Let's . . . Hey, maybe you should stay here," she said, talking herself out of taking the two of them to the emergency room with her.

"No!" Tyke countered. "We should all go."

Eva felt sick. She didn't want the boys up there, in case . . . Well, in case things really went wrong. But at the same time she needed them. And both boys were fully dressed, ready to leave the house.

The phone rang, and all three of them jerked at the noise. Eva stared at it when it rang again, and Tyke stared at her. Neither moved toward the phone.

"Do you want me to answer it, Mom?"

Eva was starting to shake. She knew they had to pick it up, but the thought of what was on the other end scared her to death.

"No, son." She tried to be brave. "I'll get it."

Holding tight to Leo, she walked over and picked up the phone as the fourth ring faded. "Hello?"

Eva? It was not the voice of her mother, or the sound of any stiff professional voice she expected from the hospital.

Eva? It took the second time hearing her name to switch gears and realize who was on the other end of the line. She had noticed that Ambro had the phone in his car, yet still it surprised her to hear him calling her on it.

"Ambro, I'm sorry I can't talk right now. My grandma's gone to the hospital." She dropped the phone back on the base, but before she could find the hospital's number it rang again.

"Hello?" This time her voice sounded impatient, on the verge of anger, and she couldn't control it.

Cara? Are you all right?

"Mama!" Eva blurted out. "Yes! I'm fine. I just got home. Is Nonni okay? What happened?"

I'll tell you all about it. Can you come up?

"Nonni's okay, right?"

Yes, cara. Just shaken up. We both are.

A gust of breath escaped Eva's lungs, and she had to fight to hold back tears of relief. "Okay, we're leaving soon."

The phone rattled horribly as she tried to hang it back on the base. Tyke was standing there, and he saw her trembling all over. "Mom? Are you okay?"

"Yes, honey." She clenched her teeth and tried to turn away, not looking at him. "I'm fine."

They all froze when the phone rang once more, only this time Eva also cursed. It was something she had only done perhaps five times in front of Tyke in the entire fifteen years of his life.

Turning back, she picked up the phone again. "Mom?"

Eva, please don't hang up! Once again, it was the voice of Ambro Procopio. *I'm on my way back to pick you up. Don't leave, okay?*

She didn't have even one second to object. The line was already dead.

"Who was it, Mom?" Tyke asked after she had been silent for fifteen seconds, staring at the phone and shaking so bad even her chin trembled.

"It was Ambro Procopio."

Tyke waited, but she said nothing more. It was all she could do to blink her eyes fast enough to control the onslaught of tears.

"Mom?"

She drew in a deep breath. "It's okay, Son." She put as much calm in her voice as she could. "Why don't you make a sandwich or something really quick, okay? We're going to wait here for a few minutes. Ambro's coming to get us." And that was that. She gave no further explanation, and Tyke was wise enough not to ask.

The moment the Le Mans screeched up in front, Tyke shot out the door with his half-eaten sandwich in hand, Eva right behind him with Leo in her arms. Ambro was only fast enough to come around and meet them as they reached the passenger side. He jerked open the door and pushed the seat forward so the boys could get in back.

When they were all settled, Ambro practically ran around the front and got in, throwing the car in gear. "I won't race," he said.

Eva almost laughed as she turned to stare at him incredulously. If ever there was a time to race, this was it. But after the way she had treated him earlier, she didn't dare say it. She only smiled and patted his arm, then folded both hands in her lap.

The five-minute drive to Sweetwater County Memorial, first down Elk Street, then onto Grant, and finally College Drive, felt like an hour to Eva when Ambro chirped the tires to a stop in front of the ER doors. He jumped out and helped Eva get Leo out of the dark back seat, then reached out and gave her arm a squeeze. "I'll park the car and come in," he said.

"It's okay, Ambro. Thank you for the ride."

"If I leave how will you get home?"

Eva froze, until a little shake of her arm from Tyke brought her out of her trance.

"Oh. Right. Are you okay to stay, Ambro? I'm sorry."

"No, please don't be! I volunteered, remember? Go find your grandmother. I'll be in soon."

With that, he hurried around and got in the Pontiac, and it rolled away.

In the examination room bed, Isabella Rossi was sedated, but not quite asleep. She managed to drag her eyes open at the sound of Eva's voice speaking with Bianca at the entryway to her room. "Oh, my dove," the old woman said in a feeble voice. "You came. Come to me, Eva darling."

Eva, with Tyke, who still held onto Leo, hurried into the hospital room. At the bedside, Eva smiled down at her Nonni. Isabella reached up and took her granddaughter's hand, giving it a little shake. "You shouldn't have worried yourself, sweet one. You didn't need to come. I'll be home soon."

Eva tried to smile when Isabella looked up at her. "It wasn't a problem, Nonni. I wanted to come. Ambrosio brought us," she added.

"Oh. He did?"

"Yes, Nonni. He made a special trip back to get us when he heard the news."

"Oh." Isabella looked thoughtful. But weariness was quickly overtaking her thoughts, and her words were drawn out. "Well, that's good. Good Italian breeding, maybe."

Eva smiled. It hadn't been so long ago when Isabella was telling her she didn't like Ambro. Then again, had she heard about his speeding problem, she would most likely have returned to her initial assessment. Eva didn't plan to tell her. Or anyone, for that matter.

"Yes, maybe, Nonni." She leaned down and kissed her grandmother on the cool, leathery skin of her cheek. "You go ahead and rest now, okay? We'll be right here when you wake up."

Of course they wouldn't be. Eva knew the hospital staff would send them packing to the waiting room soon. She was surprised they had let the boys come in even now.

When Eva left Isabella's room, her mother was waiting in the hall and gave her her second embrace of the night, a long, firm one that made Eva begin to feel healing start inside her. Maybe things would be okay. She didn't know how they could pay for this trip to the hospital, to say nothing of any medication that might be prescribed before they left, but things would work out. They had to.

Ambro came in from the outer door, searching for Eva. When his eyes fell on her, the question there was obvious. Eva nodded, and, looking relieved, Ambro walked closer.

"Your grandmother is all right then?"

"Yes. Thank you, Ambro." She knew she didn't sound as warm as she wanted to. She still couldn't quite get past her scare from earlier. The flicker of Ambro's eyes demonstrated that he sensed her coolness.

"It is no problem. Would you like something? Any of you? A drink? Maybe some coffee, or a cigarette?"

Eva shook her head. "Nothing for me. Thank you."

Ambro looked over at Bianca. "Mrs. Galanti?"

"No, thank you, Mr. Procopio. It's very thoughtful of you to ask."

Tyke, who accepted the offer of a Coke, was Ambro's only taker until he looked at little Leo, held tight in his brother's arms. This was the first time Ambro had seen Leo in full light, but his back was still to him. "And how about you, little man? I'll bet you could use a candy bar. Couldn't you?"

Ambro stepped around to see the younger brother's face, and he froze. His mouth came open, then clamped shut. He looked quickly over at Eva. It was the first time she had noticed Ambro looking what she would call disconcerted.

"That is Leo," she said in a cool, even voice.

Ambro looked back at the little boy, then once more at Eva. She was waiting for him to get over his apparent surprise and say something to her, at least to ask about Leo. He didn't.

Mr. Charisma recovered like a professional politician. "What do you say, Leo? How would you like a candy bar?"

Leo's eyes lit up, and they leaped over toward his mother. When she nodded cautiously, the boy looked back at Ambro and gave him a huge nod, and a grin the size of Wyoming.

Ambro grinned back and reached out to give Leo's arm a squeeze. "Good boy. A Milky Way? Reese's peanut butter cup?"

Leo stared at him, a wondering look locked on his face. "You don't talk much, huh, Leo? That's okay. I probably talk *too* much." He winked and reached out to tousle Leo's hair. "Okay, then my choice. Reese's it is. I'll be right back."

Ambro left, and five minutes later he returned with a cup of Coke on ice, and the promised peanut butter cup for the youngest Galanti.

Eva couldn't take her eyes off Ambro, looking so suave and polished in his black, striped wool suit and a diagonally striped

black and smoky blue tie. Ambro was not a man given to frivoli-
ty. When he smiled, it always seemed sincere. But these smiles—
more like grins—that he was giving to Leo, they could not be
denied. Ambro was not putting them on only to win points with
her.

Ambro made one-sided conversation to Leo's fixed smile as
he carefully unwrapped the candy cups, then peeled the paper
wrap off the first one, all the time watching the little boy, with
one eyebrow cocked. "Oh, this is going to be delicious, Leo.
You'd better be careful. I think your face is going to crack if
you keep smiling like that." He let out a laugh. It was obvious
he didn't know if Leo understood everything he was saying—or
any of it, for that matter. But in reality, even though he had yet
to grasp the often-unfortunate art of speaking, Leo's compre-
hension was as good as that of any boy his age.

Reaching out, Ambro held the candy for the boy to bite, but
Leo tried to take it out of his hand until Ambro eased it away.
"Oh, no. Your mama would take off a piece of my hide if I let
you get chocolate all over those precious little hands, buddy.
You just bite it; I'll hold onto it."

With a completely trusting gleam in his eye, Leo leaned
closer to the candy and bit off about a fifth of it. Ambro beamed
as he watched the little guy chew, with a marveling look of
wonder, then reach out his hand for more.

Still smiling, Ambro reminded him only to eat it out of his
fingers, and then he held it out to him again. This time Leo bit
off half of what was left. He chewed for a few moments, then
looked at his brother, whose face was only inches away. He still
had the biggest look of amazement in his eyes. One would have
thought Ambro had performed some kind of culinary miracle.

Finally, Leo took the final piece of candy in his mouth, staring at Ambro mesmerized as he chewed. It was as if he was try-

ing to figure every single thing about Ambro out in this one un-wavering study.

Licking the melted chocolate off his fingers, Ambro looked over at Eva, seeming very pleased. The smile slid slowly off his face as their eyes met. After a moment, he managed a wink at her, then turned back to Leo. "You want the rest?"

The boy's response was instant, as if he had already given it plenty of thought. He pointed at his mother.

"You want your mama to have it?" asked Ambro, showing his surprise. Leo gave him a huge nod for reply, then looked back over at his mother.

With another smile and a shrug, Ambro walked to Eva. Shrugging again before Eva as he made a broad outward gesture with both hands, he said, "Little Leo wants you to have the rest. He told me."

Eva forced back a smile, pursing her lips. "He did, did he?"

Ambro dipped his chin, looking at her as if invisible specta-cles were perched on the tip of his nose. He held the still-wrapped peanut butter cup out to her. "Want me to put it in your mouth, or can you hold it?" That got a giggle from her. "Please. Can we be friends again?"

Eva felt fortunate that she was able to hold her hand still as she reached out and took the candy. Inside, she was shaking like a vacuum cleaner about to explode. "Yes." She nodded.

"Yes?"

"Yes, we can be friends again. But from now on, maybe I drive."

Ambro's eyes crinkled up with mirth. "Okay. Maybe from now on you drive."

He watched Eva for a while as she ate the candy, then after a moment looked over at Leo. "Do you think I could hold your little boy?"

Eva frowned and shook her head. "You should probably wait. It will take him a while to warm up."

"But he was smiling at me."

"You were giving him candy."

Ambro allowed himself a laugh. "I have a way with children. I didn't tell you? If he will come to me, is it okay?"

Eva shrugged. "I guess. But it's not very likely. Don't be surprised when you find out I was right."

Still smiling, Ambro turned toward Leo as Eva and her mother watched knowingly. He stopped in front of Tyke and put his hand softly on Leo's shoulder, making him turn to look. A grin started to come over Leo's face, but then it froze, vanished, and he kept staring, his mouth open, studying Ambro intently.

"Would you let me hold you, Leo? Just for a minute?"

Eva watched with one eyebrow raised. She was always amused when strangers tried too fast to get close to her baby. He loved people, and in time he would hug them all if they let him. But at first, in spite of gifts like the chocolate, he was always reserved.

Her mouth dropped open when Leo twisted farther toward Ambro and held out his left arm. Grinning, Ambro took the boy gently from his brother's arms. "There we go, buddy. There we go."

He turned his face, and his eyes, which couldn't have been much more pleased, met Eva's. "Yes, I guess you'll have to drive my car next time we go out. I think I'll be sitting on the other side—holding Leo."

CHAPTER FIFTEEN

EVA LAY IN BED and stared into the dark ceiling, wishing as she had as a child that she could see the stars through it, and the planets, and the moon. The ultimate dream would be to see all the way to heaven.

Ambro had dropped her and the boys off back at home after her mother had insisted there was nothing further Eva could do at the hospital, and it was now only a matter of waiting to see what the doctors had to say about Isabella Rossi.

Eva couldn't sleep. Now that the excitement of the evening was over, along with the heart-jolting scares, first of the fast ride, then of finding her grandmother had gone to the hospital, two things were stuck in Eva's head, and they wouldn't go away. She guessed she had been too scared and too angry earlier in the evening to think of these two things, but now even if she tried to think of something else, her mind kept coming back to them. One of them was good: the remarkable, endearing way Ambro had immediately treated Leo, something she couldn't quite explain away.

The other thought didn't give her good feelings or bad. It was simply strange.

On the dark highway, when the deputy had come up to the car, there was no doubt in her mind Ambro was about to get another citation. In fact, someone had once told her that in Wyoming anything over ninety miles an hour was an arrestable offense, because at that point it became reckless driving, jumping from the status of infraction to a misdemeanor.

She kept trying to recall the exact exchange, and the deputy's reaction when he realized Ambrosio Procopio was the driver he had stopped. It was all pretty much a blur now. All that remained was the overriding feeling that the deputy's attitude—what she could only refer to in her head as anger—had changed abruptly and completely upon seeing Ambro in the driver's seat. Why? What could change a lawman's mind from anger to near deference in an instant? And how did the two men know each other?

It didn't seem like Ambro and the deputy were friends, nor even friendly acquaintances. It seemed more like the deputy was Ambro's underling than a civil servant sworn to uphold the law.

She tried to wrack her brain. What business had Ambro said he was in? Or had he said at all? He had said Primo Santori was his boss, but the boss of what? Did the two of them work for the local court system? Could Mr. Santori be a judge, and Ambro a lawyer? That didn't seem likely. It was a pretty small town. If Ambro were a lawyer, it seemed like there was a better than average chance that Officer Stone would know him.

She was back to Officer Stone. Should she feel guilty for not calling him? If she should, she didn't. Ambro wasn't a bad person. No person who was bad could have treated her son the genuinely caring way he had. Who was Ambro Procopio? And why did Officer Stone have his photograph? Eva had a lot of questions; she wondered if she would ever have any answers.

She finally got out of bed, went to the bathroom, then heated a cup of milk, into which she mixed a small amount of sweetened cocoa. She went to stand at the front room window in the dark, looking out through the thin drapes, sipping her hot drink.

Into her mind popped the ticket Ambro had received that evening from Officer Cohen, Lance's friend. It was obvious that

Ambro and Officer Cohen had no understanding between them such as the one Ambro had with the county deputy.

Eva's mind finally had a side trail to embark on, now that it had wandered as far as Rick Cohen, because one step farther took her to Lance Cartwright. She thought of Lance for a while. Such a big, strapping man. He was not very old, perhaps not too experienced in the ways of the world, but he made her feel so safe in his presence. It was like she was hiding behind this great big wall of goodness, a fortress that promised to keep her from harm. Rick Cohen didn't have that kind of size, but he was also a good man, she felt. And there was the other officer she had recently met, because of Lance, the wavy-haired blond, Chris Hinshaw. Would any of those men have let Ambro off a ticket he had gone so far to earn?

She let out a long sigh. Thinking of Lance and the others made her think of the bar and grill, thus led her all the way back to Benny Fitz, a disagreeable corner in which she did not want to be. She forced her mind over to Brandon Lucky. How was Brandon tonight? Was he safe? Did he feel loved? Poor Brandon. He was an ex-con, that was true. He had done things in his past that he shouldn't have. But he was not proud of them, and he had changed. Why didn't he deserve to find someone who truly loved and accepted him? Why had he stumbled into Karen, who now seemed to hold him by a ring in his nose?

Eva sipped down the last of her drink, and then she bowed her head and prayed. She prayed for her Nonni, for Tyke and his aching tooth, for little Leo, and for her mother to hold up under all the pressure on her. She prayed that Lance and Rick and all the other officers in Rock Springs would be safe and would remain good, strong men who upheld the laws fairly for all. She prayed for Brandon, in his sad life, and she stopped herself short of the blasphemous-seeming prayer that Ambro's Le Mans would suddenly break down. She almost laughed at that thought, so she prayed for the return of reverence.

Last of all, she said a fervent prayer for Eva Galanti. That young woman had a bigger load on her shoulders than she wondered if she could continue to carry.

The following morning, Eva got an early phone call from her mother. Nonni had improved greatly, and they were going to be sending her home that afternoon with some blood thinners and nitroglycerin. Eva was of course glad for the prognosis. But she had to bury her worry about how they would pay for the medication, and for the ambulance ride and the stay in the hospital. Perhaps it would not be too much. She had made a practice of steering clear of doctors, so she really had little idea what medical care might cost. It *felt* like it would be expensive, and she had only that feeling to go on when it came down to it.

The next phone call, only ten minutes following the first, was a big surprise.

Eva?

She paused, gathering her mind.

"Hi! Is this Lance?"

It is. I just wanted to check on you and make sure you're okay.

"Sure I am. Why would I not be?"

Well, I'm sorry for being nosy, but I was at the hospital last night with a guy I got in a fight with at the Silver Dollar Bar, and I saw your mom there. Is your grandma doing okay?

Eva smiled, though Lance couldn't see her. She didn't voice it, but she had to wonder how the man on the other side of Lance's fight had fared. "She is. Thank you for asking, Lance."

That's great! When I had to leave to take that guy to jail they hadn't learned anything yet. So she's coming home?

"Yes. My mother called just before you and told me they'll be releasing Grandma this afternoon."

Oh. Will that work for you?

"Why?"

Don't you have to work?

Eva was both shocked and pleased that Lance would think of that. "No, I'm still off—until tomorrow. I can go get her."

Well, that's good. Glad to hear it.

There was a long hesitation on the line. It became uncomfortable after five seconds. *So anyway, I guess I should let you go, Eva. I . . .*

He paused too long. "Yes?"

Oh. Well . . . oh, nothing. I hope you have a good day. I'll see you around, huh?

"All right, that sounds good. Goodbye."

Goodbye, Eva.

For some reason, she didn't go to put the phone down. On a whim, she cried, "Wait—Lance?"

The line was dead.

Eva stood there with her heart pounding, not knowing why. She gave a sad little frown, trying to push the thought of Lance out of her mind. He was a nice young man, but that was the problem: He *was* young. Much younger than she was.

She started toward the kitchen to see what she could fix for the boys, then stopped. There was something nagging at her. She couldn't let it go.

As she started down the hall toward her bedroom to try and find Lance's business card, the phone rang again, and she almost swore. She hesitated, wanting to continue on to her room, but finally she went back to the phone. It could be her mother.

"Hello?"

Hi, Eva. It's Lance again.

Her heart jumped. "Hi, Lance." She found herself laughing, and he let out a nervous chuckle.

Something funny?

"Yes. I was just going to look for your business card, to call you back."

You were?

"Yeah."

Okay. Well . . . Me too.

They both laughed.

So what were you going to call me about?

"You first," Eva insisted.

What's that? Lance's voice, even with the distance and her inability to look at him, came out sounding nervous.

"You first. You called me, remember?"

Again he laughed, a shy sound. *I did, didn't I? Well, it's not a big deal, and I'll understand if the answer's no, but . . .*

He hesitated too long. "What, Lance? What is it?"

I was just wondering if maybe you'd like to go grab a burger or somethin'. I mean, not for a date or anything. Just . . . Yeah.

Eva couldn't help the giggle that escaped her. "It's not a date?"

No! Of course not. Just a quick lunch.

"Then no." Eva's tone was flat, but she was holding back a mischievous smile.

After a long pause, Lance seemed to gather his strength. *Okay, I understand. Some other time maybe?* His voice seemed to say he understood there would never be any "other time".

"Another time, will it be a date?"

No, ma'am, he said quickly. *Same thing—just grabbin' lunch.*

"Then it will still be no." She gave him enough time to struggle with how to hang up gracefully, then let out a little laugh. "But Lance, if you were to ask me on a date, then yes."

Okay. Then . . . Wait—what's that?

"If you're asking me on a date, then I'm saying yes."

Really? Okay! Okay then. What time can I get you?

"Now that's a good question," she said. "I have to feed the boys breakfast, and then I kind of have to be at the house until my mom calls. I'm not sure when that will be."

Right. Well, you know what? I'll just be around home here. I might work out in the yard or somethin'. And, uh . . . Well, maybe I'll call you later, if that would work.

"Lance?"

Yeah?

"Why don't you just get in your Bronco and come have breakfast with us? My very Italian grandmother and mother aren't going to be here for it, so I'm thinking about making a very *American* breakfast of pancakes, eggs, fried potatoes, and sausage."

Dang. I just got really hungry. You mean it? Like right now?

"Yes, like right now."

Okay, it's a deal. Can I bring anything?

"Hang on, and I'll tell you." Eva set the phone down and rushed to the fridge, throwing the door open. She scanned the half-bare shelves, then frowned. Going back to pick up the phone, she drew a deep breath. "Lance?"

Yeah.

"I thought of something you could bring."

Great. What is it?

She let out a little laugh. "Well, I don't suppose you can bring some eggs, could you? And some sausage? And maybe some Aunt Jemima syrup?"

Lance's big, rollicking laugh came over the phone, the kind of laugh she had seldom heard from the gentle giant. Apparently, he was understanding now that without his coming over, she and the boys wouldn't be having much of a breakfast.

So what you mean is for me to pretty much bring everything we need for breakfast?

She giggled, feeling her face redden. "Oh, come on. It's not *that* bad!"

Just joshin' you. I'll be there in about half an hour.

CHAPTER SIXTEEN

LANCE CARTWRIGHT WAS GOOD company. He took to the boys, and they to him, and that made Eva happy. The boys needed good role models in their lives, and as far as she had seen, other than Ambro's tendency to drive too fast, both he and Lance were that: good role models. Brandon Lucky had turned his life around as well, and made himself a good man. Eva considered herself fortunate to have three good men in her life, three good men all from very different stations in life. She felt like her father would have been okay with those three taking over as his grandsons' role models.

As the meal was winding down, Eva and Lance were laughing about how bare her fridge was and how the meal wouldn't have been much without his generosity. She giggled again as she told him something her father used to say that always made her laugh: *If we had some eggs, we could have bacon and eggs—if we had some bacon.*

Lance laughed as long at her father's funny quote as she always had. She laughed too, but perhaps more because it was so funny to see his reaction.

After breakfast, Eva and Lance sat on the couch playing Jim Croce, Glen Campbell, and Cat Stevens records. She felt so much more relaxed being with Lance than she did with Ambro Procopio. Although Ambro made up the difference by being so suave and mannerly, Eva felt more able to talk with Lance—more able to tell him about herself, and about her struggles. Lance listened quietly and never tried to "fix" anything, which made big points with Eva. She knew there was no fixing what was awry in her life. She only needed a shoulder to cry on.

After one particularly long silence, when Eva had almost run out of things to talk about and was drifting off mentally and only half listening to Jim Croce sing "I Got a Name", Lance cleared his throat.

"Hey, Eva?"

She shifted her gaze to him and for a moment searched his eyes. "Yeah?"

"I wanted to ask you about something. It's none of my business, though, so I hope you won't take it the wrong way."

Eva smiled. "Go ahead and ask. I don't believe you would ask me anything wrong."

"Thanks. So . . . Well, I heard you were riding around with a guy named Ambrosio Procopio. An Italian guy."

Her stomach seemed to cramp up a little. Lance had indeed picked one of the topics she had hoped wouldn't come up. But it was a small town. Obviously. "Yeah. Funny you should ask about him. He asked me to dinner at his boss's house."

He nodded. "He likes to go fast, huh? I've seen his Pontiac around a lot. That's one of the nicest cars in the whole town."

"Yeah. It is. I love black cars, but I think if I had to choose between a black and that gold it would be pretty hard."

Lance was quiet. He was the one who had mentioned the car, but of course it wasn't the topic of interest.

"You think you'll go out again?"

"I don't know, Lance. He's kind of out of my league." She immediately thought how that must have sounded, and the look on Lance's face bore it out. "Wait—I don't mean I would *want* him to be in my league, either. I guess I'm just saying I don't really think he's my type."

Lance nodded, looking thoughtful. He seemed to like that revelation. "He's sure got some money though, huh? You could use it, I guess."

Eva laughed. "Wait. Lance! What are you doing, trying to marry me off? I just met the guy."

He gave a sheepish grin. "Oh, sorry. Yeah, that did sound kind of premature, huh? Anyway, Rick told me he gave him a speeding ticket."

"He did. But . . . when did he tell you that?"

"Umm . . . He called me last night."

Eva pondered this. Was the phone call only to make casual conversation, she wondered, or were Lance and the other officers really keeping tabs on her? If it was the latter, it seemed strange. She wasn't sure how she felt about it.

"So . . . I have to ask *you* something now, Lance."

"Shoot."

"Well, do you guys always pass around stories about people you write tickets to?"

"No, not normally, especially now that the city's gotten so big. But— Okay. Can I level with you? I hate being nosy, but well, I'm kind of a sheepdog personality, you know? And . . ."

"And I'm a special case you're trying to keep safe, right? A sheep?"

He stared at her like the proverbial deer caught in the headlights. Only when she giggled did he grin with relief. "Hardly a sheep. No, Rick knows I've been trying to watch out for you. He was just trying to be helpful. Is that okay?"

She thought about it only for a moment. "Sure. You guys make me feel safe. Now I have another question." This was one she was afraid to get an answer to, but she had to ask. "Do you know anything about Ambro? Other than about his car? I mean, is he okay? A nice guy?"

Lance shrugged even as he was shaking his head. "That I can't tell you. The only thing I know about him is he has good taste in cars. And I guess in girls too." Even as he finished that comment, he blushed, smiling shyly.

When the phone call came from Eva's mother an hour later, she and the boys got ready to go. She thanked Lance for being with them. They stood at the door for a moment while Lance tried to think of something to say. At last, the moment he turned to go, he turned back. "Hey—I don't suppose you'd like to go to a movie or something sometime, huh? *American Graffit's* showing at the theater—since you like cars."

"Cars that work!" she said by way of correction.

"Yeah. Preferably."

"I'd love to go to the movie with you, Lance. Sure. We'll just have to hope we hit the same days off and you don't get called in for more overtime, huh?"

"Yeah. Let's hope. So . . . I'll call you."

"I go back to work tomorrow at one," she pointed out. "In case you were wondering."

Lance grinned. "Thanks. That was my next question."

She smiled at him. "Hey." He looked down at her. Neither of them spoke as she stepped close and embraced him.

Primo Santori waved Ambro Procopio toward the liquor cabinet in his posh parlor, with its twin brown, leather-covered sofas, and its four-by-eight original oil painting of pronghorns flying like earthbound jets across the Red Desert of Wyoming.

"Go pour yourself some sherry, Ambro. Go on. You need to relax." Primo stood straight, easing his chin almost back against his neck and watching Ambro with a smugness that almost seemed severe.

Ambro shook his head irritably. "I'm not feeling thirsty, Primo. And I'm plenty relaxed."

"Did I ask if you wanted any? I said pour it. You aren't thinking straight."

Ambro grunted. *Thinking straight?* Was alcohol supposed to make him think straighter?

"Primo, I don't know if you are listening to me."

"I listen," said Primo in a controlled voice, his untrimmed eyebrows lowering even more. "I always listen. But this time what I'm hearing is that . . . Let me put it plainly: Your head is wrong. That woman is perfect. You know it as well as I do. I think you're getting soft."

"Please listen. I will find you others. It's a big town. There are other attractive women in Rock Springs. Not having her wouldn't be the end of the world."

"Okay, my friend. Listen. I am mixing you a drink, and you will drink it. A Brandy Alexander, eh? How would you like that? No, don't say. Just . . . sit." He jabbed his finger at one of the sofas. "Sit down. Now."

Irritably, Ambro sat on the edge of the sofa, looking out the window at the picturesque, exquisitely landscaped back yard, with its eight-foot high, seemingly impenetrable board fence, and the drab, dry mountains of the desert beyond. He glanced over at his boss as Primo filled a wine glass partly with brandy, then added crème de cacao, and a dash of heavy cream from the refrigerator. It did indeed look good. While Primo was whipping it up with a whisk, Ambro took a deep breath. At last, he eased back against the sofa.

Primo brought him the drink, and Ambro sipped it. It was delicious. It hadn't become one of the more popular whimsical drinks of the decade for nothing.

Primo paced to an obscenely large rolltop desk and opened a drawer, shutting it softly and turning back around with a pair of fat black cigars, from which he clipped the ends with a pair of short, heavy scissors. He strode to Ambro and handed one of them down to him.

"You have a lighter?"

Ambro nodded. "Thanks."

"What are friends for?"

Ambro wasn't sure at the moment. To irritate each other, perhaps. And right now the boss side of Primo seemed far more prominent than the friend side, and he was in full irritating mode.

Ambro lit the cigar only because he felt obligated; Primo had put him in no mood to smoke. They puffed in unison, and Ambro took another sip of the Brandy Alexander and sighed as the smooth liquid melted slowly down his throat.

"It is good, no?"

"Yeah. Good. Thanks, Boss."

"Boss? What is this, Ambro? *Boss?* We are friends! Amicos!"

"Of course. Friends."

"Talk to me, amico. Talk to me." Primo's voice was soothing, even if he couldn't train his fierce warrior's eyes to be the same. But even in spite of those eyes, Primo was a politician of the highest order when he wanted something. "I want this girl. I want this Eva. Please tell me you're not falling in love with her. That isn't it, is it? Ambro, don't disappoint me. You're a smarter man than that. She's just another broad."

Ambro wanted to jump up off the sofa, but there was no graceful way to do it, and he made a point of doing nothing that wasn't graceful. Even if he had to put a bullet in someone or break his legs, he found a way to do it gracefully—with style.

"Just another broad? Then why is she so important to you?"

Primo frowned at him. "You know what I mean. She is not *just another broad*. But she is not the type Ambrosio Procopio needs to be married to, either. Are you falling in love with her, my friend?"

"I'm not in love with her, Boss."

"Ambro . . ." It was Primo's warning tone.

"Sorry—*Primo*. Come on! I'm not falling in love. Give me some credit."

"Okay. I trust you. I thought you would know better. So you're trying to tell me it's really this boy? You're serious, aren't you? A dumb little retarded kid? And you're going to shrug off a hundred thousand-dollar broad for that? Use your head!"

"We have it good in this town, Primo," Ambro countered, holding his temper back. He took great offense to his boss referring to Leo that way, but he was already angering Primo as much as the other way around. It wouldn't do to push it too far. "We're making money like it's going out of style. There are other women in Rock Springs. A *lot* of them. Attractive women. We've never had trouble finding them before. And if you want, we can bring in others, from other towns."

"Not like her."

Ambro wouldn't argue with that. Yes, there was something special about Eva Galanti. He had seen it right away. Maybe too special for what Primo had in mind.

"Why her, Primo? Why do you need Eva Galanti?"

"I need her, Ambro. I *need* her. Before now, that has always been enough for you. Why has that changed?"

"I don't want to do it anymore—not with her. Come on, please—as a favor to me? Just this time?"

Primo gave Ambro a long, hard stare. His eyes looked angry, but very slowly they seemed to soften, perhaps to turn contemplative. Finally, he let out a resigned sigh.

"All right. Okay. Ambro, you're off the Eva Galanti thing. Done. Find me somebody else. Better yet, find me three somebodies. It's going to take three to make up for that one."

"Thanks, Primo. I appreciate it."

"Damn you, amico—you had better."

Ambro finished his drink, which by the last drop was almost tasteless, then went and got in his Pontiac and screeched the tires peeling out of the driveway. He didn't care that Primo Santori's help was going to take half an hour getting that rubber off the concrete.

After Ambro was gone, Primo Santori wandered around the house, still in his red satin bathrobe, looking for Serenella. He finally found her passed out on their bed upstairs, a wine glass lying on the floor beside her.

Scoffing, he shut the bedroom door and padded quietly back downstairs, where he picked up the phone and dialed a number.

"Hey, Galletto! Yeah. Primo here. I need you to do me a favor, my friend. There's a girl I want you to recruit." He went on and told Galletto all about Eva. "Why don't you go meet her, uh? Talk to her. Romance her. Take her around the town and let her see the dark side, then take her up in our neighborhood to see how she *could* live. I want her, Galletto. She is going to be one of our girls, and I think you are the right man for the job."

Gavino Berretti had always been Primo Santori's second pick for a recruiter of beautiful females. His nickname, Galletto, referred to a man who did a lot of flirting with women, and he had come by it honestly.

Galletto was the right man for this job. He had never let Primo down before.

Then again, neither had Ambrosio Procopio . . . until today.

CHAPTER SEVENTEEN

EVA SAT ON HER bed and wept. Her mother had just left the room after a short, hard discussion about her grandmother's prognosis, and it wasn't good.

Isabella appeared to be in the middle stages of congestive heart failure. She had extremely high blood pressure, was borderline diabetic, and her cholesterol was dangerously high. The doctor suspected that she needed coronary artery bypass surgery, but at her age and in her condition it would be more dangerous doing the operation than letting it go and trying to treat her with medication.

Bianca had felt forced into filling three prescriptions, what the doctor claimed was the minimum Isabella would need: one for her high blood pressure, nitroglycerin for her heart, and the third to fight the cholesterol. Between the three of them, at a cost of twenty-five dollars for one month, they had drained Bianca of all but three of the dollars she had been saving "for a rainy day". This day was about as rainy as things could get out here in the Red Desert.

Eva cried and cried, and as long as she was crying, she didn't have to think too much. It wasn't until she was about dry of tears that she really began doing any truly deep thinking, and then she started feeling like she couldn't quite catch her breath, and she began shaking all over.

Oh, what had she done with her life? She had married too young, a lovesick fool marrying a heartless one. When that man

was gone, she was a middle-aged woman with no formal educa-
tion, very little job experience, and two sons in her care, one of
them with special disabilities that required greater care than she
had been prepared for. Then, when her father died, a mother and
a grandmother who relied on her too. And her husband, once he
had spent everything and sold off all he could, had vanished.
Good riddance, too, but his disappearing act had left her sole
bread winner for five people, with blackness on a horizon that
seemed to grow blurrier every day, and no light at the end of a
dead-end tunnel.

What had she done? What had she done!

Her fevered mind burned through her performance as a barmaid. Was she doing enough to get big tips? Could she do anything else? Offer more? And what, for a self-respecting woman,
could that be?

And the lawn mowing; summer was quickly coming to an
end, and that would stop with it. Then came winter snow shovel-
ing season, but it was never lucrative either.

What else could an uneducated woman do? Where else
could she turn?

There was always welfare. Food stamps. But could she do
it? Perhaps if they all were starving to death she might consider
it. But her mother and grandmother never would, and they
would be furious with her if they found out she had gone begging to the government.

Her family was going down in flames, and she didn't have
so much as a squirt gun to put them out.

A knock came on the door, and she dried her eyes. "Yes?"

The door cracked open, and an eye peeked in. The crack
widened to reveal Tyke's face, and he came in and walked to
her. Without saying a word, he leaned in and hugged her, and it
was all she could do to hold back her tears.

Finally, she gathered strength. Still holding him, she said into his hair, "Hey, buddy. How is that tooth?" She was praying for a miracle.

"It's okay." But his voice had no conviction, and he hesitated too long.

She pushed him away, holding onto him by the shoulders. "You have to tell me, Tyke. If it got too bad it could . . ." She stopped herself short of what she had intended to say. "It could be way worse than now." That made it sound serious, but not as dire as what had been on the tip of her tongue.

A tear suddenly squeezed out of Tyke's eye. "It hurts really bad, Mom."

Eva raised a trembling hand, putting the back of her fingers alongside his cheek, which she noticed looked swollen, and maybe even a little red, unless she was imagining it.

To that one swollen spot, it felt like Tyke had been pressing a hot water bottle.

That night, when the house was quiet, Eva fell on her knees. She prayed harder than she had prayed in months. This was no memorized prayer from a prayer book. This was a deeply heartfelt prayer, her own words, from her own soul.

Her knees were going to sleep when something strange happened. Over her entire body seemed to wash a warm wave of air. It flooded all around her, up through her, penetrating her heart. It left her even a little more breathless than she had been earlier.

Everything was going to be all right. Things were going to be fine!

She lay in bed after saying amen. She stared up at the ceiling and let the warm tears run slowly down the sides of her face. God was up there somewhere, watching over her and her family.

Eva Galanti was not alone.

Patrolling. Night shift. Rattling doors. On this warm summer night, all was still. All was calm. Lance Cartwright paused at his patrol car and drew a deep breath of the sultry air.

This was his element! The night. The city. The quiet calm. A cat cut out of an alley, peered toward him, then scattered across the street at a crazy run. Soon another appeared, gave him the same glance, but slunk dead away from where he leaned on his car.

Lance thought about the stark difference between this part of Rock Springs, known as Blairtown, and the area of K and M Streets, Noble, Pilot Butte, and other thoroughfares in the bar section, where not too unlike Las Vegas the nightlife went on unchecked. Up there, nightly fights, open prostitution, gambling, and carousing were in full swing. It was no man's land, even declared so by the police department. With thousands of temporary residents in the area, that part of Rock Springs was beyond the police department's control, call volume was over five or six times what it had been prior to the boom, and no officer in his right mind would go into that district for *any* call without an army. But down here in Blairtown, other than over at Benny's Bar and Grill, everything was still, enjoying at least a temporary peace.

Lance drew another breath, and smiled. What was Eva Galanti doing now? he wondered. It was funny how being near Benny's made him think of her—as if he needed any reason. How had things gone after picking up her mother and grandmother at the hospital? Maybe he should have called. But he was worried she might think he was getting too forward, trying to intrude on her life. He really wasn't. Heck, he wasn't the marrying kind anyway. He only enjoyed having her as a friend.

What was the quote he had heard from actor Gary Cooper? A bachelor is a man who doesn't make the same mistake once? He grinned to himself in the darkness.

That was Lance Cartwright. Big Hoss. Just like his name-sake on *Bonanza,* he lived a simple, single life, and a happy one. His own father had left his mother and five children to fend for themselves when he was young. He had pretty much been forced to raise his four younger siblings while his mom worked at the factory. Lance had already raised his family. Why would he want to start that all over again? Even for a woman like Eva.

Besides, he had no idea what to do with a Down Syndrome child. He sure liked that little guy and his huge smiles, but there was a lot more to raising a boy than just liking him.

Lance grinned again and shook his head. What was he think-ing about anyway? Eva Galanti had to be ten years older than he was, and a thousand times more attractive. A woman like that would never be interested in him. He had been called handsome before, but by a woman like that? No way. Eva was simply a nice woman, too polite to tell him to get lost.

The only hope he had, really, was that she needed him be-cause he made her feel safe. He guessed that would have to be enough. And truth be told, it made him feel twelve feet tall.

He got back in his car and started cruising again. He didn't often pass through Blairtown, so much of it was strange turf. Adding to the problem, a lot of this area was newly developed and chock full of trailer houses and camp trailers, because every house, apartment, and hotel in Rock Springs was taken. It was good to know his entire area of potential response. Not that it took long to cover a town of twenty or so thousand people, at least at night when the traffic from all the newly arrived resi-dents wasn't so horrendous. But even in a town that size, there were always some obscure street names that didn't stand out after only three years living there, streets he might be called to for any emergency, on any given night. It seemed like some of the trailer parks weren't even permanent, so those in particular he was not familiar with, and he should be.

Just out of one trailer park, beyond the stockyards, and back into the older, stick-built housing, he was surprised to see tail-lights glowing half a block ahead of him on the right, and he slowed down. It always piqued his curiosity to see activity at two o'clock in the morning. He himself was a night owl, and even on his nights off he might be prowling the streets. Still, as someone sworn to uphold the law, it wouldn't do to drive care-lessly on past.

As he crept by, he recognized the dark sixty-seven SS Ca-maro that belonged to Officer Jacob Glattner. He didn't see the two human shadows standing in the dark beyond the car until after he was a few car lengths away, and he cursed himself. His powers of observation were blurred.

Stopping the car, he threw it in reverse and rolled back. By the time he came alongside Glattner's Super Sport Camaro, a car in General Motors' "deep water blue", which even in the daylight may as well have been black, the motor was still run-ning, but he could no longer see anybody around. He got out and scanned the area, and soon he saw the unmistakable perfect, wide-shouldered shape of Jacob Glattner striding out of the shadows.

"Hoss! What's up, brother?"

"Hey, Glatt! What the heck? Kind of late hours, isn't it? Hot date?"

Glattner grinned as he got close. "How'd you guess?"

Lance grinned back, knowing Glattner was joking. He had seen enough of the other person to know it was a heavyset man almost as tall as Glattner's six foot two.

"So what *are* you doin', anyway?" It wasn't any of his busi-ness, maybe. But a cop is always a cop.

Glattner's face went serious. "What? You think you're the only one who can know a beautiful woman?"

Lance stared at the off-duty officer, blinking. He recovered in a moment, and hoped it was somewhat gracefully. "Of course not! Heck, I'm sure you have five times the gorgeous chicks hangin' around that I do. But I hope they aren't almost as big as you are."

Glattner had just put a cigarette in his mouth, and as he flicked a lighter, the thin yellow glow illuminated his face enough for Lance to see his expression recover from surprise. "Oh! Oh, you mean that guy I was just talking to?"

Lance chuckled, feeling suddenly nervous.

"I have no idea who that was. I dropped my girlfriend off and he was walking down the sidewalk and asked me about Curly." That was the name with which Glattner had dubbed his Camaro.

"Oh, I get it." The explanation made perfect sense. "I can't blame him, man. I dream of having a car like that someday."

"You'll get it." Glattner drew deep on his cigarette and swatted Lance casually on his arm. "You'll get it."

"Sure. Well, what's new with you anyway, man?"

"Nothin'. Say—I'd better get rollin', huh? I have to work first shift tomorrow."

"Oh, sure! Yeah." Lance tried to switch gears in light of Glattner's sudden pronouncement. "Yeah, you'd better get goin'. I guess I'll go back up and drive the bar district."

"You're brave! Well, good luck, buddy. Stay safe up there, huh? I mean it."

Glattner turned to his car, Lance to his own, and he drove away. He only made it a few cars from Glattner's Camaro before slamming on his brakes. There on the right side of the street, but facing against traffic, was the greenish-gray sixty-nine Plymouth Roadrunner with the black hood, the car Lance had seen parked behind Primo Custom Auto Parts. Same Nevada plates and all—as if there would actually be two cars like this in a city so small.

On a whim, Lance threw his car in reverse, backing to where he had left Glattner, who was still sitting in his idling car. Lance jumped out, and Glattner rolled down his window. "What's up, Hoss?"

"Hey, man! Sorry to bug you, but did you see that gray Roadrunner a ways up?"

A strange look came into Glattner's eyes before he could sweep it away. "No, not really."

"Oh." That was not the answer Lance expected. Furthermore, it wasn't the first answer Glattner's eyes had manifested. "Huh. Okay, I was just curious if you know who owns it."

"Nope," said Glattner with a shrug. "I can't think of anybody that owns a car like that."

"All right. Have a good one," said Lance, and again he drove on, committing the Roadrunner's license number to memory as he passed.

As he was nearing the end of the block, he saw the glow of headlights on the street and on the cars ahead before another vehicle veered onto the street, coming toward him.

As the vehicle passed, he recognized the pale green and white sixty-eight Ford pickup owned by Chris Hinshaw, who was also off duty, and who like Jacob Glattner had to work the next morning.

He touched the brakes and saw Hinshaw's brake lights blink on, but then the pickup kept rolling. Pausing at the corner and looking in his rearview mirror, Lance watched the pickup, expecting it to stop near the Camaro. Although Rock Springs P.D. didn't really have partners, per se, it was widely considered that the handsome cops, Glattner and Hinshaw, were a pair—pretty much best friends, on duty or off. And neither of them lived anywhere near this neighborhood.

Strangely, Hinshaw's pickup crept right on past the Camaro without pausing long enough for the two men to say hello to each other out their windows.

Lance went ahead and made his turn, his brow knitted. What was going on back there? If Glattner and Hinshaw weren't fellow officers, that scene was certainly something Lance would have gone to check out more closely. It made it all the more intriguing knowing the relationship between Glattner and Hinshaw and seeing them both driving around this obscure neighborhood at two in the morning on a work night, and they didn't even stop in surprise to say anything to each other.

On a whim, Lance pulled into the next alley, then backed into the first open space he could find at the back of a dark house. Cutting his engine, he got out and locked the door, then moved slowly along through the shadows of the houses so he could get back and get a view of Glattner's Camaro. He had yet to see it come by, and the street was too narrow for him to turn around and go out the other way; it had to still be in the same place.

As Lance came up to a big old GMC Suburban that was parked on the corner, he saw the glow of Glattner's park lights ahead, and a moment after that a big vehicle turned off the next street and rolled slowly forward. When it got alongside the parked Camaro, it stopped, and someone got out. He could hear the hollow ring of the slamming door plainly in the night.

A shadow passed in front of the headlights, then vanished in the darkness. For a long time, Lance waited, feeling breathless. It seemed like half an hour before a shadow once again passed in front of the headlights of the vehicle stopped in the street, the door slammed again, and soon the vehicle came Lance's way.

When it turned, on the same street Lance had taken, the same street Hinshaw had come from, he recognized what he already had known he would see: Hinshaw's Ford.

Half a minute later, the Camaro's headlights flashed on, and Lance, feeling conspicuous, faded down lower behind the Suburban. The Camaro came on, hesitated at the corner, then turned and followed Hinshaw's pickup.

Lance straightened up from the Suburban and stood alone in the darkness, his heart thudding. What in the world had just happened?

A date? Lance might not have been the brightest star in the sky, but he was far from blind either. Glattner was no more on a date than Lance was.

But it was Glatt's business, and Hinshaw's. Whatever they were doing at two in the morning on a work night, they were fellow peace officers, helping to keep his city safe. It wasn't his to question their late-night activities.

One thing, however, Lance would not rest until he knew, and that was the identity of whoever owned the greenish-gray Roadrunner. He drove back to the station, where one of their two night dispatchers was performing her nightly balancing act of trying to stay awake while not overdosing on black coffee.

Lance had the woman run a license check on the Plymouth Roadrunner. It came back as being registered to someone by the name of Lucas G. Borders, age thirty-seven, who lived, it said, in Las Vegas, Nevada. The registration information did indeed match the car, listed as a gray sixty-nine Plymouth Roadrunner.

Lance wrote down all the information on a piece of notebook paper, folded it in half, and stuck it in his shirt pocket. What he had was interesting information, the kind of thing he always saved, and the kind of thing that seldom amounted to anything. But then there were those other times when it turned out to be the infamous *Golden Ticket*.

CHAPTER EIGHTEEN

EVA WAS UP EARLY, but she still didn't beat her mother to the kitchen. Bianca was making coffee and had a homemade poundcake already in the oven, and she had brought out a jar of strawberry preserves she had proudly made herself the first part of July.

Eva sat basking in the glow of her mother's presence, smelling the fresh-ground coffee, then sipping slowly on one cup, followed by another, as the aroma of the poundcake began to permeate every corner of the kitchen.

Talk was light, and they both avoided the topic of their Nonni. Bianca asked about Lance, about Ambro, and even touched on Eva's barmaid job, although well aware it wasn't Eva's favorite topic.

Forty minutes passed pleasantly before a long, comfortable lull in the conversation filled the room. Finally, Bianca came over and put both hands on the tabletop.

"Okay, my daughter. I'm going to have to ask you: To what do we owe the peaceful look on your face this morning?"

Eva drew a deep breath, smiled, and let out her breath in a sigh, resting her chin on her hands. "I'm happy, Mama. I think we're going to be okay."

"I think so too. But you didn't seem so happy last night."

"No." She frowned, dropping her hands to the table, studying them as she twisted her fingers together. "Can I tell you, Mama? Tell you what happened?"

"Of course. I hope you will." Bianca pulled out a chair across from Eva and sat, reaching across to take her hands. "What is it?"

"I prayed last night."

Bianca gave a little shake of her head. "Okay? That's all? Is that so new?"

"It wasn't like other prayers. Everything was different. I just . . . talked. You know? I didn't recite a prayer. I talked to God. And I felt this warm feeling come over me. It was . . . like nothing I've ever felt."

Bianca was nodding slowly. Tears had come to her eyes to match those in her daughter's. "I'm so happy, cara. So so happy. We're going to be all right. We are."

Then Tyke came packing Leo into the room, with both their hair all messed up and sticking everywhere, and Leo sporting his ear-to-ear smile.

Yes, everything was going to be okay.

Tyke's toothache was so bad Eva didn't want to make him go work in the heat on this hottest day yet of the entire summer. With a promise to earn enough money that day to get him into a dentist the first thing the next morning, she got into her straightest-leg jeans, a plain white tee shirt, and sneakers, put her hair back in a ponytail, and headed out to the shed to get the mower and gas can.

By noon, she had managed to make a whopping ten dollars, and three of that was considered a tip. Discouraged, but still smiling, she came home, put the mower away, and got ready for work.

Officer Buck Stone sat in his patrol car at a distance and with binoculars watched the lone-standing business with the arched sign over the door that said PRIMO CUSTOM AUTO

PARTS. He had found an anonymous note sitting on the seat of his car that morning when he came out to go to work. There was not a clue who had left it, and all it said was *Watch Primo Custom Auto Parts.* Oddly enough, he had gotten the same admonition from Chief Buyer, who apparently was a friend of the man who owned this place and claimed to be doing him a favor.

So here he was, but he didn't have enough trust in or respect for Chief Buyer to come here only at his request. He was here because of the chief's request, certainly, but only because he was suspicious of the real reasons behind it. And he was also here because of the cryptic note. The more time went by, the more he didn't know much of anything, at least not much of anything he wanted to know.

He thought about his wife, Olivia. His three sons. Those innocent guys . . . They knew nothing. Neither did Olivia. Why did *he?* Why had someone picked him, of all the officers on the department? And why pick anyone in Rock Springs in the first place? Wouldn't it have been a more sure thing to go somewhere else? The state police? The U.S. marshals? If this anonymous informant didn't trust the Rock Springs P.D., why trust *him?*

Every day left Buck Stone more frightened than the day before. He had to get out of this place, out of this police force. How could he sell his house and go, get his family somewhere safe? Who could he trust? Why had he even trusted that barmaid, Eva Galanti, as much as he had? Even if she was a good person, as he was pretty sure she was, hadn't he put her in a terrible situation? Luckily, he hadn't told her much. But then, at the time, he hadn't known much.

Now he had an apple box full almost to the top of all he soon might know, and much that he was sure he didn't want to know. The only thing he didn't know for sure was if there was anyone in his workplace that he could trust. And he still had yet to learn who was feeding him all the documents and other information. What if this person was simply making it all up? He couldn't see why they would be, though, and that was the scariest part. Besides, although he had yet to study any of the paperwork closely, he had glanced through it enough to know it would have taken hundreds of hours to compile it all. What kind of liar would it take to go through all that work for something he wouldn't be able to prove?

Stone sat in his patrol car watching the supposed auto parts business until he got a call to a civil standby and had to drive away. He had seen no activity at the business. He didn't even know what he was looking for.

Later that morning, he went out to DJ's A & W, out by the Kasbah Lounge, to grab a coffee. He came back out with the coffee in a covered mug and opened his car door, but before he could get in, he heard a voice behind him, a young voice.

Half leery, he turned to spot a skinny boy in a white and black-striped tee shirt sitting on a bike. "Hi, policeman."

"Hi, son."

"I'm supposed to give you this." The boy held out a folded piece of paper.

Glancing around, surprised, Stone stepped closer to the boy, who handed him the paper. "Thanks, son."

"You're welcome. See ya." The boy stood up on his pedals and darted away on the bike, gone behind the café in less than twenty seconds.

Looking around again, and seeing no one suspicious, Stone got in his car and unfolded the note.

At one-thirty, go to the phone booth outside of the Kasbah and wait for a call.

Buck Stone's guts felt frozen. How in the world had some random kid on a bike known he was going to come over here for coffee? How long had this kid waited here for him, and what had someone paid him to do it? Buck had to call somebody in. There were no reasonable explanations for any of this stuff, and the whole thing was getting too scary. He needed to call the authorities. But who were the *authorities?* Who could he actually trust? If the notes were true, he was starting to feel like he could trust no one who called himself law enforcement, and no one in the court system, or perhaps even the mayor's office or city council.

Stone had to go. Even if he couldn't sell his house, he had to pack up his family and leave. He was in a place he should never have been, in darkness up to his neck, and a thundercloud was coming down on him from above. This whole town—even the entire county, perhaps the state—suddenly felt evil and black.

He had to move. That was it. He would take the phone call at one-thirty. His curiosity wouldn't let him walk away right now. But then he would take everything he had, all his proof, go and turn it into the state attorney general's office in Cheyenne, and drive away.

He was a first class police officer making almost 9,500 dollars a year. That wasn't worth his life or the safety of his family.

The newcomer was dressed in a slim-fitting dark gray suit-coat and trousers, but he wore no tie. His hair wasn't long, exactly, but longish, with a wave to it especially where it curled over his collar. He had thick eyebrows that hung low over his eyes, a meticulously clean-shaven face, and a strut to his walk that proclaimed him to be perhaps unreasonably proud of his looks, since Eva wouldn't have considered him much better than average-looking, although he had an athletic build from what she could see while he was wearing the suit.

As Eva had started to get accustomed to, the dark-haired man stood inside the front door after shutting it quietly and surveyed the crowd. As of two-thirty it amounted only to seven men, four of them pool players and three of them hard drinkers who had come in, ordered a bottle and were really getting after it, two at the bar and one at a lonely table, all seeming bent on trying to get as drunk as they could in record time.

The only other barmaid in the place was Teton Belle, who was out of the room. The man's eyes settled on Eva, and an easy smile came to his lips. Even from twenty feet away, his teeth flashed in the quiet yellow light that glowed even through all the cigarette smoke.

The man sauntered toward Eva, and she met him halfway across the floor. "Hello. I'm Eva. What can I get for you?"

"Well, hello—Eva. I'm Gavino. Gavino Berretti."

Eva stared at him, trying to look calm. *Berretti!* This was the other Italian man whose photo and name Officer Stone had shared with her!

Berretti oozed his hand out to her, and she reluctantly took it, trying to seem casual while she felt anything but. When she went to drop her own hand away, he held on with quiet pressure until she relaxed. Then he nonchalantly lowered his hand. She had a sudden urge to wipe her hand on the skirt of her burgundy-colored dress, but she resisted. Who knew what kind of a tipper Gavino Berretti might be? If Ambrosio Procopio was any example, the local Italians had deep pockets and didn't mind showing them off.

"I'll take two pints of Rheingold Extra Dry—if you have it," said Berretti. "And I'm craving a grilled chicken sandwich." His making of the order without seeing a menu made Eva think Berretti had been in here before, but she didn't remember ever seeing him, at least not other than the xeroxed photo.

"Coming up," she said with her best winning smile, turning to go.

She was drawn up short by Berretti grasping her wrist and easing her back around. "Also, if the place is as slow as it looks, I'd love some company for a while."

She smiled again, allowing him to keep hold of her wrist for those few seconds their eyes met. This Gavino Berretti was very self-confident, but he didn't have Ambro's room-filling charisma. And his average looks had taken a sour downturn now that they were close and she could see his unpleasant greenish-brown eyes. They didn't necessarily have an unpleasant look *in* them. They simply weren't attractive eyes, as they were too droopy at the bottom lid, and slanted down at the outer corners. But Berretti's perfect-toothed smile improved his overall appearance, and she continued to be hopeful that he would find her service worth a good tip. Since her lack of success mowing lawns, Tyke's tooth pain depended on it.

"I'll see how things look," she told him as his hand fell away from her wrist. "I'd be happy to sit for a while if it stays slow. Thanks for asking."

Inside, she groaned. How to seem friendly and agreeable, without looking permissive? It was an age-old question that had no answer, because every person's perceptions of another's actions and voice might differ hugely. Many was the time she had smiled at one man who simply smiled back and said hi, when she might give the exact same smile to the next man and have him claim her to be a terrible flirt. To her shame, her own sex was even more vicious with such groundless judgments.

Eva passed Teton Belle coming out of the kitchen, her heart starting to pound even harder than it had from the knowledge that another of Buck Stone's faces was here, alive and in person. Belle's exit from the kitchen meant Benny Fitz was alone with the dishwasher now, and other than Brandon Lucky, none of the dishwashers here seemed to have any spine. As much as Eva disliked Belle, her mere presence would have been enough to keep Benny somewhat at bay; now there would be no buffer.

Drawing a deep breath, she stepped into the smoke-filled kitchen, careful not to slip on the always grease-filmed floor. She stopped a careful distance from Benny, who was shiny with the sweat beaded on his cheeks as he stood over the griddle. The dishwasher was nowhere in sight.

"I need a grilled chicken," she said.

Benny turned and looked at her, staring as if he hadn't heard her. She waited for the blank look on his face to fade, but when it did, it didn't help. "What's that?"

She repeated it, louder, and in well-enunciated words he couldn't have misheard.

He cupped his hand to his ear, then seemed to think better of it and waved her closer. Gritting her teeth, she walked to within five feet of him.

"I need a grilled chicken," she repeated.

"Yeah? What's wrong, Eva? You think I'm gonna bite?"

She tried to smile. She didn't want to fight today. "No, I just didn't want to get my clothes splattered."

Grinning like a happy dog, Benny stepped closer. She took one step back, but she didn't want to anger him by turning and leaving. "There. Better?"

No. Much worse, she thought.

When she didn't respond, Benny reached out and snatched her wrist, the same wrist Gavino Berretti had held, only Benny's grip was harsher. He pulled her a little closer—something like a hundred yards too close to his three-days-without-a-long-enough-good-enough-shower body odor.

"You smell good today, Eva. I was meanin' to tell you."

Benny didn't, and she had been *wishing* to tell *him.* "Thank you." She made a note not to wear the same perfume again at work—although to Benny Fitz she would most likely have smelled good even if she had smeared her body with garlic juice and rolled on a bloated dead cow.

"How about we hit a movie tonight, Eva? I want to see *American Graffiti*, but I don't want to sit there by myself. *Westworld's* playing too. Better yet, *High Plains Drifter* is at the drive-in, and I haven't had a Clint Eastwood fix for a while."

"I can't, Benny. I'm seeing someone steady now."

Benny's eyes hardened, and his whole face seemed to harden along with them. That made her cringe more than having actually let his name cross her lips.

"Oh yeah? Who's that? The damn cop? I don't like you bringing him around here." He dropped her arm—it was more like he tossed it.

"No," she said. "His name is Ambro Procopio."

Benny stared at her like his mind was trying to catch up. All of a sudden, he started to laugh. Then he laughed harder. He began laughing so hard it almost seemed like real laughter. Finally, he caught his breath.

"Ambrosio Procopio? The Porcupine? Ha! You must really be dumb, Eva. You ain't *seein'* the Porcupine. And if you are, it sure's hell ain't the kind of seein' you think it is."

Feeling breathless, and confused by his words, she backed off a couple of steps. "I'm sorry. Really. Hey—don't forget the grilled chicken."

He scoffed, and his face grew dark. "Whatever. Send Belle back in here to get it in five. I don't wanna see your face in here again today."

Spinning on her heel, hating how stiff she felt, Eva left the room, trying to catch her breath. But a breath full of cigarette smoke as she stepped back out into the lounge was no way to catch it. As she heard the kitchen door whisper shut behind her, she wondered if she should feel as upset as she did. Perhaps she should look at Benny's order for her not to go back in the kitchen as a gift from God.

Walking casually behind the bar as Jim Croce belted out "Bad, Bad Leroy Brown" over the bar's speakers, she collected a tall glass of ice and two pint cans of Rheingold, then stepped back out on the floor and looked around until she found Gavino Berretti. It seemed coincidental that he had chosen to sit at the same table where she had talked to Ambro Procopio. Teton Belle was sitting with him, laughing as if they were old friends.

As Eva walked toward the table, Berretti leaned closer and said something to Belle, then waved her off with a wiggle of his fingers. Belle saw Eva coming and stood abruptly away from the table, turning to her. As they passed each other, Belle gave her an unsettling, measuring look, and the beginnings of a smile that contained more than a little smugness.

Eva set the beers and the glass down in front of Berretti and gave him her best smile, trying to hide how shaken she felt. She couldn't stop thinking of the weird look from Belle, and the laughter of Benny when she mentioned Ambro's name, then the strange things he had said about him. And "Porcupine"? That was a nickname she had never heard. And now to have another of the men here that Officer Stone had brought to her attention! To say she felt confused was an understatement. She was beginning to feel like there was some big joke being played in Benny's, and she was the only one not in on it.

"The sandwich will be a few minutes," Eva said.

"Great. Can you sit until then?"

Eva scanned the room. She needed to sit, that was for certain. Her legs felt inexplicably weak all of a sudden. But sitting with Gavino Berretti would have been one of her last choices. "Sure, Mr. Berretti."

The man frowned. "Heyyy. All the formality doesn't sound nice. I'm Gavino to all my friends."

"Okay." She forced another smile. "Gavino. Thank you."

What was she thanking him for exactly? A future tip, she hoped.

Teton Belle had gone back into the kitchen straight away from leaving the table. Eva hadn't thought anything about it, but half a minute later she saw the door open, and Benny Fitz's face peeked out, registered on her sitting there with Gavino Berretti, and then with a sneer he disappeared again. Shortly after, Belle reappeared and started making her rounds of the other customers, pointedly avoiding looking toward Eva and Berretti as she went to hang on the pool players and flirt her way to her next tip.

Berretti made small talk with Eva for a few minutes. He didn't say a single thing that sounded like he was flirting, but everything about his body language was crawling all over her, and it was hard for her not to act uncomfortable.

They soon heard Benny yell from the newly opened kitchen door, although he didn't appear. "Belle! Grilled chicken up."

Belle went back into the kitchen and returned with a tray to bring Berretti his order. "Grilled chicken, Gavino?"

"Yes, ma'am. Thank you, doll."

Belle looked over at Eva with a little twitch of her shoulder and a smile pulling at one corner of her mouth.

"Eva, do you want anything?" Berretti asked.

"No. Thank you, though."

"Get her a nice zinfandel," said Berretti, ignoring Eva's refusal. "That'll taste good even if you're not in the mood," he said turning back to Eva.

Eva smiled. She didn't really care—as long as her tip wasn't going into the price of the wine.

Belle came back and poured Eva a glass half full of zinfandel red wine, and Eva gave it an obligatory sip. Gavino Berretti was right: It did taste good. After Berretti slipped Belle some folded cash, she smiled and winked, thanked him and wandered off.

"I'm going to take you to dinner tonight."

Berretti's proclamation was so abrupt Eva could only stare at him, her mouth open with no words coming out.

"What time do you get off work?"

"I, uh . . . I'm off at nine, but—"

"But nothing. I won't take no for an answer, Eva. And you won't regret it. I promise."

CHAPTER NINETEEN

GAVINO BERRETTI SAT OUTSIDE Benny's at precisely eight forty-five in a maroon metallic 1971 Lincoln Mark III, its vinyl landau top carefully and precisely cleaned, as was every inch of its chrome and steel. Even every surface on the inside was clean and vacuumed, and if there had been so much as a fleck of gravel on the carpeting Berretti would have been down on his knees to pick it up with tweezers and a magnifying glass if he had to.

The moment of leaving Benny's earlier that afternoon, upon finishing his grilled chicken sandwich that he had to admit was perhaps the most exquisite he had ever had Benny Fitz prepare him, Berretti had stopped at the nearest phone booth and dropped his dime to place a call to Primo Santori. He told him he would be picking Primo's new target up when she got off work at nine, and he wanted to see if there was any way after driving around with her to show her the sights that he could bring her to Primo's for supper that night, although it would be late. Primo had laughed, telling Berretti that Ambro had already had her up once. Then he thought more about it and decided it might be funny after all to have her show up again, but with a different escort: Eva Galanti, round two at the Santori sanctum.

Now there was nothing for Gavino Berretti to do but wait for Eva's appearance at the front door—although he would go searching for her at nine-O-one if he hadn't seen her yet.

He waited in high style, listening to Perry Como crooning on his tape deck while he smoked Cuban cigars and sipped from a can of Rheingold.

Inside Benny's, Eva walked away from a growing crowd of ever-more flirtatious drinkers and carousers to wash her hands in the back room while saying hi to Jud the night cook and Mark, one of the nighttime dishwashers, and avoiding Benny's gaze.

It didn't matter, though. Benny cornered her while Jud was putting on his apron to prepare for the night's customers.

"Saw you sittin' with Galletto Berretti."

"Galletto?" The name was new to Eva.

"Yes. Galletto. Who did you think that was?"

"You must know something I don't," she said. "That man told me his name is Gavino."

"Right. Whatever. You don't know what you're doin', Eva. You really that desperate?"

Eva was in no mood to play *I Spy*. She didn't like how Benny played. He might have some important information for her, or he might simply be trying to play another psychological game. Either way, she tried not to let him get under her skin with cryptic comments. She couldn't put faith in half what he said anyway. The only thing that bothered her was knowing he actually knew both of the Italians not just by their real names, but by nicknames. What was really going on here beyond her scope of knowledge?

"I have to go. Someone's waiting for me."

"The Porcupine? Or Galletto?" Benny maneuvered around to stand between her and the exit. "Or that big oaf of a cop?"

"Please, Benny. I'd rather not talk about this."

"Of course you wouldn't. Okay, so end up like Teton Belle then. Don't say I didn't try to warn you." Benny stepped aside, and Eva walked past. She threw a "good night" behind her, mostly for Jud and Mark, but Benny could take it to be for him as well if he wanted to.

She left with Benny's comments under her skin, in spite of her best intentions. And she left wondering what he had meant about Teton Belle.

Out in the lounge, she looked around for Belle. She was nowhere in sight. The two incoming girls were hard at work already, and Belle was either still in the back room, or she had gone out the back way to go home for the day. It didn't matter. Eva wasn't sure she wanted to talk to her anyway. Curiosity had killed the cat. Eva didn't need it to kill her too.

She had called Bianca on her break to tell her she would be late coming home that night, and of course her mother wished her well and told her to be careful. The warning was Bianca's usual, but lately in Eva's ears it had a different ring. She didn't know exactly why, but of late it seemed like there was much more in her world for her to be careful of.

She simply wasn't sure what all of it was.

Ignoring the last round of cat calls from around the smoky, dim-lit lounge, Eva escaped outside, sucking in a huge gout of fresh night air that, although still almost murky-warm from the torrid August afternoon, was almost as welcome to her as a slushy glass of ice water. Bill Withers was singing "Ain't No

Sunshine" on Benny's stereo, but out here, with the door shut, the volume was low enough that Eva could actually enjoy it.

Across the street a dark-colored yards-long land shark of a car was idling, and when the driver's door opened, its dome light came on, revealing the silhouette of Gavino Berretti. He called out her name and a greeting of "good evening".

"Hello, Mr. Berretti," she said as they met mid-street, dividing in half a small crowd of soon-to-be revelers headed for the bar, three of whom greeted her by name in passing.

"Ah, Eva. That cuts me. It's Gavino, remember?"

"Yes. Sorry—Gavino."

"Shall we go?"

"Sure. Is it okay if I take my car and park it somewhere else first, though? Somewhere safer? I can follow you."

"Of course. Where are you parked?"

"In back."

"Good. I'll drive around. Would you like to ride?"

"No thank you. I need to breathe some clear air for a minute and get some of this smoke out of my clothes."

"You would smell good no matter what," he replied.

She smiled at him, but the comment didn't win any points with her. They didn't know each other well enough for him to be making statements so personal.

At the back of the bar, as she was starting to get in her car, Eva saw a cigarette lighter flare up and looked into the shadows at the back of the building. "Well, hi, Miss Prissy." It was the raspy smoker's voice of Teton Belle.

"Hi, Belle."

Berretti's car pulled up in the alley.

"Going with Gavvy, huh? I'm surprised. You never seemed like the type."

Eva felt her insides tighten up. She was starting to hate cryptic people and their cryptic comments, but for the first time in a long time she wished she had a few minutes to ply Belle for more information. Whatever she thought she knew, and whatever Benny had been talking about earlier, it was more than Eva knew. And in spite of her determination not to be bothered by shadowy words from people she didn't care for, it was all starting to get to her.

"Good night, Belle."

Maybe tomorrow she would corner the other woman before or after work demanding to know what she knew about Berretti. For now, there simply wasn't time.

Getting in her car, she fired it up and backed out, then got behind Berretti's Lincoln as it inched its way down the alley and out onto the street.

Berretti drove up Blair Avenue, turned right on Alder, then drove down six streets and turned right on Woodruff, into a half decent residential area. He pulled over at a long stretch of empty curb and got out as Eva parked her ugly station wagon behind him. She imagined the Lincoln was probably champing at the bit to be away from there and was probably relieved that it was nighttime and that no one could see it together with her beat-up Valiant.

"Will this be good enough? I've been over here, and it's pretty safe."

"I'm sure it's fine," Eva said. "Anything's better than leaving it at Benny's."

Berretti nodded and pointed at the Valiant, grinning. "Quite the car, Eva. I didn't picture you in that, not at all. What you need is an immaculate white Thunderbird—say, 1956?"

"What?"

Berretti chuckled. "I guess you haven't seen *American Graffiti* yet."

"No." She shook her head. "I don't have much time for movies."

"For that one, you should. Instant classic, Eva. Real classic. And the cars! Well, there's a mystery lady in it," he said as he was walking her around to the passenger side of the Lincoln, "and she drives a white fifty-six Bird. That's what I see you in. Something sporty, and classy. It's what you were born for."

She smiled and thanked him. But what did Gavino Berretti know about what Eva Galanti was born for? In fact, what did he know about her at all?

She slid onto the perfect leather bench seat of a car whose interior cried out to be pristine but stank of a nauseating mélange of cigar smoke and jasmine-scented deodorizer.

Berretti went around and oozed into the other side, looking over at her. She didn't have her seatbelt on, and he looked down at it. "Do you want to please buckle?"

She looked at him for a moment before her heart started to race. Had she just gotten into a car with another speed demon?

"Are you serious?"

"Of course. Don't you want to be safe?"

"I guess." She sought out the belt and pulled it around her, buckling in. She couldn't say she had done that ten times in her entire life. "You aren't going to go racing this thing, are you?"

"My Lincoln?" Berretti gave out with a merry laugh. "No! No, I don't do that kind of thing—not in this car, anyway. I just believe in seatbelts. Is that so bad?"

"No, of course not. It just isn't a habit for me."

Eva thought about the oddity of a man who apparently obeyed speed limits but worried about being belted in for safety, while the last man of his breed seemed to throw all caution to the wind. And yet her gut instincts found her trusting Ambro Procopio far more than she did Gavino Berretti.

They drove around the block onto Young, then back on Alder again, almost immediately turning left onto A Street. Through ever-increasing traffic, they continued north-northeast,

finally crossed over the railroad tracks, then making their way
back down onto Front Street. Eva found herself more and more
apprehensive as Berretti drove. They were heading into an area
of town well known through common lore to be a bad place for
women to frequent after dark.

"What's over this way?" Eva asked, trying to sound nonchalant while she felt anything but.

"Why? Are you worried?"

She looked at him, but he had already glanced away.
"Should I be? I guess I just have never heard there were any
good places to eat in here."

Berretti chuckled, forced into driving less than twenty now
because of the sea of vehicles going every direction. "Oh, well,
you would be surprised, Eva. Up a little distance on Pilot Butte
there are a lot of eating places that might surprise you. Besides,
we have plenty of time for that. I hoped you wouldn't mind if
we took a little tour through this area. It's supposed to be pretty
edgy after dark, but something about it makes me feel alive."

Berretti inched northeast along Front Street. The street itself
continued to throb with activity. Indeed, it seemed in a way to
be alive itself, with traffic everywhere, and teeming with pedestrians crossing back and forth under the almost audible hum of
neon lights and through the rowdy sound of different kinds of
music pounding out of doorways along the way. Even as early
as nine-fifteen, some of the revelers were already unsteady on
their feet. Eva noticed a serious dearth of women, and not a single one of them walking without at least one male companion.
Those she did see weren't the kind Eva would likely see walking through the doors of a church.

As they were about to come up to one of the bars, its door
flew open and two men stumbled out, nearly falling. The first
one to steady himself turned and struck the other one a vicious
blow in the side of the face as seven or eight more people, one

of them a woman, piled out of the doorway onto the sidewalk and into the street to watch the combat.

Berretti brought the Lincoln to a stop. After Eva watched the vicious fight for a few moments, appalled by the onlookers who cheered the bloody battle on, she turned to look at Berretti. His eyes looked glassy and were glued to the brawlers.

"Can we go?" Eva asked.

He turned and met her eyes, looking first as if he hadn't heard, then appearing shocked. "What? It's just starting."

"I want to go," Eva repeated.

"Oh, please. All right." Giving a little honk, he started forward, right into the crowd. Eva's first thought was that one of the roughnecks in the fight was going to kick his immaculate car or throw a bottle at it. Instead, several of them seemed to recognize the car, and the group of them went two different directions. Gavino Berretti didn't seem too Biblical, but this reminded her of Moses parting the Red Sea. Waving out the window, Berretti drove through the gap.

He signaled to turn left, and Eva looked up in time to read the street sign: K STREET. Her heart leaped into her throat. This was the most infamous street in all of Rock Springs, the one place that even in seedy Benny's Bar and Grill people warned her never to go after dark.

"Don't drive here," Eva said.

"Why? It's safe enough—for us. Come on, Eva. I won't let anything happen to you."

Her heart beat wildly as the oppressive heat of the remaining day met with that rising up off the asphalt and the tight, tunnel-like collection of buildings. The smells of grilling burgers, cigarette smoke, and booze floated into Berretti's car, but he didn't seem to mind. His face was lit up like that of a child at a Christmas parade. Bold lights gleamed from the fronts of the buildings, some of them blinking harsh against Eva's eyes.

From every direction came voices calling, music blaring, the dark stares of people as the Lincoln slowly rolled down the street.

A car stopped near them, and its back door opened, ejecting a woman the likes of which Eva had never seen outside of the cinema. It didn't take even a sheltered woman two guesses to figure what this woman did for a living. So it was true: Prostitution was alive and well in Rock Springs.

Ahead of them, the street seemed to be narrowing down almost to the point of closing in, like the infamous path leading to hell, growing narrower and narrower, making the way plain before them.

Before they reached the next street, the Pilot Butte Avenue of which Berretti had spoken, Eva had seen no more than perhaps fifteen women, compared to perhaps two or three hundred men since turning onto Front Street, and even compared to the barmaids in Benny's, these women were the toughest-looking, and probably hardest she had ever laid eyes on. Other than the one just-arriving car letting off the hooker, all of those she had seen had men around them talking to them as if working out some kind of business proposition.

At Pilot Butte Avenue, which cut off K Street to the right, Berretti turned. "Well, how do you like your decadent town?" he broke his silence of a minute or more.

"I don't. I'd like to leave this area."

"Okay, we're going. I've had enough too, I guess." If he had been here before, Eva wondered how he could not have had "enough" the first time. Her whole body was shaking just from what she had seen, and she felt sick to her stomach.

Pilot Butte Avenue was a convoluted mess of a thoroughfare, but somehow Berretti managed to get through it and back out of the busier part of town. In time, they found themselves on Walnut, eventually crossing Alder, which they had been on earlier in the evening. This area was nowhere near as scary as the area along Front Street and the railroad, but Berretti kept driving and driving, and hardly talking, Eva found herself growing anxious again. Eventually, they started climbing again into what Eva would have referred to as Rock Springs' highlands, into an area of really nice homes that looked vaguely familiar to her. It had long since become obvious that Berretti, like Ambro, wasn't taking her to any restaurant; they had been out of the business district for some time. But she determined not to ask anything about it.

The first time her curiosity made her look at a passing street sign, she drew a sharp little breath, which Berretti gave no sign of noticing. They were on Palisades Way, the street on which she remembered that Primo and Serenella Santori resided.

Berretti followed Palisades around on its convoluted path, then finally pulled to the end of the street and into the Santoris' driveway and put the Lincoln in park.

Eva turned to him and frowned. "Okay, what exactly is going on? Mister— I mean Gavino, do you . . . I have to assume you know Ambro Procopio."

"I do," said Berretti with a laugh. "You've been to Primo Santori's place before, I'm told."

"Very recently." Berretti was grinning on her, but Eva didn't smile back.

Berretti reached out across the seat and tried to lay his hand over Eva's, but she casually slid hers away as if she hadn't noticed. His smile lessened, and tightened, but outwardly most of it remained.

"Then you know you can find the best Italian food in town right here at the Santoris'. And tonight they are serving a favorite of mine—rigatoni with vodka sauce. Prepare to have your palate melted."

Eva wanted to be happy to think about eating more of Primo Santori's delicious food, even though it seemed really late for supper. But there were warning bells going off in her head that she could not explain. However, she was still positive that the night before God had been answering her prayers, and what if this evening was a part of the answers? What if God meant for her to be back here? What if he was opening some huge opportunity to her, something that all her years of financial struggle made her deserving of? What if here, right inside this house, her ship was finally going to come in?

Primo Santori was almost overly gracious tonight, and for some odd reason it came to Eva that he had trimmed his unkempt eyebrows. They now matched the rest of his perfectly groomed self. He leaned close and kissed Eva on the cheek as if they were friends from far back, or even family. He laughed off the little joke that he, Ambro, and Berretti had pulled off, bringing her here now two times. Serenella came in looking sleepy but welcoming—except that her smile wasn't as polished and perfect as her husband's. There was an undeniable coldness to Serenella's face, even when her teeth were shining in all the glorious whiteness of her million-dollar smile.

Serenella this evening was dressed in a sleeveless gown of cream-colored satin that brushed the floor and revealed her every curve. Around her neck was a string of pearls, and if Eva was any judge these weren't the manmade kind. Their luster matched that of the diamonds on three of her fingers. Serenella was dressed as if going to a gala at the governor's mansion.

"I'm sorry for my clothes," said Eva, excusing her white-trimmed, short-cut maroon barmaid's outfit. She didn't even dare mention the smell. "I am coming straight from work."

"Nonsense!" Primo Santori waved the comment off, in one word excusing his wife's dress and his striped, three-piece suit and tie. "On the contrary, Seri and I are too formal for a supper at home. But old habits . . . You know."

"Of course," said Eva, as she followed Serenella to the dining room and preceded Santori and Berretti. But she *didn't* really know. There was *nothing* about this kind of life that Eva understood.

The rigatoni was exquisite, as once again was the wine and the bread. "Imported flour from France," said Santori as he explained the richness of his bread. "Only the best at the Santoris'."

Eva smiled back at him.

"So, Eva, I hear that you are driving an old station wagon to and from work. Is this true?"

She smiled, embarrassed. "Yes, I'm afraid so."

"Ahh . . . That doesn't seem right. You should be in a nice new Chrysler. Or an Audi, perhaps. Station wagon . . ." He clucked his tongue. "It doesn't seem proper for a woman of your . . . charms." He smiled. "But don't mind me. I am only prattling. How is your family, Eva? Ambro told me that your grandmother is not feeling well."

Eva froze. Ambro. Ambro. Was this the opening she had been hoping for all night? Her mother always said that breathing the wrong air would kill the canary, and certainly the "air" here could be poisonous for her, or at the very least it was none of her business. But the situation seemed so bizarre she was dying for some kind of explanation, and no one was offering one.

She lost her nerve. If no one else was going to talk about the Sherman tank parked in the middle of the dining room table, she wouldn't embarrass herself by addressing it either. Her question was, Why had she been brought to this same house two different times, by two different men, and no one seemed to want to tell her the real reason?

"She's fine now. She's home. Everyone is fine."

"Oh, well that's good. I know that kind of thing can be very hard on a person. And you certainly don't deserve that. You deserve good things in your life."

"Thank you." Eva didn't know what else she could say, since she had yet to find out why Primo Santori cared about her life.

"Yes, you do deserve nice things, darling," cut in Serenella. Her voice startled Eva a little because the woman wasn't in a habit of carrying on much conversation around her.

"Thank you," she said again.

Primo looked over at his wife, and Eva caught a look he gave her, and a dropping of his eyes, as if toward her neckline. Whatever their private signal was, Serenella seemed to take it.

"Listen, darling," Serenella said. "I don't want to be presumptuous—wait, would you like more wine?"

Eva took a moment to switch gears, looking down at her empty glass. "Umm . . . Yes. Please." She didn't need more wine. In fact, she realized she didn't even *want* more, only it felt ungracious to decline. Anyway, simply having it in her glass didn't mean she had to drink it.

Primo stood up and grasped the wine bottle, and Eva put on a smile as she listened to the tinkle of the beautiful pink liquid filling her glass. She thanked him, then took an obligatory sip before setting the glass down and turning her attention back to Serenella.

"As I was saying, dear, I have been dying of curiosity to see something. Do you mind?"

Of course Eva had no idea what Serenella's "something" was, but again, how could she decline?

"Not at all."

With permission granted, Serenella reached behind her neck and expertly unclasped her necklace, then stood, walking around behind Eva. "You are so incredible to look at, even in a pauper's outfit," said the woman with a light laugh. "I am just dying to see you in pearls."

She hooked the string of pearls around Eva's neck, then walked over to Primo's side, putting her hand on his shoulder. Eva felt herself blush as she realized all three of them were gazing at her, and Primo was shaking his head in open admiration.

With a big smile and an expansive wave of his arm, he said, "Now isn't that something? Beautiful. Simply beautiful. Oh, Eva, you have indeed missed your look in life. Indeed. You should be driving fine cars, wearing silk gowns, pearls, and diamonds. The world is missing out. What a shame."

Eva laughed, trying to hide her embarrassment. "Oh, it's all right. Thank you so much for your compliments. But I have learned to live a simple life."

"But do you enjoy it? Do you enjoy living hand to mouth and never knowing if you'll be able to pay your bills each month?" asked Serenella. "You can't possibly, can you?"

Eva shrugged. Embarrassment was beginning to turn to discomfort. "No, really, I'm fine. Thank you very much for all your concern, though. I think I should probably be getting home to my family." She looked over hopefully at Gavino Berretti.

"I am so sorry!" cut in Primo Santori. "Oh, where are our manners? We certainly don't mean to chase you off, Eva. No, on the contrary, the evening is young. We still have dessert waiting, and you certainly wouldn't want to make me feel bad by leaving so soon after all the work I put into making it."

Eva took a deep breath, trying to stay calm. "Of course not. Yes, I would love dessert. I don't mean to rush off." She looked at Berretti again, and he nodded at her and winked. She found herself fervently wishing her speed demon, Ambro, was here with her tonight. She felt so out of place, and she was certain Ambro would have sensed her discomfort and made it right.

The dessert ended up being *struffoli,* and probably the most delicious Eva had ever tasted. For a little moment in time, while all of them were peacefully enjoying it and smacking their lips, complimenting Santori on his prowess in the kitchen, Eva felt comfort again, a sense of peace that permeated her being, and which she hoped wasn't more from the wine than from an actual good feeling in the air.

"You know, Eva," said Primo as he finished his dessert and invited himself to light a long, slender cigar, "I truly can see you living a much-deserved, grand life. Can I tell you something?"

"Of course." She was half afraid of whatever he might tell her, but what if it was the answer to last night's prayer?

"I have to tell you that after dining with you twice, and after some very enjoyable conversations, I feel certain about one thing: I have been looking for someone like you, in every way. Someone who deserves to have happiness, to have a good income, to drive a nice, reliable car, to wear beautiful dresses and nice jewelry.

"Eva, what would you think about leaving that dreary bar and grill and coming to work for me?"

CHAPTER TWENTY

THERE WAS A LONG moment after the surprise wore off that Eva sat feeling flattered and excited to think maybe something good was finally happening in her life, and that perhaps, as she had felt while praying, things were at last going to turn around and her financial struggles would be over.

But then those warning bells began to chime in her head again, and she remembered one of her father's favorite sayings: *If someone starts to stuff your plate with too many delicious things all at once, after you have struggled by on rice and beans too long, you should suspect there is a turd somewhere in there.*

"Would it sound too ungrateful for me to ask what I would be doing?"

Primo smiled expansively. "Of course not, not at all. We can discuss all that in depth. I wouldn't expect you to jump at anything without full disclosure." He turned then to Serenella. "My dear, would you do me the favor of cleaning up, while Gavino and I take Eva to my office for a few minutes?"

"Certainly, dear," said the woman. To Eva, her voice sounded cool, making her words seem dull and obligatory rather than cheerfully compliant.

"Come, Eva, if you will." Primo held out a hand to her, which she took not because she needed help standing but because the man's will seemed irresistible, and she didn't want to offend her potential future employer.

The three of them trooped to Primo's office, and this time he carefully shut the door. He bade Eva take a seat on the sofa, and he lounged into one of the easy chairs, with Gavino Berretti pulling up a hard wooden chair about halfway between the two of them, then slouching onto it the wrong direction, so that his arms were hugging the back of it as he smiled at his boss and waited for him to speak. For some reason it struck Eva that sitting in his chair this way made it seem like Berretti was using it as a shield.

Primo cleared his throat. "Where do I begin, my dear Eva? I would first like to talk about the benefits of the job."

"Okay."

"Most importantly, if I may, your financial struggles will be over. Literally tomorrow, because tonight I am prepared to advance you a check in the amount of one thousand dollars."

This thought gave Eva chills, and she had to fight back the tears of happiness that tried to come to her eyes.

"That sounds wonderful."

"Yes, I hope so. Wonderful. It will be. I literally would expect—without knowing what you clear at the bar and grill—that you will easily bring your income up by five times, minimum. You will have medical insurance as well, which is a very rare thing. And for a small reduction in take-home pay we can insure your family as well. You will be able to travel from time to time and see some fabulous places you would never get to see otherwise, not to mention staying in some really posh hotels and eating at the best restaurants."

Eva's head was whirling. This all sounded too good to be true. Even in all the excitement of imagining what Primo Santori was offering her, she could hear the ring of her father's voice: *You should suspect there is a turd somewhere in there.*

Feeling breathless, when he paused, she tried to calm herself and control her voice to keep it from sounding shaky. "That sounds pretty wonderful. But what would the job part be?"

"Cigarette, anyone?" Primo seemed to ignore her question, pulling out a pack of Benson and Hedges.

While Eva waited, looking back and forth from Primo to Berretti and trying to hide her impatience, the two men lit up cigarettes and began to puff and blow smoke up toward the ceiling. It was normally a maddening habit that Eva detested, but right then she hated it for more than the usual reasons. Anyone with half a brain would have seen that Primo was purposely trying to put her question off.

"Eva, that is the good part. The job itself is so simple: sales. Basically, that is the job. Sales, but without even having to do any talking. Actually, perhaps one would call it more of a delivery job than sales, because you have to sell nothing. You will have already sold it, just by being your beautiful, lovable self."

"I don't understand." Eva looked back and forth between them. "Being myself?"

Primo waved a hand dismissively. "Yes, that and . . . Well, doing, shall we say, *female* things. Entertaining men. Some very wealthy, very influential men."

You should suspect there is a turd somewhere in there . . . Get out! Get out, Eva, said her father's voice in her head.

"I . . . I guess I'm afraid I still don't understand." But she was more afraid that she *did* understand. She was afraid she knew exactly what Primo Santori was proposing. But she couldn't simply get up and walk out; she had to hear him say it.

Primo gave her a close-mouthed smile, shrugging expansively and chuckling. "What did you think of our little downtown tour tonight, Eva? Of K Street and Pilot Butte? Front Street and the others? Not a pretty scene, was it?"

"Of course not."

Primo was still smiling. "Well, you will never need to know that life—ever. Because that isn't what I am asking of you, that kind of dangerous existence. But listen. Let's be honest, young lady. You know what to do with your body—and such a splendid body it is, I might add. After all, you have two sons, and I assume . . . Let's face it: This is a bit of a delicate topic, but we are all adults here. I really don't need to be more explicit, do I?"

"Wait. Are you suggesting . . .?"

Neither of the men spoke. Even flirtatious Gavino Berretti suddenly seemed unable to meet Eva's questioning gaze while sitting there using the back of his chair for a shield, while as for Primo Santori, he was puffing madly on his cigarette, knifing his silver-blue eyes into hers as if forcing his glance not to go away. The little smile, surrounded by his brown and silver mustache and goatee, continued to play at the corners of his lips.

As her voice trailed off, silence filled the room, a silence so profound that she became aware of the ticking of a huge grandfather clock she hadn't paid any attention to until that moment.

"Listen, Eva," Primo's voice suddenly filled the empty space. "This is literally the opportunity of a lifetime. We carefully select our clients, all right? They're nothing like the scum down on K Street. They are clean, well-off, disease-free—respectable. Men in high places, whom you can expect will go to even higher places—and take you with them, very discreetly, if you are ambitious enough to get on this train while it's at the station. You would have a very simple part in it all: providing a few high-end things these men demand. A little cocaine here, some heroin there. Marijuana, if they are the casual type. And yes, your body, which as I said, and as I'm guessing by appearances, you would be, shall we say, quite good at."

Eva leaped up off the couch, feeling sick. The room had gotten suddenly very hot, and the smoke seemed to be choking her even more so than it did down at Benny's. She turned on Berretti. "Take me back to my car. Now."

Primo stared at her. Gavino tried to, with a smile frozen on his face and the cigarette frozen between his lips. But his eyes fell away after a moment.

Primo's voice lowered and got quieter. "Miss Galanti, let me caution you. Not only is this the chance of a lifetime for you, but you never know what could happen in your life if you refuse."

"What? Now you're threatening me?"

"Oh, Eva! Don't be a child," Primo said, his face growing darker and eyebrows lowering. "Threatening you? Please. Look at yourself. A dead-end job with a schmuck of an employer, a greasy, filthy man who would have you and give you nothing in return—and hell, half his barmaids work for us already, but not the way you will be. Those others are working downtown. On the street.

"To go on further, you have a grandmother who is sick. A mother who can't work because you have a retarded kid she has to stay home and care for. What kind of threat do you think I could make to you, really? Your very existence up to now is its own threat. You've been living it. But even so, believe me . . . it could get much worse, without a second's notice. Life has a way of doing that."

"My son is *not* retarded," she said through gritted teeth. "He has Down Syndrome. That is two completely different things. I demand you take me to my car right now," she repeated, whirling on Berretti once more. "Mr. Berretti?"

Berretti looked over nervously at his boss, puffing hard on his cigarette. "Boss?"

The flat of Primo's hand shot up, silencing Berretti. "Just wait, Galletto." The older man turned back to Eva, and he pulled the cigarette out of his mouth and held it down at his side, pinched hard between his fingers and thumb. A curl of smoke crept up along his side. "Take a few days to think before you tell me no, Eva. Three days—maybe even four. Don't say no now."

"I don't need to think about it for one minute," she shot back.

His eyes flattened out. "I didn't ask if you needed to. I only said do it. And while you're thinking, think about this: We know where you live. And everything else there is to know about you. I can tell you how much your rent costs, how much you paid for that piece of junk station wagon you drive. I can tell you what utilities you pay for with the city, and with a very little work I could even tell you what you have for breakfast tomorrow morning. I can also tell you how easily a dry old, rotten house like yours could go up in smoke, taking everything inside it, including sleeping people.

"You know what we do now, Eva. Whether you are smart and ambitious enough to jump on board, you know. That puts you in a very important, very small circle of people I have trusted with this information. It puts you in an extremely delicate place. Should you choose to be . . . shall we say *indiscreet* with that knowledge, in other words, should it get to *anyone* else—say even your mother . . . Well, little Eva, I have to tell you that I have heard retarded kids like yours tend not to live anywhere near as long as normal people. Perhaps you have heard this as well."

The heat was gone. Eva felt cold all over and was shivering. She stared at Primo Santori, but now she was staring through a blur of tears. She could hardly see his flat, snake-like blue eyes anymore, and perhaps that was a blessing. Her spunky side had finally slid away. This man was threatening her Leo, her home—everything she knew, everything she had. There was a time to be brave, a time to stand up to a man like this. But there was another time when a woman in her place had to shut up and run. This was that time.

"I won't say anything."

Primo took a step closer. "What was that?"

"I won't tell anyone."

"Tell anyone what, Eva?"

She stared him down, swiping angrily at the tears in her eyes as she tried to grasp what it was he wanted her to say. "Nothing. I will tell them nothing."

He dismissed her words with a little sideways wave. "Well, after all, Eva, what is there to tell, yes? You came to my house a couple of times, we had a nice little supper among friends. I might have offered you a sales position at my manufacturing business, and you felt like you could do better on tips from Benny's Bar and Grill, so you turned me down. Very clean, very simple.

"Just don't forget, all right? Don't forget that retarded kid of yours. What was his name? Leo? He sure needs his mother—as long as he is alive he does, anyway."

Eva turned away from him, and her knees almost buckled. Berretti reached out as if to catch her, but she slapped his hand away.

She walked on wobbly legs toward the office door, hearing Berretti come along in uncertain steps behind her.

As she touched the doorknob, she heard Primo Santori's voice behind her once more. "Remember, Eva—there is still time. My offer is open. As long as you remember we talked about nothing with you but normal life, and perhaps Italian food, I will not rescind my offer. But you should always remember one thing, you of all people: An Italian does not well tolerate betrayal.

"And there is one last thing I will also tell you—something you should take with you to your grave. If you think you can get around this by going to the police—the city, the county, the state—even the FBI—think about it long and hard. I can prom-

ise you that should you do so, everything you tell them will
come right back to me. Everything. Think about that, and think
hard. Little Eva, if you betray me there is no safe place for you
to turn."

CHAPTER TWENTY-ONE

EVA FOUND HER HANDS shaking again the next day when
she was getting dressed for work. She had taken Tyke to the
dentist that morning, to the tune of twenty-two dollars. At a
wage of one dollar and fifty-five cents an hour, just five cents
over minimum, if she made a full forty hours a week, and sup-
posing zero in tips, she was averaging a gross every month of
two hundred forty-eight dollars, while trying to pay rent, a car
payment, and then clothe and feed herself and four dependents.
She had no reason to wonder why she was shaking.

Of course it wasn't only her financial dilemma—and the
dentist bill she had been forced to pay half of, which was all she
had at the time, with a promise to pay the other half the following month. Her uncontrollable shaking also came on whenever
she thought of the evening before, when the truth of Primo Santori's intentions struck home.

Everywhere she went now she thought of Primo Santori,
wondering if he or someone who worked for him was watching
her. Did they know she took Tyke to the dentist? Did they know
the exact route she drove, and perhaps even how much gas she
had in her tank? Or was much of what he had told her only to

scare her into thinking her situation was hopeless? The scary thing was there was no way she could know for sure.

Even feeling broke and forgotten by God while driving home from the dentist office, and having to pass up the gas station even though her gage showed near an eighth of a tank, Eva would not consider Primo's offer. She had always heard stories of desperate young women who felt forced into that life, and some of them had supposedly even become quite affluent. But at what cost to their souls? Eva would never have dreamed of purposely making her family suffer, and perhaps if they were near starving to death she would have had to re-think her moral convictions. But there were still other options—going to the government, for one, or going begging to her church. Or any number of other churches, for that matter.

Taking Primo up on his offer would only have been considered if it were a matter of life and death.

Why had God let her down? Hadn't he given her an answer to her prayers the night before meeting Gavino Berretti? Or had that too been wishful thinking? Did she need to pray again? Did she need to pray even harder?

Grasping onto that thought, she got on her knees again until they hurt. She prayed until she felt she had repeated every word in every order imaginable. And never did she feel any answer, or even another feeling of comfort like the first time.

Feeling wearier than she had in months, she finally struggled up off the floor and finished dressing, looking at herself in her black shoes, dark nylons, and maroon, knee-length dress, her hair pulled back in a ponytail. She stoically re-applied her mascara, which she had cried away, wiped her cheeks again, and got ready to head out, praying there was enough gas still in the tank to get her there.

Throughout her sleepless night and today, Eva had thought many times about calling Buck Stone. But every time she thought about it she thought about Primo Santori's threats. Yet even so, she still hadn't been able to shake the thought.

Just as she touched her bedroom doorknob, she thought of Officer Stone again. Taking a deep breath, she went and pulled out his business card, staring at the number he had written on it. She started to put it away again, then stopped. Finally, she went and got the phone, without an explanation to anyone, and brought it back to her room.

With her hand shaking worse now than before, she dialed the number. One ring, then two, then three. With each successive ring she was in danger of dropping the phone back on the cradle. And then it picked up.

Hello? It was a woman's voice, sounding very tentative.

"Hi. I, uh . . . Well, I'm trying to reach Officer Stone." She had come very close to disconnecting.

Just a moment, please. The woman's voice was bending from tentative toward frightened. She heard her whisper. *I don't recognize the voice, but it's a woman.*

Now a man's voice answered, and to Eva's ear he sounded none too sure of himself either, but she was pretty sure it was Buck Stone.

"Officer Stone? It's Eva Galanti." There was too long of a silence. "Officer Stone? Are you there?"

Eva! The voice came back. *Are you okay? Is everything all right?*

A chill ran over Eva's body. "Yes, I'm fine, but . . . I think I've found something out. And I'm very scared."

Eva. Listen to me, Stone's voice came again. *Those faces and names I showed you—forget them, okay? Forget they ever existed. Forget you ever saw me.*

"Officer Stone!" She didn't think about it until after she spoke, but her tone sounded almost scolding. "I have to talk to you. I have to meet with you somewhere."

Again, a pregnant pause. She half expected the line to go dead. *All right. But we might have to do it out of town somewhere. Maybe in Green River.*

"When?" she asked, feeling almost frantic now because of how he was speaking. "I have to go to work now, until ten."

Tomorrow, Stone said. *Tomorrow morning.*

"Okay. What time? Where?"

I'll call you tonight, Stone said. *Promise. Eva, don't talk to anyone. And I mean no one. If anyone asks you, you've never met me.* With that, the line went dead.

Trembling, Eva set the phone back in the cradle, resting her shaking hand there for a minute before she could find the strength to reach out and unplug the cord from the jack. Without conscious thought, she wound up the cord, picked up the phone, took a deep breath, and headed out of her room.

At the front door, she smiled and said goodbye to her mother and grandmother, then gave Tyke a long hug. It was so good to see him out of pain, although he was worn out from the Novocain, and from the ordeal of having a God-given part of his body yanked out of his head.

Smiling and begging with his sweet little almond-shaped eyes, Leo wanted to hold onto her longer, and she hated leaving him, but she had left herself only five minutes to spare once she got to work—five minutes to sign in, get her apron on, and get ready for the grueling afternoon and evening.

Waving goodbye one last time to everyone, she went and got in the Plymouth. Saying a little prayer, she put the key in and turned it. It made a strange grinding noise she didn't remember hearing before, so she turned it back, waited a second, and tried again. That time it fired up, and she pulled away and headed to work.

She found herself in the lonely, barren section of Blairtown Avenue with the railroad on her right, the brush and grass and rocks to the left. Judging by her last experience, she didn't like this location, and neither did the Plymouth.

The front end of the Valiant began to rattle. Then came a clanging sound underneath, and the rattling became so severe she almost couldn't hold the car on the road. With her heart in her throat, she veered off into the weeds, almost immediately smelling scorched vegetation.

Jumping out in the road, she was almost run over by a passing delivery truck. Swearing in frustration, she looked under the car, where smoke was curling up. The grass was on fire!

Falling back in, she turned the key again, and it made its earlier grinding noise but didn't fire up. She got out in a panic and dropped to her hands and knees. The grass along the roadside had been clipped not long ago, and the flame was already burning down, but now it had caught on some of the taller grass around the right fender.

Running around, Eva started stomping on the flames until she could feel the heat through the bottom of her right shoe. It took twenty or thirty seconds that seemed like a day before she was standing in a four- or five-foot square area of black, with the grass burned clear to the ground. She lifted her right foot to look at the bottom of her shoe, seeing only then how thin it was worn.

Looking around desperately, she saw no help. No one at all on this lonely stretch of road, just rows and rows of glowering, ominous boxcars squatting sullenly across the road. She shot a glance at her watch and swore again, glad no one was around to hear her. She had five minutes left before she was officially late for work, and it was at least a ten-minute walk.

The tears that had been waiting spilled over as she took off at a run, leaving the car sitting there with the keys in the ignition. Less than fifty feet away from the car, she stepped in a dip and almost turned an ankle, making her fall to her knees in the brittle grass and gravel at road's edge.

Feeling the pain of gravel grinding into her knees, she fell forward onto her elbows, learning instantly that there were nasty goats' head burrs growing among the grass. Ignoring the pain, she lowered her head onto her forearms and cried.

At last, Eva struggled to her feet. The sun's impossible heat was bearing down on her, and up at her from the asphalt, but she didn't dare walk in the grass anymore. She looked down at her knees and wanted to scream. With great care, she picked from her knees six burrs whose pointy ends felt like they had some kind of toxin on them, then stared at the tears in both nylons. Gritting her teeth, she went on and pulled out burrs that had stuck in her forearms when she went down.

She cried God's name out loud, then stared up toward heaven through her tears. Why had he left her? Was this a test? She had told Primo no! She had no intention of succumbing to temptation. So why? *Why?*

In desperation, she started at a fast walk, aware only of the tears on her face and the smell of ash, sun-burned grass, and hot asphalt. Something kept prodding into her brain, and now she couldn't stave it off. Primo had said he wouldn't withdraw his offer. As long as she didn't tell anyone, he had given her time to think it over. What had he said? Three or four days? What if she said yes? What if she agreed to do it for a while? A short time, maybe only long enough to pay off her bills, to buy a decent car? Would she be condemned for trying to preserve her family? It wasn't like she had never slept with a man before. It wasn't as if she didn't know how to make a man happy, and men liked her. Or maybe she could refuse to do the "entertainment" part. Just do the narcotics part. But she was pretty sure Primo wouldn't hire her if she refused to sell anything but drugs.

Five minutes into walking, with Blairtown looming bigger and uglier ahead, when it came to her what she had allowed herself to start thinking, she almost laughed. No way. No way! She would not succumb to Primo Santori's temptation, no matter if he had made a pact with the devil to torment her if she refused. There were some things a God-fearing woman simply couldn't live with.

By the time Eva turned the corner and came in sight of Benny's, she got another shock. There was Benny Fitz himself, standing in front of the entrance, arms folding across his aproned chest, searching the street. The moment he turned his head and saw her coming, he dropped his hands to rest on his hips, and his head settled back into his neck. He stood there glaring, waiting for her to get close.

She raised her voice as soon as she thought she was close enough for him to hear. "I'm sorry, Benny! My car broke down. I got here as fast as I could. I even ran." She knew her voice sounded pleading, but she couldn't help it. In her desperate state she didn't even care that she had said his name out loud.

He stared at her and started to open his mouth to say something. His mouth shut, and he gritted his teeth. Finally, he growled in her face as she reached him. "Get in there, Eva, and get working. We'll talk about this later."

Holding back tears, Eva pushed inside, the smoky room almost as black as the inside of a deep cave after so long in the bright August sun. The darkness was a blessing, and she almost ran across the room to the back, ignoring voices she was sure were calling out to her.

In the back room, she tried to clean up the best she could, washing her face and drying her eyes, wiping the blood off her knees and arms. When she went to re-do her mascara, a jolt went through her. She whirled around, scanning for her purse, but she already knew the truth: She had left it in the car!

Her first instinct was to leave and go running back to the car to look for it. But it was empty, after all, at least of any money but small change, and at least as far as she knew she still had a job, which she probably wouldn't if she left. She wasn't positive, but she almost thought she had seen a hint of mercy in Benny's eyes before coming inside. That mercy was her only hope.

Forcing herself to take a deep breath, she went out into the kitchen and pulled her apron off the hook. Benny was at the griddle flipping burgers as if nothing were wrong. In fact, he was even quietly humming "Dancing in the Moonlight," or at least a semblance thereof. And Benny *never* hummed.

Teton Belle came in walking straight and tall, pushing her ample chest out even farther than normal it seemed, and chewing her gum like a rabbit on speed. She had a little smirk on her face that Eva instantly wanted to tear off her with a hot rake.

"So you gonna be one of Primo's girls, huh?" Belle said, then looked toward Benny, whose attention her words must have drawn. He was behind Eva now, so she couldn't see him.

"I'm not anybody's *girl,* Belle, so please get out of my way, would you?"

Without awaiting a reply, she brushed past the chesty barmaid and went out into the lounge. She was immediately accosted by an already-drunk, ball cap-wearing miner named Pete Wells, who was about as wide in the chest as he was tall and whose wrists were as big around as a normal man's forearms. Wells was haired all over not much different from a black bear, and smoking a cigar that seemed to be half the reason for the air-born sea of blue smoke already clogging the place.

It was going to be the longest shift of Eva's career.

No one came in that day that Eva would have wanted to see. That is, no police officers, and no Brandon Lucky. In fact, she hadn't seen Brandon at Benny's in so long she had started to wonder if he still worked there. She had never asked, and he never volunteered the information.

To top it all off, she had tried calling Brandon at home, where she only got an angry and cold-sounding Karen and had to leave a message she knew would not be returned. The phone at the mechanic shop where Brandon worked rang a dozen times with no answer, and she never found time to try it again. She couldn't even get hold of Lance Cartwright, whom she had called in desperation hoping to hitch a ride home. In her desperation, she had even tried Rick Cohen, and last of all she had contemplated calling Buck Stone, but after the way he had sounded when they talked, she didn't dare.

Her last choice, and it was hardly a choice at this point, was Ambro Procopio. But she couldn't. Her pride had to mean something. Besides, the way things had turned out, and now assuming the real reason he acted interested in her in the first place, he probably wouldn't have come to get her anyway.

She would simply have to walk home. It wouldn't be the first time she had ever had to walk somewhere. The only thing that bothered her was the thought of walking along the roadway in the dark, and it would be almost dark even before she was off work. It really wasn't only that particular roadway, either; it was more the common knowledge that it could be deadly for any woman these days caught out in Rock Springs after the sun went down.

It was the hottest part of the day outside when Eva took her break and went to stand under the cloth awning and escape the tobacco smoke and fumes of drunkards in the lounge. In spite of the heat, she had enjoyed five minutes of her break, soaking in the quiet of the street, when the front door burst open, and Benny was standing there glaring at her. He grunted in surprise. Had he been thinking she left?

The fat man folded his arms across his chest the way they had been when she first laid eyes on him that afternoon. "Been doin' any thinkin' about how you gonna keep your job, Eva? Remember when I told you last time you were out of chances?"

She froze, staring at him. "Benny! I told you my car broke down. Please!"

"Not my problem. I told you to get a new car. You're out of chances, girl. Just so you know."

Leaving that ominous statement, like a sack of manure dropped on the sidewalk at her feet, Benny turned and vanished back inside his smoking cave.

Eva stood there feeling so scared it made her furious, and once more she began to shake and had to force back tears. She almost wished she had the gumption to quit. Where else could she go? A bank? A grocery store? A florist shop? There had to be *someplace*! But how would she find a place where she could make the kind of money she got from the tips of happy, careless drunks? In short, there was no other place, other than perhaps another bar, and she had already checked in at most of the others over the last month or so. Nobody seemed to have any openings in this town.

It took the entire rest of her break to calm down enough to go back inside, and right when she felt ready, she saw a car come strolling down the middle of the street toward her. It was a dark maroon Lincoln with a white top.

Feeling sick again on the instant, Eva whirled and threw the door to Benny's open, going inside before the car she was certain was driven by Gavino Berretti could get close enough for her to see him. What were they doing now, stalking her?

That thought instantly hit her in the guts, making her feel nauseous and making her think of trying to call Lance Cartwright again, or at least Brandon Lucky. But what could Brandon do? He already had a record, he couldn't even own a firearm, and how did a common man fight the Mob anyway? And she had a feeling just from now knowing Primo, Ambro, and Berretti were settled here in Rock Springs that there had to be more of them she didn't know. Anything she knew about the Mob told her they never worked except in packs.

She was hurrying toward the pay phone to the right, along the front wall, when she heard someone yell her name and turned to see drunk Pete Wells barreling toward her through the crowd. Now there would be no chance to make a phone call. She cursed Wells even as she smiled at his approach.

It was nearing nine o'clock, one hour from the end of Eva's shift, and she was up at one of the front tables when she heard the sound of a siren. Shortly after that, she heard another, from a different direction.

A few of the bar crowd started drifting toward the front of the room, and one of them opened the door and went to stand out on the sidewalk, soon followed by a general exodus of any customers who were near the front. The police sirens didn't sound like they were going on a straight line, but driving in haphazard patterns about town. And it wasn't town as in Rock Springs—it was Blairtown! As Eva followed the others out onto the sidewalk she could hear the nearby hard squealing of tires to accompany the wail of the sirens.

A large motor roared, and all of a sudden they could see in the gathering dusk a sleek, low-roofed car barreling down the street toward them from the left at a breakneck speed way too fast for the twenty-five mile-an-hour street. A Rock Springs police car appeared three quarters of a block behind the front car, which as it rocketed past turned out to be a Plymouth Roadrunner, greenish-gray in color, with two men in the front seats.

The police car, red light rotating on top and siren shattering Eva's eardrums as it came on, was limping. The right front fender was hanging partway off, and an ugly, deep scrape marred the side, almost all the way to the rear fender. The right front wheel also didn't seem to be rotating quite straight, and it was fast falling behind the Roadrunner.

Roaring past Benny's, the Roadrunner blew the stop sign at the corner and made the turn on two wheels, screaming all the way around. As the squad car came by, Eva thought she recognized Buck Stone at the wheel, and he blew the stop sign as well. Another squad car swept around the corner where Stone's car had first appeared, losing control and nearly hitting a streetlight post. At the last second, it pulled out of the fishtail and came on, dust flying out from under it off a street that until the last few moments had appeared to be well swept.

For another ten seconds after the cars vanished, Eva could hear the ever-increasing roar of the racing cars as they gained speed going up Blairtown Avenue, and then, when they were maybe as far as half a mile or so out, the sound of a shot jolted Eva and she jumped and put a hand to her mouth. Belle, who Eva hadn't even known was standing next to her, gasped.

A couple more distant shots erupted, and then the sound of squealing tires, and a loud crash. Someone nearby swore loudly, and one of the men started to run across the street to a waiting car. Another man ran after him, grabbing him mid-street and whirling him around. Eva could hear them arguing about getting into the middle of a possible gunfight, and after barking at each other for a while they both came walking back, the cop chaser looking properly disappointed.

Even as the two men made it to the sidewalk, another shot cracked in the distance, then another, and another. A louder boom, perhaps that of a shotgun, followed the first three.

Eva's heart was racing as she saw Jud, the night cook, pulling past, inching his car through the crowd as he looked around at everyone with frightened eyes.

The night cook! Eva jerked her hand up to look at her watch. It was only nine-0-five. Jud was an hour early. Sighing because she still had almost another hour before the end of her shift, Eva glanced toward the distant place where the collision had occurred, and where it sounded like a full-out gunfight was underway, then went back inside the lounge. She tried to hide her worry, but she felt sick about what might be happening, and whether Lance or one of the others she had recently met was involved.

One of the few people who had given up on his curiosity to come back inside ordered a couple of burgers and fries, and Eva went to the back to give Benny the order. She was shocked to see Jud putting on his apron as Benny was taking his off.

Teton Belle was back there as well, and she smirked at Eva as she walked past and returned to the lounge. At that moment, Henri, the blonde barmaid, came in through the back door, took one look at Eva and Benny, grabbed her apron, and headed for the front without a word.

"Come on, Eva," said Benny. "You an' me need to talk."

She caught the worried look Jud gave her as she passed and she reached out and gave his arm a pat. She knew he would have stuck up for her, but Jud had his family to feed just like she did.

At the back exit, Benny stopped, and Eva almost ran into him. "Leave the apron hanging. You're off work."

Fumbling, Eva untied the apron, pulled it off over her head, and went back to hang it up. She straightened the bottom part of her dress self-consciously, although it didn't need straightening, and followed Benny out into the back lot.

"All right, Eva. This is it. You're done. I don't want you back in my place tomorrow."

The shock of his words hit her like a wave, so fast she had no time to gather or marshal her pride. "No, Benny! Please! I'll beg you if I have to. It wasn't my fault. What about my family?"

"Guess you should've thought of that when I told you to go buy a new car."

"I couldn't! Benny, I can barely afford that one." It rang in her head that she had never said this despised name so many times in such a short space.

"You got one chance, and that's all." If Eva had had time to think, she would have realized this was the moment Benny had waited for, and he had been building up to this all along. But Eva was in panic mode.

"What? What, Benny? Anything you ask."

"We're goin' to spend the night at my place, Eva. No movie. No eatin' out. No nothin'. We're goin' to my pad. That's the deal. Otherwise, start walkin'."

She stared at him, and in his eyes, even in the failing light, she could see it. Benny Fitz was one hundred percent positive he had finally backed her into a corner. He knew with everything that was in him he was finally going to get her into his bed, because he knew how desperate she was to keep her job.

But Benny was wrong.

"No, Benny. Don't ask me to do that. I have a little boy. I have— No, Benny. I won't."

He took three strides toward her, and a chill washed over her body. She had never seen her boss before with a look quite this insane on his face. Yes, she had seen him angry—many times. But this was something different, something she hadn't seen since a retarded boy had gone berserk in a grocery store one day, beating his older brother half senseless with a can of string beans before anyone around could gather their senses enough to stop his tirade.

Benny was closing on Eva as she felt herself crash against the back wall of the bar. He raised one hand as if to strike her, and she instinctively threw her left hand up to ward it off. Benny grabbed her wrist as if he had been expecting her move, and as he stepped into her he shoved her arm down and grabbed her throat with his other hand.

He leaned in with his fetid cigarette and garlic breath and started trying to kiss her on the mouth, in between cursing her and calling her foul names. Somehow, in spite of her whipping her head back and forth in her struggle, he got his mouth over hers, kissing her savagely.

In terror, she brought her knee up hard. Benny grunted and ground his teeth together, and his face started to grow redder. "Well, you little—"

Seeing his reaction, she kneed him again, then once more. As he started to stagger away, dropping his hands to his groin, she ran close, screaming in anger, and slammed him on the left ear with the palm of her hand. To her surprise, Benny fell sideways, catching himself with his hand on the hood of Henri's car. He turned to look at her in time for her to come at him again in a fury she had not foreseen from herself. She brought a knee up and struck him with all her force along the seam of his pants, and as his shocked eyes flew open, he twisted and fell sideways, landing on the knee of the leg she had struck, then falling the rest of the way to the pavement, as if he no longer had any control over his muscles. Berserk, she started stomping on his middle, over and over, only half aware she was doing it.

Then in a blind panic, she turned and ran. She got almost to the corner before changing her mind and running to the back door and back inside. By now, she was crying uncontrollably with the adrenalin that flooded her body. Shocked, the dishwasher stared at her. Jud dropped his spatula and grabbed her shoulders as she tried to run by, and it was all she could do to think straight enough not to attack him as well.

"What happened? Eva! Calm down! What happened?"

She tried to tell him, but her own words didn't seem coherent, even to her. She heard Jud swearing, and he pointed toward the exit out to the lounge. "You'd better run." She whirled, and he grabbed her arm and swung her back. "Wait! Go get in the storeroom and hide. I'll tell him you ran out the front. Go!"

Stumbling, hardly able to see, and praying that none of the other girls chose now to come to the kitchen, she got to the next turn, made a right, and jerked open a door on her left that went into the room where they kept the cleaning supplies, mops, brooms, and buckets. There was also a little sink in there.

In the back of the cleaning closet, she crouched, waiting. Waiting. Waiting interminably . . .

Minutes later, she heard angry, jumbled voices. All she could make out was Jud's last words, "—through the lounge! She just ran by like she was all upset and didn't say anything."

Eva heard loud footsteps going by, and then a long silence. She waited, still on the floor against the far wall from the door, listening to her own heart pounding in her head. She shook like she had the chills.

After a long silence, she heard the lounge door slam open again, and the same heavy steps stomped by. The back exit door slammed, and after a minute she heard an engine fire up, and then a car peeling out of the lot way too fast. It was all too loud to hear through a wall, so she knew Jud must have gone and opened the back door again to look out.

After another minute, there was a soft knock on the storage room door. "Eva? You okay?"

She was so petrified she almost didn't recognize the voice. "Jud?"

The door opened, letting in a two-foot bar of bright kitchen light. "He's gone. You need to take my car and get out of here, okay? Come on, hurry."

She got up and stumbled to him, and he caught her and held her while she shook for half a minute or so. "All right, Eva girl. It's over, for now. Just get goin' before he decides to come back."

She nodded briskly, wiping at her eyes. "I'm going, Jud, but I'm not taking your car."

"Yes, you are, Eva!" He shoved the keys out to her.

"No! I'm not taking it."

"Eva? Please. You can't walk on these streets at night and you know it."

"Don't ask me anymore, Jud. I'm fine. Really. I'll be okay. I'll call the cops before I go."

"What, an' then wait here for 'em? I'm tellin' you, Eva, I wouldn't put it past that maniac to come back here lookin' for you, and he's in a blind rage."

"No, I'll leave. I'll stay in the shadows. Thank you, Jud, but it isn't that far home."

"I think somethin' happened on the road up there too," said Jud. "You might have to take a different way. You could be walkin' out there for half the night."

"I'll stop somewhere and see if I can borrow a phone and call for a ride then," she said, knowing she was probably lying and that she would likely have to walk the entire way home if she didn't take Jud up on the offer of his car.

At last, Jud let out a ragged sigh. "You won't take my car?"

"No. I promise I'll be fine."

"Okay, but I think you're psycho."

She smiled, drawing in a deep breath. "No, I think we both saw what psycho is tonight, and it's not me."

He grinned and laughed nervously, swiping at his mouth with the back of a hand. "Yeah. Yeah, you got that right. Hey, come here." He drew her into another long hug, patting her back. "Yeah, girl, you sure aren't the psycho here, I'll say that. Now why don't you split, and I'll make the call in to the cops for you."

CHAPTER TWENTY-TWO

EVA SLIPPED ALONG THE side of the road, keeping an eye out either direction for cars. It was near complete darkness now, and considering how this town was, the darker it became, the safer she felt. Full dark in Rock Springs was preferable to half-light, at least on this lonely road. If anyone drove by, she would simply lie down in the grass or get behind a cluster of rocks before they could spot her.

Part of her feeling of security came from something that also gave her the opposite feeling—a feeling of danger. That was the last gift Jud had given her before letting her leave the bar. He had pressed a snub-nose Astra 680 revolver upon her, a .38 special. Eva had fired guns many times before, and she was good at it. She had shot often with her father and with Brandon Lucky, but she had never had any reason to fire at a human being. After Benny Fitz's behavior that night, however, it wasn't hard for Jud to convince her that having the .38, at least as a threat, wasn't a bad idea.

After walking ten minutes or so, she saw headlights coming toward her from the direction of Benny's. She crouched in the shadows of the grass in the barrow pit as a sleek dark vehicle cruised past, five or ten miles over the speed limit, possibly a late model Chevrolet Caprice. It looked like the kind of car detectives and FBI agents drove on television, and for a moment she almost wished she had flagged it down and asked for a ride to her car. But it could as easily have been some member of the local Mob as an officer of the law. Besides, even when she got to her piece of garbage station wagon, what was she going to do? She still had a long ways to walk home after that, because it wasn't likely to start.

In a few minutes, it was completely dark, too dark to see anything other than to know she was walking in the lowest part of the barrow pit, with the grassy, rock-strewn expanse on her right, and the asphalt surface of the roadway two feet or so higher on her left. The ground surface was naturally a little rough, caused by clumps of tall yellow bunchgrass, but so far more than manageable to walk in because the clusters of rock were mostly scattered farther out. She had slightly twisted an ankle three or four times, but not so much as to render her unable to walk.

Suddenly, her foot hit something, and before she could recover she felt herself going down. It seemed to happen in slow motion, the way such unexpected falls do, and in the near-complete darkness she had no way to prepare for her collision with the earth. She hit harder than she expected on her elbows, feeling the sharp points of dead grass jab into her forearms before she rolled off to the left. She lay there for a moment on her back, looking up at the smear of the Milky Way and the bright pinpoint pricks of the stars, before she began to be aware of an ever-growing sharp pain in both her shins that was even worse, as it registered on her, than the little wounds in her arms.

Sitting up, she massaged her shins briskly, cringing. In a brief panic, she searched around for the revolver, crawling about in the grass. Had anyone seen her they would have thought she was mad. The revolver was closer than she thought, and she sighed with relief as her right hand closed over it. She retrieved it, holding it tightly to her as she breathed herself out of her scare.

It wasn't until that moment that curiosity struck her. What had she tripped over? This was about the same path she had taken in her earlier panic to get to work, and she hadn't seen any objects in the grass large enough to trip her.

Looking around, it wasn't hard to find the dark rectangular shape against the paler grass. Crouching, she felt the surface, half expecting it to be metal. But it wasn't. Other than the sharp edges, it felt like soft, slick leather, or perhaps vinyl—a case of some kind. Running her fingers along it, she was surprised at the smoothness of it. To be so smooth this surface hadn't been out in the weather for very long.

Ever more curious, she felt along its edges until she touched a handle, which she grasped to heft it up. It was heavier than she expected, obviously weighed down by something inside. How strange! This was a briefcase. She had seen others that looked exactly how this one felt. She was positive it hadn't been here earlier. The grass wasn't much over mid-shin. She couldn't possibly have walked past it in broad daylight without seeing it. From a passing car, on the other hand, it wouldn't have called much attention to itself, so she wasn't surprised that no one had stopped to pick it up.

She wobbled to her feet, brushing off her forearms and knees, then as much of her dress as her fingertips could get to. Reaching down, she felt around, found the handle of the briefcase, and picked it up, starting on her way once more with the revolver in one hand, the briefcase in the other.

A few minutes later, almost at the same time that the bulk of her car appeared in the shadows before her, she began to make out the glow of a flashing light farther ahead that was way out of place here in this darkness. It was almost as if a streetlight were shorting out or something, but after staring for a while, and knowing there shouldn't be any streetlights for another mile or so, she realized the glow seemed to be made by a red light, and there might have been a blue one as well. Did the police have someone stopped up ahead? Or was she near the scene of the wreck and the apparent shootout from earlier that evening?

The thought startled her because in her current circumstances she had put that incident out of her mind. She contemplated heading back toward the bar, but the possibility of Benny Fitz still lurking around made her discard that idea. Besides, if there were policemen ahead, what if one of them was Lance? A feeling of unexpected relief rushed over her. It had been a while since she felt safe, and the idea that Lance Cartwright could be close by gave her the feeling of safety she had been longing for.

Unless . . .

A feeling of sickness swept through her guts. With all that shooting, what if . . . No. No, she couldn't think about that. No, Lance was all right. She would have sensed it had he been hurt. Wouldn't she?

She stood there in the grass for half a minute, trying to work past the feeling of terror that had nearly overcome her. She had to move on. She couldn't stand here wondering. It was too late to go back and take another, much longer, path home. She started on.

Reaching her car, she went first to the passenger side door, throwing it open and making the dome light come on. She saw instantly that her purse, which she had left on the floor, was gone. Her heart fell, and her mind whirled, trying to envision all she had inside. At first, it almost made her laugh to think how disappointed the thief must have been when he found out she had no cash or credit cards. At most, she might have had thirty or forty cents. Following the humor, a feeling of anger burst over her. A feeling of having been violated. Some lowly thief had stolen her purse, and the most valuable thing in it were photos of her family.

People were rotten. Rotten to the core.

At least they had left the keys in the ignition, probably after trying to start the car. In her anger, she assumed they had tried to start it, anyway. If they were willing to steal a purse, why not a car too?

She went around and got in, said a little prayer, then tried the key. It made the same grinding noise as earlier in the day, but it wouldn't start. After the battery started to sound like it was running low, she finally gave up.

Yanking the key out, she threw open the door and got out. Holding the pistol and the briefcase, she started marching on toward home, trying to ignore her already aching feet.

She only got twenty or thirty steps before something struck her. Why carry this heavy briefcase all the way home? Her fingers were already feeling the strain of it, and she had a lockable spare tire compartment that would be perfect for stowing it. She went back to the car, opened the back door and then the steel doors that revealed her spare tire and tools.

As she was throwing the briefcase into the spare tire compartment, the flash of lights hit her, and she looked back the way she had come. A vehicle with its brights on was puttering down the road toward her.

Slamming the door, she ran to the other side of the car and crouched down behind the tire, waiting. She didn't realize for a while that she was holding her breath.

The car came on, and the closer it got, the slower it rolled. At last, she could see the bright beam of a flashlight coming from the car, flashing around in the darkness beyond her and her car. The other car was stopped in the road now, and she heard its door slam. Terrified, she got down on her stomach, immediately feeling goats' heads sticking into her through her blouse. She imagined the other person being Benny, searching everywhere for her, relentless.

After what seemed like ten minutes, she heard the car door shut again, and the car rolled on, gravel crackling under its tires. It got next to her car and stopped again, and as she squeezed the revolver tight she waited to hear the sound of the door. The flashlight burst over her car, flitting around for a while. The car drove on for a few more feet, and the flashlight beam hit the back of her station wagon, going right over the top of her head. She was hardly breathing now, and trying to decide if she should bolt and run.

The time the car sat there idling in the road, the flashlight rotating around like a beacon around a prison wall, seemed interminable. Finally, the light's beam extinguished, and the car puttered on down the road.

Eva lay there in the grass, dirt, and burs until she felt something crawling on her skin. She came up fast and swatted at it, feeling a couple of burs at the same time.

She managed to get to her feet, shaking as if she were becoming sick, and once again she knocked the burs off, something she was getting all too used to. She opened the back door of the station wagon again and locked the spare tire compartment, then shut the door and started off again toward home. It was nice only having the revolver to carry again, but somehow it felt like it weighed twenty pounds.

Eva wasn't keen on walking past the scene ahead of her, where the emergency lights were flashing brighter and brighter, but she certainly couldn't go back the other way, especially since walking that way would take her at least another forty minutes or so to get home, even if she were able to avoid running into Benny on the way.

It wasn't long before the flashing lights ahead became glaring. Another couple of minutes and she could see at least five sets of red lights, and one blue, spread apart all along the road. It was night shift, and there couldn't be too many more patrol cars than this in a town of twenty thousand people, could there? One of these cars had to be Lance's! At least one of them appeared to be a rescue truck as well.

The thought of seeing Lance, of feeling safe again, urged her into a faster walk, even though her feet felt raw and bruised from her black flats, which weren't made for walking long distances on uneven ground, besides the soles being worn out.

The closer she got to the flashing lights, there seemed to be so many vehicles, and scattered so far, that they must have the entire road blocked off. Starting to worry that they might order her to turn around and go back, she got up on the asphalt to walk the rest of the way. She would have to hope for the best.

It was a relief having a solid, smooth surface to walk on, but the damage had already been done. Having to maneuver over all the rough ground, around clumps of grass, hidden rocks, and rodent holes, had taken a toll on her feet from which it would take days to recover.

When Eva guessed she was some hundred yards from the uneven string of vehicles, some with the red and blue overhead lights, others with only their headlights glowing, she stopped to survey the scene and compose herself. She could see the bright beams of flashlights and a couple of lanterns bobbing around now and then. Sometimes one of the lanterns would come to rest on the surface of the road. There was also a mechanical chatter in the mix, and a bright light that must be coming from a gas generator.

Her heart began to pound. It might have been two hours since the shooting, and the crash. What exactly had gone down? It had to be huge for the police still to be here. It had to be huge for the incident to have shut down apparently the entire Rock Springs police department, and the main thoroughfare between Blairtown and the rest of Rock Springs.

She had the sudden feeling that even if Lance Cartwright were on this scene he wasn't going to have any time for her.

Regardless, this was her way home, if they would allow her to use it. If they sent her back the other way, by the time she got home her feet were going to be crippled.

With a lung-filling breath, she kept going, now much more slowly.

She stopped again thirty feet from the scene. In the glow of the lanterns, and what she now realized was not only one, but two brighter lights run off the generator she could hear the rattling purr of, the scene was much clearer. There were a total of three police cars with single red bubbles of light rotating on their roofs, and a fourth that appeared to have a light bar stretching from one side of the roof to the other, with two rotating red lights on the sides, and a blue one in the middle. She had started seeing blue lights on some police cars on TV, but this was the first one she could recall seeing in person. Then again, before meeting Lance she had never paid much attention to police vehicles either way.

Besides the lit-up police vehicles, there was the closer pickup that appeared to be a rescue rig and also had a red light bar, and there were two dark vehicles and one police car sitting sideways in the road with none of its lights on at all.

"Hey!"

A sharp voice made Eva jerk. She looked over to see a man standing by a dark car that only had its parking lights on. Suddenly nervous, she took a step to the right and opened her hand to casually drop Jud's revolver in the grass and dirt, then walked a ways off from it.

"Stay right there," the man's voice commanded, and then she spotted his dark silhouette coming closer.

"Hi," she said as the man got close and she saw his white shirt and paler face contrasting with a dark suit and tie.

"What are you doing out here?" the man asked without ceremony. He had his right hand suspiciously up near his chest, as if getting ready to reach for a gun in a shoulder holster.

"Walking home from work. My car broke down."

"Okay." He paused for a few seconds. "That your station wagon up there on the side of the road?"

"Yes, sir."

"All right, well you're going to need to find another way home. This is a crime scene."

Panic shot through her as she stared at what she could make out of the hard-sounding man in the dark. "Sir, please. I've already walked a long way, and it will take another hour or more to get home if I have to go around."

"Well, it's not a good idea for you to be here. This is a crime scene," he repeated, as if she might have forgotten what he said two sentences earlier. More likely, he just felt important saying it.

"Please. I won't look at anything. I promise. I can't go back that way. I was attacked by a man back there at the bar, and I think he might come back looking for me."

The man didn't reply. She could only assume he was staring at her. He could surely see her, but the lights were behind him, and mostly all she could make out from her side was his silhouette and the pale of his face and shirt.

"Is Officer Cartwright here?" she blurted out. "Or Officer Stone?"

The man was taken aback. "Cartwright . . . That's the guy that looks like a skyscraper? Yeah, he's over there."

"Could you please tell him Eva's here?"

"Eva?" the man repeated, sounding perturbed. "All right. But don't step any closer." He walked past the back end of his car, apparently to avoid the area in the center of the road, and bobbed away among the bouncing lights.

In half a minute, huge relief washed over Eva as she saw Lance Cartwright's unmistakable silhouette looming closer.

"Eva!" he called out from forty feet away. "Is that you?"

"Lance!" In spite of the suited man's order, she couldn't stay put. She ran the rest of the way to Lance and threw her arms around him, holding back the urge to cry.

He kept patting her back, talking to her soothingly. "Hey, hey. You okay? That was your car on the side of the road up there, wasn't it?"

She nodded, and after a few seconds followed it up with, "It broke down again, and I think this time it's bad. I've been trying to call you and Brandon Lucky. I even tried to call Rick Cohen."

"I'm real sorry, Eva," he said, and there was no mistaking the sincerity in his voice. "I've been tied up here quite a while, and before that they had me on a stakeout. And the other guys . . ." He stopped there.

"Who had you on a stakeout?"

"Some FBI agent. Well, that guy who came and told me you were here, actually. Agent Tervalon, his name is."

"Wow. A stakeout in Blairtown? This town's getting crazy, huh?" She thought of her wild revelation about the presence of the Mob here, but of course she didn't dare say anything. She didn't know if she would ever dare tell a soul what she had learned, even after calling Officer Stone.

"Yeah. Crazy. And you don't know the half of it."

"That wasn't you chasing a gray Roadrunner earlier, was it? Past Benny's?"

"No. That was Jake Glattner and Officer Stone."

At the mention of Officer Stone's name, she felt a little guilty. What did Stone really know about the men whose photos he had shown her? What had he been trying to learn? She should have called him long ago. But she was simply too scared. And she hadn't wanted to get involved.

"What happened?"

Lance paused, then looked around to see if anyone else was near. His voice got quieter. "It's pretty bad, Eva. I mean—*real* bad. I'd be in some deep water if they knew I was even talking about it, but the driver of that Roadrunner you saw got hurt pretty bad in the wreck; he's unconscious up at the hospital. And . . ." He stopped abruptly.

Eva suddenly noticed that her friend's voice sounded very shaky.

"And you can't tell one soul any of this, Eva, but one of our guys is dead: Officer Stone. He got a bullet through the back of his head."

CHAPTER TWENTY-THREE

EVA HAD NOT KNOWN Officer Stone very well, but the shock of hearing his life had been snuffed out like a candle, when so recently she had been talking with him on the phone, was like a kick to the guts. Her immediate thought was that Stone had been killed for some other reason besides what might seem obvious—perhaps because he was digging too deep into the activities of the Mob. That sure didn't say much for her own chances for security.

Eva more than ever wanted to tell Lance about Officer Stone now, about how they had been talking and how they were going to meet in the morning, but warning bells began to go off in her head. Officer Stone had seemed to Eva as if he trusted no one. He never gave out names of people not to trust—but he never gave out a single one he thought he *could* trust either. She felt suddenly sick, going back to her earlier fears. What if she were in danger talking to Lance? Did she really know him? Did she really know *anyone* in a position of authority in this town?

"What's wrong, Eva? Did you know Stone too?"

On the instant, she made a decision. "No, of course not. Well, I had met him, yes. But no, it's just upsetting to hear of a police officer being killed, that's all."

Headlights flashed across them from the direction where Eva's car was parked, and Lance's eyes jerked up to watch it approach. Eva also whirled around.

"Hey!"

Both of them turned at the sound of the voice yelling from over by the cars, and Eva saw the FBI agent named Tervalon walking toward them through the dark. "Officer Cartwright, it looks like we'd better get some cones across the road. Do you have some?"

"Sorry, Eva," Lance said quietly. "Hold on a minute, okay? I'll be right back. Sure I have some," he turned and yelled back at Tervalon. He trotted off toward his patrol car. Eva didn't watch him go. She had turned back toward the approaching headlights, hoping to recognize the car quick enough to run if it turned out to be Benny Fitz. With a good head start, even in her bad shoes, she could make it to where Lance and Tervalon had disappeared into the field of emergency lights.

The car stopped in the middle of the road, and a silhouette appeared. It took only a moment after it walked into the headlights' beams for Eva to recognize the lanky form of Brandon Lucky. Running to him, she threw her arms around him without shame, and he hugged her back.

"Evie! Is everything all right?" He had to speak right into her hair; her death grip was too tight for him to pull away.

"Yes, yes. Thank heavens you're here, Brandon. I've been trying to reach you. Your work phone never picked up, and then I left a message with Karen."

"She told me."

"Oh. Okay, that's good. I'll have to thank her."

"Uhh, not such a great idea. She's already mad enough about me comin' over here."

"I'm sorry, Brandon. I didn't know where else to turn."

Brandon cut her off. "I know, Evie. Your car's broke again. I saw it. And I tried to call you back earlier."

"You did? When?"

"I don't know—two times. Maybe around five, and then around seven."

"But I didn't—" She stopped, and anger flooded her chest. She couldn't keep it from her face. "Belle! She answered both your calls."

"Yeah. It was Belle. She said she'd pass the first message on. The second one she said she thought you had already left."

"At seven? No, I was there."

"Yeah. I called your mom, and she told me what happened with the car. I went to look for you just now—I thought you were supposed to be off at ten. These clowns made me drive all the way around the long way."

"Sorry," she said. "Yeah. I was supposed to be off at ten. Benny decided to let me off at nine instead. I'm sure he didn't want anyone coming to pick me up."

"Jud told me everything," Brandon said. "I'm through with that joint. I quit tonight."

"Oh, no! What are you going to do? Will your mechanic job cover everything for you guys?"

"I guess we'll see. But I ain't workin' for a guy like Benny Fitz no more."

"Thank you, Brandon. It means a lot to me that you'd stick up for me like that."

"Of course! Now let's get you out of here."

"Wait! Before we go, I found something in the grass when I was walking here that I was going to tell Officer Cartwright about."

"Really? What?" At that moment, Lance was walking toward them with his arms loaded down with cones.

"A briefcase. It was lying there in the grass, and it wasn't there earlier in the day when I went by. Weird, huh?"

"Wait—a briefcase? What's in it?"

"I'm not sure. I—"

"Wait, Evie. Don't tell the cops about it yet."

"Why?" Lance was setting the cones out across the road in front of Brandon's car.

"I just have a funny feeling, all right? What happened up here?" He nodded toward the cluster of emergency vehicles.

She lowered her voice. "Don't tell anyone. It sounds like some kind of FBI thing."

Brandon swore, then apologized. "Okay, Evie. We gotta get outta here. There's some guy in a suit walking toward us." He looked over and swore again.

Eva whirled to see Agent Tervalon approaching them. "So don't say anything about the briefcase?"

"No! Please! Just hold on for a while and let's look at it," Brandon hissed.

"Okay, I think it's time for you people to leave," said Tervalon as Brandon and Eva turned to face him. "It looks like you've got yourself a lift now," he observed.

Lance stopped near Tervalon. He looked at Brandon, seeming somewhat suspicious. Eva reached out and touched Lance's arm. "Hey, Lance, since you're busy, I'm going to have Brandon take me home."

"Brandon?" Tervalon cut in. "Hey. I know you, don't I? What's your last name, Brandon?"

Brandon stared at the agent. After several seconds, in a sullen voice he said, "DeWilde."

Tervalon kept staring Brandon down and couldn't see Eva smiling. Apparently, Tervalon wasn't a fan of Western movies, or maybe he would have recognized that Brandon was only being a smart aleck. Brandon DeWilde was the young co-star of the Alan Ladd Western, *Shane*.

"Brandon DeWilde? Have we met, Brandon?"

"You never know. I'm a friend of Shane's." Brandon refused to take his eyes off the agent's hard face.

"Well, I have no idea who Shane is. Listen, you being smart with me, Brandon? I think I know you. I have a feeling we're going to be talking again."

"Funny, I was havin' a feeling we wouldn't be. It'll be cool to see who was right."

"All right, if you two are together, get moving. You can just flip that car around and scram."

"Good as gone," Brandon said. "Come on, Evie."

Eva turned to Lance, her eyes pleading. She didn't want to leave without at least saying goodbye, but right now everything seemed so awkward. As Tervalon looked at Lance, then stalked back toward the crime scene, Lance's glance went from Brandon back to Eva. "You all right?"

She drew a sharp breath, trying to sound strong. "Sure. I'm sorry you're so busy. Like I said, Brandon came looking for me, so I'll just let him take me home."

Lance nodded. "That sounds good. Tervalon is starting to have a cow. I'll call and check on you, all right?"

"Okay. Good night." Eva had thought a minute ago about hugging Lance, but something suddenly felt strange. Was it only the way Brandon was acting? A nagging worry started to pick once more at the edges of her mind. She hated thinking it, but even though Brandon hadn't said anything about Lance by name, he had managed to heighten the doubts in her mind.

Brandon and Eva got into his car, and he wheeled it around in a couple of tries and drove back the way he had come from. At her car, he pulled up, and she looked over at him. "Brandon, do you know something about Lance Cartwright?"

"Why do you ask that?"

"I don't know. You didn't seem to like him."

"Oh, no. Nothin' like that. I'm just tense, I guess."

"Why didn't you want me to tell him about the briefcase?"

"Just paranoid, maybe. And leery of cops, no matter who they're friends with. Let's go look at that briefcase, okay? Then we'll talk about this."

They got out and went to her car, popping the back and unlocking the door for the spare tire compartment. Eva pulled the briefcase out, and as Brandon shut the door they started back toward his car.

Seemingly from nowhere, headlights flared out of the darkness from the direction of the crime scene, and Eva froze. The car that had obviously approached with its lights off for at least a quarter of a mile after coming around the last curve started toward them slowly, and Brandon's voice took on an urgent tone. "Evie! Throw that in my front seat."

Without hesitation, she opened his door and threw the briefcase in as the car came on. It stopped behind Brandon's car, and its dome light came on. Eva wasn't sure, but it looked like Agent Tervalon behind the wheel. He seemed to be watching them, then lowered his head for several seconds. Finally, the dome light clicked off, and he drove up alongside Brandon.

The dark car eased to a stop, and Tervalon got out. "Everything all right?" Eva could hear plenty in the man's voice to indicate he really didn't care. He hadn't stopped out of concern for their well-being.

"Sure, fine."

"Brandon DeWilde, huh?" said Tervalon, as if trying to prove what a great knack he had for remembering names. "I guess I'll see you around, Brandon. Just going to get some doughnuts for the guys."

With that, he sank back down in his car and drove off toward Blairtown.

Brandon got in the car and took a deep breath. "Man. You know how you asked if I didn't like Lance? Well, I like him just fine. But that FBI guy, on the other hand. He really gives me the creeps."

"Me too. Why do you think he bothered to tell us where he was going?"

Brandon thought about it for a second. "Great question. For one thing, who does he think he's kidding? There's no place in Blairtown to buy doughnuts for those guys, and he was halfway to the main part of town already anyway. Let's hurry and see what's in that briefcase." He dug a flashlight out from under the seat and flicked it on, almost blinding them both.

"Will it open?" he asked.

She tried the latches. "No."

"Okay, no prob." He fished around under his seat again until he came up with a flat screwdriver.

She laughed at him. "What *don't* you have under there?"

"A wolverine or a saddle," he said, grinning. It took about ten seconds to pop the briefcase's latches loose, and Eva threw open the lid.

The two of them gawked, and if what they saw didn't scare them out of their senses they would have been fools. With a suddenly trembling hand, Brandon reached over and picked up a paper-banded stack of twenty-dollar bills. He dug below it, and there were three more bundles under the first. He sifted around for a moment to make sure the entire case was filled with the same fresh, crisp bills, then looked up at Eva.

"We gotta beat it, Evie. Come on, let's throw that in the trunk."

They jumped out, looking around them, then popped the trunk, threw the briefcase in, and Brandon shut it tight, then scanned the darkness one more time.

They got back in the car, and he drove slowly away until Eva said, "Shouldn't you drive faster?"

"No way! And catch the cops' attention?"

"I think they're all back there."

"Yeah, well, Tervalon ain't, and we ain't takin' any chances."

Almost as if on cue, lights flared on in front of them again, and a car approached at slow speed. It didn't take long to identify the long black car Agent Tervalon drove, as if they would have had any reason to wonder who was approaching.

"I guess he didn't find any doughnuts," Eva said sarcastically.

"Nope."

After they had passed, the drivers staring each other down, Eva reached over and grabbed Brandon's leg. "Do you think he saw us with the briefcase?"

"I think he was watching. With binoculars. I don't know how much he could see from where he was."

Eva swore, and she didn't bother to apologize.

They drove straight to Eva's house, and Brandon stopped in front. Her heart had been racing a hundred miles an hour, and she finally turned to him. "Brandon, I feel sick to my stomach. Where do you think that money came from?"

"I'm scared to tell you what I think."

She gritted her teeth. "Okay, I guess you're just trying to make me feel better."

She could see he wanted to force a smile at her pathetic attempt to make a joke, but he couldn't manage it. "Evie. Whoever the cops were chasin' jetted that case out the window before they could catch 'em."

"Are you sure?" She didn't say it, but she had been thinking the same thing.

"Pretty dang sure. And who keeps that kind of money around in a briefcase?"

Eva stared at him, a chill running up and down her spine. An obvious answer had been in the back of her mind for quite a while.

"You think it belongs to the Mob?"

"Who else?"

She swore again and apologized this time, neither of which Brandon acknowledged as he kept watching her, speechless.

"What do we do with it, Brandon?"

"Hell, I don't know. You positive nobody saw you walkin' down that road before that FBI creep just now?"

"Yes. Well, no. There was one car that passed me twice, but it was pretty dark, and I crouched down. After that, you were the first car."

"Did you see what the car looked like?"

His question made her feel even more sick than before, and she didn't want to answer him. "Yes, I saw."

"And?"

"I think it was the same car: the FBI guy's."

Brandon closed his eyes and put his hand to his forehead, drawing a deep breath. "Okay. Okay, let's think, Evie."

"Shouldn't we take the money to the police?" she barged into his thoughts.

"No! Evie, you take that money to them, it's gone. The Mob won't have it, and you won't have it either—but the Mob might think you still have it anyway. I know how the fuzz work. They'll freakin' swipe it and claim they never saw it."

"But what about Lance?"

"Are you serious? Evie, I don't want to badmouth your friend, but he's wearin' a badge. You know how much they pay those guys?"

"No."

"Well, it ain't enough to keep them honest." She frowned. She didn't believe Lance would steal the money, and she told him as much. "Well, either way it won't matter. He'll have to turn it in and write up a report, and it won't make it all the way through the chain of command before it mysteriously goes missing. Hundred percent guarantee."

"Then what are we going to do?"

"I think we should lay low, for starters. I think you should hide it. And . . ." A scared look came into his eyes.

"And what, Brandon? *What?"*

"I just thought of somethin'."

"Tell me!"

"That creep was writin' my plate down, Evie—when he stopped behind me back there and his dome light came on. He's gonna know everything about me by morning."

"That's okay, right? We didn't do anything wrong—except you telling him the wrong name."

He raised a hand and pinched his lips so hard it had to have hurt. "I don't know. I don't know, Evie. I bet he'll know I was in the pen. Ah, hell. I just don't know. I think we're in it big. That's what I think. Hey. You got any place you can go stash all that money? Someplace safe where not one soul could find it?"

Eva could feel her pulse pounding in her temples. Her head felt like it was going to explode. "I guess I could find someplace."

"Well, you better find someplace. You better find it fast."

CHAPTER TWENTY-FOUR

EVA COULD NOT SLEEP. She was out of a job, her car was broken down—severely, it seemed—her grandmother was sick, her rent would soon be due, and now, buried deep in the back of her closet, was a large sum of money that apparently belonged to the Mob. Here she sat with all the money she could possibly need, and yet she didn't dare spend one bill of it.

Yet on the other hand, how in the world could she give it back?

It came to Eva deep in the night, when most foolish ideas, and a few brilliant ones, come flashing to weary minds: What if finding the money was God's answer to her prayers? She had prayed hard, and the feeling that had come over her had made it seem so certain her troubles were over—that God was ready to put a plan in place for her and her family to be taken care of. Would she be foolish to give up this money? Without a doubt, if it was Mob money, it was dirty. What if God had provided a way for it to be put to good use, to help good, innocent people? What if it turned out the most foolish and ungrateful thing she could do would be taking the money back to criminals who didn't deserve it? What if the briefcase full of money was nothing but a windfall?

She should have prayed. She normally would have. She wouldn't admit to herself that the reason she didn't pray now was that she wasn't ready to know the truth.

Somewhere in this turmoil of her mind Eva fell into fitful sleep.

The dreams were ugly and dark. Fat, greasy men were chasing her, grabbing her. There were several of them at different times, but in the end all of them turned into Benny Fitz. An austere-looking blond man in a suit pulled the side of his coat aside to reveal a revolver in a shoulder holster when she was with Brandon and Brandon started getting mouthy. It was as dark in the dream as it had been when she met FBI Agent Tervalon, but she knew the man in the dream was one and the same. She was running. Hiding under cars. She found one car and jumped in it, found the key in the ignition, and went to start it up, but a fire erupted from under the hood.

Eva woke up sweating, staring at the dark ceiling. When her heart stopped racing, she fell into deep thought again. What was she going to do?

Maybe the best thing for her was to go to a car lot, buy a new station wagon or van with all her found money, load up her family, what was left of the money, and start heading for some big city as fast as she could drive, to lose herself among the mass of humanity and pray the Mob never tracked her down. After all, what was holding her here in Rock Springs?

That was the thought in her mind when toward morning she finally fell asleep again.

In the early hours not long after sunrise, Eva's eyes popped open, and she came out of bed in a panic. Jud Shouter's revolver! She had left it lying in the grass near the scene of the gunfight!

With her mind in a whirl, Eva stumbled into her pants. Her heart was pounding so out of control she couldn't even laugh when she found she had been putting them on backwards. She had slept in her bra, but even where the edges of it dug into her skin she didn't notice the itching as she dived into a bulky gray sweatshirt and raked her fingers through her hair, glancing at herself in the mirror.

It was then, staring at her sleep-deprived face, she stopped. What was she doing? Was she planning on running all the way to the cordoned-off crime scene on foot to look around for a gun someone might already have found and taken as a potential piece of evidence? Her fingers jumped to her temples and started massaging them roughly, and she jammed her eyes shut. She wanted to cry. Jud had trusted her! She couldn't leave that gun if it was still there. She had to find a way to get it back.

In her wild panic, she thought of Lance. When had he gotten off work? She looked at her clock. It was eight-fifteen. Surely Lance would be asleep. She thought of Brandon. He would still have been her first choice, because he had been in trouble before, and he seemed to have a good grasp of how to handle it or even get out of it. But she couldn't send him down there again. She had asked too much of him already. And besides, since the gun control act of 1968, it wouldn't do for him to be caught in possession of a firearm, because of his status as a convicted felon.

She pulled the heavy mustard-yellow phone off her dresser and took it over to sit on the edge of the bed with it, cradling it like a wounded animal. She had stolen it from the other room and kept it with her for the night, in case of any important phone calls.

Realizing she was shaking, she tried to take deep breaths to calm herself. Lance. It was him she had to call. She didn't have to tell him anything about the money. It made perfect sense for her to have had Jud's gun with her, and just as much sense why she had thrown it down, simply because she knew it wouldn't look good having it in her hand, and she hadn't wanted to take a chance of being caught with a concealed weapon—besides the fact that she had no place to conceal it anyway.

With a trembling finger, she dialed Lance's home number, and waited. It rang only four times before she started feeling sick about the call and pressed down on the disconnect nob on the base. When she let off, the dial tone was humming in her ear.

She sat there in heart-pounding silence. What was she going to do? Who could she talk to? She didn't even dare bring her mother into this, at least not yet.

Feeling sick at heart, she knew Lance was her only answer. *Don't tell him anything. Don't slip. Don't trust anyone.* She was talking to herself in her mind, but she could almost hear her voice out loud. Don't trust anyone? Could she really not trust Lance? She hated admitting it, but Brandon Lucky and Buck Stone had left her with so many recurring doubts. Still, having that gun was innocent. It was! Of course Lance would understand.

She dialed his number again, this time determined not to hang up.

It was six full rings before she heard the phone rattle off the hook on the other end, and for several seconds there was silence. When she was finally about to hang up, she heard a groggy voice say hello.

"Lance? It's Eva."

A long pause. *Hey. Eva? Is everything all right?* She could tell he was coming quickly awake.

"I'm so sorry to call you so early in the morning. I know you must have worked most of the night."

Hey! No, it's okay. Really. What's up? She almost smiled as she listened to his best attempt to sound chipper and alert.

"I need your help. I didn't know who else to call. Gosh, I'm so sorry about the early hour, but I thought if I waited it might be too late."

Serious—stop apologizing. I'm good. I don't have to work tonight, so I can come back and sleep later.

She went on and told him about the gun, and about where she had dropped it. She thought she could hear him trying to get dressed even before they hung up.

Lance Cartwright sat on the edge of his bed in his Levi's and stared at his wide bare feet, thinking it was time for him to clip his nails. While Eva's voice was still in his ear, he felt almost energized and ready to meet the day. Anything to do to help her out. He was embarrassed to admit how that woman affected him. He knew she had kids and was much older than he was, but besides the fact that she was so easy on the eyes, there was something so real and kind and wholesome about her. He had never met anyone quite like her, and he was head over heels— although there was no way he would ever admit it.

But now that they were off the phone and he sat there half-dressed and contemplating the two hours of sleep he had gleaned—if he was lucky—"energized" was a word he would no longer think of to describe his current state of being. He felt more like one of the undead ghouls he remembered from the 1968 movie *Night of the Living Dead.* At least that thought got a smile out of him. When he got up and looked in the mirror, he thought at least maybe he looked a little bit better than those people—if not much.

He put on a blue and cream shadow plaid shirt, which was getting threadbare from years of wear, but was his favorite shirt. Anyway, on a cop's salary he couldn't go out willy nilly buying new shirts simply because an old one got a little thin in the elbows and worn at the cuffs.

He tugged on his brown Wrangler harness boots, which were his pride and joy and which he had had to have resoled now three times. These boots made him feel whole. Next to his dog, his Bronco, and his Model 29 Smith and Wesson revolver,

06 North Valley Center Road

they were the only things he would have a hard time parting with.

Stumbling out of his room, he ate an oatmeal raisin cookie he had started the night before and grabbed a cup of creamed coffee he had set in the coldest part of the refrigerator. He didn't know why icy cold sweet coffee tasted so good, but it did. And right now he sure needed it.

Going out into the front room, he found Moose, his gigantic mutt, sitting on the couch looking out the window. Moose gave him a smile fit for a dog his size and a series of loud thumps of his tail. Was it time to go out? That's what Moose's face was asking, but his grin vanished as if slapped away when Lance went over and gave him a quick scrub of his head and ears and said, "Sorry." Moose knew all too well what that cursed word meant.

"I'll be back in a while," Lance said with a grin, patting the dog one last time on the head. "Don't eat all the best food, huh?"

Reaching under the couch cushion, he pulled out his .44, which was in a holster but didn't have a belt, grinned at Moose, and went out the front door, his car keys jingling on his finger.

He scanned the street as he always did, looking for thugs who might want to make up for his throwing them in jail or beating them down with a night stick, jumped in the Bronco, and fired it up, then sank back in the seat, reveling in the sound of the engine's loud purr.

Off he went back to the scene of last night's investigation, praying he would be returning later with good news for Eva.

He came at the scene from the same direction the chase had taken. Before he reached it, after passing Eva's station wagon, he noticed cars strung along the left side of the road, the same side Eva's car was on. The first was a police car, as was the second. The third one was the black Chevrolet Caprice coupe driven by FBI Agent Cooper Tervalon.

Lance slowed to a crawl as he passed the cars and saw two men—but only two—wandering around in the grass at the side of the road. The uniforms worn by those two men, and the lack of a third person, made him look back to Cooper Tervalon's car, where he made out the driver inside. The man was wearing black-lens glasses, but there was no question he was glaring at Lance as he passed.

Lance pulled over to the roadside and stopped. Officers Jake Glattner and Chris Hinshaw looked at him, and both waved.

"What's up?" Lance asked, wanting to grin but confused about why two cops under the watchful eye of an FBI agent were wandering around in the weeds, rock, and desert sand at nine in the morning after a long night at the crime scene. "You guys lookin' for lucky clovers?"

Both men laughed and came walking over to him. Before Hinshaw could say anything, Glattner said, "Oh, I lost a hubcap around here in the chase. At least I think it was here."

"Oh crap," said Lance. "Want some help?"

Glattner laughed. "No thanks. By the look of your eyes, I'm kind of surprised you could find your Bronco. What the heck you doin' back here anyway? Didn't you end up stayin' out here most of the night?"

"I did. I'm wasted. But I think I might have lost my wallet in the grass somewhere. Can't find it anywhere."

"That was pretty careless," said Chris Hinshaw with a laugh.

"You know me," Lance came back. "Always losin' somethin'."

"You'd lose your mind if you didn't keep it so tight in that cage you call a skull," said Jake Glattner. "So hey—if your wallet's around here, I'd be surprised. We've pretty much scoured this place."

"Huh. Dang. Well, thanks, Glatt. Maybe I'll go look anyway—since I'm already here."

"Suit yourself. I hope you can drag your eyes open wider, though, or you won't be seein' anything."

All of them laughed. Lance started to drive off, feeling sick about the gun. He didn't dare ask if they had found it, for obvious reasons, but if they had scoured this area so well and it was right near the road, he couldn't imagine they hadn't. He thought of something and stopped.

"Hey! I was gonna ask you guys somethin'."

"Shoot," said Glattner.

"Well, I was thinkin' about havin' a summer end barbecue at my place. Might as well use that big back yard for somethin', right? Chris, you can bring your wife. Glatt, bring your girlfriend. And bring your choice of booze or whatever. I'll do the meat. You interested?"

"Sounds like a great time to me," Chris said. "Good luck with Glatt, though. He hasn't even been on a date in two months."

"Man, don't rub it in," Glattner said. "How's an ugly guy like me supposed to get a date anyway, when guys like Hoss are pickin' up all the best-lookin' foxes around here?"

They all laughed again, and Lance said, "Well, let's plan it for some Saturday or Sunday. Afternoon, evening—I don't care. But like I said, bring your own drinks. I can't afford to cover guys that drink like you two animals!"

Lance drove off not thinking about drinks or barbecues. He was thinking instead about what Hinshaw had just said, and Glattner not correcting him: Hinshaw had said Glatt hadn't been on a date in two months? But he plainly remembered Glatt telling him the night he saw him and Hinshaw creeping around in the dark that he had just dropped a date off. It was strange that when his manhood was on the line Glattner didn't even say anything about that.

Half a minute later, he pulled up to the scene, which was still coned and taped off. There was a rescue truck parked on the near edge of the scene, and a privately owned blue Dodge at the far end. He could see someone sitting in each of them.

Stopping crossways in front of the cones he had left, Lance got out and started up the side of the road where Eva had told him she dropped the gun. He hadn't gone twenty steps when to his surprise he spotted it shining up at him out of the grass. He grinned with delight, looking toward Glattner and Hinshaw. How could they have missed this? Luckily, it wasn't a rattlesnake, as the old saying went. He would have loved to rib them about their observational skills, but under the circumstances of course he could say nothing.

Getting back in the Bronco, he stuffed the Astra under his seat, then sat there a moment. He was seized by a sudden harsh thought. Buck Stone. He was dead. Just like that, Buck's life had been snuffed out. That was a hard pill to swallow. Buck was never one of the showy cops. He was never the life of any party. But he was stolid and trustworthy, big enough to be valuable in a fight, but cool and polite enough that he was never known to be the cause of any. Buck would be a hard cop to replace, and Lance was really going to miss that guy.

He thought of Stone's wife and kids, and the thought made him sick. What would that family do now to survive? For them, it was going to be a long, cold winter.

With a sigh, he headed back, stopping again near Jake Glattner and Chris Hinshaw, who looked up from their search. "Still no luck, huh?"

"No, damn it," said Glattner, and his usual grin was gone. "I guess I'll be buyin' a new one."

"Sorry, man. Still sure you don't want any help?"

"No," replied Glattner. "I think we got it covered. I don't think it's here."

"Tough luck. I'm sure they won't make you buy a new one, though. It's just part of the job."

"Yeah, sure. See ya, Hoss," said Glattner.

Lance waved and drove off. As he passed Cooper Tervalon's car, the FBI agent gave him the expressionless stare again. Of course, with his sunglasses on, he could have been asleep. Now why was an FBI agent sitting around on the roadside after being up all night on an investigation? Lance would have thought that man would be in bed, not waiting for a couple of city cops to find a lost hubcap.

He shrugged it off. Some things he simply couldn't wrap his mind around on two hours' sleep. In fact, even after another four hours he wasn't sure that one could make any sense.

Trying to fight his eyes from drooping shut, Lance drove home. He would call Eva with the good news, and then unless she insisted on getting the gun right away, he was going back to bed. Moose would just have to sit out on the sofa, dreaming about eating or going for a walk, and grin to himself. Lance would be lost to the world.

CHAPTER TWENTY-FIVE

WHEN THE PHONE RANG a second time, shortly after hanging up with Lance Cartwright, Eva assumed it was him again. She was so relieved and happy he had found Jud's gun without any issue that she would have been ready to celebrate, if it hadn't been such a long, sleepless night. She didn't know why exactly—possibly in part because of lack of sleep—but she felt almost euphoric.

She jerked the phone off the receiver. "Hello! Lance?"

There was a long pause, and she started to think no one was on the other end of the line. As she was about to hang up, a woman's voice spoke. *Is . . . this Eva? Eva Galanti?*

Taken by surprise, Eva said, "Yes, it is. Who am I speaking to?"

Miss Galanti, please listen. I have to see you right away, okay? My husband left me your number, and I have nowhere else to turn.

"Who is this?" Eva insisted.

My name is Olivia Stone. My husband was Buck, and you called him the other day. He told me I was to call you if anything happened. Miss Galanti, I don't think I have much time. I have to see you right away.

Eva could not remember hearing more fear in another adult's voice. "Mrs. Stone." She stopped. She didn't even know what to say. "Are you all right?"

I have to see you, Miss Galanti. Please!

"Do you need me to call the police for you?"

No! Olivia Stone almost screamed in Eva's ear. *No, I beg you—please! Whatever you do, don't call the police. Don't call anyone. Please drive to my house right away.*

"I can't. My car is broken down."

After another long pause, Olivia Stone said, *Give me ten minutes, all right? I have to gather up my kids. I'll come to you.*

All the fear Eva could feel through the phone line had reached her heart and head, and she was frozen. Did she dare let this woman come to her house? Did she—

The phone went dead. Eva jerked it away and stared at it as if there would be some inscription on it telling her what had happened. In a panic, she jiggled the disconnect button. Moments later, she had a dial tone. What had happened? She started to envision thugs in suits coming to Olivia Stone's house and grabbing her, maybe taking the phone out of her hand.

What should she do now? Did she run? If someone had come for Olivia Stone, would they be here next? Her family's faces popped into her head and she ran for her door, then stopped.

Calm yourself, Eva. Calm down! She had to think. Who could she call? Brandon! Brandon was the only one she knew she could trust. But what about Lance? Her head was spinning. Was Lance a good cop? Was he dirty? Had she told him anything that could be used against her if he was? Eva felt suddenly like a character in an Alfred Hitchcock movie. She wanted to run, but if she ran she had to take all her family, and where could they go? *How* could they go?

Shaking, she dialed Brandon's number. It rang and rang. At ten rings she was about to hang up when she heard it pick up.

Yes?

It was the voice of Brandon's wife, Karen. Oh, how she despised this woman. "Karen, is Brandon there?"

No. He isn't—Eva. He went to tow your piece of crap car to the shop, if you have to know. You listen to me, you little vixen— I've had about all I'm going to take from you. I'm done. Don't call here again—do you understand? Do not call this number again.

"Karen, wait. Listen." Karen didn't wait or listen. The phone was dead.

Running her fingers back through her hair and cupping her temples in her hands, Eva stared at the door. What was she going to do? Olivia Stone couldn't come here even if no one had grabbed her. She had never given her the address. Someone had Olivia Stone. Eva and her family would be next.

She thought of little old Tony Galloway, who lived about eight houses down and around the corner on Soulsby Street. Tony had always been such a kind old man. He must be in his late eighties, and he could hardly get around, so he was always happy to let Eva or Tyke mow his lawn when they came asking. Tony, a retired traveling salesman, had a beautiful deep red Chrysler New Yorker she had seen in his garage one Saturday when he took her inside to get gasoline after her mower ran dry. She had never seen the car out of his garage. Every time he got groceries, and presumably when he got gas for the mower or anything else, there was another neighbor who would pick him up. Tony's eyesight was about shot, and he had told her he was afraid to drive.

So that was it. She would see if he could loan his car to her. If he wouldn't . . . She thought of the briefcase full of cash. Surely he would sell it. Wouldn't he?

Someone knocked, and her mother spoke through the door, "Hey, cara, you coming to eat with us?"

"Yes, Mom. Thanks. I'll be right there." She didn't know how, but somehow she managed to sound perfectly at ease. Now what? Did she go lounge around and eat with her family and wait for the Mob to show up and grab her like they must have Olivia Stone?

So far, Bianca and the others knew nothing. They didn't even know for a fact that Eva was out of a job. They knew—or at least Bianca did—that she had had trouble with Benny Fitz. They knew the car was broken down again. But she had told them nothing else. Nothing about Benny's attack on her. Nothing about the shooting, the wreck, or the killings.

Changing into some more fitting summer clothing, a pair of wide-legged white slacks and a pale blue blouse with a square neck and butterfly sleeves, she slipped her white sneakers on and stepped out of the room, fluffing up her hair as she walked down the hall. She couldn't get her fear for Olivia Stone and for herself off her mind, but she strove to keep it off her face.

"What's for breakfast, Mom? It smells wonderful."

"Well, I thought I would make something French," Bianca said, "so I did crêpes. I hope you like them. I think Leo's going to clean them out if you don't get busy."

Leo, hearing his grandmother say his name to Eva, looked up at her and grinned, his mouth full of crêpes and strawberry preserves. Eva bent and kissed him, ruffling his wispy light chocolate-colored hair. "You look silly, honey bear." She looked at Tyke. "Good morning, buster. What plans do you have for today?"

She wondered how her act was going. Did she seem calm to them? She felt anything but.

As they chatted about pretty much nothing, Eva's heart galloped like a Thoroughbred on the final stretch at Preakness. The food was almost tasteless, and it was hitting her stomach like acid. She felt a need to go throw it up and prayed it wouldn't actually happen. She smiled at Tyke and Leo. She patted Nonni's hand.

A sudden pounding on the front door made Eva leap up. If she had had time to think about it, she would have been glad she didn't already have to pee.

"Who could that be?" asked Bianca. "Tyke, do you want to go see?"

"No!" Eva's voice was too harsh, and everyone turned to look at her. She forced herself to smile. "It's okay, Tyke—you just sit down and finish your breakfast. I'll get it."

Taking a deep breath and trying to fight back tears, Eva set her napkin down and started for the door, staring in fear out the front window through the curtains. Out at the street there was a long blue-gray Plymouth, and she could see someone moving around inside. A glance to the left showed her a heavy-set blonde woman she had never seen before standing at the front door in a pair of green pants and a hideous black blouse covered in nonsensical olive-colored shapes. She was holding a large cardboard box and had her head turned to look at the street.

With another lung-filling breath, Eva opened the door, making the woman's face whip toward her. She gulped a breath.

"Mrs. Stone?"

The woman nodded. "Yes. Olivia."

"How did you know where I lived?"

"It was on my husband's notebook. Listen, Miss Galanti, I'm sorry for coming here, but I have no one to turn to. Buck told me to come to you if anything happened. He said he didn't know who else to trust. Hey—I don't know how you and my husband knew each other. I hope it was . . . professional. I'm sorry. I don't know why he chose you. You didn't—" She stopped whatever she had been about to say, searching Eva's eyes as Eva tried to beat her racing heart back down to a normal pace.

"Olivia, I promise you—I barely knew your husband. He talked to me a couple of times at work, and once on the phone. Honest."

A look of relief washed over Olivia Stone's face. "Okay. Yes, I was home when you called him. Please take this," she said, thrusting the big cardboard box out and forcing Eva to take it from her. "I have no idea what to do with it, so I hope my husband gave you some idea. We're leaving town—me and my boys. I don't know what's in this box. I never wanted to know, and Buck said it would be better if I didn't look. But please be careful. Whatever's in there, I know it got him killed."

With that, Olivia Stone turned and ran down the steps, out the sidewalk to her Plymouth, and sped down the street. She had the look of a woman who would never be setting foot inside the city limits of Rock-Bottom Rock Springs, Wyoming, again.

CHAPTER TWENTY-SIX

EVA TOOK A DEEP breath and turned to the door. She hated
lying to her family, but right now the last thing she wanted to do
was admit the truth. Her first tack, Plan A, was subterfuge: head
for the bedroom without saying anything. Plan A took a nose-
dive.

"What's that, Mom?"

Plan B was to spout off with some innocent-sounding lie to
Tyke before anyone else got involved. "Just some old maga-
zines my friend Mrs. Stone didn't want anymore. She thought
there might be some recipes in them I'd want."

And thus do Plans A and B quickly begin to unravel, because now Eva's mom looked over. "Stone? Isn't that the name
of the police officer who was killed?"

Eva froze. She had purposely chosen to say nothing about
yesterday's events, but at the same instant she found herself asking how her mother already knew, she heard chatter on the radio
in the background, and everything fell into place.

"Oh, yes, I think it was, Mom."

"That was right over near your work, wasn't it?" asked her
mother then. "Oh, silly me! Go put that box down. It looks
heavy."

Eva forced a smile before marching down the hall, pushing
her door open with her foot, and setting the box on the bed. Her
heart was still smashing against her ribcage, and she struggled

for solid breath. She didn't want to know what was in this box. She almost hated Officer Stone for getting her involved.

With a trembling hand, she reached down and picked up a black and red hard-cover ledger. She opened it to a place somewhere in the middle and started scanning. It contained dates, and times, people's names, a few dollar figures. One she saw said $2000.00, with the letters "PD" scrawled across from it on the outside column. She dropped the book as if scalded and backed away, coming to an abrupt stop amid a pain in her back, and the muffled sound of her own cursing. She had run into the edge of her own door.

For several seconds, Eva rammed her eyes shut, willing the pain away, and her breath and pulse to return to normal. The three of them continued on, uninterrupted, regardless of her will.

She went out into the hall and pressed the door shut, then walked to the kitchen as if she didn't have a care in the world.

"So I didn't hear all the news, Mom," she said casually. Now she was fishing to find out how much her mother already knew. "What did you say happened?"

"Oh, they said something about an attempted drug bust down in Blairtown, and then I guess there was a car chase. Whoever was in the car started shooting at the police somewhere over north of Benny's—on Blairtown Avenue, it seems like—and then wrecked. The driver ended up in the hospital in a coma. There is a police officer and an FBI agent both dead."

"That's awful, Mom!" Eva said.

"I know. I find it hard to believe something like that can happen in a little town that was so peaceful and quiet such a short time ago. What was the FBI even doing in Rock Springs? This place has changed so much in the last year. It breaks my heart."

Eva swallowed hard. It was all she could do to keep meeting her mother's eyes, but she didn't dare look away. Her mother was too astute at reading her. A vision of Ambro Procopio, Primo Santori, and Gavino Berretti flashed across her mind, with Serenella Santori following after.

"It's pretty strange," she admitted, then smiled and reached out to ruffle Leo's fine hair. "So are there any more crêpes, Mom, or did the boys get them all?"

"No, cara, I saved you some. You know I wouldn't let you starve. You're too skinny already."

Eva laughed. "I'll always be too skinny for you, Mom. If I weighed one hundred ninety pounds you would say I was too skinny."

With a new round of crêpes on her plate, Eva covered them with strawberry preserves and rolled them up, then spooned whipped cream on top of them and cut off a dainty bite with her fork, trying to make herself look like she was anticipating the taste.

Tyke grinned. "Gee, Mom, you'll never finish breakfast if somebody doesn't show you how to get a real bite!"

"Oh, stop." She bumped Tyke on the end of his nose with her fingertip. "Don't you know that's how you stay skinny?"

"I guess so. Hey, Mom, do you think we could go to Monkey Ward and get me some new shoes sometime before school starts up again?"

She cringed inside, but on the outside she smiled. He had no idea they were as broke as dropped records, and there were no more paychecks or tips coming anywhere in their near future. "Sure, kiddo. Are your old ones really that worn out?"

In reply, he held one foot up, and Eva looked at the gray sole of it and again cringed. One place was so thin she could almost see his sock through the bottom of it. "Ohhh . . . kay. Yeah, we'd better go shopping." She thought of the money hiding in her closet. What if she took a little? Just enough to get by. Even if it was only a couple of twenties, slipped out of one of the bundles. No one would ever notice forty dollars, would they?

"We need flour too," said Bianca, from where she was scraping the last of the crêpe batter into her prize pan. She had brought home the flat cast iron pan, designed specifically for cooking crêpes, after her one trip to Europe. "And maybe some eggs. We should probably start a list. When do you get paid again, cara?"

"Umm . . . I think it's this Friday, isn't it?" Eva felt sick. She hated lying to her own mother, and she couldn't keep up this charade forever anyway. How could she even carry it past her first workday, which was scrawled on the calendar for all to see? It was either pretend to be sick and say she had called in, or she was going to have to leave and go somewhere for nine hours so they thought she was working.

And that workday started at one o'clock that afternoon.

She looked down at her plate. Half her food was still on it. "Hey, do you boys want to divide the rest of this? I don't have much of an appetite."

That was like asking dogs if they wanted a steak. Tyke didn't ask if Eva was sure. He just grabbed her plate. To no surprise, he cut off a bigger portion for Leo than he kept for himself. Eva didn't doubt he could have eaten more, but Tyke always looked out for his baby brother.

Telling everyone she was going to lie back down for a while, as Eva was walking away down the hall, she heard an unmistakable voice come over the radio: *Hello, Americans. This is Paul Harvey. Stand by for news!* On any normal day she would have stayed. Paul Harvey's *News and Comment* had always been a must-listen in the Galanti household. But right now she only wanted to lie on her bed and think . . . or not.

There was one good thought for her the moment she closed her eyes, lying on the bed, and this one thought was the one she tried to drift off to sleep to: She *would* have one more check, if Benny was honest. Even though she didn't have a job anymore, she still had one more payday . . . if she but had the guts to go pick up her check.

Lance Cartwright's eyes popped open, and he swore. His oaf of a mutt, Moose, was licking his hand, but that wasn't why he swore. He swore because out of the blue it had hit him that he had been so tired when he got off work at seven that morning that he had forgotten to turn in three citations, one for a red light and two for speeding. Moose tilted his blocky head and stared at him.

"Don't look at *me* that way, dummy. You'd swear too if you could." He grinned, feeling his eyes close almost all the way over with sleep. He swung his legs over the side of the bed, scratching all around the dog's head. "Okay, bud, I have to go to work for a bit. You can hang tight, right?"

Moose fired his tongue at the back of his hand and nailed him square with half an ounce of spit.

"Good. Real good," he said, wiping his hand off on the dog's thick fur as he stood up. "Come on, mutt."

Lance went to the kitchen, and Moose followed him. Pulling a bottle of grape Nehi out of the fridge, Lance used the back edge of a knife blade to pop it open. Moose was staring at him with those big eyes he couldn't resist, so he cupped him under the chin and trickled several tablespoons' worth of pop down his throat, watching with a laugh as Moose slurped it up.

"All right, man, that's enough. You'll rot your teeth out." Tilting the bottle up, he drained half of it down his own throat and let out a belch, then dragged the refrigerator door open again. "Don't got a thing in here do we, bud? Aw, what the heck." He took a package out that had two sirloin steaks in it and pulled them apart, throwing one in its entirety to Moose, then putting the other one back for later.

Grabbing a package of Twinkies off the countertop, he ripped it open and stuffed one whole into his mouth, then went back to the bedroom and got dressed while trying to chew the double mouthful. Pressing his hair down with the spit-moistened palm of his hand, he went to the door and gulped down the last of the Twinkie. "All right, Chubby, you stay here and guard the castle, huh? I'll be back with some food in a while."

Out of the jumble of the sentence, Moose caught the word "food", and his ears came up. "Yeah, yeah. Just . . . be good."

Lance drove to the city building at the corner of Broadway and B Streets, which was also the police station and, in the back, the fire station. It was a massive, beautiful two-story building of cut brown stone, with a decorative cream-colored clock tower capped off by a highly verdigrised copper cap and a lightning rod. Parking his Bronco out at the curb, he gathered his citations and ran up the front steps and inside, where a right turn took him into the police section. No one was around, not even Rhonda, the dispatcher. He threw the tickets on the chief's desk and scrawled a quick note to explain why he had forgotten them that morning, then headed back out to his car.

As he was stepping out the front door, he saw his buddy Rick Cohen pulling his blue Plymouth Fury up to the curb in front. He walked down the steps to meet him, intent on talking to him about his planned barbecue.

Rick got out of his car. "Hey, Hoss. What's happenin'?"

Lance explained his faux pas with the tickets, then said, "Hey, how's about a summer-end barbecue? I asked Glatt and Chris, and they're both game."

They talked it out for a minute before Rick said, "Sure is too bad about Buck, man. I think we oughtta do somethin' for Livvi. Her an' those boys are gonna have a rough time, huh?"

"Man, I know. Makes me sick every time I think about it. I don't imagine she'd wanna go to the party, huh?"

"Jeez, I can't imagine," Rick agreed. "Prob'ly the last place she'd want to be."

"Yeah. You know, maybe on my way home I'll go check on her. See if they need anything."

"Yeah? Good idea," Rick said. "Think I should go with you?"

"Nah, prob'ly not. I bet if we went one at a time it'd be easier."

"Sure, sure. Hey! I been meanin' to tell you about somethin'. Somethin' weird! And it kinda makes me mad." Rick stopped and looked at the door, jerking his thumb at it. "Anybody else in there?"

"Not in our side. Even Rhonda's gone."

"Wow. That's weird. So hey—come back in for a sec."

They went in the station, and Rick walked over to look in the chief's office, as if not quite sure Lance was telling him the truth. Lance laughed. "What's up, brother? Don't trust me?"

Rick allowed himself a nervous laugh. "Man, Hoss, it's gettin' where I don't know *who* to trust."

Lance went serious. "What're you talkin' about?"

"Well, I was gonna tell you the other day. Remember how I told you your friend Eva was riding around with a guy named Ambro Procopio, and I stopped him *screamin'* up Railroad Avenue?"

"Of course. And you wrote him a ticket."

"Yeah. That was as good as any speedin' ticket I ever gave. I think I could even have gone with reckless and arrested the guy."

"Yeah? So?"

"So I turned it in that night, but I never told you what happened the next mornin'. I had some reports that I got held over writin', so I was here when Buyer came in. I was gettin' a Coke out of the fridge, and I heard a phone call come in, which he took. What got my attention was I heard him mention my name. Yeah. He says somethin' like, 'Oh, yeah, Rick Cohen.' And then he asks whoever's callin' if there's some kind of problem. So no crap, man—I'm listenin' by the door now, 'cause . . . Well, you know—waitin' to see if I'm gonna catch flak from Joe Citizen. Anyway, Chief says somethin' like, 'All right, no problem. I see it now, here on my desk. It's taken care of.' So I took off and went in the bathroom, and after a while I heard the back door shut, and when I come out Buyer's gone, I guess to some meeting. I tried his door, and it wasn't locked, so I went in, and that ticket I wrote? It was gone."

"Gone? What do you mean 'gone'?" asked Lance.

"Gone off his desk. There was a whole pile of paperwork there, includin' a bunch of other tickets, some of them ones I had turned in at the same time as Procopio's. But his wasn't in the stack. I looked around in the garbage, and there was nothing there either. So I headed out just on a gut feeling to the garbage in front, since that was the way Buyer left. That ticket was in there, Hoss. He friggin' threw it away! I'm not makin' this up. That was something like a sixty in a twenty-five speeding ticket, man. What's up with that?"

Lance frowned. How long ago had he been in Chief Buyer's office getting chewed out for not writing enough tickets? He told Rick about that incident.

"Yeah, see? See? He's always on us about tickets, and then some schmuck calls him up and he just throws one away that was rock-solid?"

"Did anybody ever say anything to you about it?"

"No, but I took the ticket out of the garbage and took it home with me. I can't stop lookin' at it. Chief sold me out, Hoss. I don't know what to make of it."

"Good old boys' club," Lance said with a shrug. "Maybe that's all."

"Ha. Yeah. Right. Well, I guess, but it sure doesn't make me feel like ever writing any more tickets."

"No, you just have to know better than to write 'em to the Chief's friends."

CHAPTER TWENTY-SEVEN

LANCE CARTWRIGHT DECIDED TO drive by Olivia Stone's house on his way home from the grocery store. When he got there, her Plymouth wasn't outside, but he went up and knocked on the door anyway. The house had an oddly vacant look to it when he looked through the picture window in front, so he leaned closer and raised one hand to create shade, giving it a more thorough study. What he had noticed that was strange was empty walls, and now he saw not only that there were un-used nails sticking out where Buck Stone used to hang a collection of Western art he cherished, but that there was a fairly large collection of boxes over against the far wall, the wall that backed up to the kitchen. He had also noticed coming up the drive that there weren't any bikes or other toys around, and that was more than a little odd. Buck and Olivia, with their three rambunctious sons who loved being outside, almost always had stuff like that lying around.

The Stone place looked like a moving zone, yet not every-thing was gone. He made a mental note to himself. He *had* to come back and check on Olivia and the boys. What in the world would make her move, especially this fast? They hadn't even had the funeral service for Buck yet.

With a sick feeling gnawing at his guts, he went back out to the Bronco and headed home.

Admitting to her mother that she had lost her job at Benny's was one of the hardest things Eva had ever had to do. She had known it was going to be difficult, but she hadn't expected all the tears. Something was turning her into an emotional wreck lately. Maybe a *lot* of somethings.

She told her she had lost her job, but to protect her there were other things she hadn't told her. She hadn't told her about Ben-ny's attack. She hadn't told her she had been at the scene of the gunfight. And she hadn't told her about the briefcase full of money. While she was lying on her bed later, thinking about how wise it was to hide so much from Bianca, and wondering if it would come back to bite her, the phone rang. She had no desire to pick it up, and she hoped it wasn't for her.

"Mom!" Tyke's voice sailed through the closed door. Eva frowned. She seemed to have no luck with anything.

Going to the phone, she picked it up and covered the mouthpiece, yelling out to Tyke that she had it. When she heard him hang up, she put it to her ear and spoke tentatively. "Hello?"

Hi, Eva. Hey, it's Lance.

"Oh, hey! Did you get some sleep?"

I did. I sure feel a lot better.

"I'd like to get the gun and take it back to Jud, but I'm still broke down, and I haven't heard from Brandon yet," she said.

Well good. He laughed. *Sorry, that didn't sound nice. But I wanted to ask you somethin'. Oh, wait. First—do you have to work today?*

"I don't have to work at all," she said. "I don't have a job."

Oh no! Dang, that's not good.

She smiled grimly. "No, in this case it's very good."

I hope you find somethin' else soon. But in the meantime, I was hopin' I could come get you and take the gun back to your friend, and then . . . Remember you said we could go to a movie? It's the last night for American Graffiti.

Eva cringed. She had been hoping to hang out at home with the family and relax. But she had told Lance she would see a movie with him, and after his going back to the police scene and getting Jud's gun for her, especially when he had hardly slept all night, she certainly owed him, and much more than only a date.

"Okay, yeah. What time do you want to come? We won't be able to take the gun back until Jud comes in to work tonight, but we could go to the movie first. But before that, maybe . . . Oh, never mind—silly idea.

No! he said. *What?*

"Well, it sounds corny, and I'm sure you have a lot of stuff you could be doing, but would you like to come over and hang out with me and the boys for a while?" There was a pause that to Eva seemed too long. "Sorry! I knew it sounded dumb. Maybe some other time."

No, Eva—it doesn't sound dumb at all. I'd love to do that. I get a kick out of your kids.

That gave her a big smile. "Okay. Well, you could come over any time then. I'm just waking up from a nap. We could cook some hotdogs or something."

Now you're talkin' my kind of diet. Let me feed Moose and the dumb fish, and then I'll head your way. Maybe half an hour?

Eva hung up with a smile on her face. That made two of those smiles for which she owed Lance. Before that there hadn't seemed to be too much reason for smiling all day.

The boys enjoyed being with Lance. Tyke got him to play checkers, Tyke's favorite game, and they even went out on the front lawn to throw a football back and forth. Eva and Bianca took Leo out, and while Bianca sat holding Leo on a lawn chair, Eva joined her son and the over-grown boy that was Lance. A couple of times someone said something or did something that got them all laughing, and it felt so good that all the doubts about Lance Eva had allowed to pick at the edges of her mind evaporated.

They went back in the house after everyone was worn out and sweaty, boiled some hotdogs, and ate with relish—both figuratively and literally. For a little while, Eva was able to convince herself that everything was going to be all right.

Sitting on the sofa sipping Hires root beer, Lance suppressed a belch that Eva was certain would have been monumentally impressive after putting down half a glass of the ice-cold brew. Tyke, a few seconds later, had no such manners. While Eva gasped and cried out her son's name, Lance broke into laughter.

"Well, great—now you encourage him," she said.

That made Lance laugh harder. He shrugged apologetically. "Well, it was a pretty good one, you have to admit."

Eva giggled. "Yeah, I guess it was a pretty good one. You could at least say 'excuse me'," said Eva, giving a mock frown to her son.

"Yeah. Excuse me," said Tyke.

With a grunt of disgust, Eva said, "Uh-huh. I can tell you're sorry."

Tyke looked back and forth from Eva to Lance. He and Leo couldn't stop grinning.

"Hey, Eva," Lance shot all the fun in the hind-end. "I don't want us to have to rush off, but . . . Well, I was wonderin' if you could maybe go with me somewhere before the movie. I need to go see someone, and it might be good to have a woman there." That was as far as his explanation went, leaving Eva more than curious.

"Oh, yeah. Sure. Now?"

Lance looked at his watch. "Yeah, prob'ly. It's five-thirty, and the movie starts at seven."

"Okay, let me get my purse." She started to stand up at the same time he did.

"Do you need your purse?" Lance asked, making Eva stop and stare dumbly at him. The thought of leaving her purse had never crossed her mind. And then another thought came to her: She *had* no purse! She had lost it to the thieves who raided her broken-down car.

When she told that to Lance, he said, "Maybe we should go over to the station before the movie and see if anyone brought it in. Most thugs like that aren't gonna keep a purse. They'll just toss it after they get whatever they want out of it."

With that hopeful thought in mind, because regardless of its value Eva kind of liked that purse and wanted her family photos back, they said goodbye to her family, then drove straight to the city building. Lance took Eva inside with him and seated her on a chair while he went back in the evidence room, in an area where they collected things people had turned in. When he came back out, he had five purses of varying sizes. Before he could say anything, there came a loud, eerie moaning from behind a door not far away. Startled, Eva looked over at Lance.

"What was that?"

"Oh, jeez. Sorry about that. The jail's back there, and we got a strung-out girl in our padded room. I guess she got a hold of some bad LSD."

"Oh." Eva stared at him, her guts tightening up. The very thought of that made her feel sick. She guessed in spite of her job at the bar and grill she was still pretty sheltered and naïve, especially for a woman her age.

Lance shook his head and shrugged an apology when the wailing started up again. "Sorry." He hefted the pile of purses. "So any of these look familiar?"

Her attention drawn away from the distressed wailer, Eva gasped, looking at one medium-sized purse made of fake brown cowhide. "You have to be kidding me! That's it!"

"Okay, well there you go," Lance said with a big grin. "I guess I'm not just some big dumb worthless oaf after all."

A voice surprised them from around the corner: "I beg to differ!" A dark-haired, handsome man poked his head around and laughed. "Hey, Hoss! Carryin' purses these days?"

"Yeah, funny. Just bein' a lady's knight in shining armor, that's all."

The stranger's dark eyes slid over and stopped on Eva. "Wow. Oh, sorry," he said with a grin. "I didn't mean to ogle." He came around from the other side of the wall where he had been and walked over to them, introducing himself as Jake Glattner with a slight bow to Eva and offering his hand.

Eva was taken aback. This man was strikingly good-looking. She took his hand, feeling like he was a bit too brave staring her down. "Hi, I'm Eva Galanti."

Glattner seemed to freeze for a moment. The smile that slid over his face came across as a cover for his surprise.

Lance went on: "Eva, we call this goon 'Glatt', but you don't have to remember that. I wouldn't let him be around you again if you paid me."

Glattner laughed. "Are you guys on a date picking out purses?" Eva had the funny feeling he only wanted to know if they were on a date, period. She also couldn't shake the feeling that he had recognized her name. He wasn't quite able to hide his surprise on hearing it. But it could be that he had heard Lance talking about her before. It seemed that was how everyone else who worked here knew her.

"Yep. On a date," said Lance, then promptly fumbled all the purses, dropping Eva's upside down on the floor before she could catch it.

Both trying to be chivalrous, to the tune of the distressed woman wailing beyond the wall, Lance and Glattner crouched down and started picking everything up, handing it back to Eva to stuff into her purse. The last item Glattner started to hand over was a business card. Like a typical cop, his curiosity made him flip it over and glance at it.

He froze, then looked up at Eva as he held the card out for her to take. "Buck Stone? Looks like everybody around here knows you but me," the dark-haired officer said. Eva caught the snap of Lance's eyes as he looked at her, and then saw a look that passed between Lance and the other man. An uneasy feeling came over her. Suddenly, she really wanted to be out of this place.

"Did you know Buck very well?" Glattner asked, trying to pull off acting casual but failing.

"Well, no, not well. I mean, yes, we met, down at Benny's. We had talked. That's all." Glattner had hardly asked her any-thing, but with the way both he and Lance were staring at her, and with the strange aura now in the room, she felt like she was being interrogated. It wasn't a feeling she appreciated.

An open office door suddenly pushed wider to their right, and out of doorway stepped a well-built man of some fifty years old in a uniform complete with tie. He wore no gun, only a black uniform belt held up by diamond-shaped belt loops. The man looked each of them over, his eyes landing last on Eva, and his smile revealing deep dimples.

"Did I hear right, Miss? You knew Officer Stone? Oh, I'm sorry to be rude. I'm Chief Buyer. You can call me Howard." He stopped and waited, his eyes almost demanding that she give him her name.

Eva nodded and took his proffered hand. "Eva. Nice to meet you. And no, I didn't really know Officer Stone. I just spoke with him briefly when he came to Benny's Bar and Grill where I work—on a call," she fibbed.

"Oh. So, Eva . . . ?"

"Galanti."

"Ohh." He drew the word out oddly, and his eyes flitted inconspicuously over to Glattner. "Galanti. So you didn't really know Buck. Well. I guess under the circumstances that's a good thing."

"But apparently Buck was in the habit of just passing out his business card with his home phone on it to all the pretty girls," inserted Jake Glattner, grinning and winking at the chief when he looked over at him again.

The chief tried to keep a smile on his face, turning his eyes back on Eva, eyes that were somehow disturbing. She decided that the best way to describe them was crazy. He had crazy eyes—odd for a police chief, she had to guess.

"Well, I don't suppose you'll need that number anymore," said the chief. "Here, I can throw that in the trash for you."

The offer seemed bizarre—unnecessary, really—but Eva looked over at Glattner, who stepped forward and gave her the card. She instantly handed it to the chief, and he wadded it up and poked it down into the front pocket of his sharply creased black polyester pants. A smile came back onto his face, bringing wrinkles out to the sides of those crazy pale blue eyes. "Nice meeting you . . . Eva. Guys." He nodded at the others, then turned and sauntered back into his office, shutting the door behind him.

Eva shifted her eyes over to Lance, wondering abruptly if he was no longer her knight in shining armor, and if not, then why. He certainly had remained silent during most of the odd exchange. "We'd probably better go if we want to see the movie."

"Oh, sure," agreed Lance. "Good seein' you, Glatt."

"You bet, man! Nice to meet you, Eva." Jake Glattner's manner seemed as gallant and polished as anyone's, other than perhaps that of Ambro Procopio. And at least compared to the chief's demeanor, it actually seemed almost genuine.

"You too," she said, and she wanted to mean it. But she couldn't shake the uneasy feeling Glattner continued to give her.

She and Lance went outside, and he wasted no time. "So hey . . . When we talked about Buck before, you said you had met him, but you said you didn't really know him." It was a flat statement she was left to take however she wanted to. Was Lance interrogating her now too? She had known Stone much better than she had been admitting to anyone. But why did it matter? She was starting to get a sick feeling in the pit of her stomach.

"Does it make any difference?" she said, trying to keep the shakiness out of her voice. "I think I told you, he came in Benny's one time, and we talked for a little while. I guess I saw him one other time, but that's it." She didn't tell him about talking on the phone. Her bad gut feelings about the whole affair were returning to her now in force.

"I'm sorry. No, I guess it doesn't matter, but . . ."

"But what?" She was trying to stand her ground. Trying to appear strong.

"But I was just thinkin' if you knew him very well, I'm sure glad I asked you to come with me today. That place I wanted you to go with me was over to Buck's house, to see his wife Olivia."

Eva stared up at Lance. The revelation was startling, but she didn't know how to feel about it. Maybe she simply felt too suspicious about people lately, but it seemed almost as if . . . Was Lance guessing she and Buck Stone had been having an affair or something? The thought made her feel like she had been punched in the stomach. She had barely known the man! She wanted to say something, but how did she tell Lance how she and Buck had become acquainted, when Buck himself hadn't seemed to trust *anyone?* In fact, if he had trusted Lance, why hadn't he told his wife to turn the cardboard box over to him, instead of a woman who was almost a complete stranger?

"So do we still have time to see her before the movie?" To Eva's own ears, she sounded almost like a robot. She was hoping they wouldn't have time to see Olivia Stone, or that she wouldn't be home if they went. What if Olivia admitted she had already seen Eva once today? What if she couldn't hide the shock in her eyes at seeing her again? What if she instantly thought Eva was in on something with Lance? Eva's mind was in a whirl from which there seemed no escape.

"I think we might be able to squeeze it in before the show," said Lance. "Is that still okay?"

Eva almost wished she could throw up right in front of Lance, so she wouldn't even have to tell him she was suddenly not feeling well; he would see for himself. "Sure, if you think we have time."

Lance smiled. She guessed the uncertain look of it was because he was reading the looks in her face. Maybe that was the worst thing about going on dates with a cop: They were too well-trained at reading people.

As they walked by the left side of Jake Glattner's patrol car, which Eva hadn't even noticed when they first parked, Lance looked down. "Huh. That's weird."

She turned her eyes to him, drawn to the bait and almost glad to have something else to talk about. "What?"

"Well, Glatt told me he lost a hubcap in the chase. But all four of them are still on his car. That's bizarre."

"Do you think he got a new one?"

"They don't look brand-new," he said. "Besides, I think they would have had to order one in. I was sure he said it was off his

car." To clarify, he told her the story of how Glattner and Hinshaw had been walking around the side of the road searching in
the grass when he drove past her car, with Tervalon there seeming to be watching over them. "Maybe it was Chris's car," he
said, shaking his head. "But I sure would have sworn Glatt said
it was his. Oh well. Maybe they found it after I left."

They got in his Bronco and sat down. Lance fired it up, then
took a deep breath. Finally, he turned to Eva. "Hey. I don't want
to butt in on your business, Eva. I feel like a total jerk for even
askin' you anything, and you don't have to say one thing. But I
was gonna go over to the Stone place and see if Buck's wife
needs help with anything. I tried to see her earlier, and nobody
was around. When I looked in the window it even looked like
she was packin' up to move. I want to help her, but I don't want
to put you in a bad situation."

"Lance . . . If you're asking me if there was anything between me and Buck Stone, the answer will always be no." She
guessed her voice probably didn't sound overly happy with him.

He stared her down as long as he could keep his eyes there.
"I'm sorry, Eva. I can take you home if you'd rather."

She drew in a deep breath and let it sigh out, then reached
out a shaky hand and squeezed his arm. "Hey. Lance, we live in
a messed-up world. I know it as well as you do, even if I'm not
a policeman. I know things happen. I don't blame you for wondering."

She wanted suddenly to tell him about her relationship with
Stone, about the reason for his first visit, about the phone calls,
his suspicions and doubts, about Olivia Stone's earlier visit. She
wanted to tell him all of it so bad she ached. But she had to have
time to think. She couldn't remember for certain, but it seemed
like she might have promised Brandon she wouldn't say anything. She at least needed to talk to him first, although she was
pretty sure what he would tell her. In the end, in the few seconds

she had to decide, she chose to go with Lance to the Stones', and just hope Olivia wasn't there when they arrived.

"Let's go see Mrs. Stone," she said, patting his arm before she dropped her hand. "I can tell it would make you feel better."

Down deep, she prayed they weren't going to pay a visit to Olivia Stone only so Lance could try to get a feel for her and see if she knew anything. Maybe it would serve the same purpose, but for Eva, not Lance. Perhaps it was exactly what she needed to help her know for sure if he was the good, honest man she believed him to be.

She made up her mind: If a single thing seemed out of place, she was going to distance herself from Lance, and permanently. She could afford to take no chances.

CHAPTER TWENTY-EIGHT

BEFORE THEY STOPPED, EVA knew which house belonged to Olivia Stone. The blue Plymouth she had seen Olivia driving was parked in the driveway. Her heart had already been racing; now it seemed in danger of jumping out of her chest. She could hear its pulse against her eardrums, a sign she had always believed must also mean her blood pressure was ready to explode.

She risked a sideways look at Lance, hoping she would see something good in his face. Instead, she saw no expression at all—the face of a poker player. He could have been mentally trying to prepare himself to console a new widow, or he could have been figuring out how to silence her forever.

Lance threw the Bronco in first, set the brake, and looked at Eva. "It would be nice to have some moral support, but I won't ask you to go in if you don't feel comfortable."

Her mind raced. Would Olivia say anything about the box? Would she let on that they had already met? This could easily backfire. But Eva was already in it. She might as well jump. "I'll go with you. I think it will be easier for both of you."

They got out and started for the door. Before they had even reached the two concrete steps going up to the landing, Eva saw Olivia Stone. She was standing behind the glass storm door, staring out at them both. The fear in her eyes was unmistakable, and although at first she had been looking right at Lance, all her attention now was on Eva. Eva gave her a tiny but adamant shake of her head and tried to make her see the warning look in her eyes. She could only pray Olivia would know her meaning.

Eva could sense how hard it was for Olivia to push open the storm door, but she did. Her eyes were now riveted on Lance.

"Hi, Lance. Can I help you?"

Lance froze on the bottom step, Eva still on the sidewalk. After a moment, he gathered himself. "Hi, Olivia. I was just comin' to check on you. And tell you how sorry I am." Eva would have had a hard time imagining Lance looking more uncomfortable than he had when he was asking her out, but right now he did. Her gut instinct told her this man was not one they would have sent here to see if Olivia Stone knew something she shouldn't. Olivia must have seen that too.

"Thank you, Lance. Do you want to come in for a minute?"

"Sure," said Lance, and he turned to Eva to motion her up in front of him, taking her elbow. When they got in the house and the door shut, Lance said, "Olivia, this is a friend of mine, Eva Galanti. I hope you don't mind me bringin' her along."

Olivia's glance faltered when she looked at Eva. "No. No, of course not. Hi, Eva."

Eva forced a scared smile and extended her hand, which Olivia took briefly. There were three boys seated on a sofa, staring at the TV. One of them, the oldest, got up a few seconds later and came over to stop by his mom. "Hi, Lance," he said quietly.

"Hey, buster." Lance dropped to a knee, something he was probably used to having to do with kids. "You doin' okay?"

As is often the case, words of concern bring out emotions, and they did for the boy, who started to go to tears and rushed forward to hug Lance, as if to hide his emotions in the big man's shirt.

"I'm sorry, Doug," Lance said, patting and rubbing the boy's back alternately. The boy was openly sobbing now, and that set Olivia off.

The pain in Eva's eyes for Olivia must have been obvious, and Olivia must have needed someone to cling to. Eva was shocked when Olivia's face twisted with pain, the tears started, and she stepped close and hugged her, so tight it was difficult to breathe.

The two younger boys, who might have been four and six, seemed to realize the raw emotion in the room could no longer be pretended away, for they both got up, and the younger one instantly started crying and hugged his mother's leg, while the six-year-old joined the communal embrace of Lance and Doug.

Olivia, obviously embarrassed, stepped away from Eva long before the boys stopped hugging Lance, keeping him down on one knee. She went to another room and came back holding her youngest son and a box of Kleenex.

The two older boys finally managed to pull away from Lance, but then they stood awkwardly hanging onto his legs. Eva guessed considering the nickname he had for the older one that they must be pretty familiar with him. That made Buck Stone's apparent lack of trust that much more disconcerting.

Olivia was obviously striving to keep herself together. But it wasn't only her: No one in the room seemed able to find a comfortable place to put their eyes. There were tears still streaming down Olivia's cheeks, despite her best attempts to push them away with a disintegrating tissue. Lance kept trying to console her with his eyes, but it only made her raw emotion worse.

Finally, it was simply too much. Olivia was shaking, her eyes puffy and red. She set her smallest boy down and almost fell into Lance's arms, and for a long time he held her while Eva stood wishing she either knew Olivia better or that she could be somewhere else, somewhere far from here.

Lance was a huge Teddy bear, so it wasn't hard for Eva to understand how comforting it must be to be held by him. The thought crossed her mind to go back out to the Bronco, but that would be even more awkward than staying. Instead, she started talking to the two older boys, pulling their attention away from their mother and Lance and distracting them with conversation about school, and about their interests. All the while, Lance held onto Olivia and the youngest boy, and Eva guessed a good five minutes went by. It seemed more like an hour.

"Thank you for coming, Lance," Olivia finally said between sniffles, managing to pull away from him and looking down at the floor as she blew and then wiped her nose. She tried to look up into Lance's eyes, and as she attempted to speak, tears again rushed into her eyes, and she crushed her fist to her mouth. Finally, she managed to say, "Buck sure did love you. I hope you know that."

Eva looked up at the wrong time, right when tears flooded Lance's eyes and he ground his teeth together. He stepped close to Olivia again and hugged her. Anything would be more comfortable than standing there letting everyone see his tears. "Thanks for telling me that, Livvi. I sure loved him too. We'll never be able to replace that guy."

When they finally walked away from the Stone place and got back in the Bronco, Eva knew two things: Olivia Stone was moving, but she had determined to stay until Buck's funeral service was over. And there was no way in the world Lance Cartwright was on the take. Buck Stone could have trusted him. And the box full of evidence now in Eva's bedroom should have been with Lance, not with her.

But how in the world did she give it to him now when Buck Stone and his wife had both left it in Eva's care?

They went ahead and saw *American Graffiti*, down at the Rock Theater on Broadway, after leaving Olivia Stone's, and neither of them even spoke in a whisper through the entire movie. Nor did they so much as accidentally touch each other. The movie wasn't necessarily sad, other than right at the end, but Eva found herself inexplicably weepy over something about the nostalgia in it, the nostalgia of young high school friends who had graduated, ending their final summer together and heading off into the world. Maybe she was remembering all the way back to when she too had so many big dreams about what the world of her future was going to be like.

Lance took her to A & W for a burger afterward, even though her earlier hotdog would have been enough to carry her through to morning. They sat in the Bronco eating burgers and fries, and Eva ached to tell Lance everything. She wanted him to know what she had in her bedroom—both the box of papers Olivia had given her, and the briefcase in her closet. But she had made a spoken promise to Brandon about the briefcase, and an implied one to Olivia about the box. So she held her silence.

"I guess I prob'ly oughtta get you home, huh?" Lance asked after five minutes of silence. "Hey. Are you okay? Did I do somethin' wrong?"

Stunned to know his concerns, she looked at him for a few seconds before she could break her thoughts free. "No! No,

Lance, you didn't do or say *anything* wrong! No, the evening has been wonderful. I'm so sorry; I was just thinking."

"You sure?"

"Yes! Of course I'm sure. I loved the movie, and the food is great too. Really. It's been super nice."

"Okay. I'm glad. I'll get you home pretty quick, though. I'm sure you're missin' the boys."

She didn't argue. They finished their food, then went to drop Jud's gun off to him.

Jud grinned when Eva and Lance stepped back into the kitchen, where he was flipping burgers a ways from the dishwasher. Turning the last burger over, he took off his apron, threw it down, and ran over to give Eva a hug, laughing.

"You're a sight for sore eyes, little girl!"

"You too, Jud." She waited until he pulled away before lifting his gun to show him, then setting it down on the counter. "Thank you for letting me borrow that."

Jud grinned again. "Not a problem! You sure wouldn't have needed it that night, though. I ain't sure, but I heard from a little bird that Benny had to go up to the hospital after he left here. I guess you messed him up good!"

"Really?"

"Oh yeah. He didn't even come to work the next day, and he sure was walkin' with a limp when I came in tonight. I'm not sure what you did out in the back lot, but please don't do it to me."

Eva giggled, feeling a little relief and a big feeling of justice. "I don't think you'll ever have to worry about that happening to you, Jud."

After leaving Benny's, they drove back to Eva's house, and Lance opened her door for her. She invited him in, but he told her he needed to get going. "Can we go again sometime?" she asked.

He looked down at her. "You serious?"

"Of course I am."

With a big grin, he said, "You bet. Any time I'm off."

She thought about kissing him on the cheek, but it would have been a big production. With her at five foot five and him standing seven inches over six feet, she would have had to ask him to bend down. "Good night, Lance," she said, and turned away.

She hadn't gone five feet before his booming voice stopped her. "Eva! Wait!" When she whirled around, he was walking toward her, a glow of excitement in his eyes. "I can't believe I totally forgot I wanted to show you somethin'."

"What? What is it?"

"Can I borrow you again? Just for like maybe ten minutes?"

"Sure, of course. Are we going somewhere?"

"Yeah, yeah. Serious, it'll just take ten minutes—maybe five."

He got her back in the Bronco and drove a little too fast out of the neighborhood to the four hundred block of Bridger Street, a little to the southwest of Eva's place. It was dark enough other than streetlights that she couldn't see much about the neighborhood other than the fact that it was a modest one with some lawns that were well cared for, and others not so much.

Lance slammed on the brakes, making her lean quickly forward. "Sorry about that! Oh man. Can't wait for you to see this. Wait for me to open your door."

He got out and almost ran around to open her door, then helped her down out of the tall rig and said, "Okay, close your eyes."

She looked up at him, surprised. "Serious?"

"Yes, close 'em. Really."

He took her hand, and she walked with him, thinking how odd it was after all these years to be trusting a man. She hadn't walked more than twenty or thirty steps before he stopped her.

"Okay, you ready?"

"I guess. At least I hope so."

Lance giggled like a little boy. "You will be! Open your eyes."

She opened them, and as they adjusted to the shadows, she saw that he had a flashlight in his left hand, and its beam was pointing in the direction of a house—to its driveway, specifically. And more precisely to a car in the driveway. She inhaled quickly. She was looking at a black Chevrolet Chevelle with mag wheels.

"Oh, wow! You found one! What year is that?"

"What year do you want it to be? Come here."

He led her to the front, where he shone his light beam first on the big "SS" on the grill, and then on the hood, which had a wind-splitter on it, which Chevrolet had done away with in sixty-seven.

"It's a sixty-six Super Sport!" Eva exclaimed. "I can't believe it. Lance, that is the exact car I have been dreaming of!"

He motioned her to the rear of the car again, and she followed. "You didn't see that yet, did you?" He raised the beam of the flashlight to point at a white sign in the back window with black lettering on it: FOR SALE

With a fast inhale, she popped a hand to her mouth. This had been her dream car since her father bought his brand-new red one and took her on a cross-country trip through five states in it, back when Tyke was just a little boy.

She went closer to the sign and peered through the window, then turned to him in disappointment. "It doesn't have a price."

"One thousand bucks."

Looking over at him, she stared for a moment. "How do you know?"

"Because I knocked and asked him when I first saw it."

"One thousand dollars? Oh, wow. Wow. I would love to have this car." But she knew more than she knew anything it was out of sight. It might as well have cost the brand-new price of over three thousand dollars; her father had paid around thirty-three hundred because his came with all the options.

"Well, get it!"

She laughed. "Yeah, sure. Why don't I just take two or three, all in different colors?"

Matching her laugh, he said, "I know. I figured it was out of your price range, but I couldn't wait to show it to you. Hey. Here's the guy's information, just in case. He said he'd be happy to have you come take it for a spin." He handed her a folded slip of paper.

"Really?"

"Really," he said with a nod.

This deserved a hug even if dropping her off in a timely manner at her house didn't. Eva grabbed hold of him and squeezed him tight. "I can't believe you even remembered talking about these cars," she said as she pulled away.

"Right! You don't know me very well. I'd buy it for myself if I had the money. Then you could drive it all you wanted."

That night after saying goodnight to the boys and her mother and grandmother, Eva lay in bed with her lamp on and stared up at the ceiling, her fingers interlaced behind her head. Her father was walking through every little corner of her mind. Truth was, he never really was far from her thoughts, but right now, after seeing the Chevelle, it was as if he were right there with her. He would have been more like a little kid than she was if he had seen that car. They had walked all around it, using Lance's flashlight, and the car was a perfect marvel, with hardly a scratch on it. The inside was just as perfect as out. It made her heart race. She knew she shouldn't even go ask the owner for a test drive, but at the same time she knew she would. Her dad would be riding alongside her, and that was an opportunity she could never pass up.

It had to have been after two o'clock when she finally turned off her lamp and lay there in the dark, feeling sleepy. Her eyes shot open sometime after that when she thought of the briefcase full of money.

What was she thinking? She had the money for that car! She had the money, if only she had the guts to use it.

Eva finally slept sometime in the night, and surprisingly her mother and the boys all let her sleep in. When she woke, the room was throbbing with the high sun, and she almost fell out of bed in her consternation before remembering she really had nothing that needed doing today.

She stared at the clock for a few minutes, rubbing her forehead to get some blood flowing in her face as the time of nine-thirty registered on her brain. Finally, she got up and stumbled into some clothes to wander down the hall in a silent house. There was a note on the table telling her to help herself to coffee and sweet rolls on the stove and that her mother, grandmother, and the boys had gone strolling in the neighborhood. That was something new. They must really have wanted her to get her beauty sleep! And right then she sure needed it, too.

Heating up the coffee, she got on the phone with Dino's Automotive. To her surprise, someone answered, and they actually brought Brandon to the phone.

Hey, Evie, his voice came across. He was not his normal exuberant self.

"Hi, Brandon. I think I'm sensing some bad news." He hesitated for too long. "Come on. You might as well tell me."

Okay. Yeah, you're right. Oh, man, Evie. Hey. What if I try to see if they'll let me co-sign on a loan with you, huh? We might be able to find you somethin' in great shape. We could—

"Wait," she cut him off, fighting the tears that came to her eyes. "Brandon, is it *that bad?"*

Yeah. Gosh, Evie. Yeah, this thing's pretty much toast. You're gonna have so much money tied up in it . . . Yeah. You'd be better off gettin' somethin' else. I know there's cheaper cars out there than what this is gonna take to fix.

Eva stared at the wall, searching for words. She wanted to say something that would make Brandon feel better, along with herself. She could tell he hadn't wanted to give her the news.

"When were you going to call?" she finally asked.

Call? I did. I talked to your mom about an hour ago.

"Oh. Okay." That explained why her family had gone walking. They too were trying to de-stress. The only one who wouldn't understand what a dire situation they were in would be ever-optimistic, innocent Leo.

When I get off work we'll go lookin' for somethin', okay? Brandon put real effort into trying to make his voice sound brighter.

If Brandon could try to be positive, she had to as well. He felt bad enough already. "We can try, Bran. It's okay. I'll let you get back to work."

Okay, but don't you worry. I'll co-sign on a loan, or whatever you need.

"That sounds good. Thank you so much for trying."

They hung up, and Eva didn't know whether to feel worse for herself or worse for Brandon. She didn't know if she had ever heard him sounding more down. He was really taking this to heart. But of course she would never think of letting him co-sign on a loan; his wife hated Eva bad enough already.

The phone rang while Eva was sitting on the bed putting socks and sneakers on. Feeling already exhausted, she picked it up.

Hey, Evie. It's me again. Hey, my boss was sayin' he thinks if we look hard enough we could maybe find a used motor and get you back on the road for less than a hundred and fifty bucks. Two hundred, tops. He even said if we go to the wrecking yard and pull it ourselves we might could get one for a hundred or less. I'll do the work for free. How does that sound?

"Oh, that sounds wonderful, Bran. Thank you. That sounds really good. We'll talk later, okay?"

She hung up wanting to cry. She couldn't stop thinking about the fact that with tips and wages she usually grossed around two hundred eighty to three hundred twenty dollars a month, depending on how drunk the tippers were at Benny's. And now she couldn't even make that. Now she had nothing. No bank in the universe was going to give Eva Galanti a loan, even if she had a co-signer. Besides, with Brandon being an ex-con, she doubted they would let him co-sign anyway, even if Karen didn't throw a fit about it.

She didn't have ten dollars to her name . . . and yet she did.

Her heart was pounding hard and fast when she went to the closet, slid open the folding doors, and got on her knees. Reaching way back under her dresses, she grasped the handle of the briefcase and pulled it out, going to the bed with it.

How long did she have until her family came home? Her fingers were trembling as she popped the case and stared at all those crisp bills, which she had not dared look at one time since bringing the briefcase home and sliding it out of sight under a worn-out bathrobe.

She picked up one of the top stacks of bills, all of which were twenties. Calming herself down enough so her fingers would work, she counted the bills carefully. There were one hundred twenties. Two thousand dollars. Eva's head was swimming. In her entire life, she had never seen that much money in one place, and now she had a whole case full of it! As she reached for the next wad in the stack, she stopped. This one was only tens. In a strange panic, she grabbed the next one to find they were five-dollar bills.

The last banded wad in the stack was ones. She almost laughed at herself after a moment. Her first reaction to finding out that all the bills weren't twenties was disappointment. But why? It wasn't her money anyway! And besides, if every stack in the briefcase were identical, how much was in here?

She grabbed a piece of paper and did some quick math. As the total continued to mount, so did her heartrate. When she was finished, she stared at the paper on her bedspread. It took her several moments to remember to breathe.

If she wasn't mistaken in her math, and if all these banded stacks were exactly as they appeared, she calculated there were fifty-four thousand dollars in this case. Could this even be real money?

She fumbled one twenty out of a pack, then laughed at herself. She wasn't certain she had ever seen enough twenties to recognize if one were real or not. Setting the stack of twenties down, she pulled out a one and held it up to her light, tilting it back and forth. At last, she went and got another one out from a drawer where she kept a few ones for emergencies and studied them side by side.

Oh, how could she know? She was no money expert. Every one of them could be counterfeit, for all she knew.

But the one thing she could say for certain was that to her untrained eye the money in the briefcase looked every bit as real as one of the four one-dollar bills she had left to her name.

CHAPTER TWENTY-NINE

BRANDON CAME TO GET Eva on his lunch, even though she pleaded with him not to. Somehow he seemed to feel responsible for her not having a car to drive, but she knew it wasn't his fault. He had given it his all to fix her car, and even his boss had stepped in to look at it, playing that "second pair of eyes" that even the best of professionals sometimes need. They both came away separately with the same opinion about her sadly dead Valiant. It had simply been too abused over the years, and a car will only drive on the same oil for so long before the damage is irreparable.

Brandon drove them around to every car lot in town until they knew where the cheapest reliable station wagon was, and the cheapest van. They headed next to the banks, and the answer was the same everywhere. For an ex-con living in a rented apartment, running far behind on his wife's medical bills, and a woman with two children and no job, there were no loans to be had.

They next went back to try and talk to the car lots, even trying to offer the Valiant as partial payment. No one was going to issue credit to someone in a situation like Eva's or Brandon's, not even the two private sellers they found.

Brandon's "lunch" ended up being, like *Gilligan's Island,* a three-hour tour. It didn't end with a shipwreck, but to Eva and Brandon it certainly seemed like one. When they were done, they sat in Brandon's Delray at the shop, staring at and speaking poorly of her Valiant, which to her had never been very valiant.

"Brandon, I have to tell you something," she said finally, after much deliberation. "I never told you this, but one night a while ago I got on my knees and prayed really hard. I got an answer."

Brandon looked at her, saying nothing. She could tell he wanted to look like he was politely listening. Perhaps he even wanted to believe. But it seemed like Brandon had given up his belief in prayer long ago—perhaps even his belief in God.

When she was too nervous to go on, he came to her rescue. "Yeah? What kind of answer?"

"I had a really strong feeling everything was going to be all right. And it was only a few days later when I found that briefcase."

"You're kiddin', right? Evie, that ain't and kind of answer from God, or even good luck. That's the worst kind of luck! We should've left that where it was an' run."

"No, Brandon, listen. I'm serious. Listen to me. I felt really good about that prayer. I know God was talking to me. Why would I break down right there, even after you did all that work on my car? And then nobody was answering my calls, so nobody came to get me. I didn't have to walk home that way. And that car chase didn't have to go down that road. They didn't have to throw that money out right there. I could have gone to my car, seen it wasn't going to work, then turned around and come back to Benny's to call for somebody again. Can't you see? All that happened because God was looking out for me. Everything's going to be all right, Brandon. I know it is."

"Evie. Please. I'm beggin' you to stop. God doesn't help little people like us, okay? I don't want to hurt your feelings, but he just doesn't."

"He does! I know he does. It's going to be all right."

"Oh, geez! Wake up, Evie. It ain't gonna be all right! Come on! Look at your house. You can't make a payment. Your husband leaves you. You have a kid that's . . . Well, you know—not like other kids. Your grandma's sick."

Tears rushed into Eva's eyes, and they darted away. Her impulse was to jump out of the car and start walking home, but she didn't. Even in her moment of frustration and near anger with Brandon, she knew she couldn't run away. He didn't deserve that. He was only trying to help, the way he always tried to help. And right now the only way he could help was to try talking sense to her—or at least what he thought was sense.

"Let me go tell Dino I'll be back in a bit, Evie. Okay? I'll take you home."

She nodded, holding back her tears. Brandon got out and went inside, then came back out with his aging boss, Dino Priest, who came to the driver's side of the car with Brandon.

Dino leaned down on top of the door frame and looked in at her with compassionate eyes through a thatch of deep wrinkles. "Hi, Evie. Listen, everything'll be fine. Don't you worry. We're gonna find you somethin'. You just hang on tight. Do you need some cash or anything? To buy your kids food an' what-not?"

The tears Eva had been trying to hold back spilled over at the old man's generosity as if the tide had simply become too great. She gave a small, fast shake of her head. "No, sir. No, we'll be fine," she lied. "I promise."

"Okay, honey, well you just let us know, all right? It ain't just me either. I know a dozen good guys who'd jump fast to get you a five or a ten, enough to keep you goin' till you c'n get back on your feet."

"Thank you so much," she choked out. "I think we'll be fine."

As Brandon drove Evie home, both of them were silent. The only sound was the humming of his tires through the open windows and the hot afternoon wind blowing on their faces.

He stopped at her house but didn't seem to have the energy to get out and open her door, and she was fine with that. She hurriedly popped it open but then kept sitting there. He was watching her, but she continued staring at her hands. "Hey." His voice finally broke the quiet, and she looked over. "Dino wasn't just talkin', Evie. He'd help you in a heartbeat, and if he says he has other guys, that's for real. I'll help you too. I still got some money."

"I know, Bran. You've already been so much help. I'll let you know if anything comes up, okay?"

"You bet. Me too. We'll start lookin' for a motor right away." By which he meant an "engine", a word her father had been very strict in teaching her, but under the circumstances she certainly wouldn't quibble—she had learned long since that mechanics never took correction very well.

"All right. Thank you so much for everything. I'll see you later."

When Eva got out and headed for the house, she turned and waved at Brandon again as he drove off. She already knew what she had to do, and she prayed she would be all done before Brandon knew any different.

Worn out from the heat, even if it was only a walk of a little more than half a mile, Eva stopped at the 1200 block of Tenth Street a ways down from where she could see the sixty-six Chevelle parked in its driveway. She looked again in her purse to make sure she had stuffed half the stack of twenties from the banded wad into a deep pocket out of sight. The rest of the stack—fifty of them to be exact—was folded neatly in half in

her coin purse, and it was about all that little purse could con-
tain.

She walked on confidently to the house, and a heavy-set but
handsome man in a ball cap saw her and came outside as she
was heading toward the front door. "You Mrs. Galanti?"

"Yes." She didn't bother to correct the "Mrs." to "Miss". It
was probably for the best. It would even possibly work to her
benefit.

"Well, you're sure going to like this car, if you're into muscle cars."

She laughed. "My father and I used to race them."

"Great. Well, like I said . . . Want to take her around the
block a few times?"

"Why are you selling it?" she asked, not caring at the moment if she sounded blunt. It was never a good idea to sound too
friendly with anyone trying to sell you a car—at least that was
her father's philosophy.

"Because I'm dumb," the man said with a grin. "Oh—Dave,
by the way." He didn't bother putting out a hand, and she was
just as glad. She wanted only to get the car and get away.

She stood there studying him after his silly answer. When he
realized she was still waiting and didn't plan on saying more, he
cleared his throat. "Yeah, well, the thing is I bought a Firebird.
This baby's a beauty, but my wife says it has to go. No room in
the garage for two of them. It was my brother's dream anyway,
not mine. Great car, just not what I was after."

"It seems all right," she admitted. Of course she didn't say
what she really thought of it—that it was breathtaking. Proper
car-shopping etiquette demanded that she play the vehicle down
as much as she possibly could. "Has it been in any wrecks?"

"Nope. Clean as can be. The old guy that bought it first really had no business with it even when he got it. His eyes were
gettin' too old for him to be on the road, but he used to drag

race, and he just had to have one more good racer. Anyhow, the cops ended up taking his driver's license, so he sold the car to my brother, who was eighteen and hot to go burnin' rubber."

"And your brother decided he didn't want it either?"

"Oh, he wanted it," Dave said, nodding. "Justin wanted the car, and Uncle Sam wanted Justin. He only got to drive it two months before they sent him to Nam, and well, Justin never got back to his car."

When Eva grasped his meaning, her heart felt suddenly heavy. "I'm sorry. That's tragic."

"Yeah. That's what we thought. 'Specially the way it happened, him tryin' to help out a Vietnamese family, an' I guess it turned out the ten-year-old kid in the family really didn't want help. He was heading into the hooch with a grenade in a breadbasket, and when Justin thought he'd be nice and buy the whole basket from him, he got more than just bread."

Eva stared at Dave, wishing he had never told her this tale of treachery and death. But then it also put a slant on the Vietnam story that a lot more of the anti-war young people in America needed to hear. Once more, she could only say, "I'm sorry."

"Yeah. Thanks. Me too. So anyway, I'd just as soon get rid of the car now, because of the memories. Otherwise, I'd probably try to find a way to keep it."

"It's okay if I drive it?" she said to be sure.

"You bet. Want me to come with you?"

"You can. That's fine."

They got in together, and the 396 fired up on the instant. It was the 4-speed manual transmission model, and Dave told her he had made some changes to it that had the horsepower well up around four hundred twenty. It had the right sound, too, and the power of the big engine in the mid-size coupe had the whole car shivering and wanting to bolt out of the driveway.

She backed it out and revved it up, wishing she could hide the goosebumps that appeared all over her arms.

"Somethin', huh?" said Dave.

"Pretty impressive, yeah."

She drove up the street and around a few blocks without missing any gears, and with everything operating as smooth as if she had been driving an automatic. "You know your way around a stick," Dave said. "I don't normally do this, but I'm in a mood. Want to take her out on Eighty and see what she can do?"

Eva looked at him, the hoofbeats of her own heart matching those of the horses beneath the hood. "That's okay with you?"

"Sure, if you can drive out there like you drive at this speed. I don't mind. For old time's sake."

"Okay," she said, shrugging, and she took it out to Interstate Eighty, heading west toward Green River.

She stopped on the onramp and revved it for a moment, letting it rock impatiently. She could feel Dave grinning when he spoke. "You really are going to do this, aren't you? Any tickets, you pay 'em."

"Of course. I'm behind the wheel."

With that, she dropped the clutch, and they shot down the onramp, then onto the freeway. When they hit sixty, Dave almost screamed. "Damn, girl! I think you must have just hit sixty in maybe seven seconds. Less than eight, for sure!"

She tamed her foot down there and leveled off at ninety, and still they were floating along as if driving a boat on a calm lake. When she saw another car ahead, she backed way off, then took the nearest emergency turn-around. It was illegal, but the chances of any cops seeing her were about as good as the chances of her finding a briefcase full of cash.

Eva's hair was a mess now, and her heart revving like the car's engine. She hadn't felt so alive in months.

"What do you think?" Dave asked when they got almost back to the freeway exit. "You weren't kidding about driving race cars."

She smiled. She felt a little guilty for her display, but not so much as to apologize. "It's pretty nice. Probably not quite four hundred twenty horsepower, though, I'm guessing."

"Well, okay. Four-o-five, anyway."

She knew the horsepower of the car off the lot, at least the high-end one like her father's, with all the options, could get around three-seventy-five.

"Better than factory, anyway," she said. She didn't know why she was feeling so feisty—even almost obnoxious. She guessed it was partly because she didn't like it when men thought women knew nothing about cars, and partly because having two thousand dollars on her made her feel almost invincible.

Pulling up in Dave's driveway, she turned the Chevelle off and set the brake, and they got out. She had found nothing about the car to criticize, so she didn't try. It was easily worth a thousand dollars and more.

"You said one thousand?"

"Yes, ma'am. Fairly firm."

"Fairly?"

He smiled. "Fairly."

"Give me a tank of gas, some groceries, and new shoes for my son before he goes back to school?"

"What will that cost me?"

"I'll give you nine hundred sixty—seventy, if you have a ten in change."

"That's a deal. Let me go grab a ten and the title."

Eva drove the Chevelle home from getting it registered at the DMV, and insured at State Farm, wondering if her mother would be as disgusted with her as Brandon was going to be.

Right then, she didn't care. This car made her happy, and lately there wasn't much that could do that.

All the way home she even managed not to think about the Mob and their money—the Mob who could have no way of knowing where their briefcase had vanished.

That money, to Eva Galanti, was nothing but a windfall. A windfall from God.

CHAPTER THIRTY

BIANCA GALANTI WASN'T DISGUSTED with her daughter. She was scared. The same way Eva had been until she started thinking about the chances the Mob would ever learn who had found their money. The same way Eva had been until the even greater fear of her family starving had gotten the better of her. Eva had taken the plunge, and now her mother could only reap the rewards of it. She had decided the money was an answer to her prayers, and nothing could dissuade her.

She had chosen to take her mother on a long drive on I-80, out through the Red Desert toward Rawlins, so she could tell her everything: about her lost job, about Benny's predatory attack on her, the walk in the dark in fear for her life, and about finding the money. After a long struggle with herself, she even admitted to her mother about the cardboard box full of damning intelligence against the Mob and whoever else might be named in the information contained in that box. So far, she had only scanned the red and black ledger book. She hadn't gathered courage to dig any deeper.

Bianca was silent for the first few miles on their way back toward town. Finally, she took in a deep breath and sank back against the black vinyl seat, letting her breath out in a long, calming sigh.

"Okay, cara. So I think I've got all this digested. I still don't know how you expect me not to be scared, but I guess I'll just have to trust that you know what you're doing. I keep trying to go through scenarios like this I've seen on TV, trying to re-member if the bad guys had ways to . . ."

"To what? How could they know anything, Mom? It isn't like there are any cameras out there. And I can't imagine they have any kind of tracking device in the briefcase."

"But you'll look anyway, right?"

Eva smiled. "If they had a way to track it they would already have been to the house. Mom, don't worry, okay? God answered my prayer that night by making me feel like everything would be all right, and then all those other circumstances came togeth-er the way they did. How do I question something like that?"

"Yes, you're probably right. It seems like that money should probably go back *somewhere,* to someone, but I guess it's all dirty money anyway. And who would need it more than we do. Right?"

"Right." Eva smiled and reached over to give her mother's hand a squeeze.

"I'll say one thing, cara: Your father would sure be proud of your taste in cars."

Brandon Lucky wasn't like Bianca Galanti. When Eva told him, the result was a kind of reaction she had seen with Brandon before, but never any time she could remember being directed at her.

She had parked up Bridger a ways from Dino's because she was embarrassed for Brandon's boss to see her new ride. She had no idea how she would explain to him where the money suddenly came from. When she went in the shop, Dino Priest said hi and gave her his big smile, which was missing two teeth on the bottom and made him resemble a white-haired jack-o-lantern. Then the old man went back to work.

Eva went over to where she could see Brandon's stick-scrawny legs, dressed in striped coveralls, poking out from under his latest job. She always laughingly wondered why he didn't buy the blue coveralls, since stripes always adorned the clichéd clothing of a convict.

Brandon must have heard her coming, then looked over and recognized her by her shoes. Without rolling out from under the monstrously large red Suburban he was working on, he said, "Hey, Evie. Can you hand me that half-inch socket?"

With a smile, she reached over and grabbed the socket, proud that she still recognized a half-inch from a seven-sixteenths even at a glance. "You have the handle?"

He must have been preoccupied, because he didn't answer until he finally said, "Can't you find it?"

She laughed at him. "I did. I asked if you have the handle."

"Oh. Yeah." His grease-covered hand appeared, and she laid the socket in it, getting grease on one fingertip, which she wiped off on the leg of his coveralls.

"Stop! That tickles," his muffled voice came back, making her laugh.

After banging around under the Suburban for a few more minutes, Brandon said, "Comin' out, Evie. Watch yourself."

She was already a good ways to one side of the wheeled creeper he was lying on. One good time having her feet knocked out from under her by her father had long ago taught her where to stand or crouch in relation to anything with wheels on a garage floor.

Brandon came into sight, his face smeared in several different places with black grease, his jaw starting to grow in with the
dark reddish-brown whiskers that made up his goatee. He
grinned, pulling a filthy rag out of his pocket to wipe off his
hands.

"Hey. How's it goin'?" he asked.

"Good. How about you?"

"This Suburban's a pain in the neck. Otherwise, great. You
bring me lunch?" He winked after he asked.

"Want me to?"

He laughed. "No, I'm kiddin'! Look at all this fat. I could
live on this for weeks."

She looked him up and down and rolled her eyes as he
struggled to his feet. As the saying always went, Brandon didn't
have an ounce of fat on his entire body.

"Yeah, you gain any more weight and they'll have to use
that creeper to roll you around," she said, giggling.

"Hey, you want a Coke or somethin'?" he asked.

She took one, and they walked over to look at a Ford Custom 300 Tudor. It was green with trunk-length fins on either
side. Dino Priest was underneath it and never came out as they
walked around admiring it. Finally, Eva got her courage up. She
knew the time would eventually come anyway. She needed to be
the one to break the news to Brandon herself.

"I need to show you something."

He looked at her and grinned. "Oh, no you don't! I keep tellin' you we gotta keep this on a strictly professional basis."

"All right, you two," Dino said from under the car.

Brandon leaned close to Eva's ear. "He's got the ears of an
elephant!" Then he looked back at her. "So where is the somethin'?"

"Outside."

They left the shop, and Eva led the way up the hot August sidewalk, her heart pounding harder and harder even though they weren't walking that fast. When they reached the Chevelle, she stopped.

He had already been eyeballing the car. "Wow! That's a sweet ride, huh? That's what you wanted to show me?"

"Yeah." Her next words caught in her throat as he started around the car, looking at the dash, the seats, then carefully scanning the paint.

"That's one sweet rod," he said, shaking his head. "Kind of your dream car, isn't it?"

"Kind of, yeah. Brandon?"

He looked at her, and it took a few puzzled moments, but finally he read her expression like an old pro. Staring at her a little longer as his mind switched gears, at last he let out a curse. "No. No, Evie. Oh hell, please tell me you didn't— Evie, please."

He was begging her, and she wanted to say something that would appease him, but she couldn't. "I bought it, Brandon."

Brandon Lucky had always been pretty good at hiding his emotions, at least if he was upset with anything Eva did. This time he didn't try. Both grease-stained hands came up and grabbed the sides of his head, pushing his dark hair back. He swore again, his eyes sweeping the car.

"Evie, please tell me you're kiddin'. Please."

"Brandon, I'm sorry. Even if I hadn't bought this, you know I was going to need to use that money. If it wasn't meant to be, why did everything happen like it did?"

"Aw, crap. Crap. Crap. We're in a world of trouble."

Eva stared at him. It was starting to feel like there was something more to his being upset than only that he wanted to lay low about the money. "What's wrong, Brandon? Did something happen?"

He nodded slowly, closing his eyes. "Yeah. Yeah. That guy, the FBI guy. He came by here earlier askin' a bunch of questions. You didn't tell him that was your car broke down that night did you?"

She stared at him, her mind whirling. "I . . . I don't remember. I might have. Oh. Yeah, I think I did. When he asked me why I was there at the crime scene."

Brandon swore again and pinched his lips like he was trying to tear them off his face. "Okay. Okay." Again, he swore, pivoting in a half-circle before coming back around to face her. "All right. Evie, listen. We gotta fly. I mean we gotta get *out* of the Rock—as fast as we can."

Eva could feel the blood draining out of her face. "Brandon. What's going on?"

"That guy was askin' all sorts of crap. I told him I didn't know anything. I told him I barely met you. He told me it didn't matter. That he had wrote down your plate. He knows that's your car because you told him. So now he knows where you live, too—from the DMV."

"Can he—" She froze, looking at the Chevelle. "I'll hide the car somewhere."

"Did you already register it?"

"Yeah."

He swore again. She had never heard him use foul language without apologizing. It was almost like he was trying to set an unbeatable record. "Well, let's just hope he doesn't find any other reason to run your name through the DMV again. If he does, he'll find out you just registered this."

"Okay. What should I do, Bran? How would I just get the whole family packed and leave Rock Springs? This trunk won't hold even a fraction of our belongings." Which of course was a stupid saying, since a drawer full of silverware was a fraction of their belongings. Normally, Brandon would have ribbed her about that, but neither of them was in a joking mood right now.

"All right. Yeah, yeah. You're right. So let's think. We gotta think. Okay, let's do what you said. You park the car a block or so away from your house, maybe down on Soulsby or somewhere, and walk home. I'll— Aw, hell."

Eva followed where Brandon's glance had just jumped to see a by now far too-recognizable black Chevrolet Caprice cruising slowly toward them along Bridger. She swore too, only not so polite a word as his.

"Start walkin', Evie. *Walk!*" Brandon swiftly started away from the Chevelle, not back toward the auto shop, but up the sidewalk. Eva almost ran to catch him, and they were four car lengths from the Chevelle as the Caprice rolled to a stop in the middle of the street. "Keep walkin'. Keep walkin'," Brandon said out the corner of his mouth.

Eva heard the Caprice when it started rolling backward, picking up speed until its grill came into their sight and it slid to a halt on loose gravel on the street. Cooper Tervalon jumped out of the driver's side.

"I'd like to talk to you two."

Brandon looked over at Tervalon for all the world as if surprised to see him there. "Oh. Hi, Mr. Tervalon."

Tervalon, his pale-blond hair shining in the sunlight, glared at them both. He didn't bother to pull off his black sunglasses. "Get in the car."

"Get in why?" Brandon asked. Eva had seen Brandon act insolent with authority figures before. He was anything but that right now. Brandon was scared, and that ramped Eva's own fear through the roof.

"Because I said to."

"Are we . . . under arrest?"

"Listen, Lucky. Do you want to do this the easy way, or the hard way?"

Using that old cop line on an ex-con like Brandon Lucky was pushing it, and Eva knew it. Even frightened, Brandon would only allow himself to be bullied so far.

"I just asked a question. What are we gettin' in the car for? Where we goin'?"

"You want to talk right here? Or someplace shady."

"Here's okay."

That wasn't the answer Cooper Tervalon wanted, and the darkening of his face showed that. "Do you want me to get a warrant and tear up your place, smart aleck?"

Eva's heart froze. They knew about the money. She didn't know how, but they knew.

"Wait. Tear up my place for what?"

Cooper Tervalon stared Brandon down, his jaws clenched. If hatred was fire, the glasses would have melted off his face. "All right . . . *Lucky*. Play your games. I'll be seeing you soon."

With that ominous threat, Tervalon sank back down in the Caprice and drove toward Elk Street, and Brandon grabbed Eva's elbow and kept walking, distancing them for all he was worth from the guilt-ridden Chevelle.

CHAPTER THIRTY-ONE

BRANDON AND EVA HAD circled the block and come back around to the automotive shop scanning all around to see if Agent Tervalon was watching for them. There was no indication that he was.

"All right, Evie," Brandon said. "You'd better get out of here before he comes back. You see that car comin', you turn your head the other way and try not to let him see you. Okay? Go home and park on Soulsby or somewhere like we talked about."

"Okay, I will. Will you be all right?"

"Of course. Why wouldn't I be?"

She drove home just over the speed limit, trying to get there as fast as possible but without drawing attention to herself. All she could think about was all the evidence in the cardboard box Olivia Stone had given her. Cooper Tervalon wouldn't be in Rock Springs if he wasn't dealing with something federal. He had to be working on something that had to do with Primo Santori, didn't he? After all, how many Mobs could there be in one town?

A sick feeling suddenly came over Eva—a feeling about Ambro Procopio. Then she wondered why she would even care. But she hadn't seen him in quite some time. What if he was the man who had been driving the Mob car? She shouldn't care, but part of her did. She couldn't help remembering how genuinely kind Ambro had been to her boys, especially to Leo. What if

Ambro had been lying in a coma in the hospital all this time since the shootout? She couldn't explain how that thought clutched at her guts.

When Eva got near home, she parked on Soulsby Street, in front of the house of an old lady whose lawn she occasionally mowed and whom she rarely saw outside. On a whim, she went and knocked on the door, and the woman answered and instantly agreed to let her park the Chevelle in her driveway. Eva had told her it was a present for her son and she was trying to surprise him.

Feeling much better about the car, Eva thanked the woman and walked home. Bianca and her grandmother were sitting on the sofa watching TV when she came in, and Tyke hurried down the hall from the boys' bedroom, carrying Leo.

After initial happy greetings, Bianca asked Eva about the car. "Oh. I parked it over on Rigby. That old lady I mow the lawn for said I could put it in her driveway so it would be safer than out on the street."

"That's a good idea," Bianca said. Neither of them said anything more. They had agreed not to let Isabella or Tyke know about the car yet, or about the found money.

"What car, Mom?" Tyke asked—because there is no way to leave a teenage boy out of the loop when it comes to cars.

"Oh, don't worry, buddy. It's a surprise." Eva turned and pretended to be interested in the television, and Tyke and Leo went to playing in the middle of the floor. In spite of her trepidation over all that was happening, Eva couldn't help smiling. She was so happy Tyke was the boy he was. How many big brothers would care about a handicapped brother the way he did?

Eva got up during a commercial break. "I think I'm going to lie down for a while."

She went back and sat on her bed, making sure the door was closed tightly, and locked. She stared at the cardboard box she had placed against her wall, underneath some folded sheets and a bedspread. That box called to her, even as it repelled her. What might be in that box? Names? Proof of guilt of people she knew? She wanted to look, yet at the same time it was the last thing she wanted to do.

What would she find there? Some names were clear. Without any doubt she knew she would find Primo Santori, Gavino Berretti, and, sadly, Ambro Procopio. Then who knew how many other mobsters. What was a lot darker to her was the question of how many local police officers she might find implicated in that box.

She felt sick thinking about that. The name of Lance Cartwright was what had kept her for so long from digging into the box deeper, although she was positive in her heart that she wouldn't find him there. But what about Rick Cohen? What about Chris Hinshaw? And Jake Glattner? What about the police chief himself, Howard Buyer?

Finally, she lay on the bed with her hands tucked under the small of her back. She closed her eyes, wanting sleep, but sleep was far from her.

As she thought about the box, and about her current situation, a little seed of anger sprouted in her and quickly began to grow. Why had Officer Stone put her in this spot? What had she ever done to deserve this? And why had Olivia insisted on going through with it? There were a lot of people who should see that box, but she was not one of them. She had no idea what to do with it. The idea kept coming to her that she had to tell Lance about it. He would know what to do. And in the worst-case scenario, if it turned out that she was wrong, and his name was one of those implicated in mob activity in that box, as long as she told him she had never looked in it, she would be safe . . .

wouldn't she? If he was guilty of federal crimes, he could simply choose to destroy all that evidence, and what would that change? Life in "Rock Bottom" would go on as always, for both the guilty and the innocent, and Eva would be blissfully unaware.

An idea came to her as her troubled mind fell upon, sorted through, and discarded random thoughts. What about the local county prosecutor? He should know what to do. A phone call to him, even if she started out anonymously, might solve everything—or at least everything but the dilemma of the money. And she still wasn't sure that was a dilemma at all. Maybe both she and Brandon were only being paranoid.

Since she couldn't sleep, Eva got up and picked up the fat phonebook off her nightstand, looking up county numbers. It was easy to find the one for the county prosecutor's office. She steeled herself and dialed the number, asking for the prosecutor.

He's busy at the moment, the receptionist said. *If you can leave your name and number I'll have him call you back.* Apparently, Eva waited too long to reply. *Ma'am? Are you still there?*

"Yes, I'm here," Eva said. "I . . . Well, it's an anonymous call. I'm not able to give out my name right now."

She was trying to sound calm, but apparently it didn't work. Apparently all this intrigue and danger did not agree with her.

Ma'am, are you all right? Do you need the police?

"No! No, I'm fine. I—" Eva pushed down on the disconnect button and sat staring at the phone, feeling sick. Her heart was pounding so fast she wondered if she would have been able to talk even if the prosecutor had come on the line.

After sitting there for ten minutes trying to get herself back together, Eva dialed the number again, and the same receptionist answered. "Yes, I called about ten minutes ago? Sorry, my phone got disconnected."

No problem. If you still wanted to speak with the prosecutor, he's free now. Should I put you through?

Eva felt nauseous, but it was time to take the plunge. She had to find a way out from under this cardboard box, the heaviest box and heaviest papers she had ever had in her possession. "Yes, could you please?"

The phone didn't ring again before rattling off the hook. *This is James Bardo. How may I help you?*

"Umm . . ." Eva suddenly didn't even know how to bring up what she needed. "I . . . are you alone?"

Uhh . . . I guess alone enough, ma'am. What is it you need?

"Well, I have some important papers that were given to me, and I don't know what to do with them."

What type of papers?

"It's hard to say. I'm sorry this sounds so weird, but . . ." She had the urge suddenly to hang up again and not call back. She had the urge to build a bonfire in the back yard and throw the entire box into it. "I believe it's some incriminating information, possibly about the police department and some people in town who . . ."

Who is this? asked Bardo. *Who am I speaking with?*

"Do you really need to know my name?"

It would really help to know who I'm speaking with, he replied after a pregnant pause.

Eva's mind spun in circles. Feverishly, she spouted off, "My name is Thelma Robinson." Thelma Robinson! What a name for her to pull out of the blue. It sounded vaguely familiar, but she didn't know why. Probably just some name from a movie or television show she had seen.

And, Thelma, can you give me a number I can call you back at?

"No! Sorry. I didn't mean to yell. No, I . . . I'm scared. And I don't have a home phone," she said on a whim. "I'm calling you from a payphone."

Oh. Where?

"Uhh, never mind that."

Someone pounding on Eva's door almost made her drop the phone. "Mom?" It was Tyke's loud voice through the door.

Stepping over, she jerked the door open and held her finger to her mouth to shush him. Apologetically, he stepped back, and she shut the door.

On the other end of the line was a long pause. At last Bardo spoke again. *Now, Thelma, we have to be very careful to be honest with each other, all right? I don't want us to start off on the wrong foot.* That made it obvious he had heard Tyke, and he no longer believed she was calling from a payphone. She quickly pushed the subject away.

"I need your help. Okay? I have this stuff, and I don't want it in my house. It needs to go to the authorities."

There was another pause before Bardo said, *Ma'am, are you in your house now?* He was trying to get her to admit outright that she had lied about not having a home phone.

"Sir, if you can't help me and you don't want this stuff—"

Wait! No, Thelma, I do want it—I think. I'm not sure exactly what stuff *you have there, but if what you're telling me is true, and it involves the local police department . . . Listen, why don't you bring it in and let's take a look at it? When can we meet? How about tonight? Say seven?*

"I'm not sure," said Eva. "I don't know what to do."

Well, let's just meet, and we can talk about it. What time is good for you? I can think of a private place to meet if you would feel better.

"I . . . No. No, I think I should wait. I'll call you back."

Ma'am! No! Don't hang up. Ma'am, this is really important. Don't hang up.

"I'm going to need to talk to somebody. I'll . . . I'll call you tomorrow." Without waiting for a reply, she dropped the phone back on the base.

Eva's face felt hot, like she was burning with a fever. She massaged her forehead and looked around the room, pointedly avoiding letting her eyes land on the box. Her mind played back over the conversation. Something about it had seemed so strange, and she tried to remember it in its entirety.

First of all, the man had seemed immediately very interested in what she was telling him. Perhaps overly so, as if he already knew something. And then . . . Suddenly, it came to her. Why had he been so ready to meet her at seven o'clock? The county offices surely would be closed by five. And then to jump so fast to wanting to meet her someplace private. Why?

Eva's mind was in a tailspin. She needed to talk to someone else; that part of what she had told him was true. She needed to see someone she not only could trust but who knew about matters like this. Should she give in and call Agent Tervalon, even if she didn't like him on a personal basis? He was an FBI agent. This kind of corruption in a city, if the police were indeed involved, that was his job, wasn't it? Why else was he even here? She was pretty sure there was no FBI office for him to work at here, or if there was she had certainly never heard about it. Maybe Tervalon was already working the case. Maybe the box full of evidence would be as much of a windfall for him as the briefcase seemed to be for her.

Eva was going to have to take a leap of faith. She needed to talk to Lance. Whether she eventually went to Tervalon or not, right now she needed somebody she felt close to, and who knew about the law. Her stomach felt sick. It took her back to when she was first pregnant with Leo. She wanted to run in the bathroom and throw up, but she forced the urge back. With trembling hands, she picked the phone back up and dialed Lance's number.

After more than ten rings, when she was about to hang up, it came rattling off the hook. *Hello?*

"Lance! Thank heavens you're there."

Eva? Sorry, I was in the shower. What's goin' on? What's wrong?

Once again, her mood was too easy to read. She was frozen, with a dozen things she wanted and needed to say sitting on the tip of her tongue. "I need to talk to you."

Oh shoot. Can it wait at all? I just got called in to work.

"Oh." Her heart fell. "Okay, yeah. I'm sorry. I'll uh . . ."

You okay, Eva?

"Yeah. Sure. It's all right. Just . . . call me when you can. Okay?"

I will. Stay by a phone. I'll talk to you soon. Goodbye, Eva.

"Bye. Please don't forget," she blurted out, but in return she got only silence. She held the phone until she heard the dial tone, then robotically fumbled it back onto the cradle, fighting back tears. She looked around the room.

Clothing filled her closet. She had both a dresser and a chest of drawers. The former held the clothing she didn't need to hang in the closet, while the latter contained sheets, extra blankets, bath linens, and one drawer for important papers and souvenirs. She had a small bookcase with her Louisa May Alcott collection and other classics, along with picture books about wildlife and birds. In one small case she kept her jewelry, in another her makeup.

She tried to think of what her mother and grandmother kept in the room they shared, and what the boys had. All the furniture could stay here if they had to move fast. She would take some of the money, even if she ended up having to turn most of it in.

They couldn't prove she had taken any. What would the family need to take in an emergency? What if they only had five or ten minutes to vacate the place?

Something hit her, and her eyes whirled about the room as she tried to play the thought all the way through to a finish. She had been worried about the money, and about the box, but . . . Not a soul would know about the incriminating cardboard box, other than Olivia Stone. And what about the briefcase? In all honesty, was there anything other than Brandon's paranoia rubbing off on her that should be making her so nervous? What in the world could possibly lead anyone to believe she had this money? Was she only trying to ease her fears? Was there something she didn't know? Could someone even in the dark have been watching her when she picked it up?

Another big question: Was there any way someone other than the criminals could know how much money had been in the briefcase? And other than the criminals, did anyone even know it existed? Furthermore, the driver of the Roadrunner, whether it was Ambro or some other mobster, was said to be still unconscious at the hospital. If he had thrown the briefcase out of his car during the chase, he seemed to have been well ahead of anyone behind him, so wasn't there a chance that no one else had a clue there had ever been money in the car in the first place?

Eva was playing mind games, and she knew it. She could ask dozens more questions like this all day long, and still there would be not a single provable answer.

If it would ease her worries, what if she took out some money, paid her rent maybe six months in advance, opened a bank account maybe under her grandmother's name, maybe in another city, and then turned the rest of the money over to Agent Tervalon and admitted she had found it? There was no way he could prove she had spent any. Even if they learned she had a new car, how did they know she hadn't had the money squirreled away — "for a rainy day"? To the grave, she would deny spending any of it.

She had to get to Brandon. She had to use him as a sounding board, since it was he who had made her so paranoid in the first place. Maybe he could at least shed some kind of light on why he thought there was a chance anyone could know she had the money. A glance at the clock showed it was after four. He would still be working.

She called the shop, and Dino Priest answered almost on the first ring. *'Lo?*

"Hi, Dino. I'm sorry to bug you. This is Eva."

Not a problem, little lady. And I'd know that voice any-where. It's funny, I was just about to pick up the phone when it rang. I'm guessin' you wanna talk to Brandon, not this old codger.

She forced a laugh she didn't feel. "Yes, if I can."

I think I'm gonna have to start dockin' his pay, he joked. *Hang on, Eva.*

A minute later, Brandon was on the phone, and she asked if they could talk. *Right now? Is everything okay?* Her voice must have really sounded off. Dino seemed to be the only person who couldn't tell something was wrong.

"Yeah, I just . . . I need to get some stuff clear in my head. You're the only one I can talk to."

Oh man, Evie. Yeah, I can talk if you need me, but it might be an hour or two. I really have to get this Suburban done. The owner called a while ago, and he's gettin' growly about not havin' it back. Would that still work? Two hours?

She hesitated, probably too long. "Maybe let's don't worry about it, Bran. It's all right." She couldn't ask him to meet her that late. She knew Karen would start to get irritated that he wasn't home, and Karen hated her bad enough already. It seemed like she was starting to hate Brandon too—if that hadn't happened long ago.

Brandon started to protest, but she told him again that it would be okay, and she hung up. She waited, but he didn't call back.

She drew a deep breath. Olivia Stone then. Olivia Stone. She might not be a cop, but she had been a cop's wife. She had to know more about this kind of thing than Eva did, and she was the one responsible for Eva having the damning evidence in her possession, even if the actual choice had been made by her husband.

Putting her shoes back on, Eva went out to the front room to look for Tyke and apologize for shushing him. Through the picture window, she saw the boys playing on the lawn. Tyke was so good to find things Leo could do with him, even though Leo couldn't get around that well other than by doing the funny sideways scoot he seemed to have patented himself.

"Mom, do you know what Tyke wanted?"

"I think he just wanted to ask about his shoes again."

"I'm going to buy him some," Eva averred.

Her mother gazed at her, seeming unsure how to reply. Eva knew she didn't like having the briefcase of money in their house. It seemed evil somehow, and it seemed like it was painting a target on them, although neither could say why that feeling was so strong.

"I need to go see a friend," Eva said.

"A friend?" Her mom studied her a moment longer. "Okay. How long might you be?"

"A while. I'm not sure. I'll try to get back for supper." She looked over to see her grandmother watching her, for all the world as if she understood every word they were saying. She looked suddenly really old, and really tired. On a whim, Eva went and sat down by her. "Nonni, how are you feeling? We haven't been able to talk much for a few days." It felt strange speaking again in her grandmother's native Italian.

"I'm good, my dove. So very good. Thank you for asking. You aren't going to see that Procopio fellow, are you?"

Eva laughed. Maybe her grandmother understood more English than she ever let on. She had suspected that off and on for years. "No, Nonni. I don't think we'll be seeing Ambro anymore."

"Okay. That is for the best, I think. He would not have been good for you."

Giving her grandmother a smile, she said, "No, I think you're probably right." And oh, if Isabella could only know how right she was.

After telling the boys goodbye and telling them to stay close within sight of their grandmother, Eva crossed the street and walked around the corner onto Soulsby. Down the street in the old lady's driveway, she got in the Chevelle. There was a U-Haul van parked in the Stones' driveway when she pulled up, and she sat there for a few minutes and let the engine rumble. Olivia Stone really was going. She should be taking the cardboard box with her. This whole thing truly had that woman scared out of her mind, and that made Eva wonder if she, too, shouldn't be even more terrified than she already was.

Shutting off the car, she got out and started up the sidewalk. All of a sudden, Olivia Stone appeared from around the back corner of the moving van, and she gasped, her eyes flying wide in obvious fear.

"Mrs. Stone? It's me."

The woman stared at her. She had seemed nervous, maybe even scared, the first time Eva had laid eyes on her at her house, holding her cardboard box full of precious papers no one seemed to want in their possession.

That look was nothing compared to the terror in Olivia Stone's face now.

CHAPTER THIRTY-TWO

OLIVIA'S GLANCE SHOT ALL around before she looked back at Eva. A screen of anger poured over her face. "Why did you come here? You shouldn't be here, Eva."

"Olivia, what's wrong? Did something happen?"

Again, the woman looked all around, then turned to fiddle with the latch on the U-Haul door, pretending she was doing something useful with it. "Nothing happened. You just need to go."

"Stop!" Eva strode to within a few feet of the other woman. "Olivia, I didn't want any part of this! I didn't ask to have that box. Why me? Why would your husband do this to me? He didn't even know me!"

Olivia whirled, her lips pinched. She stared darts of anger, almost of hatred, at Eva. But it was an anger and hatred born of fear. "You can't be here! Leave!"

"Are you going to call the police?"

The other woman stared until tears rushed into her eyes, then whirled away. It took a moment for Eva to realize Olivia's whole body was shaking. She struggled to get control of herself. Finally, she spoke without taking her eyes off the door latch of the van. "Go around the back of the house," she said in a tight voice. "I'll go through the front door and meet you back there. If you see anyone watching you before you go back there, though, you have to leave immediately. Please. For your sake and ours."

If Olivia's fear hadn't already rubbed off on Eva, that statement did the trick. In spite of the hot afternoon air, a chill passed over Eva, and her skin rose in goosebumps. As Olivia walked away toward the house, Eva tried to look nonchalant in scanning the neighborhood. Nothing seemed out of place. She studied every car in sight. No one was sitting in any of them, and none of them appeared to be a suspicious type of vehicle anyway.

After Olivia had been gone for a minute, Eva walked slowly enough around the opposite side of the U-Haul and up the driveway to the back of the house that she appeared to be out for a pleasant stroll. It was hardly pleasant, however; she could barely feel her feet hitting the ground as she walked, and by the time she rounded the corner she noticed she was starting to shake, and didn't know why.

Olivia was sitting in a lawn chair in the shade of a roof overhang, staring out at the grass and spinning a dogfood dish around and around in her hands. Their yard was fenced in solidly with six-foot cedar boards, and Eva could see no movement at any of the houses that surrounded them. Nor could she see any dog in the yard. She walked over and sat down in another chair next to the other woman.

"We used to have a German shepherd," said Olivia quietly, as if reading her mind like so many other people seemed able to do. "His name was Nitro. Buck wanted to train him to be a police dog, after he was at a convention one time, and one of the other cops told him they were starting to train dogs to sniff for drugs."

"What happened to him?" asked Eva, to all appearances carrying on a relaxed conversation.

"First, the chief refused to let Buck use him. But he kept pushing and training him anyway. He said he would do it for free. One day Doug came out to feed him and he was dead. Somebody poisoned him."

Eva felt another chill go over her. Olivia wasn't casually telling her this story. Then again, she was suspicious of anything anyone said to her anymore. Even if there was no hidden meaning behind it at all, she had started looking for one.

"I'm sorry, Olivia."

"Me too. That's when Buck first started to figure out there was something wrong. There was no one in the neighborhood that didn't like us, Eva. And everyone loved Nitro. He was just a big, happy puppy. But he was really good at finding drugs. Too good, I guess. Buck made the mistake of proving it—to the wrong people."

Eva didn't want the answer to her own next question, but she had to ask: "Who were the wrong people?"

Olivia froze, blinking her eyes rapidly before throwing the dog dish off to one side and watching it roll to a stop in the grass. "I'm sure it's all in that box."

Eva nodded slowly. The box. Of course everything came down to that.

"I'm sorry about out front," Olivia said quietly. "I'm sorry I'm not a better cop's wife. I'm sorry I'm not strong. I know you need somebody strong."

"What happened since I was here, Olivia?"

The other woman drew a deep breath. "Some guys came. Late last night. There were four of them and they all wore masks, but I know voices, and the two I heard speaking weren't anyone I know. You can't tell a soul about this, Eva. Not ever. I'm begging you. I know they'll kill us."

Eva had heard plenty of people exaggerating in her lifetime. This was nothing of the kind. Olivia Stone seemed like a very no-nonsense woman, and she truly feared for her life.

"Did they tell you that?" she asked.

Olivia only nodded.

"Why were they here? Did they come for something?"

"Of course. The box. The evidence."

The chill that poured over Eva was like a bucket of ice water. She should have been getting used to it, but she wasn't. "What did you tell them?"

"I lied. They don't know anything. I promise." This time she managed to look Eva square in the eyes. "I wouldn't put you in the crosshairs. I hope you believe me."

Eva nodded. "Of course I do." And she did. Olivia was running scared, but not scared enough to get an innocent person killed.

They sat silent for a while, each of them pawing through her own thoughts for anything important enough to say, or that wouldn't put them in any immediate danger for saying it out loud.

"They told me if I didn't tell them everything I knew, and tell them where Buck kept all the evidence, they would take my boys." Olivia stopped, and her lower lip and chin started to quiver. It took her a few minutes to get her emotions under control, and then she looked down at her hands, twisting back and forth over each other in her lap like a couple of wrestlers.

"Finally, one of the two men who never spoke put his hand on the arm of the one who was doing the talking, and when he looked at him he just shook his head. I think that had to be someone I would know. So he didn't dare speak. He wore a mask and dark glasses. He looked at the other one who wouldn't speak, and they nodded at each other. Then the main guy who kept threatening me told me if I ever told anyone they were here they would come back and kill all four of us. He said we would never see it coming, and there wouldn't be a thing we could do about it. He said they have people all over the country, and no matter where I try to run, if I talk they'll find me."

"I'm so sorry, Olivia. I can't even imagine how frightened you must be."

Olivia nodded briskly, looking back down at her hands. "They did it all with the boys right there. They were all crying, and those men didn't care. I think they liked it. Those boys will never forget that—ever."

Eva didn't need to tell her she agreed. "What do you think I should do with the box?"

"Burn it. Burn every last piece of it."

"And let them get away with everything?"

Olivia looked Eva square in the eyes. "There isn't any way to know if who you turn it over to is square. Okay? No way. Buck didn't trust anyone, and now I don't either. Except maybe Lance. I don't even know about Rick Cohen for sure. You show that box to the wrong people, Eva, and you'll go through what I did. Or worse."

"I can handle threats," Eva said. She was feeling suddenly strong, or perhaps simply trying to look that way, for Olivia.

"I'm not saying this to scare you, Eva, but you listen to me good. I don't think for you they'll be threats. I think those two men who weren't talking were cops. They were guys I know, guys who worked with Buck. I think they didn't let those other guys do something to me and the boys only out of some weird sense of loyalty. Do you think you would have that kind of protection? Burn the box, Eva. I'm sorry I ever brought it to you."

Olivia lurched up out of her chair, so Eva got up too, feeling shaken.

"Burn the box or your life from now on is going to be hell."

When Eva got back home, Bianca told her Lance had called. She hadn't stayed near the phone like she had told him she would. He had left a number, though, and had said he was at the hospital, so she called it and got a receptionist.

Lance was on the phone five minutes later. *Hey, Eva. I can't talk long. They got me guardin' this guy at the hospital—the guy from the chase.*

"Do you know his name?" Eva asked instantly. "It's not Ambro Procopio, is it?"

Lance sat quiet for a second. *Uh, no. Not Procopio. I would have told you a long time ago if it was him.*

Eva sighed with a strange feeling of relief, but it instantly flew away. "Is he awake?" If the man woke up and started talking, Eva wondered how much of her situation would change. If he had indeed thrown the briefcase out his window during the chase, was there any chance he would tell them?

They think he will be soon, replied Lance. *He's movin' around quite a bit. They were mostly lettin' him sleep, but when he started actin' like he might wake up today, that's when I got called in, to be up here with him.*

"Who is he? Does anyone know?" she asked. Now that she knew it wasn't Ambro, she was curious, nothing more. It wasn't going to mean anything to her now either way.

Some guy from Vegas. Name's Lucas Borders, but they call him Lookie Luke.

The name wrenched Eva's guts. "What did you say? Lookie Luke?" She was speaking like a robot. She didn't need to question the name. Lance had spoken plain English.

Yeah, why?

With her mind flopping cartwheels, she forced a light laugh and said, "I think there's a cartoon called that. Maybe it's just in Europe. Not 'Lookie Luke', but close—Lucky Luke." She wasn't lying. There was such a cartoon, and she was certain it was where someone had come up with the nickname for Lucas Borders. She was also certain the reason she had remembered his name was because of the cartoon.

Lucas Borders was on the list of names Buck Stone had told her about when they met at Benny's.

She ached to let Lance in on everything she knew, but after her visit with Olivia Stone she was back to thinking she should simply keep silent—about everything. Olivia was right: The best thing anyone could do was simply shut up and go on living life. If there was Mob activity in Rock Springs, so what? Was it hurting Eva or her family? No. In fact, her life so far, at least financially, was improved *because* of it, even without taking Primo Santori up on his filthy offer of employment.

At the same time Eva was thinking she should keep quiet about the cardboard box, that she should burn it as Olivia suggested, she was thinking she wanted to be with Lance. She felt comfortable around him, and protected. It wasn't just his large size and obvious poise and self-assurance. It was more his huge, kind heart, a heart that seemed to show in everything he did.

"Lance?"

Yeah?

"Do you think they would care if I came up there to sit with you for a while?"

He paused. *I don't think they'd care, but it's pretty hectic up here right now. I don't think we'd even get to talk much. You sure you're okay, Eva?*

She pulled in a deep breath. "Yeah, I'm fine. I just wanted to spend some time with you."

Wow. That makes me feel good. Can I take a rain check, though? I think you'd just be frustrated up here.

"Yeah, it's okay. I'll talk to you later, all right?"

When they hung up, she went out and sank onto the sofa, closing her eyes. Bianca looked over from washing dishes at the sink. "You want me to make you some soup, sweetheart? Or a sandwich?"

"No, Mom, thanks. I don't have much of an appetite."

"I can understand that," Bianca said. They shared a major secret, about the found money. Bianca didn't seem to have much of an appetite either.

"Hey, where's Nonni?"

"She went to bed," her mother said. "She wasn't feeling well."

Eva only nodded. She didn't dare ask any more. She was really starting to worry about her grandmother. She didn't know what they would do without her.

Suddenly, Eva sat straight up. "Mom, where are the boys?"

"In the back. Don't worry, I can see them. Are you all right, cara? You seem really jumpy. Is there something you aren't telling me?"

"No. Sorry. I'm just playing worried mom."

Lance Cartwright was flooding over one of the normal-sized chairs in the hospital, made for normal-sized mere mortals, and sipping on what might have been his fifth cup of sharp black coffee. He was drinking more from boredom than because he thought it would keep him awake.

A nurse popped her head out of the room Lucas Borders was in, a room he had all to himself, because of his celebrity criminal status. "Hey, Lance? This guy's talking."

Lance jumped up and spilled coffee on his pants, grinned and swore good-naturedly, then apologized to the nurse. "Me and my garbage mouth."

He ducked into the room to see Lucas Borders inclined in his bed on a pile of pillows. His face was swathed in bandages, and only his red, swollen nose and lips and his right eye and cheek showed. Immediately, he was looking at Lance.

"They sent the big damn bruiser up to sit on me," said Borders in a weak voice.

Lance gave him a crooked smile. "I'm just too dumb to get out of babysitting."

The man tried to laugh. "How long I been here?"

"A while. You hit that windshield pretty hard."

"I guess. Anybody else been up here besides you?"

Lance shook his head. "It doesn't seem like anyone cared about you until you started wakin' up."

This time Borders managed a laugh, although a weak one. "Ain't that always the way."

"Not with me. I snore so loud people care more about me when I'm asleep than they do when I'm awake."

"Yeah, it's pretty bad if you snore so loud you hear yourself."

Grinning, Lance said, "I wake myself up with my snoring all the time. Only my dog snores louder."

Borders chuckled. "So hey. What's gonna happen to me now?"

"Well, it isn't like you're all healed up," Lance said. "You'll be lyin' in here a while, I'd guess."

"So you guys gotta tie somebody up here all the time guardin' me? That's some crap duty."

"Keeps me off the streets."

"Yeah. Maybe we should get up a game of cards or somethin'."

They passed small talk back and forth for a while before Borders acted like he was starting to doze off again. When Lance got up, the man's eyes popped open. "You ain't leavin', are you?"

"I thought you were asleep."

"No. Just restin' my eyes. An' thinkin'. Hey, man. You seem like a pretty square guy. You on the up an' up?"

"I'm a cop." Lance shrugged.

"Yeah. Right." Borders scoffed. "A cop. That's what had me worried."

"Somethin' on your mind?" asked Lance.

"Yeah. Lots of somethin's. Can I level with you?"

"Of course."

"Man, don't turn on me, all right? I'm serious. I've got to where I don't feel like there's one trustworthy soul in the universe—or at least not in this town, anyway."

Lance studied the man for a moment, trying to choose his words carefully. "I'm not sure what you want me to say. You seem pretty worried about somethin'."

"I am. And the only reason I'm not worried with you is I don't have your name on any list."

"Huh?"

"Your name. Cartwright? I'm a *Bonanza* fan, brother. I would have remembered that. I don't suppose your name's Eric, is it?"

"Eric?"

The man looked back and forth for a few seconds between Lance's eyes before chuckling. "I guess you don't follow *Bonanza* much. So the big, strong brother—Hoss? His real name is Eric."

"Oh. That's a new one to me. No, my name's Lance. Everybody calls me Hoss, though."

The man gave a lopsided grin. "Figure that one out." After a few more moments, he said, "Hey, can you shut that door? There's nobody else in here, right?"

"Right. Just you." Lance got up and shut the door, then sat back down on the stool the doctor normally used when consulting a patient. "Talk to me, Lucas."

"You're square right?" Borders asked. "Ha! I'm sure you'd tell me you were even if you weren't."

"I'm square, man. But you're startin' to get me worried. Why would you think I wasn't square?"

Borders scoffed again. "Are you kiddin'? Because half your department is a bunch of—" He stopped, giving Lance a long, careful study. "I'd better shut up. Hell, what am I doin'? I need to be talkin' to the feds."

"I can get 'em if you want."

Borders ignored him. "Hey, what happened with Bertil Horsch?"

Lance shook his head. "I don't know who that is."

"The guy I was livin' with. Down in Blairtown. You never heard of him?"

"No. Should I have?"

For a while longer, Borders studied Lance's face. "Well, you really must not be on the take," he finally said. "Unless you're a great actor. If you were dirty, you'd know Bertil's name right off. He's with the Mob. All the dirty cops know him."

Lance was starting to worry. Borders had been talking an awful lot about dirty cops. Was he only spouting off, or did he really know something?

"Okay, man," Borders said. He finally seemed to have made a decision. "I'm gonna talk to you, 'cause I gotta gt some protection or I'm freakin' dead. I don't know how they haven't got to me already. First off, you gotta promise me you'll get the feds in here as fast as you can. They gotta get me outta this town—in short order. I can be their biggest friend, but they gotta keep me alive or I won't be good to nobody."

"You want them here now?"

"No, let me talk first. In case I fall asleep. You can call 'em when I'm done. I'm sure I'll be tellin' this story a lot more than once before this is all over."

And so it was that Lookie Luke Borders began to talk. And Borders knew way too much, had far too many intricate details about Rock Springs and the police department, for Lance to question anything of what he said. He even had details about the mayor and city council.

When Borders had finished his story, Lance didn't know whether to be angry, to cry, or to go to the bathroom and puke.

He did know one thing, though: It had been a long time, unless he was sick, since his whole body shook so bad as he tried to fit his big, quaking fingertip into the holes in the phone dial and make a call to Cooper Tervalon, who had left his number there to be called if Lucas Borders woke up and started talking.

And Lucas Borders had started talking.

CHAPTER THIRTY-THREE

LANCE CARTWRIGHT PULLED UP in his patrol car in front of Eva's house in the darkness. He had cut his headlights when he was still down the block, so she wouldn't know he was out here, and he sat listening to Creedence Clearwater Revival pound out "Bad Moon Rising" on the local AM radio station, KVRS.

Maybe he would have turned off the car, shaken himself free of his shock, and gone up to Eva's door, hoping for a healing hug and for a few moments of pretending his entire universe hadn't just imploded, but he was so enthralled by how completely the lyrics of the song matched the revelations of this horrific night that he couldn't touch the car key until it had played all the way through.

Even as the song was going, there was a bold silver moon cropping over the desert mountain rims, a sight he would normally have loved, except for the haunting lyrics.

A bad moon was rising, and yes, he could "see trouble on the way", and "bad times today".

"Don't go around tonight—it's bound to take your life . . ."

"I know the end is comin' soon."

"Hope you got your things together; hope you're quite prepared to die . . . Looks like we're in for nasty weather . . . One eye is taken for an eye . . ."

Each time a new and gut-wrenchingly fitting lyric ground through his eardrums, another wave of chills washed over him until he felt drained completely of emotion and had sunk back against his seat and sat staring ahead into the dark.

He needed Eva Galanti. He needed her tonight. He needed to touch someone, to be with someone who in no way could improve the situation he was in other than simply by emotionally being there in this time of crisis.

What would tomorrow look like? Would he still be a police officer? Would any of the men he had thought were his friends be officers? The universe was falling inward, and here he sat at its epicenter. Tomorrow, would Lance Cartwright even still be alive?

When the song ended, he reached out without thinking and shut the car off. The warm night throbbed with evil and pain. Numb, he pushed the door open and struggled out, standing for a moment with his hands on the open window frame.

It was ten-thirty, but the Galantis' lights were on, at least the one in the front room. He had talked to Eva on the phone, and she was waiting for his arrival. He wanted to go knock, yet he didn't. He feared what his own emotions were going to do to him when he first saw her.

It was at this very moment he realized his big frame was once more shaking all over.

Forcing himself to take in and push out five lung-filling breaths, he took one last one and headed for the door of the house. It opened before he got to it, and Eva stepped out, folding her arms across the front of her windbreaker.

She walked down the steps, looking up at him to try and read his emotions in the dark. They met a few feet out on the sidewalk, and he knew she had read his emotions correctly, for neither of them even said hi. They simply sank into a soft embrace, him too drained to talk, her too polite to pry. She knew he would start talking when he could.

Lance heard a voice come over his radio and cringed. He had been wishing for a night of no calls. But perhaps a call was exactly what he needed—something to get his mind off all he had learned from Lookie Luke Borders.

The voice came again, so they walked back to the car together, and the third time it came across he heard, *Patrol One, this is Dispatch. Can you read?*

He swore and hustled up his pace to reach through the passenger side and grab the mic. "Patrol One. Go ahead, Dispatch."

Please respond to a disturbance at 1409 Pioneer Drive. Caller is a next-door neighbor, but they will be at the address given. Call is a battery, but no longer in progress. Suspect no longer at the scene.

"Roger," said Lance. "En route." He turned to look at Eva. "You sure you want to ride tonight?"

"Are you sure you want me to?"

"I think so. I've been wantin' to have you come along, and after what I learned at the hospital, this could be our last chance."

She stared up at him, her eyes concerned. He had told her only enough to make her worry.

He opened her door, then shut it when she got in. Going around, he started the car back up, and they rolled into the evil night.

Neither of them spoke until they were almost to the scene of the call. At the moment she was about to speak, Lance said, "Eva, I'll tell you everything when we get this call out of the way, okay? It might take me the rest of the shift."

"Okay. Just whenever you're ready."

He chuckled without humor. "The problem is I don't know if I'll ever be ready."

They arrived, and he informed Dispatch and then got out. Hearing Eva's voice, he looked back down into the car. "Do I come with you, or stay here?"

"Come with me. You wanted to see what cops do, right?"

He thought how ironic that question was now. Tonight, he had learned the hard way that even *he* didn't know all the things some cops do.

Eva took a deep breath and got out her side of the car, looking at Lance, who was all business now, straightening his gunbelt as he started for the address whose porchlight glared out from under the eaves. Every light in the house appeared to be illuminated as well.

A man came out on the steps of the house. "Up here, officer. She's inside."

"My dispatcher said the attacker is gone. Is that true?"

"*Attackers,*" the man corrected him. "And yes, they're gone. They left here in a long, dark vehicle, maybe a Lincoln. They weren't wasting any time gettin' gone."

The man started talking before they went in the house, and a horrific story unfolded of how the man's children, whose bedroom faced the neighbor's house, had heard screaming and glass crashing. They had wakened their parents, and this man had grabbed a shotgun and gone outside. Bravely, if foolishly, he had started yelling at the house, telling them he had a shotgun. He said three men came out, one of them also brandishing a shotgun or rifle. They had yelled back and forth, and then the three men had fled in the dark car, going up the street at well over the speed limit.

The man and his wife had then gone into the neighbor's house to find the woman who lived there battered and bloody, and her and two children crying inconsolably.

"Did they tell you anything about the attackers?" Lance asked.

"A bunch of gibberish so far," the man said. "She's shaken up worse than I've seen anyone in a long time."

"All right," said Lance. "Let's go talk to her. Can you and your wife stay for a while? It sounds like you know each other pretty well, and I'm sure she'd feel more comfortable."

"Of course. I don't think I could drag my wife away if I tried."

Lance led the way into the house, followed by the reporting party and Eva. Eva stopped just inside the door, feeling completely out of place here.

Eva stood in horror listening to the woman's story when she finally got herself calmed down enough to talk. She said she and her children had been watching TV when the door crashed open without warning, and three men dressed in dark clothing came in yelling and waving guns around. She said they kept demanding that she give them what they called "the stuff", and she had no idea what they were talking about.

One of them had grabbed her by the hair as the other two cornered her kids, both of whom were crying by then. The man had jerked her head back and screamed into her face something about "information", or "evidence". She couldn't remember exactly. They might have used both words interchangeably. They wanted everything her "cop friend" had given her, they said, but she didn't know any cops, and she had no idea what they were after.

The man had slapped her repeatedly until she was crying in hysterics. She couldn't give him anything, or she would have. He finally struck her with his fist, and that was when she decided to scream. By then she felt like they were going to kill her and her children anyway, and she was desperate enough to call for help.

When her neighbor started yelling in the yard, the man who had been beating her told her if she said one word to the cops or gave them anything they would be back, and they would kill her children while she watched, then kill her. Then the three of them left, yelling back and forth at the neighbor until she thought there was going to be an exchange of gunfire.

At the last possible moment, they went to their car and raced away.

The entire story was like something out of a bad movie, and Eva listened from in front of the door, her arms folded across her chest as if she were the only one who could give herself comfort with a hug. After listening to this story and realizing how close it sounded to things she had been envisioning happening to her, and how close it sounded to the story Olivia Stone had told, she had the urge to bolt from the house and hide in the back of Lance's car.

The battered mother had interrupted her own story several times to plead with Lance, and at the end of it she started up again. "Please, officer. They told me I couldn't tell anyone what happened or why they were here. I'm so scared they'll be back. They're going to kill me and my kids." She had thought about it too long, and she burst into tears and wailing again. It took some time for the neighbors to get her calmed down once more, and the woman took her to the couch and sat there with her arm around her shaking body for a long time before the medics showed up and checked her out, doctoring her face the best they could and telling her she needed to get some stitches in her lower lip.

Finally, the medics left, and the house fell silent for a moment until Lance cleared his throat.

"All right, ma'am. I think you'll be safe tonight. Your friends will be close by, all right? And I'll keep coming by whenever I can to check on you. Let me get all your personal information for the report," he said.

The woman looked at her neighbor. "Frank? Can we stay with you guys tonight?"

Frank nodded. "Of course, Thelma! Of course you can. I wouldn't let you stay here tonight after this."

"Thank you."

"All right, ma'am," said Lance. "Let's start with your name. I'll need your full name, or at least a middle initial."

"Okay. It's Thelma. Thelma Euneice Robinson."

Thelma Robinson might as well have punched Eva in the stomach.

CHAPTER THIRTY-FOUR

FEELING SICK, EVA REMAINED silent throughout the entire call. Frank and Helen, the neighbors of Thelma Robinson, talked Thelma into letting Helen take her to the hospital to get stitches in her mouth as the medics had suggested. When Eva and Lance were finally out in the car, getting ready to follow Helen and Thelma to the hospital because Thelma was too scared to leave the house without them, Eva stared straight ahead out the windshield. Lance started the car, then looked over at her.

"Okay. What is it?"

She looked at him, wanting to smile and pretend everything was all right. She knew he had something on his chest he needed to get off it too, and she prayed that both her something and his weren't the same.

"You were going to tell me something before we got here," she reminded him, knowing her own voice sounded monotone, almost dead.

"I will. But tell me what's wrong first. Your whole demeanor completely changed in there; did you think of something?"

She swallowed hard and fought her emotions. "Lance, I almost don't even want to tell you. I'm so scared I can hardly think."

"Me too," he admitted—which didn't serve to make Eva feel better. "Come on, Eva. Talk to me."

The car Thelma and Helen were in started moving, so Lance threw his cruiser in gear and followed. It was less than two and a half miles to the hospital. Eva knew she had little time. She couldn't remember any time in her life being more frightened, and her mind was in a whirlpool from which no coherent thought seemed able to swim forth. Her only option was simply to start talking and hope something she said made sense—and hope Lance's name was nowhere in Buck Stone's box full of evidence.

"Lance," she finally started out, "what if suddenly you found out you were working in a job where everyone else you worked with was evil and crooked and being paid off? What if you found out you were the only honest person, and that no one else wanted you to live because you could be dangerous to them?"

His attention snapped to her, his eyes incredulous. *"What?"*

She could only stare at him, feeling the electricity coursing up and down her body. It was a warm night, but she was suddenly glad she had worn her navy-blue windbreaker.

The look in Lance's eyes made her cautious again. She tried to read him, and she couldn't. "Lance . . . I promise you I don't know anything that's going on in this town, with your department or anything else. I promise I don't know anything, and I wouldn't tell a soul if I did."

He was looking back at the road again, his eyes glued there as if now he couldn't even look at her. She had the urge to throw the door open and run. Had she made a big mistake saying what she already had?

"Lance? You . . . you're a straight cop . . . aren't you? Please say yes."

"I don't even want to go to the hospital," he said quietly, not answering her question. *I want to drive some secluded place and silence you*—that was what the horrid voice inside her head said for him.

"Please talk to me," she said quietly. "I promise I'll understand."

"What happened back there at that house?" he pressed. "What did you think of? Did someone say something?"

Eva wanted to cry. She had no idea how to go on. She didn't know how to bring up Stone's box of evidence, but she had gone too far now to keep it quiet. "Officer Stone gave me something—a bunch of books, and papers and stuff. I only looked through part of one book. That's the truth. I promise I don't know anything, and I don't care." Was this only her cowardly way of trying to make it so Lance didn't feel obligated to silence her?

"*Stone* gave you something? Why, Eva? You said you barely knew him."

"I did. I hardly knew him at all."

"But you mean he gave you incriminating stuff? Probably about the police, huh?"

"Yeah. But I haven't looked through it. I haven't. Lance, I don't know *anything.*"

"Me neither," he said, his voice still quiet. He remained unable to look at her.

Those two words gave Eva a thrill of hope. Gulping another breath, she sighed it back out, and then, going on those two words, she started on down the path of no return.

"I don't know anything except I don't think Officer Stone was killed on accident. I think he was killed because of what he knew. So . . ."

"So what?"

"So I called the county prosecutor today and told him I had a bunch of stuff, and . . ."

Her pause must have been way too long. "What, Eva? *What?*" They were now pulling into the hospital parking lot behind the other car. "Come on! What happened with the prosecutor?"

"He asked me for my name, and I didn't dare tell him, so I made one up. Or I thought I made it up."

Lance swore and looked over at her. "Oh no. No, Eva. Please don't tell me. Thelma Robinson?"

Eva tried to hide the fear and sickness she felt. "I got that woman beat up, Lance. They attacked her because they thought she had the evidence. She just had the bad luck of me making up a name that happened to be someone in town."

Lance swore again. She could see by his face that his mind was whirling like hers. "*James Bardo?*" he said, his voice incredulous. "It was James Bardo the head prosecutor you talked to?"

"Yes." Her heart was racing wildly.

"We're dead, Eva," he said. "Dead. I've gotta get in here and talk to Cooper Tervalon, the FBI guy. You and me've both got to get some protection, and fast."

"Why, Lance? Why you?"

"Because this guy in the hospital, Lucas Borders, told me everything today. Or I guess at least almost everything."

"What?" She was stunned. She had been trying to figure out all along how to tell him about the box of evidence . . . and he already knew? It was the exact same thing he had been trying to tell her!

"Yes," said Lance. "Everything. That's what I was going to try to tell you earlier. He told me about Buyer and Glattner and Hinshaw. And the Mob. Even the sheriff's department is in it. But he didn't say anything about the prosecutor."

"Maybe he didn't know."

"I guess he didn't. I never dreamed Bardo would be in on something like this. Man, I liked that guy, too!" He swore again as he parked not far from the other car and watched Helen and Thelma get out and start toward the emergency room entrance.

"Let's get in here and make sure Thelma's okay," he said. "Then we'll head up and talk to Tervalon. They're gonna have to get us out of town fast."

"Should I call my mom?" Eva asked.

He turned to stare at her solemnly. "Aw, crap, Eva, I don't know. I don't know if scarin' her that bad at this point will serve any purpose. I mean they don't really know about you yet, right? If they did, they wouldn't have gone after Thelma Robinson. Maybe you'll be okay for a little while."

That thought managed to give her the first real comfort she had felt all night. He reached over to put his powerful arm around her and give her a squeeze, and that was even better. Things were going to be all right. They had to be.

They went in the hospital, where all seemed peaceful and still. One room was taken by a man who had been pronghorn hunting on the Red Desert and seen a rattlesnake only after it put its fangs in him. The doctor and nurses were monitoring him, and otherwise, Thelma was the only ER patient, with nobody else around. Apparently, the hunter didn't have local friends or family, or at least none who cared to wait with him.

Lance and Eva stayed with Helen and Thelma for a while before going out with one of the nurses. "You got any fresh coffee, Gracie?" Lance asked. "Two cups would be sweet."

"We do, but we're out of sugar," the short, compact nurse replied.

"Fine for me. I don't take sugar in it anyway."

"That's fine with me, too," Eva said. She really didn't even want coffee; she was simply too emotionally drained to refuse.

They wandered down to the breakroom, and Lance poured two ceramic cups full of coffee. He picked up a white-labeled brown bottle with bold red letters that said Coffee-Mate and smirked at it, then showed it to Eva. "You want some of this stuff in yours?"

"No thanks." Carnation Coffee-Mate hardly seemed like a natural substance, and it certainly didn't taste a thing like cream.

They sipped their coffee as they walked down the hall, then stopped out of earshot of any of the nurses. "Guess it's time to go have a talk with Tervalon," Lance said quietly. "We better get the ball rolling. Maybe you should stay clear of this whole thing until him and me figure somethin' out."

"That's fine with me," she said. "I thought about calling him too, but I don't like that guy."

"Ha! We agree there. He's a real sweet guy, isn't he?" He turned and walked to the nurse's station, and she followed him. "Hey, Gracie, the FBI guy's still down there with Lucas Borders, isn't he?"

The nurse turned and stared at him, finally reaching up with a chubby hand to push her black-framed glasses up on the bridge of her nose. "You didn't hear? Mr. Borders died."

Eva and Lance stared at nurse Gracie for several seconds. Lance found his tongue first. "What are you talkin' about? I was just talkin' to him and he was fine. I just—" He stopped to stare at her, still trying to process her revelation. "Are you sure? I mean—died how?"

She chuckled, looking nervous. "Am I sure? Lance, the coroner came a while ago and took him away. I sure hope he's dead."

"But . . . Then where's Tervalon?"

Gracie shrugged. "He left with the coroner."

"Okay. Thanks." They turned and walked away, and one glance told Eva that Lance looked as numb as she felt.

He slumped into a chair in the waiting room and took a sip of his coffee, staring at it with a disgruntled look, as if he expected a baby bass to float to the surface any moment. At last, his eyes fumbled over toward Eva and seemed finally to come into focus.

"It's all of them, Eve. Everybody."

"What do you mean?"

"The city, the county, the legal department . . . even the Feds. Borders was fine when I left here. He was fine. There's no way they can convince me he just all of a sudden died without help."

"Wait . . . so you think . . . ?" She stopped and stared at him, and the worst wave of fear she had felt yet swept over her.

"Yeah. Tervalon killed that guy. He was fine, Eva. I'm tellin' you, he was fine."

Ambro Procopio rolled into town after midnight, driving his gold Pontiac LeMans and feeling impervious to any harassment by police in this city or county. He knew both agencies, along with the legal department, were solidly wrapped up in their drug and prostitution ring. Everyone was making money except the little guys who hadn't been brought in on the pot yet, and anything they did against Ambro or any of the Mob's other people would quickly be undone by the powers at the top. His recent ticket from Officer Cohen had proved how easy that was.

Yet he drove into town slowly, simply because he didn't feel like dealing with anyone—even if he could thumb his nose at them, either at the scene or later with their superiors. He often enjoyed watching some naïve cop write him a citation, laughing inside because all the while he knew they were wasting their time. But right now he only wanted to get home and crawl into his own bed and sleep.

It had been an agonizing few days for Ambro, first because of having to spend time in the hospital in Las Vegas having his bullet wound treated, and after that because his little brother,

Donatello, was doing poorly, and there was nothing anyone seemed to be able to do for him.

Little Donatello was twenty-three years old now, and like Eva Galanti's youngest boy, Leo, he had been diagnosed at birth as having Mongolism, which recently had been re-termed Down Syndrome. Every doctor Ambro's parents had taken their baby to had insisted that the boy needed to be placed in an institution, a place where the staff knew how to handle such things. But the Procopios were very proud, and no matter what someone said was wrong with one of their children, they would fight for them. An institution was the last place Donatello Procopio belonged, in the eyes of fierce and proud Cesare Procopio and his sweet wife Lucia, and so they fought every doctor and kept their baby boy home, and yet somehow to their consternation he continued to weaken, and no one could explain why.

Little Donatello had never grown very large, which led to one of his nicknames, Piccolo, which in Italian meant "small". His other nickname, the first one given him, was a mouthful. It was Cesare who had named him Tartaruga, meaning "Turtle", because for so long it seemed so difficult for Donatello to right himself if he fell over on his back. But the little guy struggled and struggled, and in the end he always won—and always without help, because Cesare knew it would make him strong, both inside and out, to work out his own battles.

Ambro had been Donatello's valiant protector forever, much the way he saw Eva Galanti's son Tyke act toward little Leo. It was why he couldn't help but love those boys of Eva's, for in them he saw himself and his little earth angel, Donatello—the little brother about whom no one in Rock Springs knew, or would ever know. That was one thing about Donatello: To his family, he was a secret, because in the world of the Italian Mafia, one did not admit to relatives who were less than perfect.

Ambro pulled up to his duplex on Kimberly, the nicest one he knew of in all of Rock Springs, and got out to open his garage door, then drove in. He wished he at least had someone with him; with his stiff, bandaged side, where the bullet from Officer Buck Stone's .38 special had broken one of his ribs, getting in and out of the tight front seat of the LeMans was the worst thing Ambro had to do during his day, and the reason he had stayed recuperating at his parents' home for as long as he had.

Well, it was partly that, and partly because he wanted to spend as much time as he could with Donatello, because the doctors were trying to tell the Procopios that their son would not live for very many more years. The thought crushed Ambro's heart.

Ambro slogged up the two stairs to his residence, a huge place that had originally been four apartments, but had since been converted into a duplex. That was the only way to make it fit for a man of Ambro's stature high in the Mob, what one would call a segundo in the Rock Springs mob structure.

Ambro went to his kitchen and mixed a martini, then walked up the stairs to his bedroom and threw pillows up against the headboard, sitting down on the luxurious blue satin bedspread and kicking off his shoes. With a long, appreciative sip of the martini, he reached over for the phone, set it in his lap, and dialed Primo Santori.

Serenella's sultry voice answered, and brightened when she heard Ambro's voice. Sometimes he had the feeling Serenella wasn't altogether in love with her husband and that she would have left him any time Ambro asked, except she knew it wouldn't matter because both she and Ambro would have been killed. It didn't matter anyway; Ambro would have had nothing to do with the woman even if Primo wasn't around.

Ambro! came Primo's voice over the line. *My friend! How are you? How was the drive?*

"Good," said Ambro, trying to hide his fatigue. "How are things here?"

Now Primo's voice darkened. *Gone to hell, if you want the truth.*

Ambro tried to straighten up, sloshing his drink and spilling some on the bedspread. "What? Why? What happened?"

Much, replied Primo. *I wish you had called me after you left.*

"I'm sorry, Primo. I was busy hurting."

Yes, I know," said Primo by way of apology. *You were doing what I told you. But the money? It is gone.*

"Gone? How? I saw right where he threw it."

It doesn't matter. It is gone. Someone else found it before we did. And that bastardo *Lucas Borders? He woke up.*

"No! What happened? He didn't talk."

Oh, he talked. He talked, my friend. Not just to Tervalon, but to the cops.

"Who? One of ours?"

No. Not one of ours. The big one—the one they call Hoss.

"Oh hell," said Ambro. "Is he still talking?"

Not anymore. Tervalon took care of that problem.

"Okay, so now what?"

You know what. Listen, Ambro, you get some sleep. We'll talk tomorrow when you're rested. Tervalon will meet us up here at eleven. You should try to be here at least half an hour before that. That man is scared, Ambro. He is liable to do something really foolish.

"I'll be there," said Ambro, grimacing as he twisted and felt the renewed agony of his broken rib.

Rest well, my friend, said Primo Santori. *We have a lot of unpleasant clean up to do.*

"Do we have any idea who has our money?" asked Ambro.

One of two people, according to what Tervalon believes. Some mechanic named Lucky is one possibility, and you'll like

the other one: It's your foolish little friend, Eva. It looks like
fate might have caught up with that little woman after all. The
Lord works in mysterious ways, doesn't he, Ambro?

CHAPTER THIRTY-FIVE

THE PHONE RANG TOO early for Eva, and she lay there in bed almost paralyzed, staring at the ceiling, praying the call would mean nothing. She had taken to leaving the extra phone on her dresser, and mornings like this she really regretted it; that clanging bell was simply too close to her head.

Her mother's soft voice came at the door: "Eva? Are you awake?"

"Yeah."

"Okay, cara—telephone for you."

Eva rolled out of bed and sat up, blinking her eyes hard and trying to still the pounding of her heart. She was tired of this sick feeling. She had done nothing wrong. Why should she be plagued like this?

But maybe it was only Lance. Or Brandon. She couldn't give up hope.

Going to the door, she opened it and said quietly down the hall. "Who is it, Mom?"

"Not a voice I recognize. A man."

Eva cringed. "Okay, thanks. I have the other phone in here." The words were about all she could get out.

She shut her door and picked up the phone, then hesitated too long trying to get up the courage to answer.

You on the line? It was a man, but very distorted.

"Yes, I'm here. Who is this?"

I'm looking for a briefcase containing a large sum of money, said the voice. *You don't know where it came from, but you do know it isn't yours. As long as you have not touched the money and none is missing, if you set the briefcase out on your front porch tonight at ten-thirty precisely, it will be gone in the morning, and you will remain safe. Do you understand?*

"Who is this?" she asked. She didn't feel brave, but she hoped her voice made her sound like she was.

Be very careful. You aren't the one asking the questions. Very bad things happen to people who jack me around, Miss Galanti. Mark my words.

"I don't know what you're talking about," she said, keeping her voice even. "I don't have any money."

Be very careful, the voice said again. *Ten-thirty tonight. Not one minute after.*

The line went dead, and Eva started shaking. *As long as you have not touched the money, and none is missing,* the voice had said. But what if she had? She hadn't dared admit she had the money, so she couldn't even ask.

She lay back down, but of course she couldn't sleep. The phone rang again half an hour later, and again came her mom's voice at the door.

"Eva, it's Brandon. You're quite the popular girl today."

Eva was up off the bed by the end of Brandon's name, and her hand froze on the phone. "Got it, Mom. Thanks."

She picked up the handset and waited until she heard her mother hang up, then put it to her ear. "Brandon!"

Evie! We got trouble bad!

"I know. They called you too?"

Somebody did, Brandon said. *I got no idea who.*

"I don't either," Eva admitted. "How did they know, Brandon? How *could* they?"

I got no idea, but we gotta split this town today. Now.

Eva froze. The phone started slowly to drift away from her ear until she jerked it back again. "Brandon, I think I know who it was."

Who, for heck's sake?

"Cooper Tervalon."

There was a long silence on the other end of the line. After a while, Eva heard a clanking in the background, telling her Brandon was only able to call her because he was at work. She had been wondering how he was getting away with it if he was at the apartment with Karen.

It did kinda sound like his voice, Brandon said*, but I don't know why he'd be makin' a call like that.*

Eva looked at herself in the mirror and cringed. "I do."

You do? Then why?

"Because he's in with the Mob, Bran," she said quietly. "A lot of people are in the with the Mob."

Eva! Stop it. You can't be sure.

"I'm sure, Brandon. I'm one hundred percent sure."

What are you talkin' about? Did you find somethin' out?

"We have to talk, Brandon. Can we meet somewhere?"

Of course. Where? When?

"I don't care. As soon as possible, wherever you want."

Your house, he replied. *I'll drive way out of town a few miles and wait to see if anybody follows me, then drive back and park down the street from you. Does your mom know what's goin' on?*

Eva gritted her teeth, thinking about her mom, her grandmother, and the boys. "No. Not yet. Not the latest, anyway."

Well, we can talk in the back yard. Until we figure somethin' out, there ain't no use in freakin' them out too.

"Okay. When will you be here?"

I'll leave in a minute. But if they follow me I'll have to come back here and think of somethin' else. They might be watchin' for us to try and leave town.

Brandon hung up with Eva and looked over at Dino Priest's feet, sticking out from under a vomit-yellow Volvo that was so ugly Brandon would have rather walked than be seen driving it. He took a deep breath. Dino Priest was a great guy, and his patience was as long as a bad sermon, but it had to run out eventually. He was paying a good wage for Brandon to be driving around not doing his job all day.

"Hey, Dino?"

"Yeah, Brandon, what's up?" came the muffled voice from under the Volvo.

"Hey, I just talked to Eva. Do you think it'd be okay if I take off real quick? Fifteen, maybe twenty minutes is all."

Dino normally would simply have told him, *Sure, go ahead.* This time he slid his creeper out from under the Volvo and looked up. "Hey, buddy, it ain't none o' my business, but is everything all right? Man, this really isn't like you to be missin' so much work."

"I wanna tell you, Dino. I just can't."

Dino struggled to sit up, not even asking Brandon for a hand, which he normally would have. From there, he stood, also without assistance. He wiped his hands off on a filthy pink shop rag while eyeballing Brandon and ignoring the other mechanic far in the back.

"You gettin' mixed up with that girl? Is that it?"

"No! No, we're just friends. Nothin' else."

Dino looked at him calculatingly. "I trust you, Brandon. And I'm not gonna lie to you, son. I don't know how you an' Karen even stay together. I couldn't do it. And that Eva, she's a real special girl. Anybody can see that. But if you're mixin' up in that kind of trouble, I gotta tell you I think it's gonna end bad."

"I promise you it ain't nothin' like that, but it's way too much to explain."

"Okay, buddy. You know what you're doin', I guess. Just be back as soon as you can, all right?"

"Thanks, Boss." Brandon started to turn away until Dino called him back.

"You know I love you like a son, Brandon. I'd do anything for you, and I'd hate to ever lose you. Be real careful."

"Thank you, sir," replied Brandon.

Brandon went out and got in his primer-gray Chevy Delray, firing it up and driving to the street, then scanning all around for over a minute before he decided it was safe to pull out. He headed out toward Highway 187, but he had only gone four blocks before he spotted the tail.

It was some dark car, but he couldn't quite tell because of the distance if it was Cooper Tervalon's Caprice. He got on the highway and gunned it, soon moving along at fifty-five miles an hour. Out here, there were few turn-offs, and almost none that should be taken by a two-wheel-drive car like his. Whoever was back there had all kinds of time to get behind him and then stay far enough back that he wouldn't have to worry about being seen.

He was at least four miles out before he spotted the dark car behind him again, and he drew a deep breath and swore. All right. He had to find some other plan. Taking a wide spot too fast, he whipped his car back around and headed back the other way, recognizing Tervalon in the Caprice as he zoomed past it. So Eva had been right! He easily could have gotten back to town in time to lose Tervalon, but what was the point? As soon as he couldn't find him, he was just going to head to Eva's.

Brandon drove all the way back to the shop, parked the Delray, and went in.

"That was quick," said Dino.

"Yeah." Brandon couldn't help but sound sullen. "I didn't get to do what I needed to."

"Son, I ain't never dug into your private life much, have I?"

"No, sir. You been real good that way, Dino."

"I'm glad you think so, buddy. But I hope you still keep thinkin' that after what I got to say."

"Okay." Here it came. Brandon had always wondered if a day would come when Dino demanded to know more about him.

"You're in trouble, ain't you, son? Somethin' bad's happenin'. Is it somethin' to do with that Karen?"

Dino had never liked Karen Lyndsey, not from the very beginning. He had tried to mind his business and not say anything, but it didn't take a genius to see through him. Now Brandon only wished he had had the same kind of sense. It wasn't just the fact that Karen was always at the doctor or the hospital for something, either. If she had been a great girl like Eva, Brandon wouldn't have minded putting up with her health problems. It was just that Karen was a witch on top of it all. That was the real rub, and whether Dino knew it or not, Brandon sure had the same rub. But he had sworn to be Karen's for life, so what was he supposed to do? He wasn't about to be like all those other creeps he had met in the pen. He had to have some kind of honor.

"It's nothin' to do with Karen. I promise." Dino kept staring him down until finally Brandon folded, something he never dreamed he would do, with Dino or anyone else. "Ah hell, Dino. I gotta talk to you. I'm in huge trouble, and so is Eva."

Cooper Tervalon was chain-smoking blue ribbon Embassy Regals like they were the last cigarettes he would ever get his hands on, sitting in his black Caprice up the road from Dino's Mechanic shop watching for any further movement from Brandon Lucky's primer-gray Delray. He was watching Brandon because he had done enough research to know he was an ex-con, he had a good, solid car, and so he was a flight risk. That wasn't the case with Eva Galanti. She had no car to run in even if she had wanted to run. He had checked with the DMV days ago, and she had only one car registered to her, the same Plymouth Valiant station wagon that was broken down in the parking lot of Dino's shop. On top of that, she had no other family in Rock Springs, and none in any town close by, and her mother, the only one in her in-town family capable of driving, had no cars registered in her name.

Brandon was the one who could fly, so Brandon was the one who got surveillance.

Cooper Tervalon was ninety-five percent positive that either Brandon Lucky or Eva Galanti was in possession of the lost money, the money Lucas Borders had jetted out of his car when he and Ambro Procopio were flying out of town just ahead of the cops. Lucas Borders was a snitch. Procopio wasn't leaving town with him because they were accomplices. He was only leaving with him because they had been caught in a compromising position by the wrong cop, and they had to lose Officer Buck Stone before he could identify them. At least that was Ambro Procopio's hope; he had way too much to live for in Rock Springs to let himself be pinpointed in a sting with the authorities now.

Tervalon's partner, unfortunately for him, was a straight agent. He had stumbled into a situation with Buck Stone where neither of them ever should have been. The two of them had died at the scene of the wreck because both of them already knew too much, and it was no longer safe to have them in Rock Springs. They died, according to the police reports, at the hands of a passenger in Lucas Borders' car who was reported to have escaped. But the truth was both men had died at the hands of their own. Tervalon didn't like it, but he liked the idea of rotting in a federal penitentiary along with all the thugs he had put there even less.

His own bullet had taken the life of the FBI agent, while that of Jacob Glattner had accounted for Buck Stone.

Everything should have ended up fine. It all seemed to be wrapped up, with all ends tied off, when Ambro called to tell Primo Santori, before leaving town to head for the hospital, where Borders had tossed the briefcase.

But who could ever have counted on foolish Eva Galanti stumbling along in the dark going after her car, and of ex-con Brandon Lucky coming out to find her? Some bizarre circumstances simply cannot be foretold.

Now Eva Galanti and Lucky were simply two more loose ends that must be tied up, so "Rocket Springs" could go back to being a safe place in which to do business.

First, however, they had to get the money back, for two dead people would tell no tales. If they were simply killed outright, the money most likely would be gone forever.

Through his binoculars ten minutes later, Tervalon saw Lucky's gray coveralls, and he was headed for his car again. Tervalon fired up the Caprice and waited until Lucky's car was at the street. He waited until he pulled out, this time headed east on Bridger. Perhaps Lucky was only testing something he had done to the car to make sure it worked. But still he wasn't about to take a chance and let him get out of his sight.

So he followed, keeping back as far as he dared.

At M Street, the gray Delray made a right turn, now heading south. He was still traveling at a fairly sedate speed limit, an easy mark for someone like Tervalon, who had been specially trained in the art of tailing people who didn't want to be caught.

Crossing Front Street, M Street was now Broadway, one of the more irritating things about this hick railroad town. They swung quietly along Broadway as it bent around to the south-west, and Tervalon was starting to believe he was completely wasting his time. Where could Lucky possibly think he was going to go if he was really trying to make a break for it?

They made a left on F Street, and then another one on Second. There was absolutely no cause for alarm, so Tervalon found himself actually starting to get bored. They turned onto G Street and followed it all the way until it turned into Connecticut—again with the backwoods hick street changes midstream. Connecticut was a straight shot pretty much due south until they made a left turn onto Vermont. If they kept going this way, they were going to be out in the desert.

Looping around, they went left on Wyoming Street for a block or so before hitting New Hampshire and turning right. New Hampshire was more or less simply the street name for what became highway 430, a lonely desert road traveling between ugly rock formations and brush, a desolate no man's land. But the gray Delray kept going on it all the same.

Just when Tervalon was getting annoyed enough to think about pulling over, he saw a puff of smoke erupt from the Delray's dual tailpipes, a cloud of dust rose behind it, and the car was flat gone! Almost before Tervalon could mentally switch gears, the Delray hit seventy, then eighty miles an hour. Tervalon depressed the gas. Eighty-five. Ninety miles an hour. One hundred! As his own speedometer began severely to rise, he cursed Brandon Lucky out loud. That idiot was going to kill them both, driving this horrible road at a speed like this.

Lucky was making a run for Colorado! Tervalon grinned. He had him now. There was no way a thug like Brandon Lucky was going to leave Rock Bottom unless he had the money with him. And there was no way a beat-up 1958 Delray was going to outrun Tervalon's top-of-the-line Caprice.

Agent Cooper Tervalon was going to catch Brandon Lucky, and then Brandon Lucky was going to die out on this lonely stretch of freeway. There likely wouldn't be a soul to report his dead body for hours.

CHAPTER THIRTY-SIX

MECHANIC MASON WILLIAMS, DRESSED in Brandon Lucky's striped coveralls, drove the Chevy Delray out on Highway 430 toward Colorado as fast as those horses would carry him—just like Brandon told him to do.

Ever since Brandon had worked so hard getting this engine souped up to race-winning levels, Williams had been itching to drive it, and every time he begged, Brandon had turned him down. *Maybe someday.* That's all Brandon would ever say.

Someday had finally come.

There was a newer model black Caprice behind Williams on the lonely desert freeway. Brandon had told him there would be. Keep it straight. Keep it on the road. That's what Brandon had told him.

The goal was not only for Williams to enjoy the drive, but to get that black Caprice as far out of Rock Springs as his little tires would carry him.

It didn't take Williams long, however, to understand that this highway, at these speeds, was going to kill him if he didn't back off. Frost-heaved Wyoming highways didn't often lend themselves to one hundred thirty miles an hour, and that was the highest speed he attained before the ugly road, and a wide, sweeping curve to the left begged him to back off to one hundred.

Some five miles out, Williams started slowing even more. There had been too many moments already when he had felt like the car, after a particularly bad swell, was lifting right off the highway, getting ready to take to the air. Even as bad as he had wanted to race this car, rolling *any* car across the desert from a one hundred-mile-an-hour-launch was not Mason Williams' idea of how he wanted to depart life. And all the rocks out here would make certain he did indeed depart it.

Seven miles out—ninety miles an hour. Eight miles out, he was at eighty. By nine miles, he had slowed to seventy-five, and the black Caprice was pretty much on top of him.

Suddenly, a sick feeling washed over Mason Williams. This had seemed like a game up till now. But he remembered Brandon's admonition: This FBI agent would try to kill him. His only protection, Brandon said, would be that the man was looking for a briefcase, which wasn't in the car. If he didn't find it, and once he saw that Mason wasn't Brandon, Mason should be safe.

Should? The word didn't sound so promising now that the FBI was fast closing on his rear bumper.

At ten miles from town, Mason Williams pulled to the roadside. The engine was growling and purring at the same time, and rocking Williams around in the seat. The Delray was ready for another run.

In a cloud of dust, the black Caprice flew up and stopped at an angle behind the Delray, and a man brandishing a pump shotgun jumped out and started screaming. Once he was able to decipher the pale blond-haired man's hysterical words, Williams understood he was telling him to get out of the car and get on the ground.

Williams put his left arm out the window, reaching high. He opened the door with his other hand, then put it out as well, showing them both to be empty and pushing the door out with his body.

Shaking from adrenaline, he turned toward the furious blond man in the black suit, both hands high above him. "Don't shoot! Don't shoot!"

The FBI agent stared. Shotgun in hand, he stepped away from his door and stared harder. A string of curses started out of his mouth as he moved closer to Williams. "Who the hell are you?"

"Mason Williams!"

"Where the hell is Lucky?" the other man yelled.

"At the shop, man! He's at the shop. I was just testing his car out for him."

The agent threw a string of vehement curses at Williams, backed to his open door, tossed the shotgun in in front of him and jumped in the car, slamming his door. It took him three tries in the narrow road to get turned around, and then the Caprice roared back up the highway toward Rock Springs.

A weak smile slowly came to Mason Williams' face. He tried to decide if he would need to go find a change of underwear when he got back to the shop. And then he tried to decide, since he was safe now, if he should just keep driving the Delray until it was almost out of gas. That was the least Brandon Lucky should allow him to do after what he had gone through for him.

Brandon Lucky parked Dino Priest's two-tone blue 1968 Jeep Commando on a rock-studded hillside some one hundred yards behind Eva's house and waded through brittle brown grass to get back to her street. Then he went all the way around the house and came up the front sidewalk. One thing he didn't want to do right now was take Eva Galanti by surprise. He knew she had a .357 Magnum Colt Python in the house, and he also knew she was pretty good at shooting it, in spite of her thin wrists. Besides, even skinny wrists can manage one shot, and one shot to midships from a .357 Magnum would be the end of a guy like Brandon whose chest to him sometimes didn't seem much wider than a bullet.

Eva threw the door open and came running out when Brandon was halfway up the walk. "Mom isn't here!" she said. "I sent her and Nonni and the boys to a neighbor's house. Hurry! Come inside."

They got inside, and Brandon slammed the door and pulled the drapes, throwing the room into semi-darkness. He whirled on Eva, who gave him a huge hug. "Wow. I wish you'd get scared more often," he said when she pulled away.

Eva tried to smile. "Brandon, you were right: We have to get out of town."

He stared her down. "For how long are we thinkin'?"

"Forever. Remember when Cooper Tervalon was watching us that night? And driving by slow? There was never anyone else around there that night, Brandon. And the mob guy told Lance that's where he threw out the briefcase. He wasn't by himself either. Lance found out Ambro Procopio was in the car too. After the wreck, he and Buck Stone were shooting at each other, and Lance thinks Ambro got hit, because there was some blood there that nobody could tell where it came from. He's guessing it was the cops and Cooper Tervalon who killed the other FBI guy and Buck Stone to get them out of the way and to give Ambro a chance to escape."

Brandon stared at her, his narrow, more-than-normally pale face accentuated against his dark whiskers. In his eyes was the greatest terror Eva had ever seen or imagined in him. The tough ex-con was suddenly in a place where he never expected to be.

"Okay, Evie. Yeah, we gotta split this town for good. But I don't know how long we can run. The Mob is everywhere—and I mean *everywhere.* There really ain't no safe places. "

"We'll have to find someone to call once we're away from here, Brandon," she said, shrugging. "It's our only chance, right? Lance has to run too—and maybe Rick Cohen. We aren't sure about him yet. Lance doesn't even dare talk to him. He really got blindsided by all this. I think he would rather have been shot than find out all his friends are crooked—not to mention his boss."

"All right. We have to think this through. I don't think you have time to pack anything except maybe a duffel bag with some clothes. Maybe your grandma's medication. I've got Dino's Commando parked up the hill back there." He pointed. "I'll go get it and let's take it back to him, then I'll get my car, go back to my place and get some stuff and Karen, and meet you . . . Where's a good place?"

"How about Albertson's?" she said. "In the parking lot. They won't dare do anything to us there in broad daylight, right?"

He stared at her. "It's almost fifty thousand bucks, Eva. What do you think they'll dare do?"

A cold hand clutched her innards. "You're right."

"But we'll still meet in the Albertson's parking lot. I don't know what other choice we have."

Brandon turned out of habit and pushed the drapes aside to look out the front. He swore and almost tore the drapes throwing them shut again. He whirled on her.

"Evie! They're here."

CHAPTER THIRTY-SEVEN

THERE WAS NO TIME to think, only to act. Brandon turned to Eva.

"You still got your Colt?"

She froze, but only for a moment. "Yeah."

"Get it!"

"What about the money?"

Now it was his turn to stare. "Get it too! And that box of papers. These guys can go to hell!"

Running down the hall to Eva's bedroom, they burst inside, and she threw everything off the cardboard box and jerked it off the floor. Scanning the room, she spotted her pillow and ran over to take it by the case, shaking the pillow free and dumping all the box's contents into the empty case.

She turned and thrust the burden against Brandon's chest, then scrambled for the closet, throwing everything aside and grabbing her Colt Python, which she had taken to keeping on top of the briefcase. Her trembling hands fumbled open the cylinder, she confirmed it was full and slammed it shut.

Crawling backward out of the closet with the briefcase in one hand and the Colt in the other, she looked at Brandon. A weird sensation had come over her, a feeling she couldn't understand. She was scared to death, and yet somewhere inside she also sensed some anger, and, strangely, even excitement.

She tried to hand the gun to Brandon, but he pushed her hand away. "Evie! You shoot better than I do. Please!"

She retracted it. "What do we do now?"

"Run out the back for Dino's Jeep."

They had given whoever was coming after them too much time, but they had no choice in their next move. Down the back stairs they ran, and as they burst out the door Eva saw a face appear around the corner of the house. It was a man in a black shirt and slacks, and he held a gun. Eva didn't think. She only dropped the briefcase, raised the Colt, and fired, the way she had done with her father so many times, the way she had practiced hundreds of times out on the desert since he was gone.

She heard the man cry out and curse, and then she snatched the briefcase from the ground, and she and Brandon were running.

Halfway up the low hill, a shot rang out behind them. Eva heard it whistle past and slap into a rock, whining away. The sound only made her run faster, ducking low and trying to stay in the rocks as much as she could. Another shot as they neared the Jeep. She heard a pinging noise from somewhere on the metal, but there was no time to see where it hit. Throwing the briefcase through her open window, she turned and leaned against the side of the Jeep with the Colt ready, and four men she could see at the back of the house scrambled over each other getting out of sight.

They were in the Commando now, and Brandon slammed the clutch down with his foot and fired it up. Below them, they could hear angry, yelling voices, and a smattering of shots. The Jeep bounced and lurched over hummocks of earth and the light tannish-gray rocks that lay scattered all over this hillside.

Brandon steered the Commando slightly to the left. They tore down the hillside through the brush and rocks, then between two houses and jarringly went over a ditch, landing on the pavement of Mitchelson Street. The ride down that narrow street was harrowing, as was their almost sideways landing out on busy Elk Street, where Brandon nearly brought the Commando up on its left wheels as he veered hard right, trying to miss a pickup and a passenger car that missed them it seemed by inches. Eva grabbed onto the door post, clenching her teeth and cramming her eyes shut. They were going to roll!

They would die in the wreck, or the Mob and the police would quickly swarm over them, seizing both evidence and cash, and it would all be over. If they lived, it would take only moments, and bullets, to finish them off.

She felt a jolt as the Jeep flopped back over on all four tires, and the engine screamed as Brandon poured the coals to it. When she dared to open her eyes, they were well on their way up Elk Street toward the freeway.

Cranking around in the seat, she saw two police cars swerve onto Elk Street two blocks or so behind them. They were soon followed by a long red car and a second civilian car that made her cringe: It was Ambro Procopio's gold LeMans!

Eva's head spun. The closest town was Green River, eighteen miles away. There was no way this Jeep could beat Ambro's car, even if it could beat the police and the red car she recognized as Primo Santori's Chrysler. If they went the other way, toward Rawlins, it was even worse. There they would have almost one hundred ten miles of flat, open desert.

As they growled past the infamous Kasbah lounge, Eva was certain Brandon would veer hard onto I-80, headed west for Green River. What other choice did they have? But he didn't. Brandon slapped the gas the rest of the way to the floor and swung wide around a semitruck that seemed to be crawling up the road in front of them.

"Where are you going?" yelled Eva as they flew past the on-ramp toward Green River.

"The mountains! There's no way we can outrun these guys on the pavement."

Eva's guts clutched inside her. She had only ever been four-wheeling in a Jeep one time, with her ex-husband. She still wanted to kill him for that horrific ride.

The police cars, Ambro, and Primo were coming up on them quickly when Eva looked back again. She swore out loud and never thought to apologize.

Where they were driving now, up Highway 187 toward the tiny settlement of Farson, there was pretty much nothing, other than a lot of good country to run a Jeep off the road, dispose of its occupants and have no one be the wiser. There were a couple of large ranches out here, Eva had been told, and she could see at a glance there were a few scattered homes, but hardly an other sign of civilization to speak of, and growing fewer by the minute.

The police cars were right on their tail now. Brandon kept veering crazily across both lanes of the highway, trying to keep them from getting alongside him.

"Why haven't they started shooting?" Eva almost screamed over the sound of the Jeep's engine, and the wind barreling in at them.

"They can't! They can't kill us because they don't know if we have the stuff with us yet!" Brandon yelled back.

Eva was extremely comforted.

This country they were driving through like a crazy blue snake had its own kind of charm, but today, to Eva, there was nothing charming about it. On their right, it ran out across flats where possibly even the cop cars could go, while to the left there was a flat area for a while, but not far beyond it the mountains jutted up in what even Eva could see was an impassable wall, even for the best Jeep or motorcycle.

Several times it felt like the Jeep was going to tip over because Brandon swerved so hard to keep the police cars behind them. "Maybe you should shoot at 'em!" Brandon yelled over the roar of the wind.

"Sure!" she yelled back. She didn't even start to raise the gun, and he said nothing more about it.

"Well, I'm goin'!" Brandon yelled after another minute. "We can't keep doin' this!"

With a hard turn of the wheel by Brandon's strong arms, he slammed his foot on the brake and left the pavement. Almost immediately, they hit a nearly invisible rut, more of a ditch, along the roadway, making Eva's head slam into the ceiling. She grabbed frantically for the dash as they bounced up into the air again and came careening down, then almost shot once more up into the air. As they bounced like a heavily inflated football across the desert, Eva found herself intermittently shouting, screaming, squealing, shrieking, squawking, and swearing; there were a lot of "S-words" bouncing around like ricochets in the Jeep all at the same time.

The country was spotted with brush, cut with washes that only ran with water during the worst of rainstorms or briefly during spring run-off. To their left reared the threatening mountains. But even as bad as it all looked for them, it was this desert and a two-tone blue Jeep Commando that were now their only friends. It was almost forty-five miles to the tiny dot on the map called Farson, where it was almost a sure thing they would find no help. After that, it was even farther to Lander and Riverton, with no guarantee they would find any kind of refuge in those little farm and ranch communities either. Eva felt sick. They were running, with nowhere to run.

Eva's only comfort was to look to the right and see out on Highway 187, growing farther and farther away, the two police cars with lights on and sirens wailing, trailed by Ambro and Primo.

With his teeth gritted, Brandon kept trying to steer them on the easiest path through the brush, rocks, and gully-washed country, but in truth there was no easy way to go. He kept inching closer and closer to the wall of mountains, but of course they only dared get so close. Even a mile or so away from the mountains, they were running into and having to cross wider and deeper gullies, and the ride was brutal on Eva's feet and backside. Regardless, across the untamed desert face they continued to bounce, while Eva took turns clutching the dash, the top of the door, or her seat, whichever was convenient at the moment. Unlike earlier, she fought to keep her cursing at a minimum, but it only crossed her mind once or twice what Brandon must think of her and her unladylike mouth now.

They bounded down into a dry wash as, to Eva's horror, she looked over to see the four pursuing vehicles turn off the pavement and stream after them into the desert.

"They're following us, Brandon!"

Brandon clenched his teeth harder and turned the Jeep up the wash. "Don't worry. I've been over here before. They won't be following for long."

"Where does this go?"

"Hell if I know!" Eva guessed that was exactly where it went.

"I thought you said you'd been here before."

"Yeah, but not all the way up."

"Why?"

"It got so bad I had to turn around and go back out."

Eva didn't swear, at least not out loud. The word she wanted to use was a name for Brandon, and she didn't think he would appreciate it like she did in her head.

Ahead, the sides of the wash started to steepen, and the sight must have alarmed Brandon as much as it did Eva, because he grimaced, slowed, and cranked the wheel to the right. The tires hit soft dirt, and the axle ground for a moment before the Jeep heaved and shot up out of the wash back onto semi-level open country, growling along through a low screen of brush not high enough to hide them from sight of their pursuers.

Eva looked back toward the highway again, then at Brandon. "Two of them are still coming."

"Cop cars?" asked Brandon, not looking over at her as he carefully negotiated around a big cluster of boulders.

"Yeah, both of them."

Without replying, he turned toward what appeared to be a really questionable road, or at least a Jeep trail. It was badly eroded and shot through with rocks, some of them a fifth the size of the Jeep. The hideous path started climbing up and up until Eva started to think maybe Brandon was crazier in a Jeep than her ex. She was pretty sure they were going to tip over backwards.

"What are we going to do, Brandon?" she finally asked, sucking a deep breath as they topped over the bluff and looked back to see Ambro's LeMans and Primo's Chrysler limping back to the pavement, while one police car stood still, a driver standing beside it, and the other crept doggedly on through the brush toward them.

"We gotta circle back toward town. I gotta try to get Karen."

"What about my family?" she asked.

His only reply was to stand there grinding his teeth together, watching the police car crawl on toward them. Whoever was driving it was living in a dream world. There was no way a rear-wheel-drive sedan was going to follow them to where they were. But then again, was there any way out of here other than back through that police car?

"We'll figure out some way to get your family too," Brandon said after a long dearth of speaking, where the only sound was the wind sighing in the brush.

"Do you think we can get back out of here a different way?" she asked.

"I guess that's what we're about to find out."

They got back in the Jeep, and Brandon drove for a few hundred yards along the bluff before it veered down the other side. The sight of the descending road in front of them made Eva's scalp tingle, and she had to push her feet hard against the floor to keep from coming up off her seat. In the bottom, she could see a brushy gully, and she wanted to close her eyes and pretend this all away. They were heading into a death trap, and Brandon must know it too.

It took a good two hours, and turn-arounds so numerous Eva lost track of them all, but after winding and grinding their way through some of the most horrendous country Eva had ever seen, she looked back, and none of their pursuers were any longer in sight.

"I can't see anybody," she said. "Do you think they turned back?"

"I guess. But I'm not sure how we'll get back in town now. You know if they went back they're just gonna be waitin' for us."

Neither one of them spoke as Brandon started north again. After a while, he stopped, and he was looking far across the flats toward a settlement way up in the foothills. "That's Reliance," he said. "I think a lot of the construction people and miners have been movin' in there."

She didn't reply. What did it matter what the place was? It wasn't any good to them.

Far out below them she could see the long, straight ribbon of the highway, and when she turned her head back she could see in the distance the hazy horizon of Rock Springs. She wanted to go back and get her family, but it all seemed so hopeless. How could they possibly get back in town without being picked up? It was a sure bet that everyone back there would be watching for this Jeep to try and sneak back into town. Ambro and Primo, at least, would know Eva wasn't simply going to leave her family.

Brandon took a lung-filling breath and started the Jeep rolling again, this time slowly working his way down toward the highway. After everything they had already been through, even though the desert face ahead still didn't look hospitable, Eva thought they could make it out of this alive, heading north. But that still didn't answer the dilemma of reaching her family.

The Jeep finally crawled down into a shallow wash with gnarled brush flanking it on the far side, and there Brandon threw it in gear and turned it off. It was one of the first places since leaving the pavement where Eva had felt completely concealed. "What are we doing?"

"The highway's another one or two hundred yards. We'd better go up on foot and do some scouting before we get back out there. I don't want to do this all again. Plus, I'll bet you a thousand dollars they're probably getting four-wheel-drives lined up by now. We have to come back in here again it might not work out so good the next time."

"We're going out on the highway? And then what?"

"We go home."

She stared at him. "You know they'll see us."

"Maybe not. I've got an idea. We're going to try and get across there to Reliance."

She looked across the valley at the hardscrabble looking settlement on the side of the hill. Her thoughts were dubious, but she didn't voice them. "What do we do if we get back to town?"

"First thing I'm gonna do is drive over and drop you off close to your house so you can walk in there and keep a good eye out for these thugs. Do you have your keys for the Chevelle?"

She patted her front pants pocket. "Yeah."

"That's lucky."

"No, you're Lucky," she said, not mentioning how *unlucky* she thought they were going to be when they got back in town.

He stared at her for a second, then started laughing. "That was funny, Evie. I can't believe you're still in a mood to make jokes."

She wasn't. It had popped out without her thinking about it.

"Brandon, I shot that guy back there."

He frowned. That thought had hung between them like a fog now for hours. He reached out and squeezed her hand. "I know. I'm sorry, Evie. He didn't give us any choice."

She nodded. "You don't think I killed him, do you?"

He shook his head, looking overly confident. "Naw. He'll be fine."

But she had been firing a .357 Magnum. She wasn't sure "fine" would describe the man she had shot, whether he lived or died.

They got out of the Jeep on silent agreement and climbed up through the brush on the side of the wash. Staying in the low, dusty scrub growth, to be as camouflaged as possible, they scanned the layout ahead. A car came from town, making normal speed, and passed a couple of minutes later. It was a long, light-colored sedan, and it never slowed. Just some oblivious traveler.

Come hell —it would be months before this place saw any high water— it was time for Brandon and Eva to head back to town.

Pulling the Jeep out of the draw, Brandon made his way slowly to the highway, then crossed it just as slowly. He had told Eva he figured moving slower might not draw anyone's attention as much as a fast-moving vehicle would.

Brandon drove over the flats until they cut onto a broken asphalt road, which was Reliance Road. Brandon made a left onto it. In short order they came to the tiny, dirty settlement of Reliance. The town had a strange set-up, long and skinny like someone had drawn a couple of big lines for streets, with a very few short sidestreets, and then told everyone to build their houses around them.

They went most of the way through town without drawing much attention from the few people out on the street to what looked like it might be the last sideroad. Brandon didn't say a word, and Eva was weary of asking him questions. He drove out on the sideroad fifty yards or so to a dusty, sad house with two wind-scoured bay horses standing listless in a run-down corral and pulled up in the yard, looking around.

"What are we doing here?" Eva asked. She could only hold back her questions so long.

"We gotta see if we can borrow a car nobody will recognize."

There was a sand-blasted fifties Ford sedan parked in front of the house with a mismatched front fender. Otherwise, no cars were parked around. They went together to the front door of the house because Eva knew how scary Brandon Lucky could look to strangers. No one was home—or at least if they were they didn't answer the door.

Brandon went out and threw open the driver's door of the Ford, getting inside.

Half a minute later, she heard the Ford's engine trying to turn over, and soon it did. The skills Brandon had picked up in his wayward youth had finally paid off in a useful way. He sat up and put his foot lightly on the peddle, letting the car throw dust away from its tailpipe for a while before letting off the gas. The vehicle now had a satisfying rumble.

"Okay, Evie. We'll bring this back later if we can. For now, can you drive the Jeep? I'll drive up into the houses, and we can pull off and hide it somewhere then drive this back to the Springs. You with me?"

"I don't think I have much choice. Do I?"

CHAPTER THIRTY-EIGHT

THEY DROVE BACK DOWN straight, narrow Main Street, which pretty much made up the entire east end of town, then turned into a filthy, battered neighborhood that had an entire width of perhaps four streets. Driving to the farthest street north, which had the boring, if fitting, name of North Street, Brandon turned left and passed ten or twelve houses, then turned right on a stubby gravel lane and drove past a lonely, homely house with an army of mongrel dogs before finding a secluded-looking place in the brush beyond to park the Jeep. There was a notepad in the Commando's glove box, and Brandon asked Evie to write a note on it explaining to whoever owned the property that the Jeep was having mechanical trouble and they would be back to tow it as soon as possible. They stuck the note in the window, and then went back to the Ford.

Brandon pointed Eva toward the driver's side. "I was only ever a car thief who learned how to drive fast enough to get away," he said. "You're the hot race car driver."

Eva grinned at him, finding that smiling made her feel more confident than she otherwise did. She got in the driver's side and looked at him. "Okay, but I hope you don't end up being sorry. And I doubt this old beater is going to drive fast even if we wanted to."

She got the boat of a Ford turned around, then drove back to Highway 187 and sat there for a few minutes as they watched both ways along the asphalt. Two lonely vehicles came by a minute apart, a rusted Dodge pickup headed toward town, and a mid-sixties Bel Air headed north toward Farson.

"Do you think they all went back to town?" Eva asked.

"That's what I'm afraid of—that they went back and now they're watchin' our places."

"What do you think we should we do?"

"You askin' me just 'cause I'm an old criminal?"

She laughed, but she didn't feel like it. She would have given anything to pretend her family wasn't in danger. "I guess that's why," she said. "Except you're kind of a young criminal."

Brandon laughed. "Touché. Well, unless we want to run clear out of state and call the FBI, or the attorney general or somethin', I'm not sure we have much choice but to go back. That's my choice—get Karen and run."

"Wait, though," Eva said. "What about what you said? What if we go somewhere else and try to get help?"

"What happens to our families in the meantime? Are you willin' to take a chance?"

She found she could no longer dredge up a smile even if she tried. "You have to be so smart about everything, huh?"

"Yeah," Brandon said. "That's me—smartest young criminal on the block. Where do you have the Chevelle?"

"It's around the corner from my house, in the driveway of an old woman I mow lawn for sometimes."

"So in a place you can get without drivin' past your house?"

"Yeah."

"Okay. Let's go there first. I changed my mind about not drivin'. I'll drive into town, and when we get where your car is you jump out, and I'll keep goin' to my apartment."

"Hey. Before we go, I thought of something."

"What's that?"

"Well, why don't we go back to Reliance and knock on someone's door and see if we can borrow their phone? You could call Karen and make sure she's ready to run down and get in the car."

Brandon agreed, so she turned around and drove to one of the first houses off Reliance Road. They got out and nervously waded another sea of loud, rowdy dogs to get to the front door. The whole weedy, dusty, minefield of a yard smelled like the tiger pens at the zoo, and Eva felt nauseous, but at least they didn't get bitten.

A rough-looking man with scraggly-cut blond hair, in a stained gray tank top and 501's, came to the door and opened it, leaning on the doorframe. He had the bad eczema all over his cheeks and chin of someone who worked the trona mines. "C'n I help you?"

"Yes, I was hoping we could borrow your phone," Eva said.

"I reckon. Not long distance, right?"

"Nope," Brandon answered. "Just to Rock Springs."

"Come on in then," said the man, hungrily eyeing Eva while by the sly way he was acting he probably figured no one noticed.

Brandon picked up the phone and dialed his number. It took a while for it to pick up.

"Karen. It's Brandon. Listen, I need you— Hey, hang on. *What? Who?*" Brandon swore, and his face paled. "Now? They're there right now?"

A moment later, his eyes filled up with tears. "Hey, listen, you touch her and I'll kill every one of you! Hey! Hello? *Hello?*"

Shaking, Brandon set the phone down on the base and looked at Eva. "They got her, Evie. They got guys at the place right now. I gotta get in there. I gotta get in there now!"

"No, Brandon, you can't," she pled as he started for the door.

He whirled at the last second. "You better call home too," he advised. "Hurry. If nobody's there yet you can at least warn them."

With waves of electricity flooding back and forth across the stem of her brain, making her hair prickle up on her neck and the back of her head, Eva picked up the phone. She misdialed the number and had to start over. Finally, it started ringing. Like Brandon's call, it took a while for it to pick up.

An almost cloying male voice answered. *Hello? Galantis'.*

"Who is this?" asked Eva.

Aww . . . And who is this? Is this by chance Eva Galanti? She suddenly realized it was the thinly disguised voice of Primo Santori.

"What are you doing in my house?" she almost screamed. "Where is my mother?"

Well, little lady, I was hoping you might be able to answer that for me. *There hasn't been a soul in here since we got here.*

"Who's 'we'? Who do you have in my house?"

The only thing you need concern yourself with, little Eva, is that you get back here as soon as humanly possible, and you should come with two very important things: Our money, and any paperwork you may have gotten from Officer Stone or his wife. Do you understand me clearly, Eva? We are going to find your family. It's a tiny town, so they can't possibly hide for long. You will surely find them too, but the shape you find them in depends entirely on how you proceed from here. Now do we have a deal?

She paused, apparently too long for Santori's patience. *Eva? Eva!*

"What?" she almost shouted into the phone.

Oh! Becoming a little petulant, aren't you? Listen, you little bitch—I'm the one who should be acting angry, not you. I'm the one who has been robbed.

The man's hypocrisy was boundless.

"Go to hell," she said angrily.

Aww . . . Now my little Eva. That is hardly a friendly way to talk to the man who within the next hour or two could be putting a bullet in your little retard's head if he chooses to. Is it?

"What do you want me to do?" she asked, turning into a robot. Her voice seemed to be coming from someone else rather than from her own mouth.

Now that is much better. Listen, Eva, you could have had everything. You could have been one of us—set for life. If only you had listened. You know, it may not be too late.

"What do you want me to do!" she repeated, this time in a voice filled with quiet venom.

Oh, we're back to this then. Okay. As I said, you bring me a briefcase full of cash and anything you received from Buck Stone or his wife, and I won't kill your family. We'll both walk away with what we want, and no harm done. You know what happens already if you cross me. Don't you, Eva?

"I'm coming," she said, her voice grown quiet. "Please don't touch my family." She hung up the phone without waiting to see if Santori would reply.

By now, the homeowner was staring at Eva in a different way. "Hey, what the hell's goin' on, anyway? You people in trouble?"

Eva wanted to answer him sarcastically, but she didn't. She only turned and stumbled after Brandon to the door and followed him out. Unfortunately, the hillbilly also followed them out.

"Hey! What you two doin' with Cranston's car?"

"He loaned it to us," said Brandon.

"Oh, like hell he did," the man said.

Brandon and Eva didn't reply as Brandon got in the driver's seat, and Eva fell in across from him. Brandon threw up plumes of dirt getting out of the yard.

When they were gone, the man in the house went back in and picked up the phone. He dialed *zero,* and in a moment he said, "Yeah. I need the police."

Brandon drove only a quarter of a mile before another gravel road popped into view, this one to the right, and he took it. Dust boiled up behind them from the August-dry dirt as they drove up to a house that looked slightly better kept than the two they had recently seen. There were two cars parked in front of it.

"Get me some money," Brandon said.

"What?"

"Money!" It was the closest Brandon had ever come to snapping at her. "Hurry. Maybe a thousand bucks."

Eva turned and leaned over the seat into the back, snapping the briefcase open, and pulled out a stack of tens. She fell back into her seat and held it out to him.

"Sorry for barkin', Evie," he said. "But we gotta get us a different car. That clown back there, I could see in his eyes he was gonna report this one stolen."

Eva never would have thought of that. "It's okay, Bran. Here." She insisted the wad of bills toward him, and he pulled the paper sleeve off them, broke them into two wads, put one in a shirt pocket and kept the other in his hand until he had gotten out, when he slipped the second wad into the back pocket of his jeans.

They walked up to the house, where a Great Dane that wasn't as friendly as the army of dogs at the other house stood guard, glaring at them with cropped ears standing straight up, and jaws waiting partially open as if deciding to bark or to bite.

"Hello in the house!" Brandon called out. "Anyone home?"

A woman in tee shirt and blue slacks came to the door and looked out. "Jupiter isn't as scary as he looks," she said. "Just don't move fast."

"You got it," Brandon said. "Ma'am, I was wonderin' if we could buy one of your cars."

She stared at him. Her jaw had been going to town chewing on gum, but now she paused. "Now what's that again?"

"Your cars," he repeated. "Can I buy one?"

"They ain't even mine," she said. "They're my husband's."

"How about I just rent one then?"

Eva saw gears shifting in the woman's head. "Well now . . . what are they worth to you, anyway? What's wrong with your car?"

"It's just overheating," Brandon said smoothly.

"And so you want to buy a new one? You from around here?"

"Yeah. From the Rock," Brandon replied.

"How much you pay me to rent that Dodge?" the woman asked, a calculating look in her eyes, pointing out a red 1962 Dodge Dart with a white roof. Like many a vehicle along the Red Desert, the car's once-shiny paint had been scoured by sand driven by high winds.

"Two hundred fifty bucks?" replied Brandon.

The woman's look vanished in the wide-eyed expression she got now. "You serious?"

"As a broken toe."

"Could we say five hundred? That would make it easier to get Ted off my back."

"Done."

"Where you gonna leave it?" asked the woman. "You gonna bring it back, or do I have to come look for it?"

"You'd probably better come look for it. Maybe at Dino's auto shop."

"Okay then . . ." The woman's wheels were spinning fast in her eyes. Brandon had given up five hundred dollars way too easily. "What do you say we do seven hundred, and if I don't see the car again you can write me and tell me where to send the title."

"You got it," Brandon said.

"And I'll give you back the other two hundred when we get the car back," said the woman.

"Right." Brandon didn't believe her. Neither did Eva. "Don't worry about it. You just keep the whole seven. I hit it big over in Reno, and I'm feelin' flush." He counted out seven hundred as he was talking and handed it all to the woman in one stack.

Eva didn't think the woman seemed to believe Brandon's gambling story, either, but right now she only cared about getting back to town in a car no one would be looking for.

Brandon had turned away, but now he turned back to the woman and gave her a long look. Eva could see he was trying to decide whether or not to say something. "Hey, ma'am. Can I level with you?"

"Sure, I guess. And by the way, I'm Margo."

"Okay, Margo, there's some bad guys after my friend here, and one of 'em's a cop. What will it take to get your promise you won't say anything?"

Margo looked from Brandon to Eva, giving her a quick study. "You got man troubles?"

"Yes," admitted Eva. If the woman only knew!

"You don't have to give me anything more," she said with a nod, a sour look coming into her eyes. "I've had run-ins with cops in Rock Bottom. I can't stand 'em either."

"Thank you," Eva said, holding back an urge to run and hug the woman.

"Sure. Hey." Her voice stopped them and made them turn back questioningly.

"If you're hoping they don't see you . . . That Ford isn't really over-heating, is it?"

Brandon shook his head. "No."

"Okay. So what do you think about me drivin' it into town and you stay a quarter-mile or so behind me? You think maybe they'll get on me when they see the car and leave you alone?"

Brandon and Eva stared at Margo. Finally, Eva found her tongue. "Are you serious? You'd do that for me?"

The woman shrugged with one shoulder. "Sure. I have to go into town for some burger and stuff anyway. I think I know who owns that car—a guy named Cranston. I'll tell the cops he loaned it to me."

Eva couldn't hold back this time. She took several quick steps and threw her arms around the woman whose kindness overwhelmed her.

When she pulled away, the woman looked uncomfortable. "There's no need for all that fuss. I just hate to see people bein' picked on. In fact, I'd let you keep all your money if I wasn't worried what my husband was gonna say when he finds out I let you take his car."

"Don't even think a thing about the money," Eva said. "We're glad to give it to you."

If she could have found a way to squander every last dime of it she would have, to keep the Mob from getting it back. What did it matter? She had already spent some of it, so the future didn't look too bright anyway.

CHAPTER THIRTY-NINE

TRAVELING ALONG BEHIND THE beat-up borrowed Ford, when they were passing the Kasbah lounge, Eva and Brandon saw the police descend on Margo, lights flashing. Eva would have liked to hug Margo again as she saw her continue driving. Brandon backed off a ways, and they watched with fascination for a little over half a mile until Margo pulled over into the mouth of Springs Drive and stopped, with two police cars pulling in to stop behind her, and another flying up Elk Street toward them, red overheads flashing.

The oncoming police car appeared at a glance to have Chris Hinshaw driving it, and he kept his eyes straight ahead as they passed each other. Brandon kept driving, trying to look casual, as they made the gradual bend to the left, then turned onto Ridge.

"We're gonna have to hustle fast," Brandon said as he drove up Ridge and paused at Soulsby, seeing the black Chevelle parked up in the driveway two houses down. Without a word from Eva, he turned right and stopped in the street behind the Chevelle. "All right. There she is. I'll drop you off right here, and then I'm headin' straight for the shop. I'll trade out cars for the Delray and head over to the apartment. You'd better get in that Chevelle, get your family, and split as fast as you can. Can you get to where they are without drivin' past your house?"

"I guess so if I go clear down to N Street."

"Well, then do that. Or else just go fast and don't look at the house."

"Okay. But I don't understand what you're going to do. They're at your apartment now, right?"

"I assume they still are."

Eva had been thinking about Brandon's situation, and she couldn't see any way out that felt good. "I don't get how you think going back there is going to help. They won't just let you go, Bran."

She had forced herself to admit this. If they could kill her and Brandon, they would—along with anyone else who got in their way. If they said they weren't going to kill them, Eva would know they were lying. She thought about the man she had shot. She thought about the revolver she still carried. It made her sick to think of shooting someone again.

"Eva, you're right. They're gonna kill us. But I don't know who to call. I don't know what to do. I can't just leave Karen to the wolves." Eva was pretty sure Karen would have left him to the wolves, but she couldn't say that to him.

She pulled the gun from where she had stowed it under the seat. "At least take this," she said.

"No. You might need it."

"I already shot somebody. I don't know if I can do it again."

"Evie, stop. Listen to me. When I was in the pen I had to stab a guy. It was him or me, and I knew it. I had to put it all out of my mind beforehand to make me do it, and you better do that too. You start thinkin' about consequences and you've already lost. That gun might be the only thing between you and your whole family gettin' killed."

Eva stared at him, her mind whirling. "Go, Evie. Get your family, and then if I were you I'd head west for Evanston, and I'd keep it up over a hundred the whole way."

"Why there?"

"Because if you can make it that far, Utah's only a little bit farther, and maybe you can get all the way to Ogden. If you can get across the border, you might have a better chance of findin' some honest cops. But be ready to use that gun if anybody gets you stopped. You know they can't afford to let you go. They don't know how much we've seen of what Stone gave you."

"Yeah." That made her think of Lance again, and she wondered if the other cops had already found him.

"Go, Evie!" said Brandon. "Good luck."

"God be with you, Brandon," she said, and without warning she raised up from her seat and kissed him on the cheek.

"Thanks, Evie. God be with you too." The words were big, because Eva wasn't sure Brandon even believed in God anymore.

Eva raced for the Chevelle, carrying both the briefcase full of money and the pillowcase with the evidence, with the Colt Python stuffed down behind the front of her waistband.

She got in the Chevelle and fired it up, and after a careful scan of the area, she backed into the street. Driving slowly to the intersection with Ridge, she looked down the street toward her house. There was a big red Chrysler and a black Nova parked in front of it. Eva was looking at the house and the cars, gaging her chances of driving past unseen to where her family waited when out of her periphery she saw another vehicle approaching the intersection from her left, coming up Ridge.

Ambro Procopio had always thought of himself as a calm, collected person. He was well aware that everyone around him felt the same. But today, he wasn't calm. He had just received a call from Primo Santori fifteen minutes ago at Brandon Lucky's apartment. Eva had called her house, where Primo and his other people still were, and it sounded like she might be headed there right now with the money and the evidence against the Mob.

Ambro, accompanied by an out-of-town mobster named Bertil Horsch who had since gone to the Galantis', had been at the Luckys' apartment trying to use any weight his opinions might carry with Chief Buyer to keep the man under control.

The situation at Lucky's place had already gone violent, and Chief Howard Buyer had lost his patience and beaten that woman good while Ambro and Horsch were outside having a cigarette. Lucky might be her name, but she probably wasn't feeling that way right about then. Her lips were all swollen up, and she couldn't see out of her left eye. Buyer had always seemed like he could turn into a volatile person, but until today Ambro had never seen him explode. He wondered how smart it was leaving a man like that alone in the apartment with Karen Lucky, but now his main concern was Eva Galanti, and Primo had two others with him who could be just as easy to anger as he was.

There at the home with Primo Santori were Gavino Berretti and Bertil Horsch, the man whose ribs Eva Galanti had burned good with a shot from whatever pistol she was carrying.

Ambro had to get back to the Galantis' before Eva showed up and Primo had a chance to lose his cool, which Primo had been known to do more than once, with ugly results.

Ambro was coming up on the intersection with Soulsby, and he would be in front of Eva's in another twelve houses or so, when he glanced over and saw a bold black Chevelle sitting at the stop sign to his right. He didn't know why he looked at the driver—perhaps only out of instinct, to see what kind of person was driving such a beautiful Chevelle.

The driver's face hit him in the guts like a kick from Bruce Lee.

It was Eva Galanti!

Without looking over, Eva waited for the car to pass. Then she could make her right turn and drive past her place at just over the speed limit to get to Tony Galloway's house, where her family was hiding. The car chirped to a stop abruptly, and she turned to look at it.

She froze. The car stopped to her left was Ambro Procopio's gold Pontiac! And the driver was just pulling off his sunglasses as he stared at her.

Eva wouldn't have wanted to own up to the word that crossed her lips as she stomped on the gas and dropped the clutch, screaming the tires as she almost lunged into the intersection. Her wheels had already been turned to go right, which she had forgotten, so she went into a crazy swerve she wasn't expecting. It took but a second to realize she wouldn't be able to correct herself at the speed the rear wheels were pushing her, so she kept it to the floor and hit the far side of the street, which fortunately had no curb. The Chevelle launched across the dusty yard between two houses as she manhandled it to the left, spinning her rear tires as she negotiated around the back of the nearest house. She hit a low pile of stones, which jolted her as the back tires came off them and landed in the dirt.

She had no time to look back and see if Ambro was coming.

Tearing along behind the houses, praying there would be no children or animals back there in her way, she made all the speed she could as she raced west. Once, she saw someone off to her left and heard them screaming obscenities after her, but she couldn't waste time or effort looking back. She flew under a clothesline whose poles were set just far enough apart for the Chevelle to clear them, and a big brown dog hit the end of his chain, running away from her as fast as he could. Finally, she rocked and rattled and slammed her way back onto the pavement at Railroad Avenue, nearly tipped it over making a ridiculous left onto Mitchelson, then another hard left back onto Elk.

It was hardly worth trying to shift the Chevelle out of first gear. Ramming along through the city streets trying to make it to Brandon's place, now with Ambro's LeMans hot behind her, Eva was hitting speeds of over forty—the few times she had to go into second—and had narrowly missed three bad collisions so far.

She swerved right off Eighth onto N Street at over twenty-five miles an hour. This was Brandon's block. The roar of a loud engine behind her made her look in the mirror, and she gasped in horror to see Brandon's primered Delray raging up the street toward her, on a collision course. She managed to gun the Chevelle enough to keep out of his way as he skidded to a stop, sliding sideways. Eva slammed on her brakes several car lengths away and threw it in neutral, then jumped out, waving frantically at Brandon.

It was too late. Ambro's gold LeMans veered around the corner of Eighth right then, nearly running into the back of Brandon's car before it skidded to a stop. Ambro backed up, then started around the Delray, headed straight for where Eva stood with her mouth agape.

As Ambro's car again screeched to a halt, just a car length away from Eva's back bumper, she heard the squealing of Brandon Lucky's tires. She whirled to see his car flying toward Ambro's like a sleek gray ghost.

The impact was terrific. With the horrible sound of a grenade tearing open a metal box, the Delray knocked the trunk up on the LeMans and almost shoved it straight into the Chevelle. While Eva watched, horrified and transfixed, Brandon threw his car in reverse for a couple of car lengths, then revved it again as Ambro piled out of the LeMans.

He leveled a snub-nose revolver at Brandon and started firing.

As the Delray struck Ambro's car again, this time managing to thrust it into Eva's rear bumper and pushing the car a few feet from her, she saw blood splatter behind Brandon's shattered windshield. She felt adrenaline flooding her body as she dropped back into the bucket seat of the Chevelle. This was like the worst of nightmares, but the one thing she knew she couldn't do was to stay. If Brandon Lucky wasn't already dead, he was about to be. The only chance of saving him was to run and try to draw Ambro off.

Eva's mind was in a fog, but driving was second nature. She peeled away from the LeMans, smoking her tires. It didn't take long to see the move had drawn the LeMans away from Brandon. Now roaring down Front Street, at speeds sometimes nearing sixty, Eva tried to find a good place and time to flip the car back around facing the other direction in an old bootleggers' move called a J-turn, a trick her father had taught her, then admitted he never should have. But she owed him for it now.

She was over a block ahead of Ambro's damaged, struggling LeMans, when she slammed on the brakes and brought the Chevelle to a full stop. Throwing it into reverse, she saw Ambro stop his car behind her. She was going almost twenty miles an hour when she turned the steering wheel hard left and slammed on the brakes, making the car spin around. As it was about to straighten, she threw it into second gear and floored it again. There was just enough room between Ambro's car and a parked car to his left for her to shoot through like a bullet from a gun.

Ambro was trying to get turned around when Eva took the next corner, then another one two blocks down. She pulled into an alley, gave herself a minute, then took off again, praying she wouldn't run into a cop before she found a phone booth.

Luck was with her, and she slid to a stop at a phone booth, stomping on the emergency brake and killing the engine as she jerked her foot off the clutch and got out to run to the phone. Her shaking hand dropped two dimes before she could fumble one into the slot. She dialed Lance Cartwright's number, all the while scanning around her for Ambro's car. The phone rang and rang. No Lance—but no Ambro, either. She had lost him!

Feverishly, she ran back to the car. She had to get back to her neighborhood, no matter who was there. She had to try and get to her family before it was too late. She would just have to pray that Lance had made his escape before everything blew sky high.

CHAPTER FORTY

THE NETWORK OF CRIME in Rock Springs was too big for Eva to run in a car as obvious as the black Chevelle, and she should have known it. Every bit as fast as she had stopped to make the call to Lance, Ambro must have been on his car phone calling in the description of the Pontiac.

Eva never made it to her family.

Forcing herself to stay calm and drive at normal speeds, Eva was almost back to her place in less than five minutes when she saw the police car cruising along right behind her and closing in like a shark. A surge of fear ran through her. But could it be Lance? As the overhead lights came on, she slowed and tried to gauge the size of the police car's driver: It wasn't Lance.

Even as Eva started to make her right turn at the corner, where she was able to look ahead and see her house with the strange cars still parked in front of it, a vehicle appeared behind the police car. It took only a second to recognize Lance Cartwright's Bronco, traveling at a high rate of speed.

Eva gunned the Chevelle around the corner and saw the police car fishtail trying to do the same. She could see both the police car and the white and black Bronco racing, now side by side behind her. Suddenly, just as they were nearing her house, the Bronco looked like it was going to take the lead and speed past the police car, but then it did something Eva had not foreseen.

The Bronco veered to the left, slamming into the passenger door of the squad car, and there was no stopping after that. The squad car went head-on against the front grill of the red Chrysler in front of Eva's house, spinning in a quarter circle and almost hitting the next car. Eva let out a yelp as she narrowly missed a second squad car coming hard down Ridge. Lance's Bronco didn't miss it.

The Bronco hit the car in the left front quarter panel, and Eva saw the Bronco's rear wheels come up off the asphalt before it crashed back down. There was no way the Bronco would drive after that collision. Lance was trapped!

Throwing the Chevelle in reverse, Eva bore down on the gas and flew back toward her friend, slamming on the brakes at the last second and making the car slide sideways as she saw Lance and the cop disembarking at the same time. The cop must have been too dazed to think, for Lance was around the Bronco and all the way to him before the cop began to fumble his revolver out of the holster. Lance's big right fist came down hard somewhere near the man's temple, and he crumpled to the ground.

"Get in!" Eva screamed. She was wasting her breath, because Lance was already sprinting her way.

Eva guessed it was the fastest Lance had ever squeezed himself into a vehicle so low to the ground. As she saw cars moving down the street, she put the Chevelle into high motion, and after taking the turn down on N Street, then getting back onto Railroad, they hit the first hundred yards of Elk Street northbound already at sixty miles an hour. They flew past dozens of businesses, lastly the Kasbah lounge, just before I-80, where Eva tried to head toward Green River.

"No!" Lance yelled, pointing at a roadblock up the ramp.

Eva swerved away at the last second and continued up Elk Street. Within half a mile, they were bombing north up the desert highway at one thirty-five. They both had yet to speak after they had gone nearly four miles.

"You're gonna have to push it as fast as it'll go, Eva," Lance yelled over the roar of the engine. She looked at her speedometer, then at him, incredulously, but he kept talking, oblivious. "The whole freakin' world is after us. They got the word out that you and Brandon Lucky are wanted for murder, and even the good cops are lookin' for you now. They're lookin' for me too."

Shocked, she turned to look at him, staring too long.

"Hey! I'd just as soon you look at the road."

Returning her eyes to the frost-heaved highway, flying past them now at a dangerous one hundred forty miles an hour that at times made it seem as if they were about to take to the air, she managed to say, "Who are we supposed to have killed?"

"The report never said. And I only heard it because I was with Rick Cohen when it came over the air."

"Rick? Lance, is he . . ."

"He's good," Lance said. "Scared as hell, but good. He's gonna split town and head for Rawlins to try and get some help."

"Rawlins! What kind of help is he going to get there?"

"I don't know, but we don't have much choice."

"We don't have a choice," Eva said suddenly, just as she spotted a lonely ranch house ahead, some distance off the highway, and stomped down on the brake.

"What are you doin'?"

"They'll have roadblocks, Lance! We have to hide some-where until the roads are clear."

He stared at her but said nothing, which she guessed meant he was in agreement.

At the next road, which was barely a road at all, Eva turned, and both of them looked back down the highway. There was nothing but emptiness and heatwaves to greet them. With a sigh of relief, she drove as slowly as she dared up the poorly kept road so as not to raise a cloud of dust, until they came to the lit-tle ranch house, which sat in the veritable middle of nowhere like a lonely army outpost in some old Western movie. She drove around behind the house and stopped. From where they now sat, they couldn't see the road.

Lance drew in a deep breath and scrubbed at his beard. "Now what?"

Eva got out of the car without a reply, moving like a robot. Emotions were welling up so hard in her chest she could barely keep them inside. She didn't shut her own door, but she heard Lance's shut behind her, and she heard the crunch of dead grass under his feet as he walked fast to catch up to her.

She reached a side door of the house, and without waiting she knocked. She already had the feeling no one would be around since there wasn't a single car in sight, unless there was one hiding in the worn down-looking shop that sat nearby. After she knocked a second time and was waiting, Lance reached out, and his big hand closed over her upper arm. His voice was soft. She guessed he knew she was about to fall apart.

"Eva. You gonna be okay?"

The kind voice was too much. It broke her. Turning, she fell against him, feeling his arms close around her as sobs wracked her body. Brandon Lucky was dead. Dead only because of her and the money—her and the evidence she should never have accepted from Olivia Stone. Dead because she had agreed to talk to Buck Stone in the first place. Brandon was dead, Eva had shot a man, and for all she knew he was dead as well. Her family was trapped in Rock Springs where she had no way to reach them to see if they were safe, and now she and Lance were on the run from who could tell how many officers throughout the state of Wyoming. It was too much to keep inside. The dam that had held everything inside burst, and the flood from it was agonizing.

Fortunately, no one ever came to the door. Eva could only imagine someone's consternation even if they had only looked out the window to see this giant of a man holding a woman who must appear to be in the middle of a nervous breakdown. In fact, it wouldn't have surprised her if they had called the police.

When Eva finally managed to get control of herself and stop shaking, Lance let go of her with one arm and reached around her to knock on the door once more. Still, no one came, and with one last study of their surroundings he reached down and tried the knob. The door opened under the pressure of his hand.

"Let's go in, Eva. Get out of the sun for a bit."

Quietly, she turned and followed him inside. The first mission in her mind was finding some tissue to blow her nose. The most suitable thing she found was a handful of napkins on a kitchen counter covered in scarred yellow Formica. She tried to blow and wipe her nose as daintily as she could, then tossed the napkins in a nearby trash can.

Lance stepped around her and took her shoulders. "You gonna hold up?"

She nodded. "Yeah. I'll be all right." After a moment's hesitation, she told him all the things he didn't already know that had contributed to her breakdown.

"I'm real sorry about Brandon. I know he had a sketchy past, but he must've been a pretty good guy for you to be so attached to him."

"He was. He always did anything he could to help me, and he never asked a thing in exchange." Stray thoughts of Brandon shot into her memory from all sides, but she managed to fight off new tears.

The house looked clean enough on the inside, in spite of a yard that had been let go. The place was old, probably from around the turn of the century, but other than age, the appearance of the home's insides was that of a place someone cared about. They got glasses out of the cupboard and drank water from the tap. Eva was surprised at the sweetness of it.

Setting her glass in the sink, she looked around the room until she spotted a fat, wine-red telephone, hunched on its base at the far end of the counter. "I have to try to call Mom," she said.

"That's a good idea."

She heard the words, but then wondered if it really was a good idea. What would happen to her emotional state if something bad had happened—most especially if the police or the Mob had found her family?

Of course it didn't matter. She simply had to know. She went and picked up the phone, and trying to control her shaking, she dialed her home number. She didn't want to hear Primo Santori's voice again. In fact, he was probably the last person in the world she wanted to hear. But she needed to know if he was still at the house, and she needed to know if anything had changed. If all was the same as before, she would hang up on him and call Tony Galloway, the old man she had told her mom to take the family to for refuge, to hide out until she heard from her.

The phone rang twice, then picked up. Someone on the other line took a deep breath before answering. When the voice came on, it was like a punch to the stomach.

Hello? It was Ambro Procopio.

"I'm not going to quit, Ambro," she said quietly. "You people and the police have to be stopped."

The silence on the other end of the line went for five or six seconds, and Eva chose not to break it. She had to let Ambro get over his shock.

Eva, don't be a fool, said Ambro finally. *You have to come home, or go to the police station. Every cop in the state is looking for you now.*

Before she could even reply, a different voice came on the phone. It was Primo Santori. *Eva, you little fool. Why did you and your friend kill Officer Cohen? That was a naughty thing to do. Now they have a warrant out for your arrest. And cops hate it when someone kills one of the family—especially if a rogue cop was in on the killing, like your foolish friend Cartwright.*

Eva stared at the wall. "Officer Cohen? Rick Cohen?" she said, shocked. "What have you done?"

Aw, Eva, Eva, Primo's smooth, controlled voice came over the line. *It isn't anything I have done. This is all because of you. You just had to have things that never belonged to you. You simply had to get involved. You had to know when Officer Stone spoke with you that this was not going to end well for you.*

Lance jerked the phone out of Eva's hand. "You're lyin' about Rick Cohen!" he yelled into the receiver. "I was with him when the APB came over the radio about Eva and Brandon."

Eva could only faintly hear Primo's voice now. *Ahh, why Officer Cartwright. It's so nice to finally hear your voice. Did you just tell me I was lying about Rick Cohen? That's a nice sentiment, but dead wrong. The murder Eva committed didn't actually occur until after that radio report. Why, every police officer in the state already knows by now that Rick Cohen was trying to apprehend Eva for drug trafficking and prostitution and that you shot him down for it. Come now, Officer Cartwright. There is no point in playing innocent with me. The po-*

lice no longer even care about Brandon what's-his-name. He's dead anyway. Ambro made sure of that. The APB out there now is for you and Eva.

Eva had stood on her tiptoes, and Lance allowed her to get close to his face as he held the phone out enough for her to hear better. The look on his face was of shock mixed with fury. Before he could form a reply, another new voice spoke over the line.

Hoss! This is Glatt, man. What the hell are you doin'?

"Jake! You son of a bitch! I never dreamed you'd go dirty."

Come on, buddy. Stop playin' games. Everyone in the state knows you're the dirty cop. You only have one chance, man. You gotta get back here. We can iron all this out. Everyone can win.

"What are you talkin' about?" Lance growled.

It's easy, bud. Come on back, bring the cash and the stuff Stone gave you. That's all you have to do. Then we can sit and talk. I guarantee you'll like what Mr. Santori has to say. He's a very generous man, Hoss. I swear to it. Chris is here too. He'll tell you the same. Come on, man. Just come in. Come back to your friend's house and we can come to some terms everyone will be happy with.

"Right. I killed Rick, remember?"

Aw, come on, Hoss. That'll be easy as pie to figure out. Turns out it wasn't you at all. Turns out that was all just a misunderstanding, and the guy that shot Rick is still on the loose. This is all fixable. You just gotta be here to talk to us. Think about it. What's the first thing that's gonna happen if you get stopped by the state police? You know what happens in Wyoming with cop killers. Right? Come on. Get back here and we'll iron this all out. You got Mr. Santori's promise.

Officer Glattner's right. Primo Santori was back on the line. *We can forget all this, Officer Cartwright. If you and your friend there don't even want to be a part of our operation, well that's fine too. We'll give you both a big slice of the pie for now, and then maybe slip you a few bucks here and there down the line— you know, whenever you need it. We'll work it out. Come on to the house and we can all shake hands and forget about all the nastiness. Say—where are you, anyway?*

Eva reached out and pushed down on the disconnect button on the phone base, making Lance look over at her. "They're lying through their teeth, Lance. As soon as we get back they'll kill us."

He nodded. "I know. That man's as slippery as a tadpole, I can tell by his voice. And I sure don't trust Glattner either. Man. There always seemed like there was somethin' off with that guy."

"I'm going to call my mom and make sure she stays put," Eva said. "Hang on."

She looked in a drawer that was directly under the phone, the most obvious place, and found a copy of the Mountain Bell phone book that covered Rock Springs, Green River, and Farson. Her fumbling fingers found the listing: Galloway, Anthony R. . . . 362-8605

She took the phone Lance handed her and dialed two-eight-six-zero-five, then waited with impatience for the sound of Tony's warm but sadly weak voice. At last, the phone rattled off the hook.

Hello? You've reached the Galloways'.

Eva was struck strangely by the sadness of that greeting; Tony's wife had been dead for many years, and he lived alone.

"Hello, Tony! It's me, Eva. Can you put my mom on the line?"

There was a long hesitation before Tony cleared his throat. *Eva? I'm so glad you called, sweetheart. Your mother isn't here.*

A giant, icy hand clutched Eva by the heart. "What? Tony! I told her to stay there until I called. Where did she go?"

I'm sorry, Eva. I think your grandma had a heart attack. Your mother and the boys all went to the hospital.

"In the ambulance?" asked Eva after she recovered from the shock of the news.

No, your mother didn't want to draw any attention, so they took my car.

Trying not to think too hard about Nonni being at Sweetwater County Memorial again and what her condition might be, Eva let her fingers do the walking through Ma Bell's White Pages and found the hospital's number, dialing it immediately. As she expected, she reached a woman at the nurses' station and asked about her grandmother.

She's been admitted, but she's sleeping, the woman said. *Would you like me to leave a message for when she wakes up?*

"No, thank you. But I would love to speak to my mother if she's close by. She's the one who brought Isabella in."

Oh, I'm sorry, ma'am, said the kind woman. *Your mother and two boys just now left here with a police officer.*

CHAPTER FORTY-ONE

LANCE CARTWRIGHT DIDN'T NEED to be any mind reader to know with one glance at Eva that something had gone bad wrong as she hung up the phone and started to shake. The problem was he didn't know what it was, and he didn't dare ask.

Finally, inevitably, Eva volunteered the information. When she finished, they both fell silent. What more was there to say?

After a time, on a wordless agreement, they both went to the living room and sank onto an aged but comfortable couch. After a lengthy silence, Lance looked at Eva. "How many rounds do you have in that Colt?"

"Five left."

"I'm shooting thirty-eights in mine," he said. "And I still have a pocketful. You'd better take some."

She looked over at him and tried to read him for a moment. "What are we going to do?"

"We have to go back," he said. "I don't know what else to do."

"Could we call the FBI?"

He stared at her. "You mean even with the way things are with Tervalon? Well, I guess we could. But I bet it takes a while to get anybody else out here. How long do we dare wait?"

"I don't know. Let's at least try before we give up."

Lance agreed, and she followed him to the kitchen while he called the operator to get him in touch with the FBI. It took a long time to reach an actual agent, and he tried to get the whole convoluted story through to him. After a frustrating conversation, he hung up, and to Eva's questioning look he said, "Let's go sit down."

Seated on the couch, looking deflated, Lance reported on his conversation. The FBI would have two agents there tomorrow. The best they could do today was to try and get the word out to the state police that the waters in the case might be muddier than everyone believed. The feeling Lance had gotten from the FBI agent, who went out of his way defending Cooper Tervalon's record, was that he simply didn't believe him. It seemed like the man only intended to follow up on the call to cover his own butt in case there really was any truth to the massive crime wave in Lance's story.

Having another thought, Lance got up and went back to the kitchen to place a call to the state attorney general's office, but the AG was gone for the day, and he was only offered the option of leaving a message for a callback. Lance hung up without saying goodbye.

"We gotta go in, Eva. But I have an idea: Let's go without the evidence or the money. They won't dare do anything then. Maybe we can still buy some time."

"For what?"

He sighed. "I'm not sure. I guess for the cavalry to get here. I don't have to tell you no situation like this was ever talked about at the academy."

"Let's take maybe just one or two pieces of evidence," Eva said. "To prove we really have it. I don't mind if we take the whole briefcase of money. I don't want their dirty money anymore. I'd rather die in poverty than buy anything else with it."

"So we leave the rest of the proof locked in the trunk, you think? Or hide it somewhere else?"

"Somewhere else. Some place they'd never think to look."

That place was in the desert itself. Lance went to the run-down shop beyond the house to look for a shovel to dig a hole. They went off fifty yards into the brush and rock and dug a hole, pulling a few random records out of the pillowcase, then putting the rest in the hole and burying it, last of all covering it with a big, flat rock they couldn't possibly lose track of later.

"There's an old pickup in that shed," Lance said when they went to put the shovel back.

She looked at him. "Okay?"

"I think we should try it. See if it works. If it does, we'll borrow it and leave the Chevelle right here. Maybe nobody will notice us for a while."

"I'm tired of borrowing and stealing other people's vehicles," she said. "Brandon was too good at it." She hurriedly pushed away the sadness that thinking of Brandon brought her. He had given his life for her. There was a time coming when she knew she would have to sit and mourn his loss—if she survived this herself.

"So we take the Chevelle?" Lance asked, to clarify.

"Yeah. I'd like to drive it at least one more time."

"Okay. We'd better go then, huh?"

She nodded. "I've been thinking. Let me make a call one more time, just so they know we're coming. And I need to see if they really have my family."

She placed the call, and it was Primo Santori's voice that answered.

"We're coming back," Eva said in reply to his "hello". "I'm bringing three pieces of paper with names and amounts of transactions on them. And the money."

Listen, little Miss Priss. You aren't the one calling the shots here, said Primo. *You'll bring every piece of anything Stone gave you. You hear me?*

"I hear you, but three pieces will have to be enough."

The next sound on the line kicked Eva in the stomach. *Cara! This is Mom. Are you all right?*

Eva fought tears. They had them. They *had* them! Her knees wanted to cave in on her, but she fought to lock them and stay standing. "I'm good, Mom. Are you? Do they have the boys too?"

All of us are here but Nonni, replied Bianca. *But we're fine, honey. Don't worry about us.*

You should worry about her! growled Primo into the phone, which he had obviously jerked away from Bianca. *You bring the money* and *everything else, you little vixen, or we start killing.*

Eva had to play the only card she could. She had to pray that as long as Primo didn't have every shred of the evidence against him back he wouldn't dare carry through on his threats. But she didn't dare anger him any further, so she didn't tell him her plan.

"We'll be there in less than an hour," she said, then hung up before he could reply.

They walked out to the Chevelle, where Lance went around to Eva's door with her, standing in front of it so she couldn't open it. He reached into his pocket and pulled out a handful of .38 Special cartridges, dividing them roughly in half.

"Put these in your pocket. I don't know if we'll have a chance to use them, but just in case we do."

She obeyed numbly, and then he held out one more before sliding the rest back into his own pocket. Reaching down, he tugged the Python out of her waistband, popped open the cylinder and plucked out the spent casing, throwing it aside and putting the live round in the empty chamber, clicking it shut again. He carefully eased the revolver back down where she had had it.

"This might be it," he said, still standing there with her backed up to her door.

"Yeah." She looked up at him. He had been such a good friend. She wished things had been different for them. Not only their ages, but their entire situation. Who knew what might have happened?

"Eva?"

"Yeah?"

"Do you think I could kiss you?"

She looked at him and let herself smile, and he must have taken that as his answer, because he leaned down as she came up on her tiptoes, and their lips met in a soft, warm kiss. It wasn't a kiss of passion. It was the kind of kiss that says "good-bye forever".

They climbed wordlessly back in the Chevelle, drove out to 187, and headed south.

Eva had driven six miles or so when they came upon a Winnebago motorhome parked at a severe tilt on an incline along the side of the road. She could see movement off to the side of it, and as they got close it was obvious someone was attempting to change a flat tire. She slowed way down, and both of them saw that it was a woman who appeared to be up in her seventies or older. Her hair looked a mess, and she had a highly frustrated look on her face. She waved excitedly at them as they got close.

"Keep goin'! Keep goin'!" said Lance. "We can't leave your family waitin'."

So Eva drove on. But she only made it another hundred feet before easing the car to a stop in the middle of the road. "Lance, we need to go back. It's hot out there, and who knows when anyone else might come by."

He grinned lopsidedly at her. "Well, you're somethin' else. Okay. Let's go back."

They turned around, drove past the Winnebago, and found the next wide spot to turn around in, then came back and pulled up behind it. The huge smile of relief on the old woman's face warmed Eva's heart and made her think of Nonni, some ten years or more ago, when she was strong and able enough to be out on the road.

They got out, and the woman, who wasn't much over five feet tall, looked up at Lance in amazement. For a moment, her look almost seemed like fear.

"Thank you so much for stopping. It's horribly hot out here."

"Are you by yourself?" Lance asked.

"Well, kind of. My husband's inside, but his arthritis is really bad, and he can't do much. Also, he had sunstroke about eight years ago, and since then it seems really easy for him to get it again."

"So how can we help you?" asked Lance. "Do you have all the tools, and a tire and everything?" Even as he was speaking, Eva could see a big jack, so large, in fact, that she wondered how the woman had manhandled it out here onto the road by herself. There was a star wrench already on one of the lug nuts.

"I think I have everything," the woman replied, pushing her sweaty hair back from her forehead. "I just can't get any of these lug nuts even to budge. I can't believe how tight they put these things on. I haven't even tried to get the tire out yet."

Eva cringed, looking at the diminutive woman. It was probably a good thing she hadn't started wrestling the tire. The jack was plenty already.

"Well here," Lance said. "Let's give 'er a try." He put his muscle into the star wrench, and with a metallic creak it made a half-turn.

"Oh! Hooray! You got it already. Well, it shouldn't surprise me, right? You look like you could carry the whole Winnebago to town for me."

Lance grinned. "Well, let's get the rest of these off and—"

"Lance!" Eva's alarmed voice stopped him, and he whirled toward her. She was staring at a car that had just appeared far out on the horizon, coming from the north.

"Ma'am, can we hide in your bathroom till this car goes by? I'm sorry," Lance said, "I'll explain when they're past, but it's a matter of life or death—for real."

"Yes," said the woman after shaking herself free from momentary confusion. "Yes, go on. Hurry!"

Lance and Eva hustled along the side of the motorhome, staying close to it so as not to draw as much attention. They clambered in as a man looked up at them in surprise from where he sat on the bench seat at a wooden table, his face flushed and sweaty.

Lance stopped. "Hello, sir. Sorry for the intrusion."

"I heard you might be in trouble," said the old man. "I'm good, son. You just do what you need to do."

They thanked him and hurried past, and Lance leaned down to look between the opened drapes at the back of the vehicle. He swore. "It's the cops, Eva. The state. Let's wait right here. See what he says."

They waited by the open window, listening through the screen. A man's deep voice bellowed out from behind the motorhome. "Ma'am? Are you all alone?"

"Yes, sir. I was just trying to change a flat tire."

"Who owns this car?" he asked.

"I'm not sure," she said. "It was already here when I stopped." Eva's heart was pounding hard, and now it started pounding even harder. She wondered if she had parked too close to the motorhome. Was there enough distance left between the vehicles for the old woman's story to be plausible?

The police officer hesitated for a long time, then asked, "Where are you coming from, ma'am?" His voice was closer now.

"Pinedale, where our son lives. We were going to Green River to visit some friends of ours for a few days when the tire went flat."

"So you didn't see anyone around this car?" he asked. "No one around anywhere?"

"No. Is there a problem?"

"There sure could be. The people who own this car are wanted for killing a police officer in Rock Springs."

After a long pause, Eva heard the old woman say, "Oh, my! That's terrible!"

"Yes, it is. We had no idea where they went, and we're looking for them all over the state. Now I guess at least we know they can't be far, unless they got some other car. Ma'am, do you mind if I take a look inside your motorhome?"

CHAPTER FORTY-TWO

AFTER ANOTHER LONG PAUSE, the woman said, "I suppose that should be all right, but please try not to startle my husband. He isn't feeling well. And then after you look around do you mind helping me fix this flat? Those lug nuts are really tight."

"Let's take a look inside here first, why don't we?"

Somehow both Lance and Eva managed to crowd into the bathroom without making too much noise and shut the door just as they heard the creaking of the metal step telling them the patrolman was making his way up into the camper. It was only then that Eva noticed Lance had drawn his revolver.

"Hello, sir," they heard the officer say. "I don't mean to startle you. I just need to look around for a minute. Hey—are you all right?"

The old man didn't say anything back, and after a moment Eva guessed the officer shrugged it off, for she heard him moving again toward the back.

Now the step creaked again. The old woman was coming in. "Oh, officer! I want to show you something."

"What's that?" It sounded like the officer was right outside the bathroom door.

Eva froze as she heard the old woman walking toward them. "Hold on just a moment." The woman must have squeezed past the man, as Eva could hear her way in the rear. Soon, she came back. "This is our son," Eva heard the woman's muffled voice. "He was an officer out in Los Angeles, but he was killed in an automobile accident on duty."

"Oh. Sorry to hear that. Nice-looking young man."

"Yes, he was. Thank you. Well, is everything all right? Could you come and help with the tire now?"

"Ma'am, I really apologize, but with these two people runnin' around here on the loose I'd probably better not stay. Listen, I'll send someone back out from town to help you, all right?"

After a hesitation, the woman replied, and her voice showed disappointment that Eva as a woman understood, but she wondered if the officer caught it. "Oh, all right. Well, thank you."

"Yes, ma'am." The floor creaked as the man moved away, but then he stopped. "Oh, wait. What's that door? Your bathroom?"

"Oh!" The woman sounded surprised. "Why, yes, of course."

"I'll check that too," he said.

The woman laughed lightly. "Well, I'm afraid you'll have trouble with that. One of our great grandchildren locked that with the key inside a few weeks ago and we never tried to get it open."

In a panic, Eva reached up and grabbed the lock knob. She tried to turn it, and it wouldn't move. Instantly, she tried the other direction, and it moved over, smooth and quiet. The doorknob instantly rattled, and the man's muffled voice came through the door. "Huh. Yeah, I guess they got you stuck good, all right."

Soon, they could both be heard moving along the tight space, past the old man, and then down off the metal step. A minute later, the step creaked again, and soon there came a quiet knock on the door. "He's gone now," the old woman said.

Coming out of the bathroom, Eva and Lance stared at the old woman and her husband. "I don't know how to thank you, ma'am," said Lance. "You could have turned us in. What made you help us?"

The woman reached out and laid her hand softly on his big forearm. "Young man, I have always considered myself a good judge of human character, and I can read your eyes pretty well. In the first place, if you were a bad person and you were really on the run, you would never have stopped to help me. It's that policeman's job helping people in trouble, and he couldn't even be bothered to take five minutes and help me change a tire. Besides," she said, turning to raise her hand and frame Eva's chin between her thumb and forefinger. "Look at this darling face. This girl obviously adores you, and this is the face of an angel if I have ever seen one."

Eva felt foolish for being so quick to let tears fill her eyes, but lately she couldn't help it. Overwhelmed, she gave the woman a squeeze, which the woman returned in full. They stepped away from each other, and the woman said, "I don't know what trouble you two have gotten into, but I suspect it's all a misunderstanding, and I sure wish you all the best. Now I think you should go ahead and go. I'm sure someone else will come along to help me with that tire."

"No, ma'am," Lance said. "No way am I leaving you here alone."

He went out and went back to work. It took twenty minutes to get the tire changed and the rig settled back down. In the meantime, Eva was in the motorhome helping the old woman keep wet rags on her husband's face and keeping him sipping cool water. By the time Lance was through with the tire, the man's color looked better, and he gave Eva a smile.

"I'm sure glad you two came along when you did. Janet would have had a heck of a time liftin' that big old tire," the old man said.

Lance grinned. "I'll agree with that, sir. That was a real beast!"

"Say, young man," Janet said. "I was thinking of something our son told us when we called him from Farson a ways back. He said there are roadblocks all around Rock Springs right now. I guess that is probably because of you."

Lance worked his jaw muscles. "That's good to know. I'm sure you're right."

"Well, won't they know your car?"

"Probably."

"Then don't you think you should park it somewhere? We can take you to town and drop you off wherever you're going. But isn't it dangerous going back there at all?"

Lance nodded. "It is, ma'am. I have to admit we wouldn't be goin' back, but some bad men are holdin' Eva's family at gunpoint. We have to go back even if we don't like it."

The woman gasped and stared up at Lance, her face shrouded in a look of terror. She turned to look at her husband, then returned her eyes to Lance. "Young man, my husband retired from the Department of Justice, and he still knows a lot of people. Is there any way we can help?"

Lance almost leaped past the old woman as her husband stood shakily up. "You were Department of Justice?" Lance said.

"Yes, sir, I was. Thirty-two years."

"Sir. I can't believe it! I tried to get hold of an FBI agent—a man named Perry is who I talked to. He said he wouldn't even try to come look at our situation until tomorrow."

"Oh, he did, did he?" the old man said, looking perturbed. "Janet, let's get this rig rolling into town. I think I'm just going to start making some phone calls."

Lance and Eva drove ahead of the motorhome until the next decent-looking road took off to the right. They went until there was a place to park the car, then walked back to where Janet had brought the motorhome to a stop by the turn-off. Climbing in, they settled down on the couch, and Lance said, "Ready!"

The motorhome rolled on toward Rock Springs, bringing Lance and Eva ever closer to destiny.

CHAPTER FORTY-THREE

"JOHNNY WAS RIGHT," JANET said from the driver's seat. "There's a roadblock ahead."

Eva heard the old man, who hadn't been introduced to them, grumble a couple of sentences peppered with curse words.

"Honey, that young lady doesn't need to hear that."

The old man apologized, embarrassed. "I just hate dirty pool, and I despise a dirty cop more than anything else." By this time Eva and Lance had had time to fill Janet and her husband in on everything that was going on in Rock Springs, and the old man's anger was at the point of boiling over. It was obvious that he had spent years as an effective lawman, however, as he had managed to keep most of his anger under a tight lid.

"What do you kids want me to do?" asked Janet as she slowed the Winnebago down. Eva smiled to hear herself being called a kid.

"We'll get in the bathroom again," Eva said. "If they let us go through, would you keep on going for a mile or so until you come to a street sign on your left that says Ridge? That will be where we need to turn."

"You two sure you want to do it this way?" asked the old man. "I can be on the phone in less than twenty minutes, and I promise you I'll get some people moving in here real fast to take charge—some no-nonsense people who'll set these Wyoming hicks straight on the law."

That made Eva smile, although she had learned there were an awful lot of these so-called Wyoming hicks who would give even a stranger almost anything to help them out in times of need.

"I think we have to at least make an appearance, sir," she replied. "I'm afraid for my family." Every time she thought of it or talked about it, her guts tightened up fiercely and her heart started to pound hard again. It was how she used to feel every time she was preparing for a big race, or on the firing line getting ready to draw and start shooting targets with a lot of people watching.

"All right then. But I want you to write down the address you're going to," the old man said. "I'll send help there as fast as possible."

Eva looked at Lance, whose face was grim. They both knew whatever was coming would not likely last long enough for any help to get to them.

"I'll do that," Eva said. "As soon as we stop. And sir, we never caught your name."

"I'm sorry, honey. The name's Tom Rittenhouse."

Lance and Eva crowded into the bathroom again. They were so close that it felt natural for Eva to lean close and put her arms around his middle, holding onto him quietly as they approached the roadblock and finally came to a stop.

Eva heard a door open. "You managed that tire, did you?" a voice came through the bathroom door.

"We did, Officer," Janet said. "With no help from you, thank you very much. My husband got feeling good enough to do it, thank heavens. There sure wasn't any other help out there."

Sounding miffed, the patrolman said, "Go on through."

The Winnebago's motor revved again, and once more they began to move. Eva felt them turning at the next corner, and she squeezed Lance tighter. She had no idea what they were going to do, and suddenly she couldn't help feeling that they were absolute fools. But she would rather have died with her family than find out later they were all dead without her, and because of her.

When they knew it was safe, Lance and Eva came out of the bathroom and went back to the front, this time not sitting down, but holding onto whatever handholds they could find as they leaned down to look out the front.

"You'll be making this next turn on the left," Eva said, and she felt her head getting dizzy as her heart raced too fast.

When the motorhome turned, Eva couldn't speak, and she reached out and squeezed Lance's hand. "You can pull over anywhere here," Lance said, just loud enough for Janet to hear. "When you get to the next street on the right, which is Soulsby, go that way and then turn right again at the next intersection. That will take you right back out to the main drag."

The motorhome came to a stop, and Eva went closer to Tom and Janet, taking a notepad and pen Tom held out to her. She tried to hold her shaking hand still to make her name and address legible enough, then handed the pad back.

"Thank you, miss. Let me ask you one last time. You're sure you have to do this? What if I at least go make a phone call and see if I can get some high-up people to call the folks here and calm the situation down for you? That's the least we could do for now. I hate to see you two go into a bad situation I don't know how you can win."

"That would be a good idea, sir," Lance admitted after a pause. "We'll be beholden to you. If you'd do that, we can wait a few minutes before we go to the house."

"Good as done," said Tom Rittenhouse. "We'll stop at the first phone booth or store we see."

"Thank you again. Thanks for everything."

Eva thanked the Rittenhouses too, and then she and Lance climbed down out of the motorhome, carrying only their weapons, the briefcase, and the three pieces of evidence which were folded in Eva's hip pocket.

After the motorhome pulled away and then turned off on Soulsby, Lance and Eva stood there awkwardly looking around, each fighting his own thoughts and emotions.

"Lance," Eva finally managed to say in a voice that almost cracked. "I really don't think you should go with me. Nothing is going to change if you don't go."

"Right. I'm goin', Eva. I could never live with myself if I let you go in there alone."

"Do we really have to do this?" she asked.

"It's your family," Lance said. "And you know these guys better than I do. If you're thinkin' of some other way, you'd better tell me now."

"I'm not. I just . . ." Her voice failed her. She knew there was no going back, and there was no other plan. Right now, every person in this city who would have been likely to help had been turned against them.

On a whim, Eva crouched down and set the briefcase on the ground, popping it open. She pulled out two fat wads of bills, shut the case, and stood back up. Folding one of the stacks in half, she stuck it in Lance's shirt pocket and snapped it back up. The other one wouldn't fit, so she handed it to him as he watched her with one corner of his mouth up in a confused smile.

"What's all this about?"

"That Bronco's going to take some money to fix up if we get through this. They might as well pay for it."

He laughed. "You're somethin' else, Eva Galanti. I'm sure glad I came into Benny's that day."

She smiled, squeezing his hand. "So am I."

Without another word, she took a deep breath, crossed the street, and started marching up the sidewalk. Her courage wasn't going to get any bigger. If she didn't move now she risked running away and leaving her family to the wolves.

Two doors down, they paused. It wasn't the scene here that they had left behind. The Bronco and all the broken cars had been cleared out of the middle of the street. The Bronco was gone, as was the worst of the police cars. The other police car sat across the street from her house with Cooper Tervalon's black Caprice behind it, and the red Chrysler Eva knew belonged to Primo was in front of her house with the black Nova she had seen earlier. There was also another police car, one that hadn't been involved in any of the earlier wreckage.

The most jarring sight to Eva was several car lengths behind Tervalon's Caprice. It was Ambro Procopio's LeMans, now sadly battered and looking forlorn. Such a beautiful car it had been not three hours before.

With another deep breath, Eva kept going, and again they paused in front of the sidewalk going up to the house, which seemed three times longer to Eva than it ever had before. The front door opened before they had gone halfway.

Ambro stood watching them come, a gun held down along his leg. He tried to meet Eva's gaze as she forced herself to stare him down, but his own gaze was uncharacteristically weak. As she went up the steps in front of Lance, Ambro said quietly, "I'm really sorry, Eva. I never wanted it to be this way."

She turned her eyes away from him, so he stood aside and pushed open the inner door. With another lung-filling breath, Eva made her big entrance. Lance came in right behind her, momentarily blocking most of the daylight.

It took a moment for Eva's eyes to adjust to the dimmer light inside, but they settled on Primo Santori, who stood in a

slick-looking black suit staring at them from in front of the
kitchen, his hands folded in front of him.

"My, my. Isn't this a lovely picture? Little Eva and big Hoss
Cartwright." Primo laughed. "And you both have the moxie to
march in here wearing pistols? My. It's like a scene straight out
of a spaghetti Western, isn't it? *Once Upon a Time in the West*,"
he said mockingly. He raised a hand and flicked his fingers.
"Take those guns from them."

Eva's heart fell, but of course it was no surprise. She had
known she wouldn't have the Colt when it came time to need it.

Chris Hinshaw sauntered over from their left, by the TV,
and pulled Lance's gun from its holster, then plucked Eva's
from behind her waistband. Hinshaw's glance looked contrite,
and he couldn't meet either of their eyes. Eva could tell the officer wanted to look brave for everyone else in the room, but the
expression on his face said he was frightened—perhaps every
bit as frightened as she was.

Eva scanned the room. The smug-looking Chief Howard
Buyer was here, as was Jacob Glattner, beside whom Chris Hinshaw went back to stand. Cooper Tervalon sat in the La-Z-Boy
across from the couch, glaring at her and Lance. There was no
Gavino Berretti, and the other man Eva had shot wasn't in sight
either. She wondered again if she had killed him, and right then
she couldn't find that she cared.

"Where is my family?" Eva asked, her voice surprisingly
level.

Primo took three threatening steps forward, almost within
slapping distance of Eva. His eyes seemed to pierce her soul.
"Don't you even think of making demands on me, you little
witch. I see my briefcase. Where is the rest of what you were
told to bring?"

"I didn't," she said, shrugging. "I have to have some kind of
insurance you won't kill my family."

Primo took that final step, and before Eva knew it her head was ringing from the hard slap that had jolted her face to the side.

"Hey, Boss!" Ambro said. "No need to be so rough, right?"

"You shut your mouth!" Primo barked. "I don't want to hear another sound out of you until this is over."

His eyes zeroed back on Eva. "You can't tell me where your family is, huh? That's funny. You should have been here half an hour ago, when your little brat wouldn't stop screaming. Everyone within half a mile could have told you then where your family was." A smirk lifted one side of his mouth as he enjoyed watching the sick expression ride over Eva's face.

Primo looked away, finding Howard Buyer, dressed in a Western-style suit, closest to the hallway. It was a telling sign who held the real power in Rock Springs when Primo flicked his fingers impatiently at Buyer. "Chief, go tell Galletto to bring her family in here." Eva remembered "Galletto" being a nickname they used for Gavino Berretti.

Chief Buyer walked down the hall, trying to move casually and ending up assuming almost the exact same false swagger Chris Hinshaw had tried to pull off. Eva guessed the chief didn't like one bit being ordered around in front of everyone else like a common probationary patrolman. Soon, the door to Eva's bedroom opened, and Buyer leaned in. Eva didn't hear him say anything, but he backed away from the door, and Bianca Galanti appeared at the doorway holding Leo, one side of her face looking strangely dark. When she came out into the light of the living room, Eva confirmed the swollen redness on the left side of her face, and she gritted her teeth hard as tears of anger came to her eyes. She tried to give her mother a brave smile as she saw Tyke come running from behind his grandmother. At the last moment, the man behind him gave him a hard, unexpected shove, making him fall to his knees.

The man who had done the pushing was Gavino Berretti, who wore dark glasses even in the dim-lit house. He gave out a laugh that could only be described by the word evil, but it, like the false bravado of Howard Buyer and Chris Hinshaw, seemed completely assumed for appearances, making Eva wonder exactly what had happened here in her absence. All these men acted like whipped puppies . . . and it was obvious by the way Primo Santori was acting exactly who held the whip.

Tyke came back up, looking defiant. He was holding himself in now as he walked to Eva, then threw his arms around her. Leo started crying in his grandmother's arms and holding his arm out toward Eva. Primo gave Bianca an angry look and motioned her to go to Eva. "Shut that damn retard up before I do it permanently," he ordered Eva.

Bianca got to Eva and turned Leo around so he could get to his mother. Eva and Tyke held the baby boy together, and Bianca tried to wrap her arms around the entire bunch.

"Now isn't that a touching reunion," said Primo. With a smile tugging at his lip corners, he watched for a moment until Tyke and Bianca had taken an obligatory step back, leaving only Leo with his mother. "Okay, Eva. Now what do you think we should do about you and Mr. Cartwright? Oh, wait. I forgot. I don't even need him, do I?"

Without warning, he reached behind his back and pulled a snub-nose pistol. As it came around and started to level on Lance, everyone froze but Ambro, who leaped forward and caught Primo's arm. "No, Boss, not in here! Remember? We've got to get them far out of town."

Primo tore his arm away from Ambro, turning to glare at him. At last he turned back to the front, rolling his shoulders around as if to straighten his ruffled suitcoat. He laughed, trying to act like he still had control of his rage. "Oh yes, I did say that, didn't I?"

And then without warning he raised the pistol and fired one shot at Lance's chest.

CHAPTER FORTY-FOUR

THE SCREAM THAT ERUPTED from Eva's mouth surprised even her. She watched while clutching Leo tighter to her as the once invincible-seeming giant grabbed at his chest and tried with no apparent success to draw a breath. He took two steps backward before going to his knees, then falling on his face. The fall seemed to shake the whole living room floor.

"What the hell!" Chris Hinshaw yelled, taking two steps toward Primo with his hands balled in fists at his sides. "You had to do it like that, in front of everybody?"

In less than a second, the barrel of Primo's gun was pointed at Hinshaw's face, making the policeman reel backward and freeze. "Do you want to be next—*cop?* I will warn you—and everyone else—for the last time: I would watch how you address me if I were you. I own this town and everyone in it. You would be nothing without me."

With the room in dead-silent shock, Primo slowly lowered his weapon, and he deliberately panned everyone there with his eyes, letting each of them get the hard glint of his sea-ice stare. The eyes of every person were either on him or averted to Lance Cartwright or to the floor—all but Bianca Galanti, whose gaze was locked in sorrow on the mortified face of her daughter. Leo was screaming again.

"I said shut that retard up!" Primo raged. He turned to glare at Bianca. "Take him and go back to the room. Don't come out until someone comes to get you."

Bianca, in terror, hustled to obey. Everyone seemed to know Primo Santori was a tower of rage and that anything could make him snap and commit murder again.

"I assume I have everyone's attention," said Primo in a purposely subdued voice after Bianca and Leo were gone. "Good. Now. Eva." He turned so his shoulders and his entire body were squared with his head, all his energy directed straight against Eva Galanti. "What did I tell you to bring me?"

"The briefcase," she said, feeling numb.

"Yes," he agreed. "Cute. What else?"

"What Officer Stone gave me."

"Where is it?"

"It's in a safe place."

"That's ironic," said Primo, still forcing himself to look controlled even though red was spreading up his neck from under his collar. "Because you aren't. Well, my dear Eva. You and I and . . ." He scanned the rest of the room before making a decision . . . "and Chief Buyer and Ambro are going to take a trip. Before we leave, we're going to tie your family up here with cotton ropes. You know, cotton rope burns almost perfectly and leaves little sign that it was ever there."

Eva stared at him as the horrible implications of what he might be suggesting began to sink in.

"So the five of us will go find all that evidence. Every last scrap of it, mind you. If I even *think* any is missing, then nothing else is going to matter. I will simply make a phone call here on the car phone and tell Mr. Berretti and Mr. Horsch to douse this place, and your family, with gasoline and throw a match. This tinderbox will be gone in an hour, down to the ground. No one will ever know why these three poor people never got out of the fire. Now, Eva: Do you have any questions?"

She stared at him, feeling sick beyond the ability to speak. She simply shook her head.

"You can't speak, ay? Aw, well, that's okay. I think I understand. So you are taking us to what Officer Stone gave you, am I correct? To every last piece of it?"

Numb, Eva nodded.

"Good. Good girl. I knew you could be sensible." Primo reached behind him with both hands, raised the tail of his suitcoat, and situated his pistol in its holster, then took a pack of Benson and Hedges from a front pocket of his coat, tapping one out of the package and using a silver Zippo to light it. He seemed to enjoy being in the spotlight, taking a few strong starter puffs and blowing the smoke toward the ceiling. He looked around, holding out the pack of cigarettes, with the lighter between thumb and forefinger. "Anyone else?"

Not a soul spoke. A few of them, namely Tervalon, Ambro, and Buyer, stared at him, but the looks in none of their eyes were congenial. Everyone else in the room pointedly kept their eyes averted. Again, Eva thought something bad must have taken place while all of them waited here for her.

When Primo's cigarette was halfway gone, he glanced around at no one in particular, seeming to know that he had enough power to be obeyed without naming names, and said, "Get those kitchen chairs in here, take the ropes, and tie everyone up. Ambro? Go get that retarded boy and Eva's mother out here."

Ambro turned with a frown on his face and went down the hall while the mobster Primo had called Mr. Horsch, along with Glattner and Hinshaw, were bringing the chairs from the kitchen.

Hinshaw turned to Tyke. The look in the policeman's eyes was unhappy. He couldn't even look at Eva's boy as he took him by the shoulders and eased him down onto the chair. Glattner had a handful of white, braided ropes, and he brought them over and wordlessly began tying the boy to the chair as Eva saw Ambro coming back down the hall with Bianca, who held Leo. The boy had fresh tears on his face, even though Eva hadn't heard him crying since they went to the bedroom.

Hinshaw looked at Bianca. He seemed loath to speak and break the solemn silence in the room, but he did anyway, in a soft, apologetic voice. "Ma'am, you'd better sit down, all right?"

Bianca tried to look defiant, but she sat, still holding onto Leo. Hinshaw stood there while Glattner came over, holding the rope stretched out to the sides as his eyes roved around the woman and boy, trying to figure out how to tie them.

"Stop wasting time," ordered Primo. "Take the screamer away and tie him separately. You can't secure them this way."

"Why are we tying them up at all?" Ambro asked. He seemed the only one in the room still bold enough to question Primo. "These other guys will be here with them. Can't they just stay loose while we're gone?"

"We're tying them because I said to tie them. I always thought that was enough." Primo gave a tight little smile to his segundo, but the glint in his eyes was deadly—almost even insane. "What's the matter, Ambro? Don't want to hurt them?"

"I don't really see a point in it. They didn't do anything."

Primo let out a laugh. He stared at Ambro as the gleam in his eyes grew. "No point in it, you say? What is the point in anything, dear Ambro? The point is you do what I tell you, for one reason: Because I am the boss, and when people stop obeying the boss, things fall apart. And money? Well, it simply stops flowing. Doesn't it? You have all seen what happens when people start playing Lone Ranger. We lose money. We lose people."

Without a word, a smug look on his face, Primo walked to Leo. The smirk at the corner of his mouth began to grow as he took a long draw from his cigarette. Staring into Ambro's eyes, he pulled the cigarette from his mouth and lowered it until the point of it contacted Leo's thigh. Ambro started forward as smoke rose from the boy's pants and he started screaming.

Primo pulled the cigarette away and laughed as Ambro stopped right behind Bianca, his face now very close to his boss's. "Pain, Ambro? Don't you know the old saying? Pain is only weakness leaving the body. The screamer will be better for it. Shut him up!" he growled at Bianca, who did the only thing she could try to do, putting her hand over Leo's mouth.

"You're a beast!" Bianca said, earning the slap across her face she had to know would be coming.

"I am, aren't I? But it takes a beast to own and run an entire town, Mrs. Galanti. A lowlife bottom dweller such as yourself would never understand such things."

Ambro was very close to Primo—within arm's reach of him. Ambro's gun was in a holster down inside the front of his waistband, and Primo's was in the holster behind his back. Ambro reached around Bianca Galanti and put a hand on sobbing Leo Galanti's shoulder, trying to comfort him.

"You don't really plan on letting any of these people go once we get back everything Stone gave Eva, do you, Boss?"

Ambro might as well have slapped his boss across the face. Primo stared him down. A twitching beneath one corner of his mustache might have been him trying to force a smile.

"I told you to shut your mouth, Ambro."

A heart-stopping crash at the front of the house served like punctuation to the end of Primo Santori's angry statement. Everyone whirled toward it, several of them diving to the floor as a ten- or fifteen-pound rock rolled across it and came to a stop at the edge of the kitchen floor.

Other rocks, smaller ones, began to fly in, both through the gaping hole now in the picture window and through new holes where the glass continued to shatter. Out in the front, Eva could hear angry voices crying out.

Primo Santori was on his knees, crouching low. "What the hell is going on out there?" he demanded, of no one in particular.

"There's a bunch of guys!" Horsch yelped. "Like bums or somethin'! Screamin' and throwin' crap!" Another rock flew through the window and hit the far wall.

"Well, shoot them!" Primo's voice was almost a scream. "SHOOT THEM!" He staggered up, sweeping the room with wild, confused eyes.

Without sound or warning of any kind, the shape of a man appeared at the back door of the kitchen, and Eva heard the almost deafening blast of a shotgun. Horsch arched his back and fell to his knees, groaning in pain.

Eva saw Primo Santori, in a fury, reach behind his back and draw his gun, trying to turn and line his sights on the newcomer at the back of the house.

The hand of Ambro Procopio came up fast, his handgun aimed at Primo. The barrel of the little gun belched flame and jumped twice, and Primo groaned and turned his own gun, shooting into Ambro's body.

Gavino Berretti staggered up from where he had dropped to the floor with the first rock crashing through the window. Face looking savage, he advanced on Ambro, his gun out, trying to get around the chair Bianca had vacated. She now lay on the floor sheltering Leo with her body.

Gavino got a bead on Ambro and fired. Ambro jerked. Primo was lying on his side, trying to line his gun up again on Ambro, as Eva scrambled to him and managed to tear the gun out of his dying fist. She rolled over with the gun in both hands, firing a high round at Gavino just as he cracked off another round at Ambro.

Eva's shot must have hit Gavino somewhere in the nervous system, for he fell straight down and started flopping on the floor.

Out of nowhere, Howard Buyer lurched close now with his revolver drawn and aimed at Eva. Before anyone knew what happened, the end table that sat by the front window came flying through the air and struck the police chief in the back of the head, knocking him forward. From the corner of her eye, Eva saw the dark shape in the kitchen stagger in closer, and a shotgun blast drowned the room in noise once more as Buyer was trying to bring his gun back into play. Blood splattered as the chief slumped straight down onto his face.

Eva was on her knees now, not crying out loud, but with tears of shock and fear and adrenaline streaming down her cheeks. With Primo's gun locked in her hands, she stared at the man in the kitchen, the man brandishing the shotgun. Her mind was grappling with the knowledge that he should not be standing there, and yet he was. His neck was heavily bandaged, but he was standing there all the same, and very much alive.

It was Brandon Lucky—perhaps the luckiest man Eva knew.

"Get over there!" she heard the roar of another familiar voice she had never expected to hear again, a voice that almost drowned out even the sound of Leo's cries. That man would be vying for the position of luckiest man alive.

As she struggled to her feet, she looked over to focus on Lance Cartwright, standing at his full height, grimacing as he held a hand to one side of his chest, the other hand pointing at Jacob Glattner, Chris Hinshaw, and Cooper Tervalon as if he were holding them at gunpoint. The only weapon Lance brandished was his finger.

In apparent shock, the three lawmen, all of them still armed, backed against the far wall, staring at Lance, transfixed.

Tyke was crouched on the floor, his arms over the back of his head. Eva had to speak his name twice before her voice registered on him. "Come here! You too, Mom."

Bianca struggled to her feet and backed over to Eva with the wailing Leo clutched tight against her body. Tyke ran. All of them got behind Eva and Primo's gun.

But there was no need. The room was still. Brandon walked across the floor gingerly and reached down to pry the handgun out of the hand of Gavino Berretti, who now lay still in an ugly pool of blood, then went and put it in Lance's empty hand. Lance only nodded at him and advanced on his former fellow policemen, telling them and Cooper Tervalon to drop their weapons. All three of them complied without so much as a word. They all stared him down with the same ashen look on their faces. Eva could only imagine what must be going through their minds, knowing what lay ahead of them now.

Brandon walked to the front door and threw it open. Like wild apes, the crowd of rough-looking men outside were lurking around the cars, peeking up over them, apparently wondering what their next move should be.

"We got it, guys," Brandon yelled out at them. "Can't thank you enough for your help. Maybe y'all better split for now before any other cops get here. But I'll be in touch."

One of the men called back. "You sure, buddy? Man, we can stay if you need us. Holy hell, it sounded like the O.K. Corral in there. You all right?"

"I'm good, Stevo. Thanks to you guys, we're all good. Take off now, man." He waved at them, and Eva watched ten or twelve of them, all seedy-looking men from the street, weaving their way out of the neighborhood, between cars and houses, vanishing like wisps of smoke into their recovered town.

Everyone heard a moan over by the kitchen, and Eva looked down to see Ambro stirring. It seemed impossible considering the amount of blood splattered and pooled all around him.

Eva walked to him and dropped to her knees, ignoring the blood. She lifted his head carefully and cradled it against her thigh. "Ambro. Why did you do that?" She scanned his bloody torso and the pasty skin of his face. She was no medical person, but it didn't take one to know Ambro couldn't survive.

"Please take my hand, Eva," he managed to say, and she did, in spite of the blood smeared on it.

"Why, Ambro? I thought you were with them to the end."

He weakly shook his head, fighting to keep his eyes open. "I have a little brother. A brother like Leo. Sure love that little kid. Can I see him one more time?"

Eva's eyes had filled suddenly with tears. She turned quickly to seek out her mother. "Mom, will you hurry and bring Leo over here?"

Bianca did as requested. When Eva held her arms up, she placed the baby into them, and he struggled around and put his arms around her neck. "He's here, Ambro," she said, fighting the tightness of her voice. "He's here."

Ambro reached up with a shaking hand and rubbed Leo's back. "You're a good mother, Eva. I sure wish I could have known you better." There was a trickle of blood weeping out one side of his mouth now. "Hey . . ." His voice was weakening. "Damn it. Damn it, Eva, I can't see you anymore. I was . . . I was just going to tell you . . . I was . . ."

She brushed the blood off the side of his face. "Ambro? Ambro!"

He drew open his eyes that had closed, and he tried to smile. "I was just going to tell you you should check Leo's diaper soon."

The suggestion seemed so out of nowhere Eva laughed. The tears in her eyes flooded over as she smiled down at Ambro and brushed the hair back from the side of his face, smearing the blood into it.

"Okay, Ambro. I will." He didn't respond. He only kept staring up at her, a little smile under his perfectly groomed mustache, where the blood trickled away. As the pupils of his eyes grew to their fullest dilation, the realization struck Eva that Ambro Procopio, the man they called "the Porcupine", was gone.

Ambro had once told her that his full given name, Ambrosio, meant something like "he who has eternal life". Ambro hadn't lived up to his name.

CHAPTER FORTY-FIVE

THE AUTHORITIES TAPED OFF Eva's house as a crime scene under investigation. It would remain as such, with its windows boarded up, probably for days. An agent from the Red Cross came and gave Eva an address in a local, brand-new trailer park, where they would have a double-wide trailer available for her and her family. Then, while the family waited outside in a big Chevrolet Suburban Brandon Lucky's boss, Dino Priest, had brought them to use until they could retrieve the Chevelle, Eva stood outside and waited for Ambro Procopio's body to be brought out.

Chris Hinshaw, Jacob Glattner, and Cooper Tervalon rode away from the house in handcuffs. There was a long list still destined to make the acquaintance of the inside of a jail, including many men in high places in the city and county government, but until Eva and Lance were able to lead the authorities out to where they had buried all the evidence Lookie Luke Borders had collected and given to Buck Stone, the rest would wait. The clean-up process in Rock Springs was going to take time, but they had nothing left but time.

FBI crime scene investigators from Cheyenne, who seemed to have materialized as if by magic after retired DOJ supervisor Tom Rittenhouse made a few well-placed phone calls, walked around inside and outside the Galanti property, taking measurements and photographs and outlining the bodies on the floor in white chalk.

Afterward, morgue workers carried the bodies one by one out of the house on gurneys. The morgue workers patiently allowed Eva to stop them each time they came out, to raise one corner of the sheet draped over their gurney and see whose face appeared there. She felt strangely detached at the sight of Gavino Berretti, even knowing it was her bullet that had killed him.

The last body out was Ambro Procopio. Eva's shaking hand pulled back the sheet to reveal the once-charismatic face of Ambro, his eyes now closed in eternal rest, his rich, wavy brown hair plastered with blood. She had kept a wet washcloth in her hand for this moment. As she heard Lance asking the gurney-attendees to step back and give her some space, she sponged the blood off the man's face and wetted his tousled hair enough to press it back into place. He would not have wanted to go anywhere, even to the morgue, with his hair looking less than perfect. She only wished she could get all the blood out of it.

As the tears began to stream down her face, Eva bent and placed a kiss on the forehead of one of the three men she credited with the fact that she and her family were still alive. She drew the sheet carefully back over his face and tucked it in, and as the morgue-workers rolled the gurney off to their waiting rig, Lance stepped in and put an arm around Eva's back, until she turned and embraced him and quietly cried into his shirt.

Many of the day's revelations took time for Eva's worn-out mind to process. Seeing Brandon alive was one of those, along with the knowledge that it was her fast move which had saved his life after he had been shot in the side of the neck by Ambro. If she had not run when she did, Ambro could easily have finished him off, then captured her as well.

Another stunning revelation was how Lance was standing here with her now only because the .38 caliber bullet Primo Santori had fired at his chest had been completely absorbed by the rolled wad of ten-dollar bills God must have inspired her to tuck into the breast pocket of his shirt immediately before they went into the house.

Karen Lucky was at that very moment in the hospital being treated for her wounds, but she was no longer of any concern to Brandon. She had told him when he went to see her at the hospital that upon her release she wanted nothing but to leave "Rock Bottom" to go live with her mother in Denver. Brandon was a free man as far as she was concerned, and she wanted nothing more from him. She would have divorce papers sent to him the moment they could be prepared.

Thus released, Brandon went to be with Eva's family in their Red Cross-provided double wide trailer house. Lance Cartwright was with them as well. Neither of the men had any better place to go. As far as "Rock Bottom" was concerned, the Galantis were the closest thing they had to family.

It wasn't until all of them were sitting alone in the living room, eating pizza, drinking Hires root beer, and quietly discussing their recent visit to see Isabella at the hospital, who was doing well and recovering much faster than the doctors had foreseen, that the final words of Ambro Procopio struck Eva.

She had been sitting there listening in a disconnected way to the droning sound of the evening news, now and then trying to process her killing of Gavino Berretti and otherwise wondering how they would go forward with life from here; they had nothing to go forward on. It was at that odd moment that Ambro's dying words returned. It had been over two hours, yet his broken voice came back to her mind almost audibly: *You should check Leo's diaper soon.*

As the television droned on, and the others stared at it, seeming transfixed, Eva stood, Leo in her arms. He had been unwilling to let her leave his sight or even to break physical contact.

Eva needed to take her son to the bathroom. Leo might still have been in diapers, since he couldn't get around well enough yet to use the toilet on his own, but he was a smart boy, and sensitive. He needed his privacy as much as any other three-year-old.

She excused herself and went to the bathroom with another diaper. Laying him on the floor, she pulled off his little Levi's, frowning in a mix of sadness and residual anger at the new burn mark on his thigh.

As she went to pull his pants the rest of the way off, she froze. It took several seconds for her mind to process what she was looking at inside the Levi's, and when reality hit her, tears flooded her eyes and spilled down her cheeks. Wiping almost angrily at the explosion of tears, but unable to stem the tide, she reached into his Levi's and picked up just one of the banded stacks of twenty-dollar bills. There were four of them inside the pants, lined up side by side. Each stack, if they had been taken straight from the briefcase by Ambro, consisted of one hundred twenties—two thousand dollars each.

Eight thousand dollars in all . . .

Little Leo couldn't have any idea why his mother was weeping, but his nature was to comfort her, so he did. He struggled up off his back and used her arms to pull him to a standing position, then put his arms around her and held her while she was crying. All the while, he kept patting her arm and speaking the little words of comfort that he alone understood.

It turned out that Leo actually did need a diaper, but it wasn't bad. Eva doubted he was wet at all when Ambro passed on his final advice. She sat there wondering how Ambro had done what he did, and if the money had even come from the briefcase, since she didn't remember any time when he could have gotten his hands on it without Primo or one of the others catching him. It didn't matter. All that mattered to Eva was knowing she would be all right. Because of the act of a dying man, a supposedly hardened mobster with a heart that ended up being as big and golden as his Pontiac LeMans Sport in quetzal gold, her family was going to be fine.

They were going to survive.

When she walked back out of the bathroom into the smell of pizza and the feel of love, she had eight thousand dollars tucked behind the waistband of her pants, a fact she wasn't emotionally ready to talk about yet. There would be plenty of time to tell everyone about the money when she reached the point of being able to control her own emotions. There would be plenty of time to reveal what Ambro Procopio had done to show his true character.

For now, as everyone turned to look at her, Eva's hardest job would be trying to explain the paradox of the face-splitting smile she wore and the tears she couldn't stop from running down her cheeks.

THE END

Author's note and acknowledgements

It was only by sheer chance that I picked the city of Rock Springs, Wyoming, as a setting for this book. As most of my faithful readers know, I tend to set the majority of my books in my adopted home state of Idaho, mostly because very little fiction seems to be set here, and because I love this state.

I scoured Idaho looking for a suitable setting for this book, a city distant enough from neighboring communities, with a decent population base but only meagerly populated surroundings—in short, a place where such a story as this could occur. I could never find any 1970's communities in Idaho that fit my parameters.

I chose Rock Springs randomly from my memories of it the many times I have passed through there, but imagine my shock when I started to research the place and learned that not only had the city boomed in the early Seventies, but that the real Rock Springs—known in a derogatory tone by many of its locals as Rock Bottom—also had a dark history much like what occurred in the book, only revealed in 1977, rather than earlier on in the decade, as it was in the book.

I want to make a special note that in spite of that rocky period in Rock Springs' history, nothing in this novel was based off true incidents or people. I judge no person, living or dead, for anything that happened in that city, in the Seventies or any other time. Learning what happened only served to strengthen my choice of "Rocket Springs" as the setting of the novel.

There is one person in this novel whose description and character, along with his name, I took from actual life, with his permission, and that is Lance Cartwright, an actual police officer living and working in Pocatello, Idaho, today, and a man I am proud to call my friend.

Everyone else in the book is completely fictional, but I want to thank a few friends for allowing me to put their faces on the cover, portraying my characters Eva Galanti, Primo Santori, and Brandon Lucky. I of course portrayed Ambrosio Procopio, so I can't thank myself.

Following is a list of those friends, with the characters they portrayed on my cover. Thank you all so much for being a part of the fun. Having your faces in my head made the creation of this novel so much more enjoyable than simply dealing with people I made up in my head.

Eva Galanti:	Kristi Roberts
Ambro Procopio:	Yours truly
Primo Santori:	Michael Brennan
Brandon Lucky:	Doug Larson
Lance Cartwright:	Himself

I would also like to thank a very important handful of people who helped me hugely in getting the details of Rock Springs and its surroundings and colorful history together. I could never have made this book what it is without the huge help of Jennifer Messer, from the Rock Springs Historical Museum, along with her colleague Richelle Rawlings-Carroll.

I also wish to thank wonderful Rock Springs residents Delbert Kroupa and Ryan and Nicole Scott., and former residents, Hub Whitt, Sheryl Yates, Jay Bachicha, Rusty Havens, Aileen

Gronewold, and Mike Allen, whom I met by sheer chance upon his return to town to walk through the Rock Springs historical museum.

I would like to beg the forgiveness of any person I have inadvertently left out of these acknowledgments, as it seems I invariably do.

About the Author

Kirby Frank Jonas was born in 1965 in Bozeman, Montana. His earliest memories are of living seven miles outside of town in a wide crack in the mountains known as Bear Canyon. At that time it was a remote and lonely place, but a place where a boy with an imagination could grow and nurture his mind, body and soul.

From Montana, the Jonas family moved almost as far across the country as they could go, to Broad Run, Virginia, to a place that, although not as deep in the timbered mountains as Bear Canyon was every bit as remote—Roland Farm. Once again, young Jonas spent his time mostly alone, or with his older brother, if he was not in school. Jonas learned to hike with his mother, fish with his father, and to dodge an unruly horse.

Jonas moved to Shelley, Idaho, in 1971, and from that time forth, with the exception of a few sojourns elsewhere, he became an Idahoan. Jonas attended all twelve years of school in Shelley, graduating in 1983. In the sixth grade, he penned his first novel, *The Tumbleweed,* and in high school he wrote his second, *The Vigilante.*

Jonas has lived in six cities in France, in Mesa, Arizona, and explored the United States extensively. He has fought fires for the Bureau of Land Management in five western states and carried a gun on his hip in three different jobs.

In 1987, Jonas met his wife-to-be, Debbie Chatterton, and in 1989 took her to the altar. Over some rough and rocky roads they have traveled, and across some raging Leos that have at times threatened to draw them under, but they survived, and with four beautiful children to show for it: Cheyenne, Jacob, Clay, and Matthew.

Jonas has been employed as a Wells Fargo armored guard, a wildland firefighter, a security guard for California Plant Protection, Inter-Con, and police officer. He is now retired after almost twenty-four years of proud employment as a municipal firefighter for the city of Pocatello, Idaho, and works full-time job as a private security officer guarding the federal courthouse under contract with the security company Paragon Systems.

One of Jonas's greatest joys in life is watching his second son, Clay, become a recognized writer of much talent in his own chosen field, that of fantasy and science fiction, with his current series *The Descendants of Light*. There is no greater compliment a son could give to his father than to follow in his footsteps.

Books by Kirby Jonas

Season of the Vigilante, Book One: The Bloody Season
Season of the Vigilante, Book Two: Season's End
The Dansing Star
Legend of the Tumbleweed
Lady Winchester
The Devil's Blood
The Secret of Two Hawks
Knight of the Ribbons
Drygulch to Destiny
Samuel's Angel
The Night of My Hanging (And Other Short Stories)
Russet
A Final Song for Grace

Savage Law series
1. *Law of the Lemhi, part 1*
   Law of the Lemhi, part 2
2. *River of Death*
3. *Lockdown for Lockwood*
4. *Like a Man Without a Country*
5. *Thunderbird*
6. *Savage Alliance*

Windfall: Connected to Savage Law, but not part of the series

The Badlands series
1. *Yaqui Gold* (co-author Clint Walker)
2. *Canyon of the Haunted Shadows*

Legends West series
1. *Disciples of the Wind* (co-author Jamie Jonas)
2. *Reapers of the Wind* (co-author Jamie Jonas)

***Lehi's Dream* series**
1. *Nephi Was My Friend*
2. *The Faith of a Man*
3. *A Land Called Bountiful*

Gray Eagle series (e-book format only—forthcoming in print)
1. *The Fledgling*
2. *Flight of the Fledgling*
3. *Wings on the Wind*
Death of an Eagle (e-book and large format softbound)

Books on audio

The Dansing Star, narrated by James Drury, *"The Virginian"*
Death of an Eagle, narrated by James Drury
Legend of the Tumbleweed, narrated by James Drury
Lady Winchester, narrated by James Drury
Yaqui Gold, narrated by Gene Engene
The Secret of Two Hawks, narrated by Kevin Foley
Knight of the Ribbons, narrated by Rusty Nelson
Drygulch to Destiny, narrated by Kirby Jonas

Available through the author at www.kirbyjonas.com

Email the author at: kirby@kirbyjonas.com or write to:

Howling Wolf Publishing
1611 City Creek Road
Pocatello ID 83204

Made in the USA
Middletown, DE
19 February 2022

61445358R00262